THIRD
PARTY

THIRD PARTY

A NOVEL

BRANDI REEDS

LAKE UNION
PUBLISHING

Text copyright © 2019 by Brandi Reeds
All rights reserved.

Published by Lake Union Publishing, Seattle

www.apub.com

Amazon, the Amazon logo, and Lake Union Publishing are trademarks of Amazon.com, Inc., or its affiliates.

ISBN-13: 9781542044936
ISBN-10: 1542044936

Cover design by Faceout Studio, Derek Thornton

Printed in the United States of America

For my hunky husband and our amazing girls,
who taught me laugh lines are a sign of happiness.
I followed the doe, and she led me here, to the life we share.

When one is in love, one always begins by deceiving one-self, and one always ends by deceiving others.

—*Oscar Wilde*

Chapter 1

JESSICA

I know right away this isn't going to be good. I can't explain it. It's just a queasy feeling in the pit of my stomach. Sometimes it's there. Sometimes it's not. And this time, not only is it *there*, it's somersaulting.

It's barely six in the morning, nearing the end of a long shift at the fire station.

I ring the bell for the top-floor unit of a building we in Chicago call a three-flat. We're on the eight hundred block of Leavitt in a decent neighborhood, a recently gentrified section of Bucktown, where many of the three-flats have been renovated into single-family houses. This one, as evidenced by the mailboxes and doorbells on the front porch, is still home to three renters.

Red and blue lights flash in rotation against the building. In further testament to the safety of the neighborhood, curious neighbors lean out of their windows to see what the fuss is all about. Cops don't fill the streets around here every day.

The buzzer bleats to admit the fire battalion chief and me, and I yank open the door.

"Excuse me." An older couple, frantic, is suddenly at the curb, exiting their car, slamming doors. The woman is stoic; the man, fidgeting, speaks for both of them. "We got a call . . . I own the building."

The chief holds up a hand like a traffic cop, but if he hopes to stop the couple from coming any closer, it's a futile attempt. "I'm sorry, I have to ask you to wait here a minute."

"But our daughter lives here."

That changes things. The chief slows his pace and adopts a softer tone. "I've yet to assess the situation. I only just got here myself." While the chief hangs back with the couple, I begin to climb the stairs. I don't know much about the situation, except that a neighbor called for a well check. I don't know what we're going to find up there, but nothing about this scene feels remotely *well.*

"I'm the one who called," a tenant says, looking down at me from the second-floor landing as I approach. "I found this note . . . the police have it now. 'If anything happens to me, tell them it wasn't an accident.' That's what it said. Can you believe it?"

A chill chases down my spine.

"So I called, naturally, and—"

"Thank you. You've done your civic duty."

"It's just . . . she must have slipped it under my door last night. I didn't see it until this morning. Is she okay?" he asks. "The guy downstairs . . . you might want to talk to him. He says he heard her arguing with someone. A man who threatened to tape her mouth shut. Do you know what's going on?"

My breath catches in my throat, and I reach out and pat him on the shoulder. "I'll know soon enough."

"If only I hadn't gone to bed early. Maybe I could have—"

"You did what you could," I assure him.

I recognize the pair of patrol cops standing outside the closed door on the third floor.

"There's a lot of city-issue cars outside," I say. "What are we walking into?"

"You don't want to go in there, ma'am," one of them tells me.

I point to the name lettered down the right sleeve of my department-issue fleece pullover. "Firefighter Blythe. Here to serve, same as you. Called here to assist."

"No saving her now."

The somersaulting in my gut ceases, and a hundred-pound rock plummets there. "I see."

"Hanging," the other says.

She's not my first, but that doesn't mean this job is ever routine or easy. "You fellas done in there?" I indicate the door. "May I?"

One of the pair opens it for me.

The acrid stench of human decay rises up as I enter the apartment. I roll it up and mentally file it into the special place in my mind I created for moments like these on the job. Compartmentalization. It keeps me sane.

The place is decorated in a bohemian vibe. It's colorful and eclectic and airy, with vaulted ceilings and exposed rafters. A nice place to come home to, I'll bet.

Lieutenant KJ Decker, detective third grade, is standing in the living room, not far from where the victim is hanging from the rafters. His arms are crossed over his chest, and he's gnawing fiercely on a wad of pink gum. He gives me a nod when he sees me.

Slowly, I approach.

She's beautiful, even postmortem. Thin. Blonde. Wearing a red satin nightie. Well-manicured hands. Red polish on her toes. The same shade paints her lips. Even death couldn't darken that shade.

And on her right cheek: a horizontal slash, with a trickle of blood, now dried, as if she dodged a sweep of a knife.

"So much for a well check," I say.

Sometimes we arrive for this type of call and learn all is fine, or at least fixable. We come, we help. But even on calls like this one, when it's too late for intervention, they still need me.

"We're just about ready for you, Jessie," Decker says to me.

"Anything I can do in the meantime?"

"I have some difficult visits to see to." He gives me a sort-of smile. He's tired. "You wanna notify next of kin?"

I don't, but it's a task no one is going to raise her hand to do. "I think the next of kin just arrived outside."

Decker lets out a drawn-out sigh. "I don't want them to see her like this."

"The chief's keeping them at bay. But I'll accompany, if you think it'll help."

"Maybe."

It appears the evidence techs have swabbed and bagged her hands, presumably to preserve whatever evidence might be lingering in the folds of her skin and under her fingernails, which is interesting because . . .

"This is a suicide," I say. It's meant to be a question of sorts. At the very least, I'm seeking confirmation of my assessment, but after nearly five years on the job, I've learned that the right inflection is important for a woman in this profession. Too much lilt, too much emphasis on the question mark, and these guys, even those without rank, will assume I'm uncertain, and they'll be bossing me around until the cows come home.

"*Apparent* suicide," Decker says. Then, under his breath, he adds, "At least that's what someone wants us to think."

"Really. She leave a note?"

"Yeah. Brief. Along with a few Benjamins on the counter."

I glance at the kitchen and see several hundred-dollar bills fanned on the counter. The number fourteen is tented next to them, which means the techs have photographed the cash as evidence.

Another number—eleven—marks the location where a lacy red bra is lying on the floor.

"Did you find a knife?"

Decker nods. "There's one in the kitchen sink."

"What's with the note the neighbor found?" I ask. "Doesn't make sense if this was a suicide. And the first-floor neighbor who overheard an argument?"

"No." Decker shakes his head again. "It sure doesn't make sense. None of it does."

Senseless or not, there's nothing I can do to change it now.

But I can take care of her to the best of my abilities.

I call for a bag and spread it gingerly over the planks of old wood flooring in what was this girl's living room. It sounds silly, maybe, but I wish I'd thought to bring up a blanket for her. She won't know it's there, and it certainly won't warm her, but soon, the old couple the chief and I encountered at the foot of the building is going to peer into this bag. I want them to see that she's comfortable. No longer suffering the ails of this world.

Minutes later, I snip at the rope that stole her last breath.

She's placed in the bag I prepared for her.

In motion, her nightie has shifted, making visible an old, deliberate carving on the arc her right breast—the letters *A* and *J*.

"Deck, did you see this?"

An evidence tech snaps a close-up.

I straighten her nightie, pull it down over her bare private parts. She's not wearing panties. Once I ensure all of her is covered, I smooth the hair from her forehead.

I close my eyes and say a quick prayer before zipping the bag.

"Deceased's name," Decker says into his digital recorder, "presumed to be Margaux Claire Stritch."

Victims always become real to me once I learn their names, and this one, with a name like that, could have been glamorous.

"Aged twenty-two years," Decker says. "Presumed suicide by hanging. Pending positive identification and autopsy."

So young.

Not that much younger than me.

I didn't know her.

And now I never will.

Chapter 2

KIRSTEN

Life in motion.

From my position in the sunroom, balancing an empty coffee mug on my knee, I stare out at the acreage rolling all the way out to the wetlands behind our new home. Fog hangs low in the air, wrapping around tree trunks.

I'm not used to this much space. Nor am I accustomed to the solitude I feel now that Ian and I are, for the most part, empty nesters, and living farther north. Evanston may not have been the city, but it was city*ish*, at least in comparison to this hidden estate twenty-some minutes off the tollway in a sparsely populated town by the name of Mettawa. The Realtor called it a gem. Ian called it a fresh start. I call it dead quiet. We may as well have moved to the north woods of Wisconsin.

We purchased this place a few months ago, and while it was ultimately Ian's decision, I thought I'd like the land. Maybe, much to Ian's chagrin, I thought we'd get a dog . . . or horses. And besides, my old friends from Evanston vowed to visit. But it turns out no one has time to be infected with the somber atmosphere of this place, where everything moves at a snail's pace.

To be honest, I'm probably not ready to face anyone just yet, anyway. Not after the episode. It was just nerves, the doctors said. Anxiety. It happens sometimes when the last child leaves the home, when a stay-at-home mom suddenly finds herself without immediate purpose.

Wouldn't it figure it would happen to me? I started crying on a nondescript Tuesday after my daughter Quinn's high school graduation, and I just couldn't stop.

There I was, at the farmers market with my neighbor Fiona, picking through fresh bouquets, thinking, *Roses or lilies?* And Fiona was babbling about poor so-and-so at the MedSpa, who'd been lipoed to the hilt and was finally ready to show off her newly restored shape on a Mediterranean cruise . . . and her husband died on the ship.

It started with a sniffle. It was ridiculous, really. I don't know poor so-and-so. Her husband had died months previously, and the woman was already on the dating circuit. But the sniffle became a sob became a wail, and before I knew what was happening, I could hardly breathe over my heaving, let alone see through my tears.

Fiona drove me home, only I'd misplaced my keys and couldn't get into the house, and things escalated from there.

Neighbors gathered.

Someone called Ian.

Someone else called an ambulance.

I couldn't stop crying. I don't even know if I tried. All I know is that I kept thinking: *I've spent my whole life waiting for things to begin, and suddenly, everything feels closer to the end than the starting line.*

The doctors gave me a sedative and a prescription for more, which Ian filled. But I don't often take the pills. They make me groggy. Case in point: this morning.

The episode was a onetime occurrence. Just something that happened. It won't happen again. I should flush the remaining pills down the toilet.

The whole thing embarrasses me even now.

I shake my head, as if the memory will simply fall out of my brain if I lament it hard enough. I'd love to let it go. To let it dissipate with this morning's fog.

I'm certain there's a sun out there somewhere, yellow and dripping with promise, but all I see in the pale glow emanating through a canopy of leaves is impending doom—shadows and the russet tones of the oncoming season.

I blink. The white fabric of the draperies against the dark yard reverses when I close my eyes, becomes black on white, imprinting a negative on the backs of my eyelids, as if my eyes are the shutter click of a camera.

I'm trying to pay more attention to detail these days. Life in motion is made of confluence, sequence. Objects blurred with the passage of hurried time. If we don't pay attention to intricacies and specifics, we could miss something big.

I blink, take pictures with my mind. *Click. Click, click.*

I see her when I close my eyes: the girl who'd casually strolled through the ballroom at the Fordhams' wedding and placed her hand on my husband's biceps. *I need to talk to you, Ian.*

Ian.

She couldn't have been much older than our children—twenty-one, maybe twenty-two—and she'd called him Ian. Not Mr. Holloway. *Ian.*

She stood casual as can be, in her flowing, red dress, with her hand *on my husband's biceps.*

Blink, blink. Click, click.

I need to talk to you, Ian.

If I didn't think Ian would assume I'm having another episode, that I'm about to lose it again, I might scream.

If I'm losing it, it's warranted this time.

I can't get her out of my head, that gorgeous barely-a-woman with a touch so familiar to Ian that he hardly moved a muscle when she laid a hand on his arm. Yet Ian carries on as if our world didn't shift with her sudden appearance at his cousin's wedding a few weeks ago, as if all is business as usual, as if we're the only two in our bed late at night under the covers.

She's here with us. She always will be—the unwanted third party in an institution designed for two.

Red chiffon skirts.

Hand on his biceps.

I need to talk to you, Ian.

Ian.

Ian.

Ian.

Anger rumbles in the pit of my gut, and I close my eyes.

And there she is: a haunting image in negative.

Her cute, twenty-something ass twitching as she pivots to lead him away from me.

"You okay?"

I startle when I hear Ian's voice, but I turn toward him in anticipation of a goodbye kiss.

He smells of some clean Dolce & Gabbana scent.

His cheek, devoid of whiskers and nearly as smooth as his baritone voice, meets mine.

His left hand trails over my abdomen, and a split-second memory illuminates in my mind: his palm on my very pregnant, seventeen-year-old belly.

It's the same hand. Just older.

But somehow, it doesn't feel as if he's the same man.

"Everything good?" he asks.

"Fine," I say. "I just didn't sleep all that well last night. I kept waking up."

"Take a pill tonight."

"I'm pretty sure that's why I'm feeling this way this morning—I took one last night."

"It's perfectly fine to take the meds two nights in a row. You have to take care of yourself."

"How very *Yellow Wallpaper* of you." I smile.

He kisses my lips. "Can you take my suit to the cleaner's today? The one I wore to Doug's wedding?"

"What? Oh, yeah."

"I don't mean to nag, but it's been a few weeks now."

"No, I know. Sorry I keep forgetting, but it's just that by the time I remember, I'm already halfway to Evanston to do the shopping, so . . ." My phone chimes with a familiar ringtone. It's a text from Quinn: FaceTime?

I reply, Anytime.

"Maybe try to find a cleaner's around here." He winks and points to my phone. "Say hi to our girl for me."

He takes a few steps toward the door but then turns back, presses his lips to my forehead once again. "Love you, Kirstie."

And then he's gone, off to help couples at the end of their rope dissolve their marriages. Off to save a child from an abusive parent, or to prove said parent is reformed. Such is life in the realm of family law. Sometimes you're a hero. Sometimes you're a slimeball.

A series of chimes alerts me that Quinn is FaceTiming. Just seeing her name on my screen is enough to make me smile.

"Quinny!"

"Hi, Mom." She's walking through campus, probably on her way to her first class. Her hair is pin straight and nearly black. Her eyes, a pretty shade of hazel green, practically sparkle when she smiles.

I never knew I was beautiful until I saw shades of myself in my daughter.

"You doing okay?" she asks. "You look tired."

"I am. And old."

"You're not even forty yet."

It's still surreal that suddenly, I'm knocking on forty's door. I graduated high school with my son kicking me from the inside, and my children and I passed through all major milestones as a team. Yet as their lives begin, mine feels as if it's nearly over.

"Thirty-nine is close enough," I assure her. "I think I need the works. Botox. Lipo . . ."

"You don't need plastic surgery, Mom. Look. Just because Dad's cousin married some twenty-four-year-old bartender—"

"You don't like Donna?"

"It's not that I don't like her. I like her fine. But she's bailing out of opportunity. She's taking the easy way out, stealing a married man, then marrying the guy probably because he has money, and quitting her job. It's just . . . frustrating. How are we, as a gender, supposed to aspire to greatness when all we're doing is knocking each other down?"

"I don't think that's how it happened. I think Doug and Lena were unhappy for a long time, and he and Donna happened to meet at the right time. She's a sweetheart."

"Regardless, marrying someone so young is ridiculous at Doug's age. It doesn't mean Dad's suddenly going to expect you to look younger, but if he does, it says something about *him*, not *you*. And, I'm sorry. Doug's covering his gray with that awful inky dye—"

"Ah, yes." They've been graying since they were twenty-one. It's the only flaw in their perfect family genes, and it landed on my son, too. "Dad has a bottle of the stuff, too, now."

"Do not even tell me. And it's obvious Doug's had some work done around his eyes. Whatever happened to growing old with grace and distinction? Donna's just another midlife crisis, like the motorcycle, and I wish you wouldn't measure your worth against her."

"How about against her body?"

"Mom."

"I'm kidding. But Donna's not the reason I'm feeling this way." But I'm not sure she isn't, now that I think about it. Donna represents something I'll never be again—young and full of promise. Just like the girl at the wedding.

I need to talk to you, Ian.

I shudder with the memory of it.

"Then what is it, Mom?"

"I look in the mirror, and all I see, despite the constant yoga, despite the organic diet, despite the antiwrinkle skin cream, are sag and laugh lines."

"Laugh lines aren't a sign of age. They're a sign of happiness."

"That's a good one." How I managed to raise a confident, intelligent, feminist daughter is beyond me, considering I jumped into forever before I even knew who I was. I make my way to the kitchen. "I'm going to write it down."

"I'm serious."

"So am I. I'm writing it down." When I reach the island, I grab a pen and a pad of paper. While Quinn rambles about the dangers of elective procedures and the message they convey to young girls, I scrawl her wise words across the top of the page. As I'm writing the last word—*happiness*—I realize I'm writing on a note Ian must have left before he headed to work:

Don't forget my suit. Xoxo.

"Your dad's dry cleaning." Something curls in my stomach. Feelings of inadequacy? Stupidity, maybe? I'm glad he left a note. I was about to forget all over again.

"What about it?"

"I keep forgetting to take his suit in."

"He left you a note." She rolls her eyes.

"He also brought me a nice bottle of wine and flowers last night. See?" I turn the camera toward the twenty-four long-stemmed red roses filling a Waterford vase on our island.

"Does he still leave his empty deodorant can on your vanity when it needs replacing, too?"

I laugh. "It's a system. It works."

"You know what else works? Saying, *hey, hon, I'm out of deodorant. Would you mind grabbing some if you're going to be out and about?* Or better yet, stopping at the Walgreens to get it on your own on your way back from lunch. It's insulting, the way he stacks his empties for you to deal with."

Quinn doesn't understand that this isn't a statement about how important Ian thinks I am. It's a division of tasks. When you spend the latter portion of adolescence as parents, you divide and conquer. What Quinn sees as demeaning, I see as my part in running a successful household. Yes, Ian *expects* me to do these things for him, but it's become a way of life. I don't question it.

"Mom? Do you feel as if you've *chosen* this life? Or as if it's just something that happened to you?"

I stop moving for a moment. It's not as if I've never thought about it before, but to have your nineteen-year-old daughter put the question to you . . . well, it makes you pause.

When I turned up pregnant at seventeen, my father suggested abortion, then adoption. When I opted for door number three, he kicked me out of the house, and the Holloways took me in.

So now that I think about things, I suppose I didn't have many options being a young, uneducated, unemployed mother of two. But I decided to keep Patrick. I decided to raise him. So that's a choice, and I made it. In many ways, that one profound decision snowballed into a lifetime.

I glance at Ian's note. "I'd better put the suit in the car now. Where's the dress you wore to Doug's wedding?" I ask. "I'll take that, too."

"It's in my closet. In the dry-cleaning sleeve I picked it up in a week after I wore it." She pauses for effect. "See? That's what responsible people do. They wear clothes, they clean them."

"There are worse things than learning to rely on someone."

Quinn counters, "There are worse things than learning how to take care of your own burdens. I know you'll keep doing things for Dad—but you don't have to. If you died tomorrow, you know, he'd have to figure things out."

"What a lovely thought, Quinn. A bit morbid, perhaps, but every day"—I glance at my reflection in the nearest mirror and pull tight the skin above my left eyebrow—"I see the evidence that I'm closer to death."

She rolls her eyes. "On that note, I have to go. I have a study group."

"Okay. Study hard."

"Mom? You *don't* need plastic surgery."

"Love you."

"Kiss, kiss," she says. "Love, love."

I hang up and drop the basket of dry cleaning—much more than a suit; I've really let it pile up—in front of the door. I won't be able to forget to take it in if I have to keep walking past it, will I?

Maybe I should just take it now.

I grab my keys.

———

"One sec." The girl working at this Laundromat–slash–dry cleaner hybrid on the main drag closest to this rural burg barely awards me a glance when I walk in. She fixes her gaze on the television screen mounted in the lobby. "God, this is just awful."

I hoist the overflowing basket of my husband's clothes to the counter and glance at the morning news. "Usually is," I say. "That's why I try not to watch it."

"Looks like a spot of something on the collar here," she says. "Spaghetti sauce?"

15

I'm surprised she noticed it, given she can't tear her attention from the news.

I run my thumbnail over the spot on the shirt Ian was wearing yesterday. It looks like a teardrop, about half an inch in size. "He brought home a bottle of red wine last night."

"Next time, don't try to lift the stain on your own. It can embed deeper into the fabric."

"I didn't."

"Someone did." She points to the faint red ring around the mark. "I'll work on it for you, but a stain like this . . . I'm not sure I can lift it."

"Thanks."

She counts the remaining items. "Twelve shirts, nine pairs of pants, one suit jacket. Pick up in two days?"

"Sure."

She's tapping keys on the computer as I spell our last name, and again, she looks up at the television. "She was just so young. Tragic."

Finally, I turn to the television to see what's going on.

I gasp.

It's her: the girl from Doug's wedding. The one who touched my husband's arm.

My spine softens, and I catch myself against the wall.

Her name appears on the screen:

Margaux Claire Stritch.

I can't help but cover my mouth in horror. It's her. And she's . . . *dead*?

Tears well in my eyes.

She was so young.

Like Quinn.

A whole life ahead of her—gone.

And the things I'd thought about her! Heaven help me, but I'd nastily pondered how much better my life, my marriage, would be without her. I'd wished her out of existence, it seems. I'd wished her gone, practically hoped some evil would befall her, and now . . .

Now it has.

She smiles at me from the television screen—happy and bright and absolutely, downright gorgeous.

I hiccup over a sob.

"Mrs. Holloway?"

Just a few weeks ago, she was moving through the wedding crowd, making her way toward Ian, as if desperately wanting to reach him. She couldn't have hoped to be covert about it—not in a dress like that—but there was a discreetness about it, too. The way she clung to the perimeter of the room until she reached him. A girl like that . . . I'll bet she commanded every room she entered, just by being in it, and now . . .

I catch two words, blurted out as if they don't carry the weight of the world:

Presumed suicide.

No.

The camera zooms in on a female firefighter—the name lettered down the right sleeve of her jacket: BLYTHE—climbing into an ambulance next to a bagged body.

"Lieutenant," a reporter on screen asks, "given the victim is the adopted daughter of Alderman Akers, is it possible there's a link to his sudden leave of absence? Can you confirm you're now investigating this case as a murder?"

Murder?

I freeze.

"Mrs. Holloway? There's something in the pocket here."

I wipe away a tear and glance over my shoulder at the counter girl.

She pulls her hand from the inside pocket of the suit jacket Ian wore to the wedding.

A red thong—silk and lace—dangles from her index finger. She drops it into a plastic bag.

And slowly, my grief morphs to something akin to anger.

I see them like a montage of pictures at the end of a movie—Ian and this now-deceased beauty—walking through the reception hall, going somewhere to talk, somewhere private.

I take the plastic bag, and therefore the red thong, from the dry cleaner's outstretched hand.

The red thong . . .

(Something a twenty-two-year-old might wiggle her way into.)

. . . pulled from the pocket of my husband's coat.

Chapter 3

JESSICA

I can't believe I did this. Again.

Granted, it was a tough end to a long shift, but I've got a good thing going. I don't need this drama.

"Where you going, Jessie?" Decker hooks a finger under the side string of the panties I've just now put back on and gives me a yank back toward the bed.

He wraps a strong arm around my waist and pulls me up close to his warm body.

It feels good to be with him. Familiar. Easy.

But if the past year or so has proven anything, it's that there's no forever here, stuffed into Decker's one-bedroom hole-in-the-wall.

The whole place is cramped, but I guess that's the way he likes it. No room for anyone else. And the view isn't much to write home about, either. I'm presently looking out a third-floor window, across a filthy gangway, at the drawn shades of another third-floor window.

The light from the bathroom—I must have forgotten to turn it off—glints off the brass of Decker's badge, still encased in its sleeve. It's the reason he is the way he is. Herculean. Determined. Unavailable and preoccupied. Suspicious of everyone and everything. Including me.

When you repeatedly see the ugly side of humanity, day in and day out, it's bound to change you. After a decade on the force, Decker has hardened. He expects the worst out of every man—and woman—he meets.

But he's a damn good cop. Damn good in bed. Unfortunately, that doesn't mean he's a good choice. Life with Decker would be wrought with perpetual moodiness and contemplation, and chock-full of constant interruptions and *Gotta go, babe.*

But we understand each other. I've done my fair share of leaving in the middle of birthday parties and uttering my own *I gotta go, babe*s. When I'm on call, I'm on call. Burning buildings don't wait until your nephew blows out the candles on his cake.

I understand Decker's commitment to the job, and he understands mine, but that doesn't mean our lives could meld, even if we wanted them to. I think about things sometimes, revisit the last incident that effectively terminated our official relationship, and I still wonder if maybe I overreacted.

Dinner plans. Eight o'clock. Meet at the restaurant.

He didn't show.

He didn't call.

He didn't answer when I called him.

I didn't see him or hear from him for days, and I found myself scanning articles for news of a dead Chicago detective and checking up on him at the station—like a neurotic mother.

When he finally resurfaced, he offered no explanation, no apology. He simply said it was *part of the job* and suggested I was too angry, too upset, too *fragile* to handle a relationship with him.

I was pissed.

Fragile women don't do what I do on a day-to-day basis.

So I suggested maybe he was too immature for a grown-up relationship with anyone. You can imagine how well that went over.

We stopped making plans to see each other after that.

Didn't stop *sleeping together*, but that's another story.

I dodged a bullet when we broke up. I don't know why I'm tempted to reload the gun every time I see him.

"Still getting to you?" His breath ruffles my hair, and his biceps flex when he pulls me just a tad closer.

"Yeah." The scent of the loft revisits me now—human excrement and rot—and a shiver runs up my spine. I fear I'll see her every time I close my eyes.

Her red toenails and lips. The red nightie. The overturned chair beneath her hanging body.

I much prefer sprinting into burning buildings to calls like the last. Such a personal thing, what I did at the residence of Margaux Claire Stritch. I feel forever connected to her, yet she never knew I existed. Funny that she will always be a part of my life, but I was never even a blip on her radar.

I wonder how she gathered the nerve to strap that rope around her neck and step off that chair. Did she change her mind a moment after it was too late?

What drives someone to take such drastic measures?

"Listen to me." Decker presses a kiss to the top of my head. "We were involved first. Doesn't that make me an exception to the rule?"

It takes a minute for me to shift gears to Decker's train of thought. He assumes what's getting to me is my bad decision du jour—i.e., my slipping between the sheets with him *again*—and the effect it might have on a relationship I've recently kick-started. And maybe that's part of it, but . . .

"So you've gone out with him a few times." Decker drops a smooth, wet kiss onto my inner wrist. "There's no talk of being exclusive with him, right? You're fair game."

"It's not *that*, exactly."

"We're just blowing off steam, you and me," he says. "After that suicide . . . we deserve it. Brutal call, wasn't it? Brutal scene." He licks his lips and stares at the ceiling, and I know he's revisiting the call in his mind. "But if that was a suicide, I'm Gandhi."

"You're not Gandhi."

"I could be Gandhi."

"Gandhi wouldn't be doing what we do."

"No one knows that for sure. I suspect he kept a few surprises under those robes."

"I should tell Jack about us," I say. "I'm going to. It's only fair." What I mean is that I won't. But I should.

"What's fair? You've only gone out with the guy a couple times."

"I just . . . I *like* him, I guess." Which is exactly why Jack should never know about Decker and me. "I should tell him."

"He's too square, too proper for you."

"Mind your own business, Lieutenant."

"Lieutenant?"

I raise a brow.

"There's a lot of weird guys out there," he says. "Are you careful? You meet him out, right? He doesn't come to your place?"

"Not that I need to clear it with you, but no. I haven't invited him over yet. So far, we've only met at restaurants. And he drops me off at the curb at the end of the night."

"So it's just the opposite of you and me."

"Yeah. He actually shows up."

"Ha-ha." He nudges me. "I mean *we* don't waste our time in public."

"I mean it," I say, maybe because I can't stop thinking about the day he didn't show up at the damn restaurant and kept me waiting—and worrying—for days. "This is the last time."

"In that case . . ." Decker slips a hand down the front of my panties. He's still nude, still semihard. He never quite deflates after the adrenaline of calls like the one we hit early this morning, especially when he suspects there's more to the story. It's almost like seeing death and destruction day in, day out, inspires him to live to the fullest. "I want a five-star review."

"It *was* good."

"*Good.*" A guttural sound, half breath and half groan, escapes him. "That might be the most inconsiderate thing you've ever said to me." He gives his head a small shake, just enough to tousle his hair—a bit longer than he usually wears it—so it drops over his left eye.

"It was—"

"Phenomenal?" He blows the hair from his forehead now. I feel his stare, as if his eyes simmer with actual flames instead of desire. "Mind-blowing?"

He's spot-on with that terminology, but he hardly needs the ego pump. I cup his face in my hands. His stubble scratches my fingertips. "Solid. Good. It always is."

"If at first you don't succeed . . ."

My good sense—the modicum I'd just regained, anyway—melts away the moment his calloused fingers twitch in my panties. Sometimes the reminder that life could end in a snap inspires me to keep living, too.

Our tongues meet. He tastes like bourbon.

Another bad decision: the bourbon for breakfast. It's why I opted to stay longer than I should've.

"I should go."

Maybe I will.

I will.

I'll go.

But I've already crossed the line once today.

And this doesn't count, anyway.

Decker was here long before Jack walked into my life. And he's brilliant. Take today, for instance. Woman hanging from her rafters. Apparent suicide. But he sees things others don't see.

If anyone else had been on that call this morning, this case might have been open-and-shut. Suicide. But because Decker was the detective in charge . . .

"What did you say?" I ask between kisses. "*If* it was a suicide . . ."

"Mm-hmm."

"You said something about that at the scene. The techs bagged her hands. Is it just the note the neighbor found that has you thinking it was more?"

"Hmm." His guttural groan at my ear sends a shivering vibration to all the parts of me that count. "Maybe."

"It couldn't possibly have been a break-in. There were four or five hundred-dollar bills left there on the counter."

"Look at you, the amateur cop! When are you going to stop dancing around the fact that you're part of the wrong force and join us in blue?"

I like being a firefighter, but I'd be lying if I said I'd never thought about making the switch.

"Maybe it *was* a suicide." He yanks me back that inch, smashing me into his chest. "But she wasn't wearing underwear."

"Yeah." Like a snapshot in my mind, I see the scrap of red bra in the corner of the living room. It was one of only a few items seemingly out of place in her loft, and the panties were nowhere to be seen—not on her person, and not dangling from some corner of furniture. "Maybe she just didn't wear underwear. It's not that strange."

"She had an entire drawer of sexy little things in her dresser. She wore underwear." His fingers trail up from the small of my back to my shoulders. "But there was also a vase in the sink. Half-filled with water."

"Any decaying flowers in the trash?"

"Trash was recently taken out. No bag in the can."

"So someone could've tossed out key evidence."

"I've got some lackeys wading through the dumpster behind the building. We'll know soon enough. But my guess? She'd been strangled before that rope was strapped around her neck."

"Strangled?" I stiffen in his arms. The images of her swaying body, of the chair knocked sideways, haunt me, like a slideshow replaying in my mind.

"Strangled." He gives me a roll so I'm pinned beneath his lithe body while he works my panties off over my hips.

What the hell.

Like I said, I've already crossed the line once today.

Chapter 4

Kirsten

I drive home from the dry cleaner's, over hills still draped with fog and around curves, in a daze.

That girl is dead.

And it sounds like she may have met with foul play.

My husband obviously knew her.

I saw her at the wedding. I'm pretty sure Quinn did, too, though she didn't mention it to me. Who else might have noticed Margaux and my husband sneaking off together?

I tighten my grip around the steering wheel.

Think.

Would anyone else at the reception be able to make the connection between the face on the morning news and the gorgeous woman in the red dress?

If the police start poking around, are they going to connect Ian to this girl? Are they going to start asking me questions?

What time did Ian come home last night?

I don't know. I felt a little off yesterday, so I took a pill, turned in early, kept waking up. I heard him come in, and suddenly, he was just there. He brought me a glass of wine. It was nice. This morning, there were roses in a vase in the kitchen. And the bottle of red was open and unfinished on the island.

What was his state of mind? Did he act strangely?

Nothing was out of the ordinary.

Until that girl turned up dead.

I glance at the resealable plastic bag poking out of my purse. The thong.

I press a button on my steering wheel. "Call Ian."

A computerized voice confirms: "Dialing. Ian. Mobile."

"Fordham, Holloway, and Lane."

He must have forwarded his calls to the office.

"Hi," I say to the receptionist. "This is Kirsten Holloway. I need to talk to Ian."

"I'm sorry, Mrs. Holloway. Mr. Holloway is out of the office."

"Oh. When's he due back?"

"I'm not sure, ma'am. Perhaps late afternoon."

"He's in court?"

"I'm . . . hmm . . . not sure, actually. His schedule is just blocked off."

What does that mean?

A nervous feeling spins in my stomach. Suppose the police have already connected Ian to Margaux? Suppose they're questioning him right now?

"Would you like his voice mail?"

"No, thank you. Is my son in, by any chance?"

Patrick is interning with Ian's firm, a fact that makes my husband nearly giddy. The plan is for Ian and Doug to bring Patrick on full-time once he finishes law school.

"He just stepped out, ma'am. Maybe an hour or so ago. I expect he'll return shortly. Would you like *his* voice mail?"

"I'll just speak with him later."

I take my eyes from the road for just a second—to terminate the call, to again regard the panties in my purse—and when I shift my gaze back to the road . . .

"Oh!"

I slam on the brakes but still clip the rear right quarter of an enormous deer crossing the road.

The car skids to a halt.

My heart feels as if it's leaped into my throat, and adrenaline pumps through my system. My hands tremble as I put the car in park.

Deep breath.

The animal is getting back to her feet.

I bring a hand to my heart.

My gaze trips into the deer's, and for a moment, we're locked in a stare—me, trying desperately to catch my breath, and the deer, limping onto the shoulder of the road.

Is she going to make it?

Her leg buckles, but she manages to regain her balance and picks up her pace.

Then, still favoring her rear right leg, she darts into the woods. Perhaps to rest before going home. Perhaps to die.

I want to follow her, to make sure she's okay, but what can I do if she's not?

Should I call someone? Animal control and rescue, maybe?

I sit for a few seconds before deciding there's nothing I can do. I put the car in gear and again begin toward home.

Our driveway is long and winding through the woods, and one might miss it if not for a gate marking its location at the county road. The gate bears the name previous owners endowed upon this property: *Giardino Segreto.*

Secret garden.

Maybe if I hadn't landed here after (because of?) the most humbling and humiliating experience of my life, I'd find such a thing charming.

But as things are, I long for my smaller house on a postage stamp–size lot in Evanston. Or maybe I long for the days before all our neighbors and friends watched me fall to pieces, the days before my phone ceased ringing, as if the episode were a contagious plague that might befall anyone attempting a conversation with me.

I turn onto the driveway. Did I leave the gate open when I left with the dry cleaning?

Maybe I did.

But I don't think so.

When I see Ian's car parked on the motor court, however, I breathe a sigh of relief. If he's here, he opened the gate. If he's here, I'll be able to talk to him about these red panties. If he's here, he's not at the police station, so maybe no one knows about his connection to Margaux Claire Stritch.

I park next to Ian's BMW, inspect my SUV and find a crack in the grille where the doe and I collided, and enter the house.

I see him standing on the back porch, right hand in his pocket, his cell phone to his left ear. I hear him laugh.

I approach the french doors leading outside and hope to catch a word or two to determine to whom he's talking, and about what.

I take a step closer.

He turns toward me and instantly ceases conversation.

"Patrick," I say, when he says, "Mom."

To whomever is on his phone: "I'll call you back." My firstborn pockets his phone and approaches me with open arms. He walks into mine.

"God, from the back, you look so much like your father." And he does. His posture, his mannerisms, even his haircut are reflections of Ian, but he's a nice mix of the two of us, resembling my side of the family in facial features. "Your father's car is in the driveway, and I just thought—"

"Yeah, I took his car in from the city," he says. "Dad's in court, but he said you didn't seem right this morning, so—"

"I'm fine."

"—he asked me to pay a visit."

"Just trouble sleeping last night."

Patrick's gaze narrows. "You seem rattled about something."

I glance at my purse atop the island. I could tell Patrick about the panties, which would certainly explain things.

"You sure you're okay?" He slides a hand back into his pocket.

But if I tell Patrick, he could go straight to Ian and forewarn him that a confrontation is coming, and I'm counting on the element of surprise to garner my husband's genuine reaction. Besides, do I really want my son to know these sorts of things about his father?

If, that is, he doesn't know already. I've considered more than once since they've begun working together that Patrick may now be part of a traditional boys' club. And men stick together.

Already, I know Ian and Patrick concealed Doug's affair with his current bride from his ex-wife. During Ian's best man's speech, he'd said, "I've gotten to know Donna over the past six months." But Doug had divorced his first wife only three months prior.

"There was a package for Dad on your porch," he says. "A padded envelope. Probably another one of his autographed golf balls or monogram tees. I left it in Dad's study."

I nod. "Okay."

"You sure you're okay?"

"I'm fine." I take a breath. "At the cleaner's, the news was on, and there was a girl . . ." Tears threaten to well in my eyes, but I ward them off. "They think she might have been murdered, and she was so young and beautiful."

I pause to gauge his reaction, but there's no recognition there. If he's seen the report of Miss Stritch's death, or if he knows about any affiliation his father may have had with her, he's wearing a poker face. "That's terrible."

"It just got to me," I say. "She was so young. I couldn't help but think of Quinn."

He opens his mouth to respond, but I don't want to hear another dissertation about cutting apron strings or about the natural order of things, and I can't listen to one more word of pity regarding the episode—or worse, warnings that another may be coming and I ought to medicate, *take care of myself.*

"And to top it all off," I say before Patrick can go there, "on the way home, I hit a deer, so if I seem shaken—"

"You hit a deer?"

"A doe. A big one, too. She ran into the woods. I don't know if I should call someone, or—"

"If she ran, she's probably fine."

"Yeah."

"Any damage to the car?"

"It's minor."

For a few seconds, neither of us says anything.

"Mom, maybe you should find something fun to do." Patrick leans a hip against the porch rail. "A hobby."

Something to keep me busy, he means to say, while his father romances young girls. I shake my head and sigh.

"Join the women's league, or something," he suggests. "A tennis club. Take up golf."

"Golf? Please. Patrick, I'm *fine.*"

He chews his lower lip, and his brows come together, as if in deep contemplation. "I just want you to know you can. If you want to."

"You even sound like your father these days."

"Well, like I said. He's worried about you. We all are."

I can't say it aloud, but to be honest, I'm worried about Ian, too. This girl is dead. Possibly murdered. Panties matching the color of her

31

dress were stashed in his jacket pocket. If Ian had anything to do with her death . . .

"How'd he seem this morning?" I ask.

"Fine, Mom."

"Not at all upset about anything?"

"No." He shrugs. "He just wants you to adjust, you know."

"I'll adjust. I'll settle into this place."

"Do you like it here? Because if you don't, you could always find another place. Maybe not Evanston, but Winnetka. Lake Forest, maybe."

"I *will* like it here. I *will*. Once I start to meet people. And I'm sure you have better things to do than babysit me." I hope it doesn't sound like a brush-off, but he doesn't appear to be affected by this girl's death, and if I expect to breathe today, I have to learn as much as I possibly can about the end of her life. If Patrick doesn't know anything, I'll find someone who does.

"We are pretty busy, actually. Dad's got me working on a continuance for this millionaire so we can protect his assets from his bimbo third wife. I mean, come on. They were hardly even married. Six months doesn't amount to half his life's work, am I right?"

"That's what they have you doing? Cheating some poor girl out of a marital settlement?"

"Not a *poor girl*, Mom. A gold digger. There's a difference."

I try to smile. "Well, I'd better let you get to it, then."

My son wraps me in another hug. "I always enjoy seeing you, Mom."

"Love you. Close the gate when you leave, okay?"

I watch until my son, in my husband's car, rounds the first bend and is out of sight.

Then I pounce on my laptop to see what I can learn about the girl found dead in Bucktown.

Chapter 5

Jessica

Jack canceled our lunch plans via text: I'll make it up to you. So sorry.

The truth is that I'm not like other girls.

The youngest of five, with four brothers, I grew up as the only female in the household once Mom and Dad split. Mom rarely exercised her every-other-weekend visitation, so maybe I didn't have a strong female example to follow, or maybe my brothers teased me if I became overly sensitive about something girly and I simply learned to toughen up. But I don't care about my birthday. I don't worry about a few extra pounds—drinking beer does that, you know—and I couldn't care less about a guy canceling a date . . . as long as he calls or texts and doesn't leave me waiting like *some* people I know.

I'm sure Jack expected me to throw a fit, and I really was looking forward to seeing him. But when you're dating a financial analyst, there are going to be times he hops a flight to New York at a moment's notice.

And then there's the matter of my commitment issues. I sort of like that he's not hovering over me all the time. Truth be told, I don't know that I would be in this relationship with Jack if his career didn't afford me a certain amount of freedom.

I text back, Totally fine. See you when you're home.

Before I put my phone back in the breast pocket of the flannel shirt I'm wearing—it's Decker's; I wore it home after our tryst, and shared shower, this morning—I send a text to the detective I can't seem to quit: Late lunch?

A girl's got to eat, after all.

After a few minutes, he returns: Meet me at the station. 2:00.

I draw in the faint scent of Decker's cologne, still lingering in the threads of the shirt fabric, and I wish I didn't care that the scent of him comforts me.

———

I'm late to meet Decker, but it hardly matters. He's not at the station when I arrive. I tell the desk sergeant at the door that I'll be waiting at the lieutenant's desk.

"Go ahead," the sergeant says with a chuckle. "*Someone* oughta use it."

"I suppose." I laugh at the joke I've heard dozens of times.

"By the way, food for thought." The sergeant slips a form of some sort beneath the glass window. "Could use another good soldier."

It's an application for employment with the Chicago Police Department. "Very funny. Do you know how long it took for the *fire department* to take me seriously? And you think I want to go through that initiation again with the PD?" It wasn't the only reason I'd opted to join the fire department—the biggest reason being a plea from my father, who thought the police force too dangerous for even a *tough broad*, his words, not mine—but cops were known for being considerably harder on female applicants.

"Hey," the desk sarge says, "we give *all* rookies a hard time. Not just the ones with tits."

"Excuse me . . . have you seen some of the veterans around here? The chief himself, I'll bet, could fill a C cup."

The desk sergeant holds his gut while he laughs. "See? You can hold your own."

Maybe I can. I keep the application.

I wind through a maze of metal desks and canvas partitions, where everyone's too busy to pay me any heed, to Decker's cubicle. For as cluttered as Lieutenant KJ Decker's apartment is, his workspace practically advertises that he's always in the field. Fat files are rubber-banded and labeled and lined up in straight piles on his desk. Someone has been compiling reports and evidence for him.

I take a seat and fully intend to busy myself with a game of solitaire on my phone, or maybe, while I wait, I'll get my online grocery order ready so I can eat something other than takeout this week. But the file atop the stack may as well have a neon arrow blinking at it: open me, open me, open me.

There's just something about Margaux Claire Stritch that I can't stop thinking about. I know my experience at the scene is still fresh, and I ought to give myself time to process it all. I also know delving into the details isn't going to help me put it behind me anytime soon, but I pull the file from the top of the stack and loosen the band.

After a quick look around—everyone here is preoccupied—I open the file.

There's not much in it yet, but that's not surprising, considering it just happened.

I sift through copies of photographs—evidence, pictures printed off the victim's social media pages . . .

I practically gasp when I see her suicide note.

Short and sweet, as they say, Margaux's suicide note—separate from the note she left her neighbor—is composed of seven words: I'M SORRY. I CAN'T DO THIS ANYMORE. It's written in measured block letters, but the signature has flourish: Maggie.

It seems to be written in pencil.

It could be that's all she could find at the moment. But the message's length is rather interesting. Given she'd taken the time to put on lipstick, she'd recently gotten a pedicure, and she was wearing a nightie when she died, her final words seem cold and impersonal. The scene of her death was intimate. The bra in the corner of her living room. The lingerie and the absence of panties. Nothing impersonal about it . . . except for this note.

I peel a sticky note from the stack on Decker's desk and write a notation regarding the lack of intimacy in her last words.

On a second note, I jot, *Short suicide notes=usually written quickly. This lettering is too precise. Writer was not in a hurry.*

A third: *Female victims/younger victims usually write longer notes.*

And there's something else about the signature that doesn't ring true . . . it appears she lifted the pencil tip from the paper several times while signing her name. I slap another sticky note to the margin of the photo and draw an arrow to one of the incidences: *Indication of forgery?*

Now that I'm into it, I can't wait for Decker to research the possibility and fill me in, so I pull up a graphoanalysis site on my phone. While I know it won't be admissible as exact science in court, graphoanalysis might jump-start some theories, which will lead to asking the right questions, which might lead to answers.

I scribble onto another note: *No X-formations or strike-throughs in the signature. Usually see these things in the penmanship of suicidal people.*

Narcissist indicators here: writing in all caps. Do narcissists kill themselves?

And there's something else bugging me. It's about the name she signed. Sure, *Maggie* could be a nickname, but something tells me that if she were going to sign a nickname to her suicide note, she'd probably address the note to someone specific. I could be wrong, but I write a note suggesting Decker follow up.

Just for kicks, and because I have time to kill, I do an internet search of Margaux's name. She has a Facebook page, an Instagram, and a Twitter account. I can't access all her information, but nowhere is it suggested that she'd ever used the name Maggie. I write down the names of a few of her friends. Maybe Decker can interview them to find out.

While surfing through the little bit of publicly accessible content on her pages, I come across a picture of her with an older couple . . . the same man and woman the chief and I encountered on the way into her building early this morning, the same people Decker approached, with me at his side, to tell them Margaux was dead. Her adoptive parents.

I stare into Margaux's eyes on my screen.

"What happened to you?" I ask her smiling, two-dimensional face.

The question is coming too late, I know. The time to ask would have been prior to the final event—when there was still time to prevent it.

I google her adoptive mother's name, Helen Akers, and learn that she's a former journalist turned philanthropist, a staunch Catholic woman who, when she isn't campaigning for her husband, volunteers and raises funds for Catholic charities. Margaux's adoptive father is a councilman for the city of Chicago, Alderman Richard Akers, nick-named "everyone's granddad," who recently announced a leave of absence.

Further digging reveals the alderman is under investigation for misuse of public funds . . . and that he has a gambling problem.

Ah.

That explains all the media attention.

She's related to a politician. And not just any politician. A politician under investigation.

The next article reveals that for the past several months, Margaux was a dancer at the Aquasphere Underground. I haven't heard of the club, but it raises an obvious question: Did an obsessed regular stalk her and kill her?

But murder by hanging? It's just so . . . weird.

If it's murder, the hanging is a cover-up for whatever really happened. A strangulation, perhaps—as Decker speculated.

As I read on, I learn that the deceased was just accepted to law school.

> "Dancing was a means to an end," a source, who prefers to be identified only by the name she used at the club, Gail Force, revealed. "She was saving for tuition. She was good, an amazing performer. But that's not all she was, so don't turn her story, or her life, into something sleazy. She was smart, intelligent enough to know how to make money fast, because she didn't have time to waste earning it by waiting tables." Force recently retired from the underground scene, but when asked whether her departure was prompted by a choking incident involving Stritch, as some patrons have said, she declined to comment.

I take a screenshot of the quote and text it to Decker.

I put the pieces together: Margaux needed money fast for school. Everyone's granddad had money problems. Are the two issues connected?

Maybe. But the fact remains: Margaux had planned the next phase of her life. While she probably wasn't thrilled with having to dance in order to garner an education, it was working. Why go through the trouble of making that happen if you're only going to end it?

I slap a sticky note, on which I've scribbled this question, on the inside flap of the file, and turn to the next photograph. It's a somewhat grainy image of the vestibule out front at this very station, a snapshot captured by the station's security camera.

I check the date and time stamp.

In the days before she died, she was here.

The next image, time-stamped less than five minutes later, has her exiting. I doubt she was here long enough to file any sort of report, but if she did, her complaint or concern could point Decker in the right direction.

Was she here because she was afraid of something . . . or someone? Or because she knew something she shouldn't have known?

But when I leaf through the file, I confirm that no report was filed. Likely, she left the station before she spoke to anyone.

My stomach growls.

When I hear someone moving on the other side of the cubicle, I quickly close the file.

"Jessie?" I look up to see one of Decker's colleagues, his sometimes partner, Lieutenant Jimmy Oliver, peering over the cubicle divider. There's a mug in his right hand.

"Hey, Ollie."

"Was that your stomach? Jeez, eat something."

"Yeah, I guess I should be heading to lunch."

I check the time.

I've been waiting here nearly an hour and a half.

I scroll through my text messages and, of course, find none from the elusive lieutenant alerting me he's had a change of plans.

"I'm guessing Decker isn't going to show."

"If you're waiting for Decker, you might be here until Christmas. We're partnered up this month, and I hardly see him." He sips from his mug. "You guys back together?"

"Um, no. That's a *big* no. Just wanted to talk to him about the case we were both called to this morning."

Ollie points to the application for employment. "Are you finally gonna bite the bullet and join us in uniform?"

"I wear a uniform," I remind him.

"You could make a real difference here."

"Yeah, yeah. Hey, by any chance do you know . . . this morning's victim . . ."

"Heard you cut her down."

"Yeah, I did." I nod. "Any evidence of sexual assault?"

Ollie raises his brows.

"It's just that I know what she was wearing, and I just stumbled over an article that stated she was an exotic dancer. The more I think about it . . ."

Ollie shrugs.

"Right," I say. "You can't tell me."

"Like you haven't been thumbing through that file for the past hour?"

Busted.

"I can't tell you because we don't have the autopsy report," Ollie says. "But if I have to guess . . . I'd say odds are better than average."

Time tumbles backward for a moment, and suddenly I'm there in Mom's trailer—the place she holed up in after she left us. And there he is: the guy she'd dragged home from the bar that night. And the way he's looking at me . . .

"Jessie?"

When I hear Ollie say my name, I shiver and force myself back to the present. It was so long ago. Not nearly as bad as it could've been. And I survived.

"You okay?"

I blink away thoughts of the past—that monster's stale breath and coked-out eyes—and meet Ollie's glance. "Yeah. I just must be hungrier than I thought. I'm gonna jet. Good to see you."

I stuff the application for employment into my shoulder bag and stand.

"I'll tell Decker you stopped by," Ollie says.

"Oh, that's all right. Don't bother. It's no big deal." And then, perhaps with a pace bordering on rude exit, I head toward the door.

Chapter 6

KIRSTEN

I print out the article I found via an internet search.

Margaux worked at the Aquasphere.

Hmm.

It's a bar downtown, hip, with separate underground facilities catering to the sexual fetish crowd.

I know Ian has been to the Aquasphere.

I've been there with him. Not in the tawdry Underground, of course, but we had drinks in the upstairs bar with a couple we used to hang out with last year before a Blackhawks game.

It's the same bar Donna tended before she and Doug hit it off.

The same bar where she and Doug—and Ian, who was there that day for drinks with clients—met.

I lean back in my chair and nibble on the arm of my reading glasses.

So the plot thickens.

I need help sorting it all out. I want answers.

Again, I try my husband's cell phone, which still routes to reception at the law firm: "*No*, Mrs. Holloway, he *isn't* back yet, and *yes*, I'll be sure to tell him you called. Again."

The red panties practically glare at me from my purse.

I wonder if Donna knew Margaux. Or if Donna knew that Ian did.

I navigate to Facebook and find Donna's page, which is littered with photographs of her and Doug holding colorful, frothy drinks with a variety of Caribbean backdrops. A quick scroll through her friends list tells me they weren't connected on social media. I don't see any pictures of Margaux, and there is no reference to her whatsoever in Donna's recent history.

She posts selfies chronically, so I can see exactly what she's been up to and where she's heading.

Last night, she wore a black dress, pink pearls, and fuchsia pumps. She and Doug were out to dinner.

This morning, she was nursing a hangover in Hello Kitty pajama pants.

I'm about to message my new cousin-in-law, requesting a lunch or a conversation, when another update pops up on her page.

Now her selfie tells me she's getting ready for yoga.

Well, I suppose I know where to find her, then.

I glance down at what I'm wearing. Perfect.

One perk of running my husband's errands all day is that I perpetually live in yoga attire. I pull my hair back, grab my mat and a water bottle, and am out the door.

I make good time to the studio I used to frequent when we lived in Evanston. When I walk in, only a few minutes late, I spy my husband's cousin's new bride in child's pose near the front of the studio.

We exchange a glance during our first warrior pose.

I offer a wave, which she returns.

Ian hasn't called all day, despite my leaving several messages, and it's after three.

I might be the only person constantly checking her watch at yoga class, but I can't relax, even in Savasana.

The girl at the Fordhams' wedding was a dancer at a fetish club.

Her panties are in my purse.

She's dead.

My husband is avoiding me.

And I'm supposed to namaste my way through this?

Relaxation is a pipe dream at this moment.

Donna seems just as fidgety.

For someone who just recently returned from a long honeymoon in Aruba—and boy, does she have the tan to prove it—she seems off, disconnected. Or maybe she's just losing her fight with the hangover.

Once class comes to a close, I approach the newest member of our family. "Coffee?"

She pauses for a second too long before nodding. "I only have a few minutes."

"To go, then?"

———

"So tell me all about it." I pour a fourth sugar into my latte at Backlot Coffee on Central. "How was Aruba?"

"It was amazing," Donna says. "I wouldn't mind staying there through the winter months. Two days back and I wish we'd never left." She hasn't once taken her gaze from her coffee cup, which she stirs with a stick incessantly as we exit the café and begin to walk toward the parking garage. She's distracted. Or maybe she simply doesn't want to be here with me.

I understand the latter. Given we have very little in common, we'd make unlikely friends.

"At least our weather is still pretty decent," I say. "Though we had some insane fog this morning in Mettawa."

"What?" She looks up finally. "Oh yeah. But how are *you*?"

The tilt of her head and the pout of her lips tell me she, like the rest of my family, is under the impression that I'm still not managing the transition to an empty house.

I hate that that was her first impression of me a few months ago—as an out-of-control, sobbing mess. No wonder she'd rather keep her distance.

We stop at a traffic light and wait for the walk symbol. "I'm fine," I say. "I'd rather just move on and forget it happened altogether, but no one seems to allow that."

"I didn't mean—"

I silence her with a hand on her forearm. "I didn't mean *you*." I smile and roll my eyes. "I meant my husband."

"The only reason I mentioned it at all is that you look sad today."

"Actually, so do you." And maybe it's not socially acceptable to say what I'm about to say, but . . . "It's a strange feeling, isn't it? To suddenly be someone's wife? To have their aspirations precede your own?"

"Who says that's going to happen?"

"You quit your job, right?"

"I'm relieved," she says without hesitation. "I tended bar for the money, and now I don't have to put in those long, late hours."

"Still, I'm sure it was empowering, in a sense. All those men thinking you're gorgeous . . . which you are."

"Thank you, but . . ." She shrugs. "That's actually one of the reasons I'm relieved. I mean, no one aspires to be a bartender. Trust me, if I could have afforded an education, I'd rather have landed *anywhere* but the Aquasphere."

"Tell me: What did you want to be when you grew up?"

A weak smile begins to form on her lips. "Oh, it's silly."

"Nothing's silly about childhood dreams."

"I wanted to be a wedding coordinator," she says after a minute. "I saw *27 Dresses* when I was in high school, and I thought . . . how great would it be to help people get married?"

What a lovely thought, and if her wedding is any indication of the events she'll put together as a coordinator . . . "You should do it. Go get your degree in leisure. Doug will help."

"What did *you* want to be when you were a kid?"

I laugh. I haven't thought about that in years. Maybe a decade or more. "I wanted to learn how to fly an airplane."

"You wanted to be a pilot?"

"No, I just wanted to know I could do it." Back then, I had a million aspirations—like a mountain range: at the top of one peak, I could be a pediatric nurse; another, an artist or a fashion designer; another, a journalist.

I was without direction, for sure, but I always thought I'd reach a peak one way or another. When you're young, you don't realize time eventually ends.

Like for Margaux Stritch . . . suddenly opportunity just fizzled out. Suddenly, it was over.

We begin to cross the street.

I clear my throat. "Listen. I saw a report on the news this morning, and, full disclosure, it's the reason I hightailed it out here for yoga. I want to talk to you about it."

"I didn't watch the news. I tell you, give me vodka by the boatload and I can handle it, but"—she massages her right temple—"I *cannot* handle red wine."

"Yeah. You should try taking ibuprofen before you go to bed."

"I'll do that."

"Listen. A girl died last night."

Donna whips her head toward me, and for the first time since I walked into the yoga studio, I feel like I have her full attention.

"Or early this morning," I say. "I don't really know when. They're not saying."

Donna raises a brow. "Why'd you want to talk to *me* about it?"

"She worked at the Aquasphere Underground," I continue. "And I also saw her at your wedding."

"*My* wedding?" She shakes her head. "I didn't invite anyone from the bar to my wedding, and I didn't interact with many people in the Underground. It was a job, that's all. I don't want people to know Doug met me in a bar and get the wrong idea."

"I understand." But whether or not she was invited, she was there.

I imagine Margaux up against some wall at the Fordhams' wedding venue, Ian between her thighs, with a hand beneath her dress, working that scrap of satin and lace over her supple ivory hips.

Why am I doing this to myself? I didn't follow them; I can't possibly know they disappeared that night to have sex. Rationally, I know it's unlikely, actually. Why would Ian risk it with his wife and children nearby? But I can't get the image out of my head.

And thinking of it, I slip back into an ugly, jealous place, where I realize things might be better at home now that she's dead. Since I first saw her, I've wondered every time he leaves the house if he is sneaking away to be with her. Now that she's gone, I can stop wondering.

But I hate feeling that way—relieved. She was just a girl, and despite her connection to Ian, her life is over now.

"Regardless, I was wondering if you knew her," I say. "Margaux Stritch?"

For a second she just takes another sip of her coffee and stares up at the traffic light at the next intersection we've come to. Finally, she speaks. "If she worked the underground circuit . . . look, no one uses their real names down there. I doubt I knew her, but even if I did, I wouldn't recognize her name."

"How about a picture?" I'm already trying to juggle my coffee and my phone, trying to call up the picture that's been pasted all over every news outlet in the city. I finally manage to scroll to the right image, and Donna barely glances at it before she shakes her head.

"Did *you* know this girl?" Donna asks. "I mean, why do you care?"

"I think Ian screwed around with her."

"Shoot, I'm going to be late," Donna says.

"I'm sorry. I didn't mean to make you feel—"

"No, *I'm* sorry, I really should—"

"Okay."

I stand on the curb as she races in the opposite direction, calling over her shoulder, "I'm sorry. I just have somewhere to be."

Well.

That was interesting.

THEN

MARGAUX

"Helen?" Margaux's voice echoed in the marble-clad entryway of the large, Victorian-era house in the historic district of Chicago. The neighborhood was called the Gold Coast for a reason. The place reeked of old money.

She grew up here, which wasn't to say she belonged here, but she had called the massive place home for nearly half her life, since the rest of her family perished in the car accident. Only she had been spared. She walked away with a sliver of glass lodged in her right cheek, just below her eye. People called her lucky. Two inches higher and she would have been blind in her right eye. If she'd been sitting anywhere else in the minivan, she'd be dead. She was lucky.

Lucky.

She touched the scar on her cheek. Although it was nothing more than a slightly raised line of flesh, a symbol of her survival, it was also a constant reminder of how she'd come to be here. There's nothing lucky about losing one's family.

She always thought of them when she walked through the door—Mom and Dad; her sisters, Kendall and Chelsey—and even though over a decade had passed, it still felt as if she were entering the place for the first time with a duffel bag stuffed with things that weren't really hers. Things she'd acquired through the department of child and family services over the several weeks she'd spent in a group home.

The state social workers had taken her back to her house to gather her belongings to take to the Akerses' place, but being the middle child, she realized that almost everything had been handed down from her older sister.

Nothing was hers anymore, if it ever was, least of all choice. If she had one, she wouldn't have elected to live with two people old enough to be her grandparents. And that's what they wanted to be called, too—Granddad and Grandma. It hadn't felt right to call them that when Margaux was a child; it felt incredibly wrong now that she was older.

Still, Helen Akers was a philanthropist, willing to take in a skinny twelve-year-old with "a mouth on her," and Helen's husband, Richard, was highly respected in the city—a career councilman. He was, at times, jovial; his wife had the personality of a pinched nerve.

It could've been worse, as the caseworker pointed out. At least she was going somewhere with substance. And her parents' life insurance would be put into a trust, which would take care of her for the rest of her life. With someone so wealthy to adopt her, she wouldn't have to worry about the funds being mismanaged. Most kids in her position would be lucky to have any funds at all.

The always-dim house, cold and museum-like, was looming and foreboding, and she was still afraid to touch the soapstone chess set always displayed, but never played, in the front parlor. After the scolding she'd received after daring to feel the smooth contours of the bishop's hat one day, she wouldn't dare lay another finger on it even as an adult.

Technically, this was home, but it was far from comfortable—and never had been.

"Helen?" With fat envelopes in her grasp, she meandered farther down the hall, toward the first-floor study, where a lamp burned in the eerily quiet space. "Richard?"

Margaux peeked inside to see Richard seated in his usual leather club chair, his head in his hands. A cocktail glass stood sweating on the old, embossed table to his left. She inhaled the scent of aged scotch.

For a second or two, she flashed on the first time Richard put his hand on her knee. She'd been with them for a few months, and it was Kendall's birthday. She was sad—bawling—and Richard helped her through it.

Only years later had she realized he'd gained pleasure from those touches. Only years later had she recognized the insidious purpose with which he had made himself intrinsic to her survival.

"Where's Helen?" she asked.

He looked up at long last. Instantly, she knew he wasn't only drinking, but drunk. Which meant that Helen had either locked herself in a room upstairs, or she was out.

His smile was wide but tired. "There's my girl." And he patted his lap, as if he actually expected her to sit there, to pretend she'd always been his real granddaughter, to pretend he could possibly love her the same way other grandfathers loved their offspring's offspring.

"I got in." She lingered cautiously in the doorway and displayed the envelopes one by one. "John Marshall. Loyola. UIC . . . they all accepted me."

His expression morphed from absolute elation to regret to sorrow in the space of four or five seconds. He emitted a loud, dramatic sob and again patted his lap.

"Your granddad is proud of you." *Pat, pat.* "Come here."

"What's wrong? Where's Helen?"

"She's going to leave me," Richard said.

"Why? What happened?"

"It was a sure thing, babydoll." He swept his scotch up in his hand. It sloshed out of the glass when he brought it to his lips. "I had a line on a horse, and the damn horse lost."

Oh.

"It lost!" He threw the glass at the walnut-paneled wall upon which she was leaning.

Shards of glass and ice and splashes of scotch ricocheted. One shard embedded in her wrist. "Ouch! Richard, stop!"

Pillows hit next.

And when he rose and attempted to pick up the chair he'd been sitting on, she screamed again—"Stop!"—and took a step back out the doorway.

He let out another whale of a sob and put the chair back down. He stumbled back and collapsed into it. "Come here. Your granddad needs you."

Margaux plucked the glass sliver from her arm and, pressing an acceptance letter to the puncture, took another step toward the front door.

Soon she was running and wiping the tears streaming down her face.

When she reached the door, she heard the weight of steps on the grand staircase. "Margaux."

She looked over her shoulder and met Helen's gaze.

The older woman wore a navy pantsuit, devoid of even a single speck of lint. Her graying hair, cropped in a feathered bob à la Laura Bush, bounced as she descended, and her lips were pressed so tightly into a thin line that they took on a colorless tone. "Leaving so soon?" Helen said, even as she lugged a suitcase behind her.

Margaux sniffled. "I just came to tell you . . . I got in. Everywhere. I'm going to law school."

Helen shook her head. "He lost your tuition."

She said it as if Richard had simply misplaced the funds, as if she expected the money to turn up any day now.

"He lost everything," Helen said. "There will be no law school for you."

"But my parents' insurance—"

"Gone."

"My trust is supposed to be—"

"Don't be naive. He had to pay back the funds, don't you see?"

"Funds?"

"Do you think it was his money he lost?"

"It was mine?"

"It was everyone's. The whole city's."

Margaux took the suitcase from Helen and set it closer to the door. "Where will you go?"

"Go?" Helen shook her head. "I'm not going anywhere. But your granddad is heading to the streets for all I care. He's bottomed out for the very last time."

"But if my money's gone . . . What about my expenses?"

"You'll continue to live rent-free in our building, but as for the rest of it . . . You'll be on your own for a while, but nothing to worry about. You'll be no more on your own now than you were at age twelve."

"But it was my money," Margaux says. "It wasn't yours to use."

Helen turned her back on her. "You'd better go. You know how he gets when he's drinking."

"I need that money. I'll tell the authorities what he did if you don't give it back."

"Do that and you'll destroy him. What kind of selfish daughter—"

"He's done plenty to destroy me," Margaux said.

Smack!

Helen's open palm landed square on Margaux's cheek. "That's the thanks I get? For taking you in? For giving you a good home? That's the problem with your generation. You don't think you have to work for anything. You don't think you have to *wait*."

Margaux took another step toward the door, her hand to her reddening cheek. "But this is wrong. That money was for my education, my *future*."

"Goodbye," Helen said.

Margaux didn't look back, just ran.

She boarded the L and cried softly while staring out the train window at the city lights zipping by. An hour ago, she had the world at her fingertips with a choice of three graduate schools. Now, it seemed she'd have to turn them all down.

A group of girls in short dresses and strappy heels boarded a few stops later and chatted nonstop about the fabulous dinner they'd just shared, about the hip bar in Lincoln Park they were en route to now.

That's what I'd be, she thought, *if my life hadn't happened to me.*

She exited when they got off the train car, a few stops earlier than where she usually did, and hung back about twenty or so feet behind.

One of them pointed to a bar and said, "That's it!"

"We came all the way out here for *that* place?" another said. "I ain't drinking in a church."

Margaux's gaze trailed to the old Gothic church across the way. A turquoise neon sign glared from the shingle—AQUASPHERE—and on the opposite end, an arrow pointed down a flight of stairs and blinked: UNDERGROUND.

Margaux knew the bar. She'd never been there herself, but she'd heard classmates talking about it. She looked down at her clothing. The jeans and Rolling Stones T-shirt weren't quite suitable for a club, but after what she'd just learned, she didn't care.

Richard had lost her tuition money.

Lost it.

Screw it. She was going to drink alone tonight.

She climbed the steps and entered what must have been the original vestibule of the building. For as large as the church was, this bar was positively tiny.

Three sets of doors behind the bar, those she'd assumed would have led to the open space where parishioners heard services, were barred. Signs warned off drinkers: NO ADMITTANCE. She walked to the far corner and tucked herself into a hole where she could sip a cocktail out of the way of everyone else.

But getting a drink proved difficult in a place that could double as a sardine tin packed to the hilt. Catching the bartender's attention would be a feat within itself.

A flyer posted to the wall caught her eye: *Dancers needed. Apply underground.*

"What are you doing here?"

She flinched when he touched her knee but soon found herself face-to-face with a man who obviously thought she was someone else. "I'm sorry. I thought you were . . ." He threw his head back and chuckled. "Forgive me. You look like someone I know."

She narrowed her gaze at him. He was good-looking.

He held out a hand. "Arlon Judson."

"Margaux."

"Classy name for a classy dame. Can I buy you a drink?"

After the whole ordeal with one of her prelaw professors last semester, Mr. I Swear I'm Nearly Divorced, she couldn't be too careful. She glanced at Arlon Judson's left hand and saw no signs of a wedding band—no tan line, no dent at the base of his knuckle. "If you promise not to shell me with cheesy lines . . . sure."

"So, Margaux. Has anyone ever told you that you look like Marilyn Monroe?"

She rolled her eyes. "Really? That's the best you can do?"

"Blonde. Bombshell. No-brainer. It's not a line, it's just the truth."

When she didn't respond, he tried again: "And let's be honest. Deep down, you're more of a Maggie than a Margaux, aren't you?"

"Always been Margaux. Never Maggie."

"Do you believe in love at first sight, Maggie?"

"That's actually why I came here underdressed tonight. To fall in love at first sight."

"What do you drink?"

"Finally, a question I don't mind answering: gin and tonic with two limes."

"That's my favorite drink. You're quickly becoming my favorite person."

"Why am I not surprised?"

The bartender leaned toward them. "Everything all right here?"

"Two gin and tonics. And I'll be right back. Left my jacket over . . . one second."

The bartender buffed the bar with a turquoise rag. "You okay?" she asked.

Margaux quickly checked the perimeter before realizing the question was directed at her. "Me?"

The bartender nodded toward the man, who was on his way back to the bar with his jacket. "Be careful. Seems like a nice enough guy, but . . . be careful."

Margaux nodded.

Arlon Judson returned. "In all seriousness, what brings you out tonight?"

"To be honest, I had a rough day with my family."

"I'm sorry to hear that."

"Thank you."

"Anything I can do to help?"

Arlon Judson was being polite. Or he obviously wanted to get into her pants. No one offered to help a stranger, especially without knowing what type of help she needed. And while she knew Mr. Judson likely had one underlying motive in mind, his smile was so genuine that she softened.

"At the risk of sounding like a line," she began, then shut up. "I was going to ask if you came here often."

"Often enough," he admitted.

"Have you ever been downstairs?"

For a second he didn't answer, but his grin told her everything she wanted to know. He knew the place well, if she had to guess. She looked again to the flyer on the wall. "What happens downstairs?"

"Sweetheart, what doesn't?"

"Anything goes?"

"Anything and everything. Ironic that this place is a church, isn't it?"

"On the contrary, I think it's honest. I was raised by two of the most outwardly Christian people you'll ever meet. They're not good people."

"It's loud in here. Do you live nearby?"

"I do."

"That'll be convenient then. At closing time."

"Fine line between confident and cocky. I'll drink with you, but I'm not going to sleep with you."

"Maybe not tonight." Arlon raised his glass. "But here's to someday."

She laughed.

"Seriously, let me walk you home. You can tell me all about it."

"That's a nice offer," she said. "But after the day I've had, I'm not ready to go home."

"Okay."

She sighed. "My whole life, I've tried to do everything right, and you know what? It doesn't help. It doesn't get me where I want to be, it doesn't stop bad things from happening to me, so . . . I'm done. Done doing what I'm supposed to do."

"What did you have in mind? Because I *know* you're not interested in a one-night stand."

"Let's take a detour," she suggested. "Let's go downstairs and see what happens."

Chapter 7

KIRSTEN

Her case is on the news again.

Margaux's neighbors place flowers and teddy bears and lipsticks near the lamppost outside her building at the corner of Leavitt and Webster in tribute to a life lost too soon.

As I watch the news, I pace around my living room, periodically eyeing the half-finished bottle of wine Ian brought home last night, recorked on the island. I don't want to drink it in case I have to drive later. But I can't sit still.

What the hell. I yank out the cork and pour a glass.

Breathe.

When my phone chimes, I pounce on it, although the ringtone alerts me that it's an incoming message from Quinn, not her father, who hasn't returned a single call or text all day.

Are you watching the news?

She's hella familiar.

Sigh. She probably recognizes Margaux from the wedding.

And I'd interrogate Ian about the girl, but he's MIA.

Something must have happened to him. And no one wants to tell me about it.

If he were in an accident, I'd surely know by now.

If he were staying late at work, I would know that, too.

And not a single judge in America is holding court well into dinnertime, so I'm not buying that he was in court all day.

But suppose Ian was brought in for questioning in the death of Margaux Stritch? Doug might be willing to tell a white lie to conceal that fact, and Patrick wouldn't want me to worry. He'd keep it from me, too.

I glance at the television, where they're rerolling the footage of the firefighter climbing into the ambulance, accompanying Margaux's dead body to the morgue. I'm glad they didn't toss her, lifeless, into the back like cargo. I'm glad she had company. But how must it have felt for the firefighter? Being alone with a dead body?

I text Doug, Patrick, and Donna—all on the same thread: Has anyone heard from my husband?

Because I can't risk anyone assuming I'm about to have another episode—and I've been bothering these three people all day, so they very well may already be there—I add: Starting to miss him. ☺

I sip my wine.

Pull the panties out of my purse.

Take another lap around the kitchen island.

The police are asking the public to call the station with tips, but I call for another reason.

"Yes, I'm wondering if anyone's been arrested in conjunction with Margaux Stritch's murder. No?" I sigh in relief. "Okay, thank you." Tears begin to build, to the point they might become a vicious storm. What if the police were lying about no one being arrested? They can probably do that. They can probably do anything they want to do, if they think it'll help move the investigation along.

I imagine Ian sitting in some cold room with harsh lighting discussing Margaux Stritch with a team of investigators.

What if he tells them I can account for his whereabouts?

I can't. Not for the entire evening, anyway.

And how am I supposed to hide the fact that there was a freaking red thong in his jacket pocket?

There's nothing I can do. If Ian had anything to do with this girl's death, I can't help him.

Or . . . suppose he fled town to avoid facing charges, and he's left us all alone to deal with everything?

I've relied on him my whole life. Can I possibly make it on my own?

I ball a hand into a fist and scream until my throat is raw. When I'm out of breath, I lay my head down on the cold granite countertop and cry. "Ian, where are you?"

"Kirstie?"

I bolt upright. "Ian?"

He's there, with car keys whirling around his finger, looking at me like I'm nuts. "You okay, hon?" He grips me under the elbow and helps me toward a chair at the island.

"I'm fine," I say. "I don't want to sit down."

"No, you were screaming. For no reason. I think you should—"

"I've been worried." I slide the chair back under the countertop and refuse Ian's offer of a seat. "I've been calling you all day, and you're basically ignoring me, and after everything going on—"

"Sorry. I had a full docket, and this evening, after hours . . ." He sits next to me. "Well, I brought something for you."

"For . . . for me?"

"You seemed sad this morning. And I figured, now that you have some extra time on your hands, maybe you could use an outlet."

"Where've you been, Ian?"

"What happened to the car?"

"The car?" I cradle my head. "Oh. I hit a deer this morning." It seems so long ago. "I thought Patrick might have told you. But listen, there's something you should know—"

"Can it wait?" He smiles.

"Ian, have you seen the news today?"

"The news?" As if he finally realizes it's on in the next room, he pivots toward the television.

Margaux's face fills the screen. A reporter's voice: "Authorities were called to the scene when a concerned neighbor located a suspicious note reportedly alluding to foul play."

I keep a close eye on my husband.

His hand shakes a little as he reaches back for a counter stool.

He swallows hard.

His flesh pales. He doesn't say a word, but his silence says enough.

"Did you know her, Ian?"

"No. I mean, yes. Not very well."

"How did you know her?"

He presses his lips together, as if to show me his lips are literally sealed.

"Where did you meet her?"

He shakes his head. "Kirstie, you don't have to worry about it. It's not what you think."

I wipe a tear from my eye. "Not what I think." I reach for my purse. "I'll tell you what I think." I toss the thong to the island.

His stare is directed toward the underwear for long, uncomfortable seconds. He finally glances up at me.

"Well?" I plant my hands on my hips and stay rooted.

"What?"

"What do you think?"

One brow rises. "I haven't seen you in something like this since—"

"I'm not offering to wear them. The dry cleaner found them in your suit coat."

"*My* suit coat?"

"Yes. The coat you asked me to take in. And that girl. Margaux. I saw you talking with her at your cousin's wedding."

"You're mistaken."

"She touched your arm and called you Ian."

"So you heard that."

"You don't deny it."

His lips form the word I don't hear him say: "No."

"What were you doing with her, Ian? Why were her panties in your pocket?"

"I don't know why *your* panties would be in my pocket, let alone someone else's."

"She's dead."

His Adam's apple bobs with a hard swallow. "Such a tragedy."

"Well?" I nod toward the panties. "What do you know about it?"

"I . . . nothing! I just found out right now, this minute."

"Do you know what it's like, hour to hour, waiting for your husband to call? Waiting for a smidgen of confirmation that he hasn't been hauled into the police station for questioning when a girl he's been sleeping with turns up dead?"

"Sleeping with? Hey, now—"

"Her panties were in your suit coat."

"You keep saying that. *Her panties.* Surely, you're not suggesting that I—"

"Whose are they, if they're not hers?"

"How should I know?"

"If you have another woman's panties in your jacket—"

"I. Don't. Know." He shoves the bag containing them toward me. When he slowly rises from his seat, I'm forced to take a step back.

"I hung the jacket on the back of my chair at the reception," he says. "It's a basic black jacket. Any man, especially with the amount of drinks flowing that evening, could've mistaken the coat for his. Anyone could have slipped anything into those pockets. Is it just possible that our son mistakenly grabbed my jacket when he went out for a cigar? That the panties belong to his girlfriend? He's much more of the age to be looking for a quick tryst in an alleyway than I am, anyway."

"Don't play lawyer with me."

"Damn it, Kirsten. Stop accusing me of something you know I didn't do!"

"My whole life, I've done nothing but believe in you, Ian." I'm pacing again. "At the wedding, I saw you talking to her. I gave you the benefit of the doubt. I've seen signs, and maybe I should I have pressed the issue sooner. But I didn't because I was afraid. Afraid of what the truth might lead to. Afraid that you'd do what you're doing now . . . that you'd try to make me feel as if I'm crazy.

"But it doesn't make sense. I saw you talking to her—you still haven't denied that—and now she's dead, and the thong was in your pocket, and it's too coincidentally similar a color to the dress she was wearing that night. It doesn't make sense."

"You're right, it doesn't. I hardly knew her."

"She knew your name."

"You know what? I think you're still not quite right after the episode. Are you listening to yourself?"

"And still you haven't told me: Who is she? How do you know her?"

"It's not relevant." He pinches the bridge of his nose and sighs deeply before again meeting my gaze. "You need to trust me on this. If I tell you who she is, I risk someone else's confidence. It's privileged."

"So she's a witness in one of your cases?"

"Privileged."

"If you don't tell me, I can't trust you."

"You can trust me. Kirstie, after all these years . . ."

"After all these years, I never expected to find another woman's thong in your pocket. I can't trust you if you don't explain: How do you know her?"

He regards me with an expression of surrender. "Doug had an affair with her."

He fiddles with the band of his Tag Heuer. I lock my gaze on it.

"She showed up at the wedding," he continues, "ready to make a scene. I was running interference that night."

"And the panties?"

"Honestly, Kirsten, I just don't know. On the life of our children, I just don't know how they'd end up in my pocket."

I study him, look him in the eye.

He can't hold my gaze.

I drive the heel of my right palm into his shoulder. "You swore on the lives of our children," I say. "And you can't even look me in the eye."

Silence hangs between us.

After some time, he clears his throat. "You know, I think I'm going to the city tonight. I'll have dinner with Patrick, and I'll stay at his place downtown."

"What?"

"For a day or so. Two, three."

"Ian, wait."

"I, uh . . . I think I'll go now. Give you some time to come to your senses."

"Come to *my* senses? Why is it that every time we get into an argument, you tell me I'm nuts and you leave? Normal couples talk it out, spend the night together. Ian, if you leave, you're giving me all the more reason to think you're hiding something."

"You're not making any sense. You've had a long day, with the deer, and with the news . . . and you've let yourself fill in the blanks. Once you're thinking clearly, you'll see that I had nothing to do with this girl."

"Ian."

"No, Kirsten." He raises his voice and points a finger at me. "I've never given you any reason to doubt me. I've been faithful to you since we were fifteen years old. I don't deserve this."

"You have to admit this is an unusual circumstance. This girl is dead, for God's sake, and a pair of panties was stashed in your suit coat. And you were gone all day, and no one knew where you were, and you came waltzing in *hours* after the close of business. What am I supposed to think?"

"You want to know why I was late today?"

"Ian. There were panties in your suit coat. And a girl is now dead."

"I drove out to Blick studios. I bought you an easel and canvases, and brushes, paints. I know you wanted to be an art major."

"Seriously, Ian? I don't paint."

"I thought you did. You won a prize, didn't you? At the art fair our senior year?"

"It wasn't for a *painting*."

"Well, whatever. The point is that you need something to occupy your time. My heart's in the right place."

"Don't distract me. I mean, thank you. Thank you for doing that, but you're skirting the issue!"

He turns toward the stairs. "I'm going to pack a bag."

"Ian, please."

"I think you need time. Take a few days," he says. "Let me know if you think you can put this negative energy toward something useful and satisfying. If you want to reconnect with friends from Evanston, or make friends here . . . you let me know. But if this is what you want to do with your life . . ." He waves his hand at me, as if he's swatting me away, as if I were a housefly.

"We should talk about this girl. No matter how much time passes, she'll still be here, standing between us."

"Christ, *think about it*! If I knew there were a pair of underwear in my suit, would I be nagging you to take it to the cleaner's?"

I shut up.

"Her death, while tragic, has nothing to do with me. Once you're thinking clearly, you'll see that."

Chapter 8

JESSICA

I decide to wear my department-issue jacket, even though I'm not at the home of Helen and Richard Akers in any official capacity.

They don't have to talk to me, but I'm hoping they will.

I walk up to their enormous brick residence and ring the bell.

The missus answers, perfectly coiffed and wearing a rust-colored pantsuit and black pumps. I can tell by the widening of her eyes that she recognizes me—you don't forget the people who tell you your loved one is dead—but I introduce myself anyway.

"Jessica Blythe." I extend a hand. "Chicago Fire and Rescue. I was on the call . . . with your . . ." Granddaughter? Daughter? "Margaux."

"The police already came by." She hitches a hip. "Unless . . . do you know when they're going to release her to me? I'd like to see to the arrangements."

"I'm sorry about that, ma'am, but I don't know. I'm not here for the city. I just thought I'd check with you to see how you're doing."

"Oh. Well, come in." She steps aside.

I enter.

The place doesn't feel lived in. Rather, it feels like one of those houses photographed for an interior design magazine. And there's not a single family portrait anywhere to be seen.

"I apologize that my husband won't be able to join us," she says. She perches on a small sofa in the foyer.

"That's all right." It's clear I won't be admitted any farther. I take a seat in a chair opposite her.

"He's indisposed, dealing with some personal issues." She says it as if half the city doesn't know he's under investigation. "I'm sure you understand. Margaux's death has crushed him."

"I imagine."

"Well . . . the Lord must have a plan. We go through trials at his whim, don't we?"

"Was Margaux a believer?"

"That's how I know she didn't take her own life. I sent her through catechism classes, and she went to church with us weekly until a few years ago. She knew the gargantuan sin it would be. She'd fallen out of practice, but I still feel, in her heart, she wouldn't have done it. May the Lord save her."

"You know, ma'am," I say, "if there's anyone else you think I should pay a visit to . . . a boyfriend, maybe?"

"She *was* seeing someone. Arlon Judson. But they'd broken up."

I nod and commit the name to memory. "Any idea as to where we can find him?"

"I don't know more than the name."

"Or friends? A colleague at work, maybe . . ."

"Margaux didn't have friends. And she didn't work outside of school."

"Everyone has people," I say.

"Margaux didn't."

"Hmm. Why do you think that is?"

"She'd been through a lot in her life. I suppose others couldn't relate to her."

"I know something about that. Too bad." I nod. "She had a job, though. At the Aquasphere Underground."

"That's a ridiculous accusation. I read about it in one of those gossip rags, and it's disgraceful what people are allowed to print."

I try another angle. "You know, Mrs. Akers, I appreciate everything you do for Catholic Charities. I, myself, went through a counseling program with the organization when I was young."

"Oh, really?"

"My mother had a problem with addiction."

Her brows slant downward, and she nods, as if urging me to continue.

"One of her boyfriends took certain liberties with me that he shouldn't have."

Her lips thin into a white line, her brows come together, and she begins to wring her hands in her lap.

She looks angry.

I suppose I can understand that. It's a terrible reality.

"If not for people like you," I blurt out, "I don't know how I would've survived."

"Do you think I don't know what you're inferring?"

"Ma'am, I'm not inferring anything—"

"Do you think I don't know Margaux spread those dirty lies among our friends? Complete fabrications! She could have ruined us, you know. Such accusations! To think anyone would believe my husband would have been inappropriate with Margaux . . . it's ludicrous. Is that why you're here? Are you looking for some way to pin motivation to kill her on me? On my husband?"

"I don't know anything about that. Like I said, I'm not with the police. I'm here to check in with you. To see how you're doing."

"And to invent a personal abuse story to get on my good side! Have you no morals?"

I stand. "I suppose I should be going."

"If you want to bother someone, if you want to know who's responsible for Margaux's death—"

"*I'm* not investigating. I only came as a courtesy—"

"—look at the obvious suggestion. Arlon Judson."

"I'll inform the police."

"Please do."

"I'm sorry for your loss," I say as I edge my way toward the door. "I'm sorry to have upset you. I really was here only to see if you needed to talk."

She crosses her arms over her chest.

"But I didn't fabricate what happened to me," I say. "I was hurt, and I survived. And if that sort of thing happened to Margaux, too . . . well, maybe she could have used some compassion instead of your judgment."

With that I place my card on a small table—if she wants to talk later, she can call—and head out the door, quick to text Decker: Call me. I might know something.

THEN

MARGAUX

Arlon knew the password to gain entry—*whip it good*.

He paid her initial membership fee, an exorbitant $1,000, and a guard—a tower of a man whose shirt was labeled PAGE—gave her a special card with a scanner code and a gold bracelet with the same code stamped on the underside. "You'll need both to enter," the page said. "Guard them with your life."

Then Arlon paid the cover charge, an additional $200. Each.

And the moment she and Arlon set foot on the subterranean level of the Aquasphere Underground, Margaux's nerves awakened.

She felt the music in her bones, and the beat settled deep down in places she wasn't supposed to talk about. Instantly, her flesh was dewy with the heat of the room, and she swayed against her new acquaintance's body.

The place smelled of something sweet, like cotton candy, and scantily clad waitresses roamed the floor with test tubes of a glowing purple liquid.

"Aphrodisiac," Arlon told her when she asked what it was.

And the next she knew, she was throwing one back.

Naked men and women alike danced in cages and on stages, some alone, some in pairs or triplets, and black doors lined the perimeter of the place.

"There's only one rule here," Arlon said. "What happens at the Underground stays at the Underground. That means no pictures. No videos. Nothing posted online."

"I can see why," she said.

"And I have the same rule. Nothing posted online."

"I abhor social media."

She took Arlon by the hand and pulled him toward the closest door. A gold star on the door bore a label: **WATCH ME.**

The next door: **PARTY OF THREE**

The next: **TIED UP AT THE MOMENT**

And the next: **WAX ON, WAX OFF**

PAINT BY NUMBER.

DRAG DAY.

They had another drink.

Then two, then three.

Another shot of aphrodisiac.

Another dance.

"Look," Arlon whispered. "It's the ultimate act of trust."

She followed the point of his finger to a window across the hallway, where a dominatrix gave commands.

A woman was tied to a table, and her man was honest-to-goodness having sex with her while a crowd gathered around. The dominatrix gave an order. The man obeyed . . . and closed his hands around the woman's throat. She writhed in both panic and pleasure. Just when Margaux was sure the poor woman would die of strangulation, the dom whipped the man's bare ass—"Enough!" He released his hold, and the bound woman practically squealed with the delight of orgasm.

"Ohhh." Margaux, mesmerized, felt hot and pink and pretty everywhere. "Yes, yes," she said along with the woman on the table.

The stranger she'd met tonight, Arlon . . . *oh my God*, he palmed her ass and squeezed. "Someday, you'll trust me like that," he whispered.

He was just what the doctor ordered, just what she needed to forget about Richard and Helen and the money and the future they stole from her.

And then, as if the mere thought of his name made him appear, there he was: everyone's granddad, himself, exiting one of the perimeter rooms, this one coined **Babysit Me**.

She knew what sorts of things probably happened in *that* room. Resentment coiled through her. Disgust.

She kept her gaze fixed on him, and he stood there, mute, mouth agape, staring back. Pain registered in his eyes, but not of the physical sort. He was looking at her as if to say, *how could you?*

He was wondering, no doubt, how she could disgrace him and Helen by walking through the door, by allowing someone she'd only just met to stand so close to her.

Wasn't it just like a man to assume she should never engage in something he'd been doing for years, if not decades?

Arlon's hand was still on her ass, and he was already biting at her neck.

Margaux, with her eyes boring holes into Alderman Richard Akers's, brought her hands to Arlon's fly, unzipped, and took him into her hand.

Chapter 9

KIRSTEN

"Patrick?" I hear the sound of bass-heavy music in the background and the nearby giggle of my son's girlfriend. "Are you out with Becca? Clubbing?"

"We're out, yes," he screams into the phone. "Not sure you could call this place a club, though."

"Do you have a minute?"

"Sort of . . . hold on a sec."

The music fades away, and I ascertain he must be stepping outside. He clears his throat. "What's up, Mom?"

"Your father left. He's on his way to your place."

He sighs. "I know. He already called me. What's going on?"

"I'm worried, Patrick." I begin to fill him in on the day's newsbreak, Margaux Stritch's suicide-slash-murder.

"I know, Mom," Patrick says before I even get halfway into all the reasons I'm concerned. "He told me."

"He says this girl was having an affair with Doug, but it doesn't make sense. Doug left Lena for Donna. Does that mean he was cheating on the girl he was cheating on his ex-wife with? It's all so contrived. Doesn't sound right."

"I don't know what's going on with Doug, but if Dad says that's what happened, well, that's what happened."

"They're saying this girl—the one who died—might have been a dancer at the Aquasphere Underground, and—"

"Oh. Okay, then, that makes sense. That was part one of Doug's bachelor party—that's where we kicked off the night. So maybe . . ."

"That's all fine and good," I say, "and maybe it even adds up. But if this girl had been with Doug, why would her panties have been in—"

"In the jacket pocket, yeah, yeah. He told me about that, too."

I wait.

"Have you considered Dad might be right? That you just need to relax a little? It hasn't been that long since you . . . you know, since your episode."

"Okay, I was upset and a little out of control when Quinn told me she was moving out before the semester even began. I acknowledge it. But it has nothing to do with the fact that the dry cleaner pulled a red thong out of your father's suit coat."

He sighs. "Look, Dad talked to me about it, and I have to say you're way off base. There's no way he'd do what you think he did."

"He seemed to think you might have borrowed his jacket that night. When you went out for a cigar."

"I was a little overserved, Mom. I might've."

"So you're saying the underwear could be Becca's."

"Probably is."

"But Becca stayed at the table with Quinn and me when you went—"

"Not every time. Look. Just throw them away, okay? You're making yourself crazy. Dad says he didn't do it, I don't really remember, and you've been married for a long time. Have a little faith, okay?"

"Yeah, maybe you're right."

"I don't know everything, Mom. But I know Dad. He wouldn't dare. The alimony would kill him."

"The alimony—"

"It was a joke."

But . . . I feel my shoulders go lax. "Is it?" I've never earned a dime of my own money. If Ian wanted out, he'd have to take care of me. For the rest of my life. "If Dad doesn't see divorce as an option, he could feasibly find someone to see on the side."

"That's ridiculous."

"No more ridiculous than to consider I have no choice but to stay. He could hide assets and leave me destitute."

"Mom."

"You just told me you were doing it for another case, so don't tell me your dad can't finagle it. And Patrick, they're saying this girl might have been murdered. If they connect her to your dad—"

"Mom! Relax. You need some sleep. You need to stop jumping to conclusions and trust me on this."

I take a deep breath. "Patrick, just once I wish you'd see things without your father's influence, through your own filters."

"What?"

"I raised you. *I* did. Your father is always your hero, but don't forget that before you were an aspiring law student, you were a kid who couldn't lose a tooth without your mommy's help. Stop placating me. I'm not some idiot housewife you're protecting assets from so you can screw her over in court. *I'm your mother*, and I deserve to be taken seriously."

"Who says you're not taken seriously?"

"You're so busy protecting him that you're not even listening to what I'm saying. She's *dead*, and sooner or later, someone's going to realize he's been involved with her—on some level."

"What do you think I'm protecting him from?"

"I'm going to bring the panties to the police station. Tell me: How confident are you that your father's DNA won't be found on them?"

"Mom."

"Tell your father to be home by morning, or that's exactly where I'm going and that's exactly what I'm doing."

I hang up.

Chapter 10

JESSICA

Amid a noisy crowd at a sushi restaurant off the beaten path, a ruby pendant stares up at me from a bed of black velvet.

"Put it on." Jack rises from his chair, walks around our cozy table for two, and picks up the box the necklace sits in.

"It's too much," I say as he clasps it around my neck. And it is—on two levels. We haven't been dating that long, for one thing, and for another, this looks like an actual ruby. A real one. And I'm wearing one of exactly two dresses in my closet, and all I can think about is how I'm going to keep this damn strapless bra from slipping off the girls all night. I don't know when or where such an elegant accessory would be appropriate in a life like mine.

"Beautiful." I trace the outline of the stone with a fingertip.

"I know you've had a hard week." He resumes his seat. "You were on that call—the suicide."

"I was."

"And I wasn't here for you. I should've been."

"It's not the first dead body I've ever moved."

"Still, it's awful."

"Brutal. But I got through it okay."

"How do you get over seeing something like that?"

If I knew the answer to this one, I wouldn't be waking up several times a night thinking of her, but my best guess is you drink too much and end up in bed with the detective in charge of the case, fucking it into oblivion, that's how. "You just gotta roll," I say. "There's nothing else you can do."

"Is it true they're saying she was murdered?"

"They don't know yet. But it's an interesting case, for sure."

"Mmm." An appetizer arrives at the table. Jack spoons a fried dumpling onto my plate before taking one for himself.

"Jack, have you ever been to . . ."

"This looks good. Sorry, it's just that I'm *starving*." He grins. "I feel like I don't eat unless I'm with you."

"Yeah, I have that effect on a lot of people."

"No, I *like* that you eat. It's crazy how many dates I've been on where she'll nibble on a side salad and not even finish it!"

"Well, you won't have that problem with me."

"Glad to hear it. And go on. You were saying?"

"I was wondering . . . have you ever heard of the Aquasphere Underground?"

"Yeah. Over on . . . Western, is it?"

"You ever go?"

Effortlessly, he wrangles a dumpling between his chopsticks and pops it in his mouth. "Trick question."

I laugh. "It's a yes-or-no question. In no way trick."

"Well, if I say yes, admit I've gone—"

"Ah. So you have."

"—you think I'm some sort of pervert. I go home alone. If I say no, you think I'm a prude, that I'm not good in bed. I go home alone. Lose-lose."

I laugh. He's funny. I like funny.

He flashes a brief smile. "Either way, I'd gladly go with you." He reaches across the table and brushes a few fingers over my knuckles. "Maybe it's time we talked about us, where you see this going."

My chest tightens. Shit, I don't want to have this conversation. I don't want to have to define anything. Talking draws a line. Definition means limits, which equals no Decker.

God, am I ready to never see Decker again?

I *should* be. No good could possibly come of the merry-go-round we've been on since I was inducted into the CFD, when our paths started to cross.

Talk about spontaneous combustion.

We met the night of a warehouse fire—an arson case—and we crashed into each other and didn't come up for air for nearly two days.

I just need to quit him. Rip him off like a Band-Aid.

"You're a different type of girl than I'm used to," Jack's saying.

"Yeah. Apparently I eat, when the rest of the female population nibbles."

"You're strong. Independent. You don't need me any more than I need another headache. But we enhance each other, don't we? And if you want to talk about doing things together, like going to the Underground—"

Double shit.

He thinks I asked because I'm curious, because I'm into the sort of kinky things that happen at the underground club. I can't backpedal now. I can't tell him I want to go to see if I can track down the girl quoted in the paper, Gail Force, or anyone there who knew Margaux. I want to know if anyone there knows anything about Arlon Judson, or anyone ever saw any red flags between him and Margaux. But Jack thinks I want to take things to the next level—that I want to *skip* levels, actually. Skip the basic sex and go straight to kinkville.

I've been hanging out with Decker too long. With Decker, it's sort of understood that every conversation is going to revolve around a case or a call or a cold file. I guess normal guys don't think that way.

As if he sensed I was thinking of him, Decker chimes in with a text message: Free?

I cover the screen with my hand and glance up at Jack, who doubtlessly saw the name Decker light up my screen. I silence the ringer and refocus on Jack.

"This is *good* between us. I only see it getting better." Jack winks and tops off my wineglass, which didn't need another filling. "Lately, you've been much more of a distraction than I expected. Even when I'm halfway across the country, I find myself thinking of you, always wondering what you're up to."

A sense of guilt rises in my gut. When he's halfway across the country, I'm fairly certain he wouldn't approve of what I'm doing. I reach for my wine, and because I feel as if I should say something, I mutter, "I aim to please."

God, I'm a shitty girlfriend.

"And I want to go to Aquasphere with you. I want to go to a lot of places with you."

My phone alerts again—vibrates this time—with another text from Decker.

"Jessica."

I meet Jack's glance across the table.

"I just want you to know I'm here for you. I'm sure there are other people—your colleagues on the call with you—you'd rather talk with about this stuff. Other people you're used to relying on . . ."

Is that a veiled accusation? Does he know about Decker and me?

"And maybe I can't understand the job the way they do. But I'll always listen. So if you want to talk, spitball theories . . . whatever. I'm here."

For long moments, we're locked in a stare across the table.

Finally, he offers a hand, and I slide my fingers into his palm. "And maybe someday you can put it all behind you. Maybe someday you'll find you don't want to do it anymore."

I refuse to blink. And even when he kisses my hand, he maintains eye contact.

I get the distinct impression he's not talking about my career.

He wants me to put *Decker* behind me. He's hoping I don't want to do *Decker* anymore.

"It's none of my business if you're seeing someone else, I guess," he says.

"I'm—"

He stops me with a shake of his head. "We've never said either of us couldn't. But I'm hoping you'll want to change that."

I have to do it, or I'm going to lose Jack: I have to rip off the Band-Aid and quit Decker cold turkey.

Chapter 11

Kirsten

I have to go to the police station or no one is going to take me seriously. When I told Patrick to give Ian my ultimatum last night, I 100 percent assumed Ian would be home before midnight. I didn't think he would actually call my bluff, and now I'm in a tough spot.

Like many women in my position, I've folded more than once over the course of my marriage, but this time I just can't bring myself not to follow through with my threat. The problem, of course, is that if I do, my husband could be in real trouble.

Real. Trouble. Life-in-prison trouble.

I know enough about the law to know that the truth doesn't always prevail in the courtroom. It's more about proof than truth.

And here's the rub: *I don't know the whole truth.*

In desperate need of advice, I'm sitting in the holding tank sandwiched between Doug's office and my husband's, with my purse clenched tightly in my lap. This is a gamble, showing up here, at the boy's club of Fordham, Holloway, and Lane.

I stare at the firm's logo: FHL in the center of the universal symbol for infinity.

Doug's longtime paralegal is periodically glancing at me, although she's trying her best to camouflage her observance. I don't have an appointment, and it's good of Doug to see me on short notice less than a week after his return from his honeymoon. It's equally very likely Doug would have already phoned Ian to tell him of my arrival under normal circumstances, so I conjured an excuse, naturally, to keep him from making that call.

"A surprise party?"

For a split second, when I look up, I think it's my husband leaning into the reception area. But it's Doug, with one hand lingering on the office doorknob and a warm smile on his face. I think Quinn's right about Doug's having had plastic surgery. He and Ian are maternal cousins, born less than a year apart, and their mothers are identical twins. They grew up as close as brothers, and our less informed classmates in high school assumed they were twins. But these days, Ian looks a shave older than his cousin. It's the eyes, as Quinn suspected.

Doug juts his chin toward the nicely appointed digs beyond the door. "Come on in and tell me all about it."

I have no intention of throwing a party for Ian. The element of surprise is what I'm counting on, however, to learn what I need to know—if my husband is completely full of shit—so I have to choose my moment carefully.

"Please, please," Doug Fordham says. "Sit."

I do so, in the leather chair closest to the door, where I'm most likely able to read Doug's expression, as he won't be apt to turn his back to me.

"I have just a few minutes, but I like what I'm hearing." He leans a hip against his desk. "For his fortieth?"

"I was thinking so. I know he doesn't want to make a big deal out of the big four-oh, but I think it's warranted."

"I agree. Count us in. I'll be sure to distract him when the time comes and help get him to whatever location you need."

"Great. Thanks so much, Doug. He works so hard—"

"Don't mention it." He's getting ready to close our meeting, and it just began. I have to work fast. "We'll have to work around the court schedule," he's saying.

"Of course."

"But by mid-December, maybe things will have slowed down. And maybe Donna can help you plan it. She has a knack for that sort of thing, and you gals should get to know each other."

I blurt out, "I wonder about Margaux."

Fordham's brows come together. "Who?"

"Margaux Stritch."

I wait.

He folds his arms over his chest. "Why is that name familiar?"

Because her name is all over the news.

"She's a friend of yours, I hear," I say.

Slowly, he shakes his head, searching some imaginary horizon for answers. And so far, I don't know one way or another if he's keeping secrets for himself, for Ian, or if he really can't place the name. It wouldn't be out of the question, if he doesn't know her, for him to have missed the news of her death. He's been back from Aruba for only a couple of days.

His wife hadn't heard, and judging by the way she rocketed away from me the moment I started a conversation about her, Donna likely didn't rush home to spill the news that someone at their wedding had been murdered.

"Adopted daughter of some political figure?" I offer. "She worked at the Aquasphere. I believe she was at your wedding."

"In that case, she must be a friend of Donna's. You might ask her."

No man would suggest I speak with his new wife about a girl who crashed their wedding, a girl whom his cousin had to divert from making a scene there, if he were sleeping with that girl. But I never bought Ian's explanation, anyway.

"I didn't think you knew her," I say. "But Ian did."

He glances at the clock and pushes away from the desk. "How does Ian know this girl?"

"Do you know where Ian was the night before last? How late he worked?"

"He, uh . . . he's been working late, I know that much, but I just came back to the office yesterday. I don't know what time he left the office. The paralegals are usually gone around four. If he stuck around, he could've been here until ten or later."

My hand is in my purse; I tighten my grip on the resealable plastic bag containing the red thong. Doug can't provide an alibi for Ian. I can't, either. If I bring this evidence—is that what it is?—to the station and establish a connection between Ian and Margaux, it won't matter if he killed her or not. It'll be the end of us. He won't forgive the lack of faith, or the accusation.

But if I don't . . . and he did it . . .

"Why?" Doug asks.

"You know, I've taken up enough of your time." I stand. "How silly of me to waste your time with details. I'll give Donna a call to sort out the guest list."

"That would be best." Doug offers a hand for a shake and pulls me closer and kisses my cheek.

"Donna's lovely, by the way," I say. "I'd love to get to know her better."

"You should. Why don't the two of you have lunch?"

"I'd like that. She made an absolutely beautiful bride."

Doug chuckles. "Don't ask what she's doing with me."

"Nonsense," I say over my shoulder as I approach the door. "You're a catch. It's in the family genes."

"Kirstie."

I turn back toward him.

"You and Ian never had a wedding."

I shake my head. "The drama of being knocked up in high school and all."

"You've overcome some great odds together. Who'd have thought, after all you've been through, you'd still be here, standing strong together?"

"I admit I had my doubts." I try to laugh. "I traded college enrollment for onesies and the Playtex bottle system. It wasn't exactly a sure-fire way to find happiness."

And that's not all I sacrificed. I lost my whole family the moment I decided to pursue this path with Ian. Both my parents are gone now. They were dead before I turned thirty, but I'd said my goodbyes and mourned the loss before I was twenty. If I lose Ian now, it'll be like I've lost everyone who's loved me in my lifetime. I'll still have Quinn—I don't think anything will ever come between us—but I'm not sure about Patrick. Funny how he's the reason I'm still here (not that I regret it), but he's so in awe of his father that I might lose him, too, simply because I may opt to do the right thing.

"Consider a double event," Doug is saying. "A vow renewal *and* a birthday party. Give our grandmother an excuse to have another glass of champagne."

"What a thoughtful idea."

"And well deserved. You've been putting up with my cousin for long enough to be sainted."

For a moment, I stand there with an expression on my face that I hope conveys amusement. He means it to be funny, but given recent events, he doesn't know how true his statement is.

I'm numb as I descend the stairs and make my way through the maze of cars in the Ohio Street garage.

Everything is falling apart.

My marriage is in pieces.

I've got one kid lecturing me and the other placating me.

And worst of all: a young woman is dead.

I sit for a minute in my car, tears welling in my eyes.

Ian is all I've ever known. I've built my entire life around his goals, his needs, his *dry cleaning*. I sacrificed my college education, and a career, to have his children, to raise them. And it's not that I regret doing so. I take pride in the fact that I've raised two amazing people. But now that that job is all but complete, it's supposed to be time to reap the benefits of all the sacrifices I've made.

And now my husband is already traveling another road, and I'm hitting a dead end.

What happened? What went wrong?

I start the car and pull out of the garage, the bright sunlight practically blinding me as I emerge.

But I've been blind enough, it seems.

I steer the car toward Bucktown, toward the fourteenth district police station.

Right is right.

THEN

MARGAUX

"Someone requested you for a private dance." The dominatrix known as Gail Force placed an envelope on the makeup table in the dressing room. "He paid up front for half an hour."

"Half an hour? What the hell am I going to do for *half an hour?*" Margaux, known in the Underground by her code name, Babydoll, opened it. An old-fashioned skeleton key fell into her hand. "Tell me it's not someone creepy. Or . . . or, God, what if it's Arlon? He'll absolutely *die* if he finds out I'm working here." Thus far, she'd been fortunate enough to schedule shifts only when she knew Arlon would be working out of town, but she was playing with fire. It could only be a matter of time before everything came crashing down.

"I don't know who it is," Gail said. "I'm just the messenger."

"I guess there's only one way to find out." She rouged her nipples and stuffed her breasts back into a lace demi bra. She shoved a wig of long, red hair—her trademark in this place—over her blonde curls. With her eyes lidded with glittery lashes, and an entire drugstore's worth of makeup on her face, she didn't resemble herself as much as she looked like a caricature of someone she'd never be. But at least she felt anonymous in this getup.

"You know what's crazy?" Margaux said. "The first time I came here, as a spectator, I was floored. I couldn't get enough of this place. Everything was so exciting and liberating. And now . . ."

"It's sort of like being backstage at a magic show," Gail said. "But hell. Beats paying the cover, right? This way, you get paid *and* you get off."

"Not entirely. I don't get off dancing."

"Keep your eye on the prize, girl." Gail patted her on the shoulder. "Eye on the prize."

"Law school." Margaux stared at her own reflection and repeated the words a few more times. She closed her eyes, took a deep breath, and, key in hand, left to pursue a portion of her tuition money.

She walked through the crowds to private room number nine, where her client was waiting behind a red drape. Another deep breath.

"Good evening," she said. "I'm yours for the next twenty-nine minutes and forty-five seconds. No touching of any kind. We're on a monitor, and if you neglect to abide by this one simple rule, security will, in a flash, flood this room, and you will be escorted out. No refunds will be given for either your private dance or your cover charge. The Aquasphere Underground not only will eject you from the premises but reserves the right to send video footage to law enforcement and local media outlets to best pursue your prosecution. Any questions?"

"Just one: Why Babydoll?"

She froze.

She knew that voice.

She peeled back the curtain.

Richard "Granddad" Akers sat on a red velvet throne, awaiting her. He wore khakis and a light-blue button-down, now untucked over his slight paunch. His full head of hair, salt-and-pepper, was mussed, as if one of the girls had already run her fingers through it.

"It's because I used to call you that, isn't it?"

The music filled the room while tears filled her eyes.

"Why are you here?"

"Because I miss you. Because you left, and you won't return my calls."

"You lost my money."

"I see you're putting all those years of ballet classes to good use," the alderman said.

"Quiet, please. Let's not talk."

"That wasn't the rule."

"Since when do you care about the rules, anyway?"

"We waited until you were eighteen," he said.

"We waited to do the deed," she said. "That's true enough. But the rest of it . . . all the presents, the looks and the touching . . ."

"It wasn't wrong."

"Maybe it was just a hand on my thigh or a hug that lingered too long, but you knew where it was leading. And the night it happened . . . I tried to stop you. You're my legal guardian. It wasn't right."

"You needed love. I gave it to you. Morally, it wasn't wrong."

"I'm not sure Helen agrees with you."

"She doesn't know."

"Oh, she knows."

"How do you know she knows?"

"Because after we started, she only got meaner."

"She's stern, always has been, but—"

"I don't want to talk. I'll just give you what you paid for."

"I want *more* than what I paid for. I want you back home for Sunday dinners. I want to know what you're up to, day in, day out. I want my family back."

"I want my tuition money."

"Is that why you're working here?"

"Why else?"

"I don't like it."

"Neither do I, Richard. But you left me with no other options."

"I'm working on it, you know," he said. "Working on getting your money back."

"You'll lose it again."

"I'm not drinking anymore. You know I only crossed the line with you when I was drinking." His hand went to his crotch. "God, the way you used to look at me."

"You were my savior," she said. "The only light in my life. You were *nice* to me, and she *hated* me! What did you think was going to happen when you climbed in my bed? *Of course* I thought I'd fallen in love with you. You're the only one who was even remotely kind to me. You took advantage of a naive girl desperate for love."

"Margaux."

"Uh-uh." She waggled a finger. "That's not my name here."

"Tell me about the new guy."

"No."

"Is he good to you?"

"None of your business."

"Come to dinner this Sunday."

"Not a chance."

"I'll give you a thousand dollars for every dinner. I want my family back. Time to heal, the three of us. Together."

"You want me to earn my own money back?"

"That's what you're doing now, isn't it? Do it my way, and you don't have to take off your clothes. That new guy never finds out what you've been doing here."

"He already knows."

"No, he doesn't. I know you. I know this isn't who or what you are, and you're not proud of what you're doing. It's the same way I know you didn't tell him about what happened between us. So what do you say? Dinner, and I'll pay back what I took."

"At the rate you propose, I'll never make it to law school. And if you have that kind of money, which you must if you're getting off in a place like this, you should be paying back what you stole from me, regardless of whether or not I sit at your table and pretend everything's fine."

"Down payment." The alderman placed a stack of bills on the side table, where his drink would normally be sitting.

"I'll think about it."

"Don't think too long."

———

"I think it would have to be roses." Margaux walked home from the L stop with her phone at her ear. With all the paint and glitter washed from her face and body and the leather and lace replaced with a T-shirt and jeans, she felt like a completely separate entity from the girl who'd danced for Richard.

Arlon made it easy to push all those terrible memories into deep, dark closets in her mind.

"I'm partial to red ones," she continued. "But roses are kind of like chocolate. You never look at them and say . . . *eh*."

"On that note, what's your favorite chocolate?" Arlon asked.

"White. Definitely."

"Red roses. White chocolate. How do you feel about panties?"

"I wear them."

"Say I'm coming over, and you haven't seen me in a week. And you know I'm dying to see a show."

She paused for a second. Was this a trick? Did he know she'd just come from the Aquasphere Underground?

"I have a few interesting things you might like. Leather, mesh."

"Anything a little softer?"

"You'd like that?"

"I'd love to watch you cook in a red nightie. Red satin, with a lacy G-string."

"I'll have to put that on my list of must-haves."

"You're my kind of girl."

"And you're my kind of guy. So . . . what's happening in Houston at three in the morning?"

"Nothing. Anywhere without you is boring."

"Ditto."

"Where are you, anyway?"

"I'm almost home, and thank goodness, too, because I think a storm is coming, and I didn't bring an umbrella."

"You shouldn't be walking so late in the city alone."

"Well, you're not here all the time, and I have to fill the void *somehow*. I couldn't sleep." And now, time for a lie: "Went to a midnight show." Or performed one . . . fine line between the two, but what he didn't know wouldn't hurt him.

"Hungry?"

"Starving! But the only place still open anywhere close to home is that little diner."

"Want to have a three a.m. dinner together?" he asked.

"Sure. I'll grab something to go. Skype you when I'm home?"

"I knew you were going to say that."

Margaux rounded the corner. Her building, with a lantern illuminating the front porch, came into view.

And so did Arlon and a porch full of presents.

He held up a bag of carryout.

"You're always reading my mind." She terminated the call and ran toward him.

They met on the sidewalk, and she threw her arms around him. His lips instantly found hers.

"Turns out, I know you pretty well," he said between kisses. "Red roses. White chocolate. Cheeseburger. And this . . ."

A small bag from a lingerie boutique on State Street dangled from his hand.

"This is actually a present for me, but . . . you get to wear it."

"You're amazing," she said. "How did I get so lucky as to find you?"

A flash of light cracked the darkness.

"What was that?" she asked.

"Lightning," he said on a breath at her neck. "Storm's coming."

It seemed more like the flash of a camera, but she was too excited to see him to argue such a silly point.

"Dessert first?" He leaned to her lips. "You? Nightie? Making love all night on your rooftop in the rain?"

"Luckily for both of us," she whispered into his ear, "I suddenly have a craving."

Chapter 12

JESSICA

"Arlon Judson," I say when I walk up to Decker's cubicle.

"Who?" He barely looks up when I walk in, but I forgive it because it's near the end of the night shift—about six in the morning—and if the guy's slept, eaten, or showered since I last saw him, I'd be surprised.

"He's someone you should talk to." I lean a hip against his desk, where I see he's filtering through all the notes I left him the day he blew off our lunch plans.

"Okay. Who is he?"

"Margaux Stritch's boyfriend, and I'm guessing the reason she has an *A* and a *J* carved into her breast."

He awards me a split second's worth of eye contact. "Interesting. And how did we come across this information?"

"I texted you, remember? Said I might know something? I paid a visit to her adoptive family. The alderman wasn't in, but his wife . . ." I whistle. "What a treat. But she said you should be looking for Arlon Judson."

"Any clue how to find this Arlon Judson?"

"Can't do your whole job, Lieutenant. Just part of it. Is the autopsy report back yet?"

"It is."

"What do you hear?"

"It's classified. Part of an ongoing investigation."

I roll my eyes. "Come on. The reason no one's heard from your sorry ass since this whole thing happened is because I analyzed your meager little file. Gave you plenty to chew on, didn't I?"

"Don't you have a kitten to pull out of a tree or something?"

I help myself to a tin of peanuts open amid the clutter on his desk. "I'm not on shift until tomorrow morning."

"Yeah," he says. "Me neither."

"Anything in the trash at Margaux's building prove helpful?"

Decker leans back in his chair and slowly shakes his head. "No half-dead bouquet of flowers, if that's what you mean."

"So what's with the vase, then?" I pop a peanut into my mouth.

"I don't know." He reaches for me, draws a line with his finger from midthigh to my knee.

His touch sends a shiver straight to all the parts of me that count in the middle of the night.

"Want to grab a bite later? Maybe rent a movie?"

"Can't. I have a date."

"With boy wonder?"

"His name's Jack. And occasionally he cancels on me, but you know what? He texts me to let me know he's not going to show. Christ, Deck, I waited here for you over an hour the other day."

His gaze hangs there, tangled with mine, and I know that suddenly—judging by his touching his lower lip with the tip of his tongue, the slightly askew tilt of his head—he's trying to find something witty to counter my logic. He presses his lips together, as if holding back the words he knows neither of us should say, and the silence, in the space of only a few seconds, grows absolutely unbearable.

"What?" I say. "Stop looking at me like that."

"You're pretty incredible, you know. And it's not that I can't grow up and have an adult relationship. It's the job. The commitment to the cases I work. You'd be the same way if you were on the force. It's tough for people to commit to cops in the long term."

"You push people away."

"You decided it wasn't enough for you," he says. "And I don't blame you. You need what you need. And, apparently, you need someone more grown-up than me."

"How old *are* you, incidentally?"

"At heart? Or in years?"

"Either way, does it matter? We decided we didn't work."

"And yet our paths keep crossing."

In the space of a breath, I remember how it felt not to be sneaking around with him—as if I'd just bought a great pair of one-of-a-kind strappy sandals. And they're comfortable, and sexy, and they go with everything, but after slipping them on a few times, I notice they're not holding up against normal wear and tear. Lieutenant KJ Decker is like those sandals. He's great to a certain point, but then the buckles start to fall off and the leather becomes unstitched, so to speak. And he's still beautiful, and I keep taking him out of the box to look at him, but I know if I test him out again, on actual pavement, it's only a matter of time before I'm barefoot.

Just when I think I can't handle another second of the silence, he intentionally taps a file on his desk, and it spills to the floor. "Aw, man. Would you look at that?"

I instantly crouch to help gather its contents.

He's crouched next to me.

We make eye contact when I see an autopsy photograph.

This one is of Margaux's bruised neck, and I zero in on what he wants me to see: an oval smudge of black and blue, roughly the size of . . . "Is that a thumbprint?" I ask.

"Sure looks like it, doesn't it?"

"Strangulation. Made to look like a hanging. Up close and intimate. And considering she wasn't wearing panties . . . lovers' quarrel?"

"Very good. So you can imagine how much I appreciate the intel about Arlon Judson."

"Yeah, but where to find him?"

"I hope to know more about that as soon as the analysis comes back. The perpetrator left some DNA for us to play with."

A sinking feeling dances in my gut. "She was raped?"

He shrugs a shoulder. "All I know is there's evidence of intercourse. It was likely of the rough variety, given the bruises on her inner thighs—old bruises, mind you, occurring a few days before her death. But not necessarily against her will."

I feel a little better hearing she might have consented, but—

I think about the cash left on the counter at Margaux's place. The panties in the drawer of her bureau, but none on her body. The reports of her working at the Aquasphere Underground. "Was she a call girl?"

"Why do you ask?"

"The hundred-dollar bills left on the counter. Four or five of them, right? Rough sex. Maybe someone was paying for it the way he liked it."

"Maybe. But I'd assume any john would take his cash with him after he committed a crime of passion."

"Unless it was an accident. Unless he got attached to her and felt remorse for what he'd done."

"Accidentally murdered her, then staged a hanging?"

"In a panic. It could happen. I mean, a guy paying for sex isn't going to want to call the cops if something goes wrong midromp."

"I guess."

"But either way, there's evidence left behind. That's good. You'll catch him."

"I will."

"Do me a favor: catch him enough for all the other bastards who got away with doing the things he did to her."

Decker's stare is sober and focused. "It's not too late, you know."

"Forget it." Decker's heard my tales of woe before, but now's not the time to hash it out. Now he should be centered on Margaux. "I shouldn't have said anything."

"We can track the guy down and prosecute."

"It was too long ago. I don't even know if he's still alive."

"Your statute of limitations runs out in two years, ten years past your eighteenth birthday. That's plenty of time for me to find him. And I will. If you want me to."

I stare into his eyes.

"Your experiences could be the reason you're always doing my job," he says. "You want justice to prevail. And it didn't for you."

"I . . . Deck . . ."

He raises a brow, reaches for a strand of hair that's escaped my ponytail. Such a gingerly touch. It feels good. Comfortable. But I know if I let it continue, I'm only signing up for a lifetime of waiting at diners for a guy who'll never show up.

"I gotta go." I stand.

"Talk later?"

"Yeah," I say over my shoulder. "Fine."

He knows I'm avoiding the conversation, but that's okay. He should get a taste of his own medicine.

When I near the lobby, I see a woman clad in Lululemon. A pair of sunglasses sits atop her head, holding back her dark hair. She's somewhere pushing forty, and she looks as if she hasn't slept in nearly a week. "I just want some information," she's saying to the desk sarge, who's barely glancing at her as she speaks. "They're not saying on the news one way or another, but . . ." Her hand dips into her purse and almost pulls out a plastic bag. Almost. At the last minute, however, she shoves it back in. "If Margaux met with foul play—"

"You related to the deceased, ma'am?" the sarge says.

"What? No. I'm . . ." She fumbles over words. "Not *family*, but sort of . . . I guess you could say we were friends."

"Sort of, huh?" The sarge looks at her over the rims of his glasses. "If you have information for the detective working the case, I'll call him. But if you don't, you'll have to wait for the breaking news."

She steps back. "I'm sorry to have bothered you." The plastic bag is still in her grasp when she leans against the door and exits.

It's obvious she's conflicted. Maybe she knows something. Maybe she doesn't. But one thing's for certain—if every city employee blows her off, we'll never know.

I follow her and have to break into a light jog to catch up because she darted around a corner. "Excuse me. Ma'am?"

She turns toward me.

I glance down at the bag she's holding.

Is that a pair of red underwear?

The scene of the incident replays in my mind, as if on a loop: Margaux's body on the floor as I straighten her red nightie over her bare lower half.

"I couldn't help but overhear." I thumb behind me. "At the station."

"Are you a cop?" She regards me with caution.

"No. Firefighter."

"Wait. You're Blythe, right?"

"Yeah."

"Not too many women on the job. I saw you on the news. Your name down the side of your jacket. You were there."

"Yeah," I admit.

Her face lights up with a smile. "Female firefighter. Good for you. Thanks for your service."

"Just my job, ma'am."

"Is it? Because I'd think that's quite a calling."

"Well, the priesthood it's not, but yeah, I guess."

A wave of pedestrians walks around us as the crosswalk alerts them to continue flowing down the street, but we stay put.

"Hey, I noticed the sarge was blowing you off back there, but . . . are you okay?"

It's hard to tell if she's crying, because she's pulled the sunglasses back over her eyes, but she takes a long, deep inhale and swallows hard.

"You were a friend of Margaux's?" I ask.

"I don't really know how to classify the connection," she says. "But I feel just awful about what happened."

I nod. "Me, as well."

"I suppose I just wanted to talk to someone about it." She shoves the bag back into her purse.

"I can understand that. Have you had lunch?"

"My treat," she says. "It's the least I can do for the potential sacrifices you make day to day, not to mention putting up with the boys' club that must come with a job like yours, and we girls have to stick together, don't we?"

"I appreciate that—"

She juts her hand out in front of me. "Kirsten Holloway. Homemaker."

I shake her hand and say, "Jessie Blythe. Fire and rescue."

THEN

Margaux

It wasn't the first time Arlon spent the night, but it was the first time he was still in her bed, asleep, when she awoke in the morning. She snuggled up close to him and breathed in the fading scent of his cologne, which she knew would linger in the threads of her sheets long after he'd gone.

A girl could get used to this. Presents all the time. Flowers and chocolates every time he returned from a business trip.

How many days between visits would it be this time?

Her body still hummed with satisfaction and practically purred with the memory of sex on the rooftop, the sounds of the city astir below.

And speaking of stirring down below . . .

She trailed her fingers down his chest to his hips, then lower. She closed her fist around the hardest part of him.

He groaned as he roused, his lean body ready and waiting. "Maggie."

She felt a rush every time he called her that. He rolled her over.

She wrapped her legs around his waist, and he crushed her lips under his. In an instant, he was inside her.

Soon, she neared the brink of orgasm, and as she tensed, he stroked the length of her neck with the tips of his fingers.

"Choke me." She placed her hands atop his and started to squeeze.

"No, no." He batted away her hands. "Not today. Not yet."

She slapped his cheek. "Do it."

He caught her wrist. "No."

She slapped him again with her other hand. "Do it!" And again. And again.

Until he finally closed his fingers around her throat. "Yes," he said through gritted teeth. "Yes!"

Her senses heightened as her throat began to restrict.

"Breathe," he whispered and closed his fingers around her neck. "Breathe."

And even as he moved above her and drove her closer to the breaking point, his fingers tightened and constricted.

"Breathe," he said.

Her eyes widened, and she gasped for breath.

Oh no. This was a mistake. She flailed on the bed as best she could to escape, but he was too strong. She had no breath with which to scream their safe word. He was going to kill her. With one hand pinning her by the throat to her bed, the other slipping beneath the small of her back so she was truly captive in his arms, he continued his controlled rhythm, as if she weren't hanging in the balance between life and death.

"Breathe."

His fingers tightened further.

She couldn't breathe. She couldn't even move.

Her flesh broke out into a fine, misty sweat, and although her air supply was dwindling, and she was light-headed, fixating on the determined expression on his face—he wanted to kill her, he wanted her gone—a sort of ethereal sensation came over her as he worked her down below with precise strokes.

Suddenly, she wasn't trying to breathe.

Suddenly, she was trembling with pleasure, and . . .

He released his grip on her neck.

Oh my God.

She drew in a lungful.

She quivered beneath him.

"There's nothing quite like it, is there?" he whispered against her lips. "To put your life in my hands and to trust that I'll spare it every time?"

"How did you do that?" she asked.

"*I* didn't. *We* did."

She drew her fingers in circles around his heart.

He groaned. "I think I love you," he said.

She melted in his arms.

Chapter 13

KIRSTEN

The busing staff cleared our lunch dishes nearly an hour ago, but I'm still sipping on my second glass of wine, and Jessie just ordered another beer. For dessert, she said. I study my new friend across the table. Our conversation has been easy, if not polite, and if circumstances were different—if I weren't on the brink of marital turmoil, and teetering on the edge of breakdown—maybe we could be friends, despite the age difference.

I know she's the youngest of five, the only girl, and while she hasn't come right out and said it, she's excited about the new guy she's dating. He—Jack—doesn't seem to be intimidated by her strength. She's also struggling to give up an old habit she picked up by the name of Lieutenant Decker, but she hasn't admitted that in so many words, either.

I smile for the first time today. "Do you have a picture of your guy?"

"Jack? We're not quite there yet."

"Hmm."

"Anyway . . ."

She's about to change the subject. She doesn't like talking about herself, I can tell, and she feels as if she's already said too much. "Why did you want to talk to the detective?"

I could tell her truth. I could whip the red thong out of my purse and cry into my wine. But it all seems too much for a first meeting, so I shrug and say, "I just can't help it. She's not much older than my daughter, and I feel as if—I don't know—no one's missing her. I didn't know her all that well"—a slight stretch of the truth, but both harmless and necessary . . . I can't change my story now—"and I feel like I'm the only one shaken up by all this. Her adoptive parents haven't made any statements, and I think that's strange, given his status with the city is the likely reason her case has gotten the media coverage. And her neighbors are piling teddy bears and lipsticks and silk floral arrangements at the lamppost in front of her apartment, but none of those people knew her. No teary-eyed boyfriend, no family members pleading for the resolution of the case . . . For all the media attention there is, it just feels rather . . . contrived. Or plastic, maybe. Less than anyone deserves."

"Agreed." Jessie takes a pull off her longneck bottle when the waiter brings it. "This girl's life was beyond private. A lot of people knew who she was, but no one knew her well, it seems. There *was* a boyfriend, apparently. And if he had anything to do with this, Decker'll get him."

I dawdle for a second, weighing whether asking the question will seem as if I'm too nosy and therefore raise flags, but what the hell. The worst that can happen is she won't tell me. "What's the boyfriend's name?"

"Arlon Judson."

"Interesting name." Ian isn't on their radar. At least not yet.

"Are you *sure* you're all right?" Jessie asks.

"No," I admit. "Lately, I feel like my husband is keeping secrets from me."

"Why do you say that?"

I sigh and glance at my purse.

Her eyes shift toward it, too. "Oh my God," she says after a second or two. "You think your husband was sleeping with the deceased."

Damn, this girl is *sharp*.

"He denies it," I say.

"Don't they always?"

Quinn texts: FaceTime?

"I should go." I signal for the check. I should catch up with Quinn.

"I'm sorry," Jessie says. "We can talk about something else."

"Oh no, it's fine. It's just . . . my daughter wants to talk this afternoon, and I have a few errands to run."

"We should do this again sometime," Jessica says.

"That'd be nice."

"And if you ever want to talk, about Margaux, or anything else . . . you know, if your husband really did cheat on you, and you have proof he's connected to a girl who just turned up dead . . . I'm sure you're conflicted, but it'd be due penance to turn it in."

I nod. "Agreed."

"If you need anything . . ."

"Thanks."

———

"I texted you a link last night," Quinn says. "There's this studio in Door County. They have programs for all the arts: creative writing, pottery, photography, painting . . . You apply for one of twelve positions—"

"Wait. *Apply?*"

"And go up there for a week—"

"I can't be gone for an entire week."

"Mom. Why not?"

"Because there are things that have to be done here at home."

"More grocery lists, honey-dos, and dry cleaning?"

"Thanks, Quinn, for reducing my life to a cliché."

"What I mean, Mom, is that arguably, the toughest part of your job is over. Patrick and I are out of the house. You've raised us. Isn't that why you never went to college in the first place? Because someone had to raise us? Well, it's done. It's time now for you to do something for *you*. Something to make *your* life better. And you love Door County. This class—"

"It's too late. I can't even fathom starting something new at this point—"

"Shut. Up."

I look at the phone this time. "Quinn."

She sighs and rakes through her hair. "Talking to you sometimes is like talking to the Colosseum. You've been rooted in the same place for so long, it's like you forget you can still be useful to yourself."

"Useful? What I do—what I've done all these years—isn't useful?"

"Not to you, it isn't. You help everyone else. None of us would be where we are without all the sacrifices you made."

"Just doing my job."

"I want you to try to think about this, okay? Imagine you're seventeen again. You're *not* pregnant, and you have your whole life ahead of you. Do you go to school? Do you pursue your passions? Or do you stay home and fold Daddy's socks because that's what he wants you to do?"

"You're oversimplifying things."

"No. You're overcomplicating things. It's just that easy, Mom."

"How did you get this way? How did I raise a daughter like you if I'm such a pushover?"

"I'm not saying you're a pushover, but that's sort of my point. If you raised me—and you did . . . all on your own—I'm saying there's someone in that stubborn head of yours who knows I'm right. It's time to seize the day."

I take a seat at the breakfast table, where I put a tea bag in a cup of hot water a while ago. But I'm too distracted to drink it, and it's cold now, anyway. "Honestly, Quinn. The world you believe in . . ."

"It exists," she says. "And I know you believe it, too. I hear your voice in my head all the time. Making sure I know I'm good enough, teaching me how to love myself and other people. If you didn't feel this way about the world, too, as if it's full of possibilities, I wouldn't think this way."

I'm dumbstruck, staring at her beautiful face, trying to see myself in my daughter. If what she says is true, I must be in there somewhere.

"I know your parents didn't really give you a choice. I know you were between a rock and a hard place, and Patrick and I are forever grateful that you chose us instead of the path of least resistance. But you can still grasp your brass ring, Mom."

"You're my brass ring."

"Promise me. Look into this Door County thing."

"Okay. I promise."

"And Mom? Whatever's been bothering you the past few days? If you want to talk about it . . ."

"I'm fine."

"Patrick said you and Dad are having trouble."

"Yeah, well, it happens sometimes."

"You're strong with or without him, you know."

"You're incredible, Quinn."

"I know. I take after my mommy."

I smile because I know that's the only way to get her to stop worrying about me.

"You okay?" she asks.

"I'm fine. Go to class."

"Do me a favor: stop thinking about whatever's going on with you and Dad. Do something for yourself. Right now."

"Fine."

"Kiss, kiss. Love, love."

"Love, love."

She blows me a kiss, and then she's gone.

Something for myself . . .

How about pay the bills? Most of them are on automatic draft, but there are a few I still pay by hand.

I sift through the stack of today's mail and sort out the bills from the junk mail.

I log on to our bank account online to check the status of our accounts. Managing our finances is the one household responsibility Ian prefers to maintain, and to be honest, I don't know how well we're doing—or not, as the case may be—now that we have two kids in college.

The log-on circle stalls about halfway through.

Then a window pops up: invalid password. I reenter it and concentrate this time, ensuring I don't miss a keystroke, but I get the same result. Access denied.

I text Ian: Did you change our bank account password?

Ian: . . .

The ellipsis disappears.

His lack of an answer is all I need to know that he did.

Me: I can't get into the account. I didn't change the password. Did you?

Ian: Yes.

Me: Why?

Ian: A few strange transactions. I'm looking into it.

Me: Maybe the transactions are mine.

Me: I'll review it.

Ian: I'll go over it with you later.

Me: What is the password?

Ian: Not over text.

Ian: Plenty of money in there for the groceries, etc. Plenty to cover the bills.

Me: I have a right to access our accounts.

Ian: When you put a dime in, I'll consider them ours.

Me: EXCUSE ME?

Me: I contribute.

Me: I make your life possible.

Me: What are you hiding?

Me: How stupid do you think I am?

Ian: We'll talk when I'm home.

Me: When will that be?

Ian: That depends.

Ian: When do you plan on stopping all this insanity?

No *love you*, no *miss you*, no *see you soon*.

And after all these years, in the absence of such a sweet nothing, a hollow feeling settles in my chest. How long would it take him to text a quick heart emoji, for the love of God?

Me: Do you even still love me?

Ian: You're making it very difficult.

Ian: But yes.

Ian: Take a pill tonight

Ian: Get some sleep

Ian: And start making sense tomorrow.

I'm tired of everyone assuming that I'm out of control, that I'm making more of this situation than I should, that I'm creating drama or jumping to conclusions.

Add to that my having possession of a pair of panties that may or may not send Ian to the gallows, and it's like a slap in the face, how secretive he's been and how he's forsaking me. If I'd forsaken him to this extent, the red thong would be at the police department right now.

I storm to Ian's study and sift through the piles of paperwork on his desk for the new password.

I tear through the place, dig through files, and leaf through books—and find nothing but a vintage issue of *Hustler*. I sigh in disgust and whip the magazine against the wall.

When it lands, however, a five-by-seven-inch manila envelope—not unlike the one Patrick found on our porch yesterday, which is still sitting on Ian's desk—flops out of it.

I crouch and retrieve it. It's addressed to my husband at our old house in Evanston. The postage was canceled months ago, a few weeks before we moved, shortly before the episode.

I open the envelope. A typewritten note, along with a flash drive, falls into my palm. I tend first to the note:

> Mr. Holloway,
> For continued discretion, I request a monthly fee. Meet at Daley Plaza to discuss the arrangements. Monday, 3:00 p.m.
> As promised, I've enclosed proof. Copy 1 of 3.
> If you don't show, Copy 2 goes to the lady of the house.

The note isn't signed.

The flash drive weighs heavy in my hand. I have a pretty good idea of what I might find on it. Still, it takes incredible nerve to look.

I plug it into my laptop.

"Oh God."

If the police get ahold of this content, the name Arlon Judson won't even be a blip on their radar.

I flip from image to image.

My husband . . . *is that my husband?*

With Margaux Claire Stritch.

His hands around her neck.

I'm going to be sick.

You can prepare for it all you want.

You can play out scenarios in your head every which way you can imagine.

Suspecting it was happening . . . that's one thing.

Actually seeing it . . . that's another.

My stomach churns as I scroll through the images, which appear to have been taken from the outside looking in through the glass of a window and past the open sheers that usually cover it:

Ms. Stritch in red satin, cooking in her kitchen.

Ms. Stritch nude and bent over her kitchen countertop with a male hand—it looks like my husband's—lost in her blonde curls and holding her in position.

I flip faster now, searching for an image that concentrates more on the man than her, some concrete evidence that I'm looking at pictures of Ian having sex with another woman. But every image captures him in shadow, as if by design.

And then, an image of the naked length of him, pressed up close and personal to the recently deceased—the side of a breast bulging between their bodies. His face, darkened in shadows, nestled in the hollow of her collarbone.

But I've seen enough to confirm it's my husband when I zoom in on his right shoulder and see the tattoo of his law firm's logo.

I flip to the next pictures:

Ian's nude body leaning over her.

Her long, ivory legs locked around his waist.

Her hands gripping his shoulders . . . a ring on the fourth finger of her left hand. I zoom in on the ring. It's not a diamond. But a girl that age . . . would she wear a ring on that finger if she weren't engaged?

And I practically feel the rhythm between them, practically experience the slow build of energy, as I flip from frame to frame.

Every ounce of fear, dread, and anger in my system culminates into a ball in my stomach, rolling there like a hurricane about to wreak havoc upon landfall.

My fingertips tingle, and pain pierces between my eyes.

I'm going to be sick.

I'm looking at photographic proof.

If these photographs fall into the wrong hands, our family is going to be thrust into the spotlight.

I consider destroying the thumb drive.

But then I think of Quinn. If something happened to her, I'd be devastated. I'd feel as if I'd failed her if she killed herself. And I'd surely want to know if she really didn't take her own life.

Besides, these images are on a thumb drive, and the note claims there are three copies. Destroying the thumb drive couldn't ensure no one else sees these images.

And if it gets out that I had stumbled across potential evidence and destroyed it . . .

I pull Ian's leather trash bin from beneath the desk and spill the contents of my stomach into it. As if spewing out all the terrible things—the worst a woman can think about in the dead of night—can cleanse me of the memory, I keep heaving over that bin long after I've emptied my stomach.

My God.

What am I going to do?

Suspicion of an affair is totally different from seeing it with my own eyes.

I wish I'd never seen what I just saw.

When I've calmed down enough that I'm no longer shaking, I text Ian:

Just found your vintage Hustler.

The ball is in my court.

I'm calling the shots now.

Get home, and we'll discuss.

For a few minutes, I stare at the screen, anticipating his reply.

When it doesn't come, I find myself on the verge of texting Quinn. I have to talk to someone about all this, and even though my daughter is hardly the ideal audience, who else am I going to talk to? My old neighbor, maybe. Fiona already thinks I've lost my mind, so it can't hurt to lose it in front of her again.

Or maybe . . .

Jessica did say if I needed anything . . .

I take deep breath and eye the second envelope, still sealed on the desk. Now or never. I tear it open.

Chapter 14

JESSICA

A chick flick plays in the background while I navigate to the Aquasphere Underground website. I pop some corn, settle back on the couch with my laptop, and pay an exorbitant fee to enter the site. Fifty bucks. Just to browse for the night. Yikes.

First, I'm prompted to select a username. I choose the default—Sexy451—and enter a chat room.

Sexy451: Looking for Gail Force.

KittenSlut: Everyone is these days.

HunkOfBurningLove: No one has seen her in a month or so.

HunkOfBurningLove: Miss the fuck out of her.

Sexy451: Does anyone know what she did at the Underground?

KittenSlut: Dominate.

HunkOfBurningLove: Ruled the world.

Sexy451: I need to get in touch with her.

KittenSlut: Leave her a private chat.

HunkOfBurningLove: Doubt she'll answer.

HunkOfBurningLove: When people leave the forum, they leave.

Sexy451: Why did she leave?

I wait, but the slut and the hunk seem to have disappeared.

Sexy451: Hello?

Sexy451: Can anyone tell me why Gail Force is no longer with the Underground?

KittenSlut: Please review etiquette of the Underground.

KittenSlut: Rule #1

KittenSlut: Never ask why.

Jesus.
I begin typing an apology, but another window pops up.
It's an invitation to chat privately with HunkOfBurningLove.

I accept.

HunkOfBurningLove: Are you into men or women?

Oh wow. This interrogation could go in a whole new direction. I'm almost tempted to log off right now, but seeing as I already paid fifty bucks, and in the interest of gathering intel . . .

Sexy451: Men.

HunkOfBurningLove: Send pic?

Sexy451: After.

Sexy451: Do you know what happened with Gail Force?

HunkOfBurningLove: She was performing at the Underground.

HunkOfBurningLove: Erotic asphyxiation in a triple-play scenario.

HunkOfBurningLove: She lost control of her bottom.

HunkOfBurningLove: He wouldn't stop.

HunkOfBurningLove: Almost killed another performer.

HunkOfBurningLove: Not sure that's why she left.

HunkOfBurningLove: But she wasn't around after.

Sexy451: Did you see it happen?

Sexy451: Were you there that night?

HunkOfBurningLove: I streamed it from home.

HunkOfBurningLove: It was the hottest thing I've ever seen.

HunkOfBurningLove: Never came so hard in my life.

HunkOfBurningLove: Pic?

Sexy451: Do you know Gail Force's real name?

HunkOfBurningLove: You're more into Gail Force than me.

HunkOfBurningLove: You sure you like men?

HunkOfBurningLove: See ya.

He terminates the chat.
Oh well.
I open another window and search for erotic asphyxiation.
Wow.
It's choking for pleasure during sex.
People actually do this?

It doesn't escape me that this could be how Margaux died, that it could have been a tragic accident in the middle of sex—Decker did say she'd recently had sex.

My phone buzzes with a text from Kirsten Holloway:

Sorry to bother you.

I just found pictures on a thumb drive in my husband's desk.

My husband and that girl.

Margaux.

And then the pictures come in rapid succession:

A woman, whom I can't deny is the same I cut down, nude, lying in wait on a bed.

A shadow of a man. I can't see his face. Only his back.

And several images of them together, entwined, having sex.

I text back, How do you know this is your husband? Can't see much of him.

But even if it isn't Mr. Holloway, it's definitely concerning that the missus stumbled over these pictures.

Kirsten: Infinity tattoo on the back of his right shoulder.

It's his law firm's logo.

It's him.

I've known that body my whole life.

I scroll though the pictures, which drip with sex and steam, and enlarge one with a good view of the right shoulder. Sure enough, there's a tattoo there—a sideways figure eight. The pictures are provocative, to say the least, and although a dead girl is the subject, I'm sort of turned on by what I'm seeing. This sex is close, personal, mouth on mouth. Hot.

But these pictures were taken by someone else, from the outside looking in.

The lighting is terrible, and some of the pictures show more shadow than subject, or glare off the window through which they were taken. Some frames highlight the dirt on the windowsill, while others appear to have been taken from such a distance that I have to zoom in on a human shape.

I imagine some hired PI standing on a rooftop across the way, aiming and clicking away.

There's usually one reason that happens.

Pieces of a theory fall into place:

Kirsten's husband and Margaux were having an affair. Someone could have been using these photographs for blackmail. It's logical to assume Margaux wouldn't want the pictures leaked, even though she was single and free to do whatever she pleased with whomever she chose. Alderman Richard Akers and ultra-Christian Helen certainly could have been hurt by a scandal like this.

Still, it would stand to reason Kirsten's husband would have been the target. But of whom?

Who would dare to use this information against him? Who would threaten to go to Kirsten and his family, or even his clients, with these pictures?

If someone were blackmailing him, however, he could have tried to end it with Margaux.

And if she didn't take it well, the breakup could have been bad and could have gotten physical. Probably did, given the slice on her cheek. Maybe a physical altercation resulted in her death. Or maybe the cutting thing was erotic, too. I conduct another search, this time for erotic cutting. Bingo. People do that to get off, too, which might explain the letters carved into her breast.

None of this makes Mr. Holloway a killer, of course, but if he were paying someone off . . .

I text Kirsten:

First

I'm sorry.

Second

Is there any money missing from your accounts?

She replies:

I wouldn't know.

I don't have access.

He recently changed the password.

Jeez, this isn't looking good.
Kirsten: Why?
I reply: Someone sent these pictures to your husband for a reason.

And if you suddenly can't access the account, he could be hiding something.

Large withdrawals

Hush money

She texts: Can you meet me tomorrow? For lunch?

I text: Probably.

Then I text Decker: Have something that might interest you.

BTW, research erotic asphyxiation and erotic cutting.

I attach links.

The buzz of my doorbell startles me for a moment. I'm not expecting anyone.

I settle back against the pillows on my sofa, toss a piece of popcorn into my mouth, and turn up the volume on the movie I'm streaming.

About thirty seconds later, I hear the doorbell across the hall, followed by the long, annoying hum of the buzzer that tells whomever is on the doorstep to come on in. This happens a lot in the city. Someone forgets a key and leans on any old button until one of us lets him in. It defeats the purpose of a security buzzer, which is why I never let the doorbell disturb me.

I divide my attention between my movie and the erotic play I'm researching. I imagine what it must have felt like: the fear of a blade touching her skin, hands closing around her throat, maybe slowly, as if with intent to catch her off guard, as if to toy with her until airflow is constricted . . . and she starts to panic.

When did Margaux realize, I wonder, that her night was about to ignite with a passion more intimate than sex? Because that's what murder is. The ultimate stealing of another's freedom—personal and invasive. Could anything be more intimate than wiping out someone's existence?

I pick up my phone to text one last message to Decker: Talk soon.

Knock, knock, knock.

I fumble my phone when I hear the three quick raps on my door, then quickly recover it. There's no denying I'm home. I'm sure the sound of my movie is filtering into the hallway. I look toward the door, willing whomever is on the other side of it to just go away. I don't want whatever they're selling, and it's too late for unannounced visitors, besides.

But when the knocker persists and pounds this time, I tiptoe toward the door and peek through the peephole.

"Jessica?"

Jack!

And, God, he looks good.

He's standing there in khakis and an untucked button-down, one hand slipping into his pocket after the knock, and the other grasping a bundle of fresh roses.

I gasp.

"Jessica?"

Oh no. I look around at my cluttered apartment. I'm going to have to let him in.

The place boasts unwashed dishes, a basket of dirty laundry waiting by the door for the day I'm motivated to hike to the basement facilities—and then I glance at what I'm wearing.

One of Decker's old flannels.

Thick, mismatched socks.

And, God . . . granny panties. Tonight could be the night Jack expects to finally take things to the next level—I don't know why else he'd surprise me with flowers—and I'm wearing undergarments that might double as something that covers the infield during a rain delay.

I could ignore the knock and tell him later I was in the shower, sorry I missed him, yada yada yada. I'm not ready for him to see the real way I live.

But . . . the roses.

He went to the effort to surprise me.

That doesn't mean I'm in any condition to accept visitors tonight. The last time I saw him I distinctly got the impression he suspected—correctly—I was seeing someone else.

If I don't answer the door now, it might lend more to his suspicions, and he might decide to disappear.

He knocks again. "Jessica?"

"Just a minute." I pull the band from my hair, releasing the snarled ponytail, and step out of my cotton briefs and kick them into my laundry basket. I check my reflection in the tiny square mirror hanging near my door.

Do I look all right?

Eh. But it's the best I can do on a moment's notice.

I open the door.

"I had to see you." Jack crosses over the threshold and tosses his arms around me. "I would have called, but my phone died, and I was halfway here anyway—"

"I'm glad you're here."

His lips land on mine, and for the first time since we met, I don't feel as if Decker is in the room with us.

Jack's hand lands on my ass, and he practically groans as he discovers I'm not wearing panties.

Next I know, he's furiously working the buttons on my shirt and walking me to the sofa, where he leans over me and coaxes me onto my back.

And suddenly, what's been at bay for weeks feels more than urgent.

Despite the element of safety I usually feel around him, the way I feel about him is almost dangerous right now. Because he ignited me with only a look. And I suddenly *need* him. All of him.

I'm working at his belt and then the zipper on his khakis. I rip at his buttons, but there's no time to undress him, and the next I know, we're making out like teenagers. His shirt is only half off, his pants are at his ankles, and my arms are still imprisoned in flannel sleeves, but I feel him against me. A pair of flimsy cotton boxer shorts are the only thing standing between us.

He burns a stare into my eyes as he bruises my lips with kisses.

He caresses my neck with his fingers, drawing slow circles with his thumb, and I have to wonder if this is how it started for Margaux Stritch, if her killer caught her off guard, wooing her with caresses, and suddenly squeezed the life out of her.

Jack holds me tight to his body, and I register details—his rhythm, his demeanor, his expression. None of it is indicative of any violent intentions, but I can't stop imagining things taking a turn, his hands tightening at my neck.

Jesus, this case is really getting to me.

"God," he whispers into my ear. "You know when you just can't stop thinking about something?"

"Yeah." Recently, I've been borderline obsessed with Miss Margaux Stritch.

"It's *you*. I just can't stop thinking about you." He rakes a few fingers against my neck, then lowers his lips to breathe a kiss there. "Where've you been, Jess? Where the hell have you been all my life?"

He palms my cheek, his thumb brushing against my chin, then pressing lower, lower, lower, until his hand is at my neck—squeezing.

The look in his eyes . . . pure determination, focus.

His grip on my neck tightens.

"Wait," I manage.

He only constricts his fingers around my neck.

His lips part to reveal clenched teeth.

He's going to kill me.

Is this what Margaux felt in her last moments? In her last breath?

I'd scream if I could catch breath enough.

The ringing in my ears—

I pull back and punch.

My fist lands square on his cheekbone.

"Jessica."

I gasp and cough and scramble out from under him. "What the hell was that?"

"What you wanted, I thought."

"Why would I—"

"All that talk about the Aquasphere. And . . ." He indicates toward my laptop, which has two windows open:

The Underground Online chat room.

And images of erotic asphyxiation.

"Oh." I straighten my clothing. "Jesus, ask a girl next time."

"Okay, I'm asking. You're not wearing underwear, you've been chatting on a sex site, and you've got pictures of people choking each other on your laptop screen."

I almost laugh, but he's so upset that I quickly contain myself. "I'm just doing some research for a friend."

He rubs his cheek where I hit him.

"You okay?"

"I'm sorry," he says.

"Yeah." My phone starts to ring. "Me too."

"I thought . . . ," he says. "Damn it."

I reach for my mobile phone. It's the station.

I hold up a finger and answer the call: "Yeah, what's up?"

It's the battalion chief: Froman has the flu. I have to go in to cover his shift.

Jack's dressing by the time I hang up. "I understand if I screwed this up. I don't know what came over me, but I saw the pictures and saw that you'd been online, and I thought we were finally going to make a commitment to each other, and . . ." He sighs. "Sorry."

"I want to talk about this," I say. "I really do. But I have to go in."

"Okay."

"Really. I'll call you, okay? We'll set something up."

He leans to me, cups my chin in a hand, and drops a soft kiss onto my lips. "I'll believe it when I see it."

"Good night." I watch him walk out the door.

My phone is ringing again.

Decker's name appears on the caller ID screen.

I answer: "What's up?"

"You had company tonight."

"What, are you spying on me?"

"You texted me a hundred times."

"So you text back, you don't stake out my apartment."

"I was in the neighborhood. Thought I'd stop by until I saw two silhouettes in your window."

I glance down at the street below my window and spy Decker's nondescript tan sedan, the beater he uses for work, parked in a tow zone. "You saw—"

"Is he gone? Was that him I just saw walking out?"

"Yeah, but I have to go into the station."

"Great. We'll talk on the way. I'll give you a lift."

"Oh." So this is a business call. "Okay. Give me a minute."

"Sweetheart? Shake a tail feather. What I've got? It's good."

THEN

MARGAUX

Margaux straddled Arlon's back and treated him to a rubdown. "Do you want kids?"

At this, he shifted and looked at her over his shoulder. "I think we'd make beautiful children together."

"Me too."

"Babe, you'd make gorgeous kids with *anyone*."

"How many kids would you want?"

"Four, I think. Nice round number."

"That's a lot of kids."

"Would you do that for me?"

"Of course I would. And since it seems law school's on the back burner—"

"Why?"

She sighed. "The man who adopted me . . . Richard—he's an alderman, Everyone's Granddad Akers . . . ever hear of him?—he has power of attorney over my trust, which is supposed to come to me on my twenty-fifth birthday, *or* upon completion of a postgraduate degree, whichever is first."

"Ah, so you can be my sugar mama."

"It's not *that* much money. Just enough, you know, to be comfortable. But Granddad's got a problem. With gambling."

"Oh no."

"Oh yes. He gambled most of my trust away, and I have to wait now for him to replenish it."

"Maggie, I . . . God, babe, that's awful."

"You don't know the half of it."

"Why? What else happened?"

"I don't need to talk about it. *Can't* talk about it, actually because . . . well, the media. He could . . ." She nibbled on her lip. "Never mind. It's just family business."

"Tell me."

"Suffice it to say there are consequences to talking. I once slipped and told someone outside the family something I shouldn't have told, and we had to pay people off to keep it out of the news, and then there's his depression . . . And when he down-spirals, there's the drinking, and he's an angry drunk . . ."

"Toxic. You need to cut him out."

"What do you mean . . . cut him out? I *have* sort of—"

"You go see them every Sunday."

"That's to pick up an installment of what Granddad has to put back into my account. It's not for the pleasure of the company, believe me. But I have no one else. I mean, they took me in. They didn't have to do that. I owe them—"

"Listen." He rolled her over. "You're not alone anymore. What have we just been talking about? A family. Kids."

A smile slowly crept onto her face. "Do you think we're there?"

"Don't you?"

She wrapped her limbs around him. "Maybe, from now on, you can come to Sunday dinners to collect."

"I wish I could. Sunday is usually a travel day, and I should get going. I still have a sales report to file."

"Oh. Okay."

"But maybe I can send you on your way with a little extra spring in your step."

"Did you know you're the first person I've met since my parents died who puts me first? I'd do anything for you."

"Anything?"

"Mm-hmm."

His slow smile morphed to an expression of determination.

"Listen," he said. "It's been hot, what we've been doing . . . the choking."

"Tell me about it."

"But I could kill you, baby."

"You're not going to kill me, Arlon."

"If anything happened to you, I wouldn't be able to forgive myself."

"I think I can deal with bringing in a tutor. If it'll help you feel better about it."

For a moment, he appeared to be deep in thought. "I'm going to run an errand."

"What? Now?"

"I'm going to let you go," he said. "But only if you promise not to move a muscle until I get back."

She nodded.

He kissed her lips. "Promise?"

"Yes."

His weight now lifted from her body, but as agreed, she lay perfectly still, even when he ripped her tank top to expose her breasts, even when he tore the panties from her body. He positioned her legs uncomfortably wide, but she remained still.

When he was satisfied with her positioning, he stood above her, his erection bulging in his boxers. "Open your mouth."

Her lips parted.

"Wider."

She obeyed.

He took one pass around her body splayed on the thin area rug. Already her back began to ache against the hard floor.

"Not a muscle." He stepped into jeans and pulled on his sweater.

Where was he going?

But she didn't dare ask.

He pulled his keys from his pocket. "Don't move."

She didn't.

Not even when he exited the apartment.

He didn't lock the door, and she was lying there, uncomfortable, spread-eagle, and naked as the day she was born, ready for anyone to pounce.

Surely, he wouldn't be gone long.

But the numbers on the clock ticked off minute by minute until nearly twenty had gone by.

What was he doing? And why? Was this some sort of test? If so, she'd pass. She'd prove her loyalty, her dedication, her *obedience* to him.

She wasn't about to ruin this. She'd given a great deal of herself to Arlon, and he'd given back just as much. Finally, someone made a priority of her, someone saw something special in her, and she wasn't about to risk it for the sake of being comfortable.

So she stared up at the exposed rafters in the loft above the kitchen, at the raw beam that ran over the length of her living room, at the tiny scuttle hole that led to her rooftop patio.

And just when she thought she couldn't take it anymore, she heard his footsteps on the stairs and in the hall.

She heard the door open, but still, she held her position—mouth, arms, and legs wide—without flinching.

"Ahh," he said. "Good girl. Good, good girl."

A length of rope flew up into the air and hooked over the exposed beam in the living room.

"I like a girl who follows the rules." He took up her ankle—the change in position instantly relieved the ache in her back—and bound it with the rope.

First one ankle, then the other, was looped into the rope, followed by her wrists. She was bound to the room, anchored by the beam. And completely at his mercy.

But something few people understood about being a bottom: the submissive was in complete control, because it was her choice to give the gift of dominance to her partner. Few things were more titillating than knowing that a man wanted her so badly he would stop at nothing to have her—even if it meant he had to tie her to restrain her.

"Let's get something straight," he said. "I don't need a tutor."

———

Margaux zinged with the memory of pleasure as she made her way to the Gold Coast.

The moment she entered Helen and Richard Akers's home, Helen embraced her, then stepped back and held her at arm's length. "What's happened to your neck?"

"What does it look like?"

"It looks like someone strangled you."

"I let him do whatever he wants."

"No."

"Sexually, masochistically, *whatever he wants.*"

"What kind of a man *wants* to do these things? Margaux—"

Margaux whispered into Helen's ear, "Aren't you married to a man who *wants* to do these things?"

Helen's eyes widened, and her jaw set. "What have we done to deserve this?" She spoke through gritted teeth. "Whatever it was, I'm sorry, Margaux."

Margaux whispered, "I am, too.

"I'm sorry," Margaux continued, "that I've been silent so long. I'm going to tell the world what Richard did to me, and what he took from me, and I'm not talking about the money."

Chapter 15

KIRSTEN

Maybe it's childish.

But I guess I don't care. I feel entitled to handle this news poorly, entitled to behave a little less like an adult in its wake.

Earlier, I stocked up on glossy photo paper and ink for my printer. Now, while eating a half gallon of mint chocolate chip ice cream, right out of its cylindrical container, I'm printing every last photo stored on the thumb drive I found in *Hustler*. Twice. I'm hanging them around the house—in every possible location Ian might encounter.

On the underside of the toilet lid in every bathroom, except Quinn's and Patrick's, because he never goes in there.

On the shelves in the refrigerator and pantry.

On his computer monitor in his study.

On the treadmill in the basement workout studio.

In the compartment of his golf bag, where he keeps extra tees.

He won't be able to explain away these pictures the way he danced around the pair of red panties. If he refuses to discuss his cheating, at least he'll have to stare at the proof of it. And if he tears the photos to pieces, I'll have replacements ready.

Serves him right.

And when the time is right, I'll deal with what I found on the second drive that was recently mailed to him.

It's getting late, and the millions of tears I shed today have taken their toll on me. I'm tired.

Maybe I'll finish the ice cream, put down a glass of wine, pop an Ambien, and sleep.

Maybe when I wake up, I'll realize this was all just a bad dream.

But I know it's far worse than that.

It's a nightmare.

And I'm actually, truly living it.

Ian's not only been sleeping around, but the other woman is now dead under what might be questionable, and definitely mysterious, circumstances. What he's done to this family . . . it's unforgivable, despite the fact that I do want to forgive him. I want to put it all behind us, repair, and move on.

I also want to scream, claw at his face, and throw every breakable thing in this house at him.

We'll see which happens first.

He'll be home soon enough. Maybe I'll manage to compose myself by then.

But not tonight. I scoop the remaining heaping spoonful of mint chocolate chip from its carton. Just as I stick the spoon in my mouth, I hear a jingling of keys on the front porch.

Maybe I'll start throwing things after all.

The door hinges creak slightly as the door opens.

"Hello?"

Shit.

It's Quinn.

And she's probably about to open the front hall closet to hang her jacket.

And she's going to see the photograph I pasted there: her father's nude, muscled body sandwiched between the long, ivory legs of the lady in red.

And with a mouthful of ice cream, I can't even call to her to distract her. I force it down—brain freeze—and bolt out of the study, tearing at photos along the way. I can't let her see them, so I stash them in the island drawer. "Quinn!"

"Mom?"

I'm practically shaking.

But I don't think she saw anything.

Chapter 16

Jessica

"What I'm about to tell you stays between us for now," Decker says the moment I slip into the car next to him. "The PD's counting on withholding this information until we get a DNA read."

"Ooh. So you want to trick someone into incriminating himself."

"I wouldn't say that officially, but . . . yeah. I guess that's the long and short of it sometimes."

I give him a playful nudge across the center console. "So why are you telling me?"

"You're my sounding board." He nudges back. "I need your take on something, your being a woman, and all."

"Thanks for noticing."

"The real issue is that the Akerses are putting pressure on the department to release the body, and the captain's patience is running thin."

"Did you find Arlon Judson?"

"Well, I found someone *named* Arlon Judson, but he lives in central Illinois, and currently he and his wife and four homeschooled children are at Disney World. And when I showed a picture of the guy's license to Helen Akers, she said she'd never actually seen the guy. As a matter of fact, no one seems to have seen Margaux with *anyone*. The people at the Aquasphere . . . hell, they're so tight-lipped they should run the Secret Service. Something needs to stick soon, or I can forget trying to prove this poor girl didn't off herself."

"And where do I come in?"

"The autopsy report and labs came back," he says. "She was ten weeks pregnant."

"Oh wow."

"So you can understand the urgency in finding Judson."

I have to tell Kirsten. She knows her husband was with this girl. It could have been Arlon Judson's baby, but it also could've been Mr. Holloway's. I take a deep breath. "Actually, Deck, there's a chance the baby was someone else's."

"Whose?"

"His name's Ian Holloway."

"Who is Ian Holloway?"

"He's this guy . . . his wife is pretty sure he was sleeping with Margaux." I take my phone out of my pocket, intending to share the photos Kirsten texted.

"And you know his wife?"

"Well—sort of." I open the text thread.

"Do me a favor: keep this news to yourself. Don't tell this guy's wife—"

"I'd rather she hear it from me than some emotionally inept cop, no offense."

"Valid. When it's time, *if* it's time, I'll call you in, but until then, not a word."

I get his point. I don't like keeping this from her, but all I need is to let the news slip, word gets out, and then the entire force will be scream-ing about some broad with loose lips fucking up the investigation.

"So, talk to me," he says. "What's going through a girl's mind at ten weeks pregnant?"

"How would I know? I've never *been* ten weeks pregnant."

"Your friends, then."

"None of my friends has a uterus. In case you haven't noticed, I tend to hang out with guys. Occupational hazard."

"Your sisters-in-law, then. Surely, you must know—"

"I don't *know*, but I'd guess at that point, she had to have known she was pregnant. And she was nearing the point of no return. I'll bet it was weighing on her."

"No record of an appointment with an ob-gyn."

"Okay. If you know you're pregnant, and you're happy about it, you make plans. You go to the doctor. If you're not happy about it—and maybe she wasn't if she didn't know who the father was, or if the father's married to someone else—you're in denial. Researching options. Maybe you go to the doctor. Maybe you don't."

"There's more," Decker says. "Seems the good alderman has been abusing his power of attorney for Margaux's trust. The trust lawyer I spoke with says the trust was put in place to secure her education, but that as executor, Alderman Akers had access and opportunity to dip into it, and let's just say he didn't so much *dip* as *swallow whole*. Now that the girl's dead, the alderman doesn't have to either pay tuition for the law program she was just accepted into *or* replace what was lost. The money becomes, essentially, his and his wife's."

"The alderman has motive."

"So I've finally got the captain's ear, and he thinks my theory might actually hold water, but—"

"Wait a minute. When I paid the Akerses a visit, the wife got really defensive. She said something about Margaux spreading lies to ruin their reputation." I pause to gather my thoughts. "Maybe she meant Margaux told people about Akers stealing the money. But Helen Akers raised the issue right when I started to talk about what happened to me when I was younger. You don't suppose Margaux was telling people that the alderman had been inappropriate with her, do you?"

"Shit." Decker shakes his head. "Now I gotta go back there and have another conversation. Why didn't you tell me this before?"

"I didn't make the connection, for one thing. For another, that old woman is a *pill*. She took issue with *everything* I said." I look back to my phone and scroll through the pictures Kirsten just sent. "But . . . you should find this interesting."

Decker takes the phone from my hand and whistles, as if to say *wow!* as he flips through the images. "Where'd you get these?"

"Wife of this guy." I point to the man on the screen. "She texted them to me tonight."

"How'd she get them?"

"I don't know."

"Can you ask?"

"I'll introduce you. *You* can ask." As soon as the words fly out of my mouth, it occurs to me that maybe Kirsten shared the information with me because I'm not a cop. I hope she understands that I had to tell Decker about the pictures. I should tell him a lot more, too. About the underwear Kirsten was worried about but didn't want to mention. About the password on the bank account.

"How do you know this woman?"

"I met her at the station. The day you stood me up for lunch, your boys were blowing her off, and she looked like she needed a friend. So I listened."

"Ah. You *listened.*"

"You should try it sometime."

"So we have a dead pregnant girl. Possible fathers: Arlon Judson, Ian . . ." Deck's brows shoot up in question.

"Holloway."

"Arlon Judson, Ian Holloway. And maybe, if your hunch is correct and Margaux hinted that she had a not-so-father-daughter relationship with the alderman, maybe even Richard Akers could've been the father."

"God, I hope not." I shift in my seat. "We know she was seeing this Arlon Judson, and she was obviously having an affair with Holloway, so she wasn't monogamous. She could've slept with anyone at that fetish club."

"I'm going to need copies of those pictures," Decker says.

"Of course."

"I'm going to need the wife's contact information."

"Naturally. But you have to be nice to her. She's been blindsided with all this, and it's a lot for her to take. It's a mess."

"And I'm going to need you to sign a statement detailing how these pictures ended up in your possession."

"I wouldn't dream of refusing. Now please. Take me to work."

Decker drops my phone back into my tote bag and puts the car in gear. "So how'd it go with Mr. Wonderful?"

"Let's not talk about him, okay?" I redirect: "Do you think you should also be interviewing the alderman? About an inappropriate relationship with a girl who was his legal daughter?"

"I'll snag an appointment with him. He's in inpatient rehab—rational emotive behavioral therapy, they call it. Supposed to help with gambling."

I wonder if it helps with quitting guys who are no good for you.

A few blocks later, Decker pulls onto a side street around back from the firehouse. I gather the straps of my tote bag and open the door. "Thanks for the ride. And for treating me like a hostile witness along the way."

Just as I'm about to climb out of the car and onto the sidewalk, Decker grasps my wrist. "Jessica."

"Don't worry about it," I say. "I know you don't mean to be an asshole."

He reaches for me, touches my chin, and for a second, I think he's going to kiss me.

I pull away. "Don't."

"Wait." He peels back the collar of my jacket and brushes a finger along my throat. "What happened here?"

"What?"

"On your neck."

"*What?*" I flip down the visor and open the vanity mirror. A red marring, fairly the size of a thumbprint, glares at me. "Oh. That was . . . it was Jack."

"You let him choke you?"

"No. It was a misunderstanding."

"I'm going to want to get a picture of that *misunderstanding*. You're bruised."

Looks like it. I swallow over a lump in my throat, and the panic of not being able to breathe returns to me.

"And I don't have to tell you—so was Margaux."

"Look, it's not what you think. I'll explain, but I really have to get going."

"Where'd you meet this guy?"

"We've been over this. At a bar."

"Which bar?"

"River Shannon."

"Lincoln Park."

"Yes."

"Where's he live?"

"Lincoln and Clark. Near the River Shannon."

"You know his address?"

"Yeah."

"Text it to me. How old is he?"

"I don't know . . . a little older than me, maybe."

"You don't know how old he is?"

"I didn't ask."

"If you had to guess."

"You saw him leaving my place. What if *you* had to guess?"

"Jessie. I barely looked at the guy. Besides, it's dark."

"He's got a young face, but he's graying at the temples, so . . . I don't know. Twenty-four to thirty? Thirty-five maybe?"

"What's his last name?"

"Wyatt."

"Middle name?"

"I don't know."

"How do you not know?"

"Because I don't know! Christ, I don't even know your *first* name beyond the initial K. You want to know his shoe size, too?"

"If there were any footprints left at the scene, I absolutely would want to know his shoe size." He glances at me. "And what do you mean? You don't know my first name?"

"How would I know your first name? Your badge says KJ. Everyone calls you Deck."

"I know your middle name. You don't even know my first? Jessica Jane Blythe, your boy is now a person of interest in this case."

"First of all, it's easy to know middle names when you have access to the state database. Second, maybe you're reading too much into this. He only tried the choking thing because of the research he saw on my laptop—research I was doing for you. Jack's a financial analyst. What would he want with Margaux Stritch?"

"It's my job, Jessie, to read too much into *everything*. But I'm not overreacting. The River Shannon is a ten-minute walk from Margaux's loft. How do you know they didn't cross paths?"

"You've gotta be kidding me," I say under my breath.

Decker looks over his shoulder to check his blind spot and immediately pulls the car over to the curb. Now that the car is in park, he turns toward me. "Tell me everything he said tonight, word for word."

"I have to get to the fire station, Deck."

"I'll write you a late pass to class. Talk."

THEN

MARGAUX

Arlon bound her wrists and ankles.

"They call this hog-tied," he says. "Appropriate, isn't it? No more chocolate for you."

With only a sheet beneath her bare body, and all the windows in the place open, she shivered and uttered their safe word: "Black crow."

"Have you ever heard of erotic cutting?" He produced a utility knife—a box cutter with a blade about an inch long.

"Black crow!"

"Oh no. No, no, no, no, no."

"Arlon. I'm begging you. Please. Black crow."

He put the knife aside.

She sighed in relief. "Thank you."

"Reset?" he asked.

"Yes. Yes, reset." Out of the corner of her eye, she caught sight of a flash outside, like lightning. She glanced toward the window, but in the dark night couldn't tell if it was getting cloudy. "Was that—"

"Look at me."

She did.

He pulled another implement out of his bag of tricks—a vibrating button, which he placed between her legs.

Her eyes rolled back in pleasure, yet a second later, she heard the tear of tape.

She flinched. Before she could say the safe word, he'd strapped a length of silver tape across her mouth.

The button fell to the floor beneath her.

"Now. Have you ever heard of erotic cutting?" The blade was back in his hand.

Her eyes were wide and sprouting tears.

She shook her head but couldn't say no, couldn't stop him.

"This is for your own good. You're mine."

She shook her head more profusely.

"I'm going to mark you now."

No. No, no, no.

"It's going to hurt. But this way, no man will dare to take you from me."

No!

He brought the blade to her right breast.

And he began to carve.

Chapter 17

Kirsten

"Quinn!" I pounce into the hallway.

Quinn flinches. Her hand is on the closet doorknob. She's half a second away from seeing her father in a position a girl should never see.

"What a nice surprise." I go to her, wrap her in my arms, and inhale all the Quinny smells: her clean-scented shampoo with the faint hint of mint, her preferred perfume, Daisy by Marc Jacobs.

"Mom, what's going on?"

"I should be asking you the same question." With an arm about her shoulders, I lead her farther into the house, away from the closet where I hung a photo of Ian doing his young girlfriend from behind. "You have classes tomorrow."

"I was worried about you," she says. "And I talked to my professors. They know I have an emergency at home." She narrows her glance at me as she takes a seat at the table. "Are you okay?"

I join her. "I'm not quite at emergency status."

"Mom . . . what's going on?"

"Nothing, Quinn. Nothing that should concern you."

"I talked to Patrick. I know you and Dad aren't speaking. Dad told him you were hysterical. Accusatory."

"Accusatory."

"*Out-of-control* accusatory. If you want to know the exact term."

Anger flares up. To think he told our son that I overreacted . . . Ian must have painted a picture of my being out of control and accusing him of outrageous things, and Patrick swallowed the tale hook, line, and sinker.

And Ian, I know, is everything Patrick aspires to be. His father overcame great odds. From a boy who got his girlfriend in trouble in high school, to partner in a law firm, his is a true story of grit, hard work, and achievement.

Either Patrick has absolute trust in his father and thinks his father is too sophisticated to do such a nasty thing as seduce a young girl behind his wife's back, or Patrick sees having other women as Ian's right, given how hard he's worked. I don't know which it is, but either way, my son is way off base.

"He said you accused Dad of having an affair. Mom, you don't actually think he would—"

"He said I was hysterical?"

"Mm-hmm. Do you really think he's screwing around?"

"I more than think. I *know.*"

"I never wanted to tell you this, but . . ." She chews on her thumbnail for a second. "I told Patrick months ago that I thought something weird was going on with Dad."

"Like what?"

"I don't know. He seemed distracted or something. I got a weird vibe. I told Patrick I wouldn't put it past Dad to cheat."

"Really, Quinn? You'd talk to your brother about this, but not me?"

"You had enough to deal with . . . with the episode, and besides, Patrick didn't agree with me. So what are you going to do?"

"I don't know yet. But Patrick obviously thinks it's okay to cover for Dad."

"Please, Mom." She rolls her eyes. "Patrick doesn't know the meaning of the word *faithful*. He was looking at engagement rings last spring, right? He said once he was finished with law school, he wants to marry Becca. If that's true, why was he out with another girl just last month?"

"You know this for a fact?"

"I didn't see it with my own eyes, if that's what you mean. But people talk."

"Does Becca know?"

"Well, I'd gladly tell her, but it won't make for a very nice Christmas. He'd be *pissed*."

"We're probably not going to have a great Christmas this year, anyway." I hate thinking it's true, but she's old enough to deal with some harsh realities. "Maybe if Patrick has to bear the consequence of what he's doing, he'd stop doing it."

"Okay, so what's the consequence going to be for Dad?"

"I don't know. I have to get my ducks in a row, I guess. I don't have a job, I've never worked outside the home . . ."

And Ian recently changed the password on the bank account, so he's probably getting his ducks in a row, too.

"You have to start pursuing your own interests. Make friends. You used to have friends, Mom. You used to have parties. Have fun."

"Parties take *work*."

"I know you and Aunt Lena were close before she and Doug split, but . . . maybe you could call Donna. Be friends with her."

I don't tell my daughter about my last encounter with Donna, when she blew me off after yoga and coffee at the mere mention of something uncomfortable.

I look to my Louis Vuitton tote, which is spilling out onto the counter.

Quinn's gaze follows the direction of mine.

I'm sure she sees the red thong, still wrapped in the plastic, reclosable bag.

She blinks away and meets me in a stare.

"Mom?"

She doesn't ask the question I know is lingering on the tip of her tongue, but she doesn't have to.

My heart tightens. As much as I want to prove to the world that Ian's wronged me, that I'm *not* hysterical and I'm not overreacting, I always wanted my kids to believe in their father. I know the pain that comes from realizing your dad has flaws, that those flaws can draw a line or build a wall between you.

The wall between my father and me was never broken down, and I am permanently fractured because of it—even now, years after his death.

But I'm not the one who did this. If Ian's relationship with our children suffers because of those panties in my purse, it's both his fault and his responsibility to repair it.

Quinn's brows slant slightly downward, and she tilts her head to one side. "Please, Mama."

I choke on a sob. *Mama*. She hasn't called me that in years.

"You should leave." She swallows noticeably, and I know by the pricks of tears in her eyes that she's trying not to cry. "You should go. I'll help you."

"Believe it or not, Quinn, I've already put some pieces in place."

"Like what?"

"Like where I want to live, what I want to do."

"You can't do this on your own. It's a big deal. It's okay to rely on people. Your old friends from Evanston . . . you're more worried about the episode than any of them. They understand. Half of them are on Prozac, anyway."

"I want to start over," I say. "When I had that episode, Quinn, it was like a catharsis, a fresh start. And maybe you haven't seen the evidence of my starting over, but it's been happening." I tap my temple. "Up here. And this is something I have to do on my own, sweetie."

I know she doesn't see me as strong. I know that for most of her life, I've played the role of a passive participant in a game where her father is king.

But that's about to change.

Earlier, I took a call from Lieutenant Decker, a detective with the Chicago Police Department. I have an appointment with him tomorrow morning.

I'm about to show my daughter just how strong a woman like me can be.

THEN

Margaux

Someone was sitting on a stoop in the alleyway behind the Aquasphere, leaning up against the wall, reading a novel. Margaux had just left another Sunday dinner at the Akerses', where Richard had pleaded, to no avail, for her to stop dancing at the Aquasphere Underground.

Before dinner, he showed her the balance in her trust fund account—$1,000 fatter, as promised. But she made twice that some Saturday nights. She left him with an ultimatum: double the weekly stipend, or she'd start talking about everything that he'd done to her. She'd already drafted a letter to NBC Chicago, detailing the way Everyone's Granddad had celebrated her eighteenth birthday.

She slipped a copy of the letter into the desk drawer in his private study as a reminder. Just in case. The possibility Helen might find it should be threat enough.

She pulled her keys from her handbag and stepped to the left, around the person reading, to get to the door leading to the dressing rooms.

"I know who you are," the stranger said.

Margaux's pink Mary Jane heels clicked to a stop on the landing.

She looked down through glasses with rose-colored lenses. Her keys dangled from her hand, the miniature pink Eiffel Tower swinging from the chain like a pendulum. It was then she noticed the bruise circling her right wrist—a rope burn, to be specific—was at the visitor's eye level. With a gasp, she tucked the hand behind her back. "Do I know you?"

"You don't realize it yet," the stranger said. "But yes. Deep down, you know who I am."

"Let's end the suspense," Margaux suggested. "And you can just tell me your name."

"Consider me a concerned third party."

"Concerned why?"

"We have a mutual acquaintance."

"Who's that?"

The concerned third party raised a brow.

Slowly, realization dawned. Margaux's eyes widened, her jaw descended slightly, and she covered her "Oh!" with a hand. "You've watched us before." She pointed toward the building she was about to enter.

"I've seen you before. I wouldn't call it watching."

"What do you want?"

"How involved are you with this man?"

"I don't see how that's your business, but—"

"You're not the only one. There are other girls. Have been. Will be. Others."

In a flash, a memory flooded back: the first night she met Arlon. The bartender had warned her to be careful. But that was a long time ago. Whatever he might have done before he met her wasn't her business, just as her dirty past wasn't any of his. "If that's true, and I don't buy it, I'm the only one who matters."

"Don't you think *all* women ought to matter?"

Margaux stepped back. "What do you want from me?"

"I just wanted you to know."

"Now I know."

"Then my work is done."

Chapter 18

JESSICA

"I did some poking around." Decker brushes up against me as he enters my apartment. It's seven in the morning, but it feels as if it's late in the evening after a night on the job. "That woman's husband? The one in the pictures? He's a *lawyer*. Well-respected one, too. I can't get anywhere near him without a warrant, so I'm in a holding pattern."

"Why don't you come in?" I say after he's already entered, but my friend with benefits doesn't have time for my sarcasm. I engage the dead bolt and chain lock on the door.

"First of all, the pictures are electronic copies, and any lawyer worth his salt is going to be able to call reasonable doubt. Besides, they prove an affair, but they don't do shit to prove murder." He's already sitting at the breakfast bar in my tiny kitchen, popping cups of dark roast out of one of those cardboard carriers from the coffee shop down the block. "Second, no Jack Wyatt owns or rents an apartment in the Lincoln Park building you mentioned."

"I've been there. I met him in the lobby once. I know he lives there. Maybe he sublets."

"It's not listed with the association as a sublease. Maybe he met you in the lobby because he wants you to think he lives there."

"People don't always report subleases."

"I'll let you know what I find."

"Well, it's a good thing you pulled me away from a long-awaited soak in my tub to tell me you might have something of interest to report later this afternoon."

"Jessie, listen." He fiddles with the heat collar on his coffee cup. "I can appreciate, coming from me, this probably doesn't hold much water, but I don't have a good feeling about this guy."

I cross my arms, lean a hip against the countertop across from him, and treat him to a stare. What does he expect me to say?

"It's not just that the apartment isn't really his and he led you to believe it was." He takes the lid off the second cup of coffee and pours a cream and three sugars into it. Just as I like it. "Here." He drops a stir stick into the cup and scoots it across the breakfast bar, toward me. "It's that in the city limits, I can't find a single early-twenties to midthirties Caucasian in the six-foot range with the name of Jack Wyatt. I've tried versions of the name: John, Jackson, Jackie. Wyatt with an *I*. Wyatt with one *T*. No dice. Always something a hair off about all of them."

"So . . . what are you saying? That the guy doesn't exist?" I stir my coffee and take a sip. "At least not in the city limits?"

"That's what I'm saying." He nods a curt nod. "And it's a big city."

Even I have to admit it's strange. When I met Jack, he said he'd lived in the city most of his life. *Decades.*

"But I found this guy." He opens a file and presents an eight-by-ten color copy of an Indiana driver license. The name: Jack Wyatt. Age: thirty-nine. "He's the closest match."

"That's not him."

"Of course not. If I can't find the guy," Decker says, "I can't rule him out for Margaux's murder. Not that I have enough to go on for even a warrant."

"Right. You don't have enough to go on because there's no connection."

"Except that your injuries match that of a dead girl."

"I told you how it all happened with the bruise on my neck, and yeah . . . it's silly and ridiculous to consider he jumped to the conclusion that that's what I wanted in a first romantic encounter, but isn't it also a little crazy for you to assume he has anything to do with Margaux?"

"Call it a hunch."

"Or call it my ex-boyfriend not wanting me to move on with another guy."

"That's not what this is about. It's that *nothing* is adding up. Has your guy ever been to Aquasphere? Maybe he met her there."

I chew on my lip for a second. "Actually, he sort of sidestepped the question when I asked him about it."

"Interesting."

"Hmm." I don't want to admit it, but the truth is that if Jack went to that place, there's a chance he ran into Margaux. "She could have met all three of them there."

"I've got a mysterious Arlon Judson, too. Not a common name, but the one I did track down has alibis, lives four hours away, and wasn't even in the state of Illinois at the time of Margaux's death."

"Helen could have gotten the name wrong," I suggest. "To be honest, it didn't seem like she was a big part of Margaux's life for the past few years. If she never met the guy Margaux was dating, maybe she just didn't know much."

Decker considers this. "Akers was pretty sure of his name. But if the girl had a boyfriend at all, why isn't he anywhere on her social media pages? A girl that age? With a steady boyfriend? You'd think the pages would be riddled with his face."

"Yeah, that's strange."

"Plus, I got a Jack Wyatt not officially living where he says he's living—and not really living anywhere else."

I look to my sofa, the site of the heated, intense, if not brief encounter I shared with Jack last night before I was called into the fire station.

"I'll ask him about the sublease. Maybe that's all it is."

"Everyone's a suspect," he says, "until they're not a suspect anymore. It's a long shot, anyway, pursuing your guy, but I'd feel better ruling him out. When it comes to your safety, I can't be too careful."

"How'd it go with the alderman?"

"Typical politician responses. No mention of the pregnancy, which is fine—he probably didn't know—and no indication that the rumor Margaux worked at Aquasphere was true. He seems to think it was all hype. Just gossip. People like to talk about sex and scandal."

I start to nod, but Decker's talking again:

"However, he owned up to mishandling the tuition funds but stated he was already replenishing the account—and provided proof that he had been. And he confirmed Margaux was involved in a relationship with a gentleman—his words, not mine—by the name of Arlon Judson, and that despite his requests, she refused to bring Arlon around. He says on numerous occasions, there were marks on her body. Bruises on her wrists and ankles. On her neck, not unlike the mark you have on yours."

"So you don't like Akers for the murder."

"He's a politician. Possibly even dirty, given his gambling addiction. And wouldn't it just figure? Another dirty politician in Chicago? He's about as clear from this case as mud on a windshield, but I gotta be honest: if he's already putting funds back into the account, a thousand here, two thousand there, and before the girl died, the motive is rather weak."

"What about Helen accusing Margaux of spreading lies? Ruining their image could be motive."

"If I could find anyone she told the lies to, I'd feel better about it. Just like I'd feel better finding Arlon Judson. Just like I'd feel better ruling out your guy."

"Fine. What do you need to effectively rule Jack out?"

"A cup he drank from, a pizza crust he gnawed on—"

"A condom full of spunk?"

"Do you have one?"

"No, but I can make it happen if it'll shut you up."

"That would do it."

I hesitate for a moment. He's daring me to sleep with Jack, if not outright asking me to do so.

It's not exactly the reaction I expected.

"I'm kidding," he says. "Plenty a killer has been nabbed with saliva. No need to take the guy to bed."

"Is there anything else you'd like me to secure for you? Hair from his shower drain, perhaps? Scrapings from beneath his fingernails?" There's a frosty edge to my tone, which I can't help but instantly regret.

He grasps my wrist.

My glance meets his.

"Hey."

I raise a brow. "What?"

"I do want you to be happy. I hope I'm wrong about this guy."

"Kirsten Holloway's husband is far more interesting a suspect than the guy you won't admit to being jealous of, but I'll accept your apology when you realize you're wrong."

But secretly, I'm terrified that it won't happen that way.

Decker's hunches usually lead somewhere.

THEN

Margaux

Margaux perused fresh fruits at a farmers market when, out of the corner of her eye, she saw a familiar face. "Hey!"

The concerned third party caught her glance but quickly started moving toward the sidewalk and soon was practically running in the opposite direction.

"Wait!"

Maybe the stranger was tired of running. Maybe it was time for another dose of reality. But either way, with the adopting of a slower pace, Margaux caught up. "Are you spying on me?"

"I didn't come here looking for you."

"Why are you running away from me?"

"I'm trying to respect your privacy—and guard mine."

"Did you hire someone to follow me? To take pictures of Arlon and me?"

"What? No!"

"I think it's happened a couple of times now."

"It's not me."

"I want to know what you're doing here."

"I already said what I wanted to say. You ought to know you're not the first. You're not the last."

Their gazes met.

"You know that now, right?" the stranger asked. "And the way he treats you . . ."

Margaux brought a hand to the bruise forming on her cheek. Apparently, her efforts to cover the mark with makeup were futile.

"Did he do that to you?"

"He didn't hit me. It was . . . up against the wall. Role-playing. Fantasy."

For the moment, the concerned third party looked just that— concerned. "Fantasy of what? Rape?"

"And what if it is?"

"Is that something you wanted?"

"Don't you dare judge me," Margaux said. "It's exciting, all right? And it's *my* choice. For once, it's *my choice*, got it?"

"Yeah. I understand. I just want to make sure it's something you really want. You don't have to do it just because he expects it."

"I do what I want."

"Okay, then." For a few uncomfortable seconds, silence gnawed at the air between them. "What does Akers say about all the marks he leaves on you?"

"Richard is the one who taught me I didn't have a choice about much in this world. I couldn't care less about what he says."

"Okay. As long as you're sure, and as long as you're okay."

For a minute or so, Margaux gauged her acquaintance's expression and found honesty, concern.

"He lost my tuition money, you know." Margaux sighed. "God, I don't know why I'm telling you all this, but I was set for life. And if anyone else had adopted me . . . I'd be enrolled, ready to go."

"That's not fair."

"I'll tell you what's not fair: a man in good standing grooming a poor kid until she doesn't realize what's right and wrong."

"Did that happen to you? Did the alderman—"

"I don't know why I'm telling you." Margaux sniffled. "You don't care about this stuff."

"I care. Margaux, *of course* I care. You can talk to me. You can always talk to me."

"Well, I don't want to talk about it anymore."

"That's fine, too."

Margaux wiped a tear from her bruised cheek, and for a moment, all was silent between them. Finally, she spoke. "It started innocently enough. I was thirsty for affection. I took any I could get. Even the wrong kind. After a while, I craved him, you know?"

She talked for nearly half an hour. "And when we finally actually did it . . . I was scared. You're not supposed to be scared, are you? But he was drunk, and Helen was just down the hall, and I was afraid that if I didn't do it, he wouldn't love me anymore."

"No one deserves that."

"Now, he just can't stand it that I'm with someone else. I think he's actually *jealous* of Arlon. Sometimes I wonder if it's why I started the relationship—any relationship, really."

"You know, maybe your precious Arlon can be useful, after all. Not sexually, if he's only hell-bent on making you feel like a whore. But he could foot the bill for the tuition Akers lost."

Margaux shook her head in puzzlement. "You mean, *use* him for *money?*"

"Why not? He's using you to fulfill his every sexual fantasy. Not a bad way to earn tuition, is it? And then you won't be roped into seeing your worst perpetrator week to week. Margaux, he *abused* you, and you're still playing by his rules."

"I can't. I'm sorry, I just can't. I love Arlon, and he loves me. I can't use him that way."

"He's not capable of love, and you've been through enough. Trust me, Margaux. You're wrong about Arlon. I'll prove it to you."

"If you really care, you'd just stop. You'd forget this crazy obsession with Arlon and me, and you'd go live your own life. I should call the cops. There are probably laws against the things you do. Following me the way you do!"

"You followed me today."

"It's *unsettling*. You're scaring me."

"You don't have to be scared."

"Then stop. Whatever it is you're doing, whatever you get out of this sick obsession with Arlon and me . . . *stop*. Please. We're happy."

"Anyone can be happy two nights a week. What do you think he does on the other five?"

"He'd be with me all the time, but he has a job. Just trust me. And stop doing this. Let me be. Let *us* be."

"He's seeing someone else."

"He wouldn't."

"He's *involved* with her, and the sooner you realize it, the better. When you take off the blinders, I'll stop coming around."

Chapter 19

Kirsten

The weather has turned colder today. It's that time of year in Chicago when it could be eighty, or barely fifty, degrees, and today, we're hovering at the low side. I'm bundled in a warmer jacket and ankle-high boots. I'm meeting Jessica in the city for lunch today, so I thought I'd get some errands out of the way and head out early.

Namely, I'm dropping off some evidence at the fourteenth district—a certain pair of panties and a flash drive full of photos. I told the detective I would do as much when he called yesterday.

If I'd consulted my husband, or his cousin, they'd tell me I had a right against self-incrimination, that in this state, a wife can't be forced to testify against her husband. But justice is due.

I drive down the county route toward Interstate 94, past mounds of golden leaves in the fields. For a minute, I remember the early days of our marriage. The kids were little and we were barely adults ourselves, and we'd raked up the leaves in the yard, let the kids wear their Halloween costumes, and we took turns jumping into piles.

I can nearly feel Ian's cold cheek against mine, his arms around me, and our babies between our bodies, all huddling to stay warm.

Laughing.

Kissing.

Singing nursery rhymes: *roll over, roll over. So they all rolled over* . . .

We were beating the odds.

Together.

I never thought any odds could beat us, but things are different now.

I'm not sure how it happened.

Little by little, I suppose.

An inch here, an inch there.

Over the course of so many years, hairline fractures left unrepaired have split into canyons between us.

It feels like only a moment ago.

Little children, full of promise, Mommy and Daddy so necessary for their happiness and survival.

When I think of their little faces, their sticky hands and sloppy kisses, I want nothing more than to somehow stop time in its tracks, to keep them little and safe and happy with parents who love each other.

I want to wake up from this nightmare, or at least to zero in on a way to fix it.

But I can't rewind time and undo the things Ian's done or may have done.

Suddenly, I'm on one side of a gorge, and Ian's on the other—and there's a beautiful, dead woman standing between us.

Or maybe the distance has always been there, but with little children at home I was preoccupied, busy, living life in fifteen-minute increments. It was easier then not to see the vast, growing space.

I don't know if there's a bridge strong enough or long enough to connect us again.

And now the truth of what's happened to our marriage, and to Margaux Claire Stritch, is hanging somewhere in the balance.

Infidelity is hard enough to survive, but considering someone died—and I can't honestly say I don't think my husband is capable . . . or responsible . . . I wonder if there's a prayer to save any marriage under these circumstances, let alone one that was, as society assumed, doomed from the word *go*.

I pull over to the side of the road to compose myself, but the tears only overcome me. I can't help it. We had high hopes, and now the last of them is circling the drain.

I cry until I'm practically wheezing.

And suddenly, I get the sense that I'm being watched.

I look up.

And I'm staring eye to eye with a doe. Near her, yet farther in the distance, are two fawns, already growing winter coats and losing their spots.

For long minutes, I watch her, and she watches me. Her posture is graceful yet stoic, as if she's a statue, instead of a real, living being.

There's a patch of her coat missing on her right rear quarter, and I have to wonder if she's the same doe I collided with the other day. I hope so. I want to think she survived.

After what feels like hours, but could only have been minutes, or even seconds, she turns and leads her family back into the woods. Finally, I put the car in gear and get going.

Chapter 20

Jessica

I'm fresh out of the tub, and I can't get Decker's commentary out of my head. He's right that he can't be too careful. And maybe, if I weren't apparently addicted to this case, I'd sit back, let him do his thing, and wait for the final report.

But it's obvious Decker's exhausted, and considering his partner hasn't seen him much all month, they're dividing and conquering the tasks related to Margaux's case. There's just not enough time in a day.

However . . .

I have an inside track on one of the people Decker's zeroing in on.

I pick up my phone and text: Breakfast?

Jack texts:

Good to hear from you.

Sorry about last night.

Was sure I wouldn't hear from you again.

Me: A girl's gotta eat.

Jack: Leaving at nine for airport.
Me: Your place then?

I'll bring breakfast.

I can be there in half an hour.

Jack: ☺

———

I enter the building Jack says he lives in with buttermilk biscuits and gravy I picked up along the way.

As instructed, I give my name at the door, and—no questions asked—a doorman sends me up to the eighteenth floor.

Proof that Jack lives where he says he lives: check.

Jack is fastening his cuff links when he opens the door. He presses his lips to my cheek. "Thanks for coming. I don't have but half an hour."

"That's all right. I don't have much time, either."

When he backs off, he glances downward. "Oh God." He brings his fingers to the bruise on my neck. "Did I do that to you?"

"It's all right."

"No, it's really not." He seals his lips at the mark. "Usually, when I leave a mark on someone . . ." *Kiss, kiss, kiss.* ". . . it's because I can't stop sucking on her." He brushes a thumb over the bruise again. "And usually . . . usually I'm a lot more fun in the sack."

I laugh. "It was still fun."

"Until you belted me. They used to call me Action Jackson—but that wasn't quite the kind of action I used to get."

"Yeah, well, I guess I should apologize again for that, too."

"I deserved it."

"Glad I didn't leave a mark on you. That could've been difficult to explain at the office."

"Yeah." He chuckles. "Will you excuse me a minute? I have to finish getting ready."

"Sure, I'll just be in the kitchen." I meander farther into the place.

The apartment is decorated with neutrals—grays, whites—and the place suits the Jack I know. It's minimalist, sleek, clean, and linear. The floor in the open area is white marble, like the steps of some important government building, or maybe a museum, but I see it gives way in the hallway to a soft, plush carpet. A large suitcase waits there, packed to the gills and ready.

The draperies across the way are wispy and white. I can't imagine they keep much hidden. Then again, at this many floors above the lakeshore, I wonder how modest one has to be when standing at the window.

God, what a place this is!

"Where can I find plates?" I ask.

"Second cabinet to the right of the dishwasher," Jack says. "So I take it you're not into the Aquasphere Underground culture."

"Uh . . . we can talk about it." A quick look over my shoulder tells me he's busy finishing prepping for his trip. He's shaping his hair with gel. I begin to open cabinet doors and drawers. I'm not sure what I'm looking for, exactly, but so far, I'm not finding anything beyond standard kitchen gadgets in a room so clean I could eat cereal out of the sink.

"That's all right," he says. "I'm perfectly happy taking you to Irish pubs."

"This is a great place," I say. "Incredible view."

"It's why I bought the place."

Confirm it's Jack's place and not a rental: check.

Decker's way off base here.

I pull plates from the cabinet and find a couple of forks.

There's an open laptop with a prism screen saver morphing from blue to green to yellow on the table.

When I move it to set it aside, the screen saver dissipates to reveal an article Jack must've been reading when I interrupted him.

My breath catches in my throat.

It's an article about Margaux titled Babydoll: Murdered?

Maybe he's reading it because it came up in his daily feed. Maybe he's reading it because of my connection to the case. Or maybe he's reading it to see if the police have made any progress in uncovering clues.

I look toward the bathroom to confirm he's still messing with his hair.

A closer look tells me he has several windows open on his computer; one of them is Aquasphere Online. Another is a second online news rag detailing a scandal between Everyone's Granddad Akers and his adopted daughter. The final window is none other than Arlon Judson's Instagram page.

The page is riddled with pictures of kids. The profile pic is a family of six posing with Mickey Mouse.

I feel a hollowing in my chest. It's proof Margaux was dating a married man.

More concerning: Why would Jack have this page open unless he knew him? Or unless he knew Margaux was dating the guy?

Prove that Jack has no interest in the Margaux Stritch case, let alone a connection to it: game-show buzzer.

My hackles are up.

Lots of criminals revisit scenes or clip articles about their crimes to relive the moments it happened, or to look for a heads-up—like when it's time to leave town.

I look again to the hallway leading to the bedroom, where a suitcase sits. It appears he's leaving for much longer than his usual day-long jaunts to NYC.

"Long trip this time?"

"I'm not really sure." The water in the bathroom turns off.

I quickly close the laptop, but I wonder if it was fast enough because he's suddenly right there.

"Should be only a few days, but I have a meeting that might have to push, so . . . What's for breakfast?" He puts his arms around me from behind.

"Biscuits and gravy." My heart is beating a little too fast. I hope he didn't see me snooping through his internet searches. I hope he can't tell that I'm nervous.

I bring my hand to my heart. Is it obvious?

My fingers graze the necklace Jack gave me.

"Oh, you're wearing it," he says.

His mouth again lands on my neck.

He seems awfully interested in my neck. Coincidence? "It goes with everything," I tell him.

Get sample for Decker: task pending.

It's the one thing I figured I wouldn't have to do, but Decker did say saliva would work, and Jack's is all over my neck.

"Thanks for bringing breakfast."

"My pleasure."

I wait a beat. He doesn't seem to notice that I'm frazzled. "Can I borrow your bathroom?"

"Sure."

It doesn't escape my notice that he's watching me as I close the door behind me.

I turn on the water and breathe.

Everything I've seen here could be coincidence.

Nothing proves he has anything more than a mild interest in a case that, let's face it, has been plastered all over the news.

Still . . .

I pull a plastic bag from my pocket and reach into the shower drain. I pull out a small clump of gray and brown hair and seal the bag.

Just in case, I check the medicine cabinet, but I don't find anything but Tylenol.

I open the drawers in the vanity and see a *GQ* magazine. The mailing label is worn, but I can tell this apartment wasn't its original destination. It originally arrived on Oakley Street. No idea of the house number, except that it ends in a five. No apartment number listed.

This, too, doesn't mean anything. For all I know, Jack lifted the magazine from his oil change venue, or from his dentist's office.

Or maybe this partial address will tell us something about Jack—where he really lives, who he really lives with, or even where he works.

I snap a picture, yet I don't text it to Decker just yet in case he decides to get into a conversation about it. That's all I need—Jack realizing another guy is texting me. And better yet, texting about reasons to suspect *him*.

Another deep breath. Time to face him.

I flush the toilet and exit out into the room.

THEN

MARGAUX

Margaux left the Underground, exiting into the dark gangway. Her boobs hurt from being pinched into a tight corset, and her thighs and lower back ached, thanks to the client who'd paid her to stand bent at the waist, her rear to him, for nearly twenty minutes.

She found herself muffling a sob. She couldn't keep up this lifestyle forever. And even though the money came quickly, would it ever be enough for school? Living rent-free didn't feed her or pay the utility bills.

Maybe the third party was right. Maybe it was time to ask Arlon to finance her education. It could turn out okay. He'd already talked about having kids, so maybe it wouldn't be out of line to ask.

"Hi."

She startled when she heard the voice behind her and practically yelped.

"Sorry to scare you," he said. "I just saw you inside, and I couldn't help but notice . . . on your breast . . . Did someone *cut* his initials into you?"

"That's none of your business."

"Maybe not. I just wanted to be sure you're okay, so if you are . . ."

"I am."

"Are you sure? Because it looks like you're crying."

"What if I am?"

"How about a cup of coffee?"

She took a few steps down the gangway. She didn't owe this guy any sort of explanation for her tears. He didn't have to know her life was spinning out of control.

"Tell you what," the nice guy said. "I'm going to be in the diner on the corner. You want to join me, great. If you don't, I understand that, too. Just thought we could talk, that's all."

Margaux kept walking.

"Suit yourself," he said.

She emerged from the gangway on one side of the old church and turned right toward Western only to see her new acquaintance standing on the opposite side of the Aquasphere, ready to cross Western, too.

She watched as he crossed, looked at her over his shoulder, and beckoned for her to follow.

What the hell.

Arlon wouldn't like it, but he was presently in a city far away.

And what if the third party was right? What if she wasn't the only one Arlon was carving his initials into?

Chapter 21

KIRSTEN

"Thanks for meeting me out," I say. "It's just been one of those insane weeks when nothing feels right."

"Tell me about it," Jessica says. "I just came from my boyfriend's place, and nothing felt right over there, either. My cop friend, Decker—he's the one I told you about, the guy I used to . . . anyway, he got it in his head that Jack's got something to do with Margaux, and I took it upon myself to secure a sample for him this morning."

"A *sample?*"

"I went there thinking there was no way in hell Deck could be right. But once I got there, I started noticing things that made me think maybe Decker *is* right. I pulled hair from his shower drain." She wrinkles her nose. "Is that insane, or what?"

"Why do the cops want a sample like that?" But less than a second passes before I cover my mouth. "Oh. They're looking for a sample to match DNA on her body."

"Well . . . on her body, sure. But . . ." Her glance shifts, and she busies herself by straightening the salt and pepper shakers. Whatever she has to say must not be easy.

"But what?" I ask.

"It isn't public knowledge. It's part of the investigation, and Deck would kill me if I leaked it."

"My lips are sealed."

"Even so, I shouldn't. But given the pictures you found . . ." She sighs. "This sucks, and I'm sorry, but Deck will fill you in . . . *if* he thinks you should know, but I can't. I'm sorry."

"I'll keep it to myself. I promise."

"I can't," Jessie says.

For a few moments, neither of us says anything. She wants to tell me whatever she knows. I can tell.

"But the sample I gathered from Jack's shower," she redirects. "It could prove interesting."

"They honestly think your boyfriend had something to do with this poor girl?"

She shrugs and zips the pendant on her necklace to and fro.

I stare at it.

"Maybe," Jessica says. "It seems she was seeing more than one man, so . . ."

My heart rate quickens. If there's a chance Margaux was seeing someone else—someone else who might have had something to do with her death—I might've just set Ian up to take the fall. If there's any of my husband's DNA on Margaux's body, or in her apartment, and Ian is innocent, it might be hard to exonerate him.

Oh God.

My cheeks flush with heat, and for a few seconds, I feel like I felt at the farmers market with Fiona—at the onset of the episode.

I take a deep breath.

My throat is dry.

I cough and reach for my water.

Calm. Calm. Calm.

Another deep breath. "Do *you* think your boyfriend had anything to do with Margaux's death?"

"I don't think Decker has much basis, except that the other night, Jack surprised me at my apartment, and long story short . . ." She moves her hair aside and exposes a faint bruise on her neck. "Decker doesn't think it's a coincidence."

"He choked you?"

"It's kind of a funny story—at least it was funny until I found the guy checking up on everything related to the case this morning, but . . ."

"Wait a minute." I pull out my phone and call up a picture of Ian and Margaux. "Jessie, have you noticed the charm on your necklace looks an awful lot like the ring Margaux is wearing in these pictures? Same pear shape, both rubies. It looks like it could be a set."

She looks, and I can only assume agrees with me when she suddenly looks tired and removes it from her neck. "I'd best get this to Decker, too, then."

"It's a simple design," I offer. "Lots of jewelers mix diamonds with rubies. It could be a coincidence."

"I'm growing tired of coincidence," Jessica says. "But you know, I don't think she was wearing a ring the night she died. One sec." She's texting. "Deck'll check on that. Maybe if we find the ring, we'll find whoever knows how or why this happened to her. Or maybe prints off this necklace will be enough."

"You sure you're a firefighter and not a cop?" I ask.

"You're not the first to ask."

"Maybe this is none of my business, but . . ."

I gauge her expression—raised brows, as if she's intently listening.

"If my daughter came to me with this sort of information, I'd tell her to stop seeing the guy," I say. "You can't risk continuing the relationship when there's a question like that hanging over you. You don't need to give him an explanation. Just stop. Whether or not he's capable of doing what someone did to Margaux—if someone did *anything* to

Margaux, that is—this . . . what he did to your neck . . . it's no way to start a relationship."

I don't expect her to heed my advice. Looking back, if some strange woman I met on the side of the road had told me not to pursue a relationship with Ian, if someone had warned me that falling for him would mean sacrificing my hopes and dreams, I wouldn't have listened. I don't regret it, either. I have my children, and they're worth every sacrifice I've made.

"What about your bank account?" Jessica says. "Do we know if there's money missing?"

"I'm working on the password," I say. "But Ian did admit there's been some strange transactions. I'll let you know when I know."

THEN

MARGAUX

"I can't wear this, Arlon." Margaux stood in front of a full-length mirror and studied the deep purples and blues of bruises on the small of her back—mementos of last week's stint on the fire escape. "Look at this." Her backless black catsuit—a gift, of course—put the marring on display. And the metal clasp at the top cut into the bruise he left on her neck, and it *hurt*. The front consisted of a deep vee that exposed the sides of her breasts and plunged to her navel.

"It's not a question of can or can't. You *will*." He circled her, like a shark swimming around a seal, contemplating, judging. "More eye makeup."

"Really? I have two coats of mascara on already."

"And darker lips. I want them red. Bloodred."

Okay. She returned to her mirror and heavily lined her eyes and replaced the pink lipstick with red. God, she looked like she was about to climb into the cage at the Underground. But if this was what he wanted . . . "How about now?"

He looked up from a wad of cash in his wallet and pulled out another hundred. "You look hot." He put the bill atop the other four on the table near her front door.

For long seconds, she stared at it, the concerned third party's suggestion ringing in her memory. Arlon could help financially. "What's the money for?"

"You're asking a lot of questions tonight."

"I just wondered—"

"If you're going to act like a whore"—he grinned—"I'll treat you like one."

So it was a game. Okay.

And if he really wanted her to wear the catsuit, she could endure it.

She stepped into heels much higher than she usually wore, but Arlon had not only requested the shoes but had purchased them *especially for the occasion*. The shoes pinched her toes, too, but she had to admit it was a stunning ensemble, despite its being on the slutty side.

"Where are we going?"

"Out."

"Anywhere in particular?"

"Don't worry about it."

She wasn't worried as much as curious, but his message came across loud and clear: she shouldn't ask any more questions.

They exited her apartment, and he instructed her to walk ten feet in front of him.

When she looked over her shoulder to ensure he was following, he texted:

This is a game of trust. If you trust me, you'll do what I say.

She didn't look back after that.

He texted instructions. Turn left here, take the alley there.

After several miles, her feet positively ached—how much farther could they go?—and she wondered why they couldn't just take a cab. Especially when they wound up in a neighborhood she could only describe as unsavory.

She crossed her arms over her middle and carried on past groups of despicable characters drinking liquor out of brown-bagged bottles and a clan of teenaged delinquents smoking weed and whistling at her.

Arlon texted:

You're coming to a door propped open on the left.

Go inside.

The door was soaped over, like a storefront under construction, and the innards of the space were dark and dank.

But he wanted her to prove she trusted him, so she did as he asked.

She awaited his next instructions, but none came in the next few minutes.

The place creaked and cracked with the wind outside, and it smelled like a urinal, but she trusted that given he'd requested her outfit and gone through the trouble of planning, there must be some amazing club up a few flights of stairs.

It was *Arlon*, for the love of God, and he was always full of surprises.

Soon, the minutes lingered well past her comfort, and she edged her way around the space, which felt like a concrete box. There was only one way in, one way out, and the longer she paced in here, the more likely it seemed she'd encounter something—or someone—dangerous.

"Arlon?"

She made her way toward the door.

Just a peek out, to see where he was.

But not a hair past the door, she was whisked back inside, a hand over her mouth, and shoved, face-first, against a concrete wall.

"Arlon?"

She recognized the scent of his cologne, the rasp of his whisper: "Quiet."

He held her there. "When were you going to tell me you've been dancing at the Underground?"

"I'm . . . Arlon, you're hurting me."

He put more pressure on her back. "You fucking whore."

"But anything goes," she said. "That's the deal with us, isn't it?"

"Imagine my surprise when I come home early from a trip and find your apartment empty."

She winced when she felt a thick rope wrap around first one wrist, then the other.

"I went to Aquasphere for a little relief that night, and imagine my surprise when I realize the redhead I paid to bend over, the one I'm rubbing one out to, is actually the girl I'm supposed to love and trust."

"But if you were rubbing it out to someone you thought wasn't me, I'm willing to overlook it—"

He yanked on the rope, and next she knew, she was suspended a few inches off the ground.

"Ow!" Hot tears crept down her cheeks. "Black crow!"

"And then, I waited to see what you would do," Arlon said. "And you met someone else at the diner down the street."

"It was just coffee, I swear. Black crow, black crow, black crow."

"If you want to act like a whore, I'll treat you like one."

"I only dance. I'm not a whore."

"Tell me you love me."

"I love you," she whispered.

The clasp on her halter top fell free, exposing her breasts. Her nipples raked over the cold concrete wall she was up against. He shoved the catsuit down over her hips.

She was completely naked now, and the door was still propped. Not twenty feet beyond the door, thugs drank from bottles in brown bags and threw dice and played cards. They could come in at any time.

"Remember." Arlon slipped a hand between her legs. "I paid you in advance."

A shadow passed over the door, but Arlon was too busy to take heed, already lowering the zipper on his pants.

Margaux's eyes widened when she saw someone standing in the doorway.

Staring right at them.

The voyeur stayed only half a minute or so, then turned and disappeared down the alley.

When Arlon was done, he released her bindings.

She crumpled to the concrete floor.

"Remember this. *This* is how whores are treated."

He shoved his cock back into his pants and headed toward the door.

"Arlon!" she cried, attempting to get to her sore feet. "You can't leave me here."

But he kept walking.

And he'd damaged the clasp on the catsuit when he tore it off her, so she couldn't refasten it. And she couldn't run after him unclothed because the street outside was populated with thugs who would do God knew what to her.

She had no money in her handbag—she'd left the money Arlon gave her on the counter—so she couldn't call a cab.

She couldn't call the Akerses, either. Not for something like this.

But she had the phone number of the guy who'd bought her a cup of coffee.

She dialed.

"I need help," she said when he answered. "Everything's different now. Everything's changed."

She couldn't see Arlon anymore.

But she couldn't be the one to end it. He wasn't going to go quietly. The only way a man like that would leave her alone was if he grew tired of her and left on his own. He had to think ending the relationship was his idea, or he'd never give her a moment's peace.

Chapter 22

Kirsten

I stop at the bank on the way home for a physical printout of the past months' transactions. It's a joint account, and as I told Ian, I'm entitled.

Once home, I peruse the pages and highlight several transactions that aren't mine, transactions I consider unusual.

For one thing, I see that twenty grand has been transferred out of the account monthly for the past six months.

Holy hell, that's a lot of money.

I'm about to scribble a note about it, when another charge catches my eye:

Seven hundred seventy-five dollars at a women's clinic on the outskirts of Chicago.

A women's clinic.

I do a quick search of the clinic and see on their list of services: abortion.

I pinch my eyes shut and take a deep breath.

I call Ian's mobile.

He answers. "Not a good time, Kirstie."

"Make it a good time."

"Patrick says he explained everything about the underwear—he said he told you they're probably Becca's, see?—so now you know the truth. Things can go back to the way they used to be. Before all this nonsense. Before the episode."

"Ian, please."

"Kirstie, let's put it behind us, take a breath, and have a good weekend."

"I need you to come home."

"Kirstie, I can't—"

"Do you think a young girl might be depressed after she aborts a child?"

"What?"

"Depressed enough to want to kill herself?"

"Kirstie, what's going on? Is something going on with Quinn? She said she came home this week for a night."

"She did."

"What happened?"

"Quinn's fine."

"Thank God."

"Come home."

"Okay, I'll try to get out of this dinner, but I can't promise I'll be—"

"Now, Ian. We need to talk about Margaux Stritch." I pause for a beat, let it sink in. "And her abortion."

Only silence answers me.

"Now, Ian."

"For Chrissake, Kirstie. You know you're not well—"

"Come home." I hang up and open the door to Ian's study, where I pull his prized, autographed Jack Nicklaus golf club from its display case on the wall and drive it right through the wall, slam it over his desk and scratch the hell out of the vintage mahogany patina.

My phone is ringing, but I ignore it. I tear through the house and smash a picture of the two of us on our anniversary last year and a picture of us when we were teenagers.

And in our master suite, I take the club to virtually everything I see that's even remotely important to my husband.

There. I'm nearly out of breath when I'm done, and I've made a god-awful mess. But damn, do I feel good.

My phone hasn't stopped ringing, so I take a seat, try to compose myself, and answer it: "Patrick. Hello."

"What's going on, Mom? Dad said you're hysterical. He's on his way home."

"I'm not hysterical. Angry? Definitely. Cheated? Absolutely."

"I'm sending an ambulance. You sound rattled."

"Patrick, stop! I don't need an ambulance."

"It's on its way. Dad asked me to call, and when you didn't answer right away—"

"Call and cancel it."

"Maybe some time to regroup, Mom. They have programs now—"

"I don't need a program!"

"I always thought that just a recentering after Quinn left home . . . with professional help—"

"Shut up, Patrick! Shut up, shut up, shut up! I'm *fine*. I'm just pissed, and I should be pissed after what your father pulled!"

"You're screaming at me."

"You need to listen. If you listen, I won't scream."

"You don't sound fine. You sound hysterical, just like Dad said. Should I come home? I'd feel better . . . you know what? I'm on my way."

"If you walk through that door, I swear to God, Patrick." My phone beeps with another call. "Your sister's calling. I have to take this."

"I'll hold."

"*Goodbye*, Patrick." I click over to answer my daughter's call. "Hi, Quinn."

"Mom, what's going on? Dad says you're having another breakdown?"

I sigh. "No."

"He said there was some bogus charge on your account and that you're not listening to reason about it. He asked me, until he had time to get proof and get the charge reversed, to tell you it was mine."

"I know it's not your charge, Quinn. I know you didn't visit an abortion clinic."

"What? *That's* what the charge was for? Why would he ask me to do that?"

"He's counting on your wanting us to stay together. He's counting your worshipping him the way your brother does, no questions asked."

"Mom . . . did he knock someone up?"

"Quinn."

"It's okay. I'm old enough to know men are sometimes assholes."

I hear the whir of an ambulance siren approaching the house. "I'll call you later, okay? I promise. But I can't talk just now."

"And you're okay?"

"Honestly?" I look around at the mess I've made. "I feel pretty good."

The gate buzzer sounds. I touch the button to open the gate.

A few moments later, a pair of paramedics rushes to the door, where I greet them.

"We got a call, ma'am, for a well check. May we come in?"

I step aside. "Pardon the mess."

They enter into shards of glass, splinters of picture frames, and eight-by-ten glossies of my husband and Margaux.

"Your husband says you have a history of anxiety, that you've been hospitalized in the past. Is that right?"

"I had an episode a few months ago."

"This is your second?"

"No," I say. "I'm just angry." I walk down the center hallway and indicate a grainy photograph. "This is why."

"Who is this, ma'am?"

"That's my husband. And as you see, that's not me with him."

One of the paramedics lets out a slow whistle while the other says, "Oh boy."

I lead them to the kitchen. "Would you like a glass of water? Coffee? Wine, maybe?"

"We have to take your vitals, ma'am."

"All right." I fill a glass with water and sip. "I'm sure my blood pressure is a little elevated, but I'm sure you can understand why."

"Are there any weapons in the home, ma'am?"

"Just the golf club. You're welcome to take it with you when you leave. It was autographed by the Bear."

"No, we don't—"

"I insist." I find the club where I tossed it and hand it over. "It's the least I can do for your trouble."

"The Golden Bear, huh?"

"It's not in mint condition anymore." I smile at my own joke.

Within a few minutes, the pair is convinced that I'm all right. I sign a refusal of ambulatory services. They drive out.

Chapter 23

JESSICA

I report to the firehouse for my shift and settle in to wait for an emergency.

For the third time today, I call up the articles I saw on Jack's laptop and reread them. It seems a girl who used to dance at the Aquasphere Underground—her call sign: Babydoll—is suddenly missing from the scene. This lends credence to what the gossip columnists have been reporting since day one: that Babydoll was none other than Margaux Stritch. The Akerses deny she worked there. But if she was the performer who has suddenly disappeared, some portion of the underground claim they know who killed her—the guy who lost control with her during a performance led by Ms. Gail Force. In which case, Gail Force might know who killed her, too.

The trouble is that the Aquasphere culture is anonymous. I looked into it. Everything underground is executed on a cash basis. They take credit cards, but most people who go there don't want to leave a paper trail. So they pay cash for an annual membership just to step in the door. The membership is tracked with a bar code. There's no name attached to it, so members are known only by their codes. They pay a nightly cover. In cash. And then . . . anything goes. The article quotes someone as explaining that the man who lost control with Babydoll lost privileges, but if he wanted to, he could simply enroll again, pay another membership fee, and receive a new bar code.

Which means, if he did kill her, he could do it again.

I text Kirsten: Did your husband ever go to the underground club at Aquasphere?

I'm figuring that Jack's been there, even if he doesn't want to admit it to me. Depending on whether his hair sample matches the DNA found on Margaux's body, his interest in Margaux's case could range from a mild curiosity to murder in the first.

I log on to the Aquasphere Underground Online site and again pay fifty dollars for access. I try again to garner information about what may or may not have happened in that club.

Sexy451: Looking for Gail Force.

I wait.

Sexy451: Does anyone know what happened to Babydoll?

I wait.

My phone rings. It's Decker. I answer, "Hey."

"Hi."

"Hi," I say. "Have you found another Arlon Judson yet?"

"No, ma'am," Decker says. "But I'm on my way to sit down with that lawyer."

"Kirsten's husband?"

"Yes."

"What can I do to help?"

"I just wanted to call. To see how you're doing."

"I'm fine."

"I know you're pissed at me, Jessica."

"I'm over it. You actually had some valid points. Purely circumstantial, but . . . I get it. It's fine."

"I've got Ollie working on who owns the apartment. Thanks for providing the unit number. It'll help rule him out."

"I hope so."

"I wouldn't be this far with the Stritch case without your help. I want you to know it hasn't gone unnoticed. Maybe you'll let me take you out for dinner when all this is over. To say thank you."

"Are you asking me on a date? Like, a real date?"

"I guess I am."

"Ask me again after the sample comes back from the lab."

THEN

Margaux

From the cage at the Aquasphere Underground, Margaux saw him coming.

And there was anger in his eyes.

Arlon stopped short and crooked his finger at her in a silent come-here gesture.

She wasn't alone in the cage tonight. She danced with two others: a woman and a man.

They sandwiched her when they sensed she was being summoned, and while it was a measure of security for her, the heat of their bodies, dewy with sweat and slick with oil, both thrilled her and terrified her. Thrilled because she loved the thought of Arlon's jealousy. Terrified because she knew Arlon would sentence her to due penance.

It didn't matter that she hadn't taken his calls since he left her in the abandoned store. It didn't matter that she'd texted him to keep his distance, that she never wanted to see him again. He'd shown up at her apartment last night, and for an hour he leaned on her buzzer until she let him in.

That was her first mistake—assuming they could talk it out, that she could hint that things weren't working, and he'd break it off to save face before she dumped him.

But it didn't happen that way.

He burst into the apartment, fucked her, paid her, and left.

It wasn't all bad. She had a good time and had gotten richer in the process. Maybe the new arrangement would work out just fine.

And now he stood there, arms crossed over his chest, and watched her until Gail Force eventually came to pull her out of the cage at the manager's behest.

"He's making everyone uncomfortable," Gail explained. "Honey, you can't keep dancing here if he's going to keep showing up."

"It's not that big of a deal," Margaux said. "He's all thunder and no rain."

"What was cutting you, then? The lightning? The guy carved his initials into your boob, for Chrissake."

"I sort of deserved it."

"No one deserves that. He ignored your safe word on more than one occasion. I see signs in him . . . this isn't about liberty with him. For him, this isn't about mutual fun and respect, Babydoll. It's about control."

"Please," Margaux said. "I can't explain it, but it's more than expected now. It's more than routine for us. It's sort of . . . addictive."

"You crave it," Gail said.

"It's the most amazing thing I've ever felt. Hell yes, I crave it!"

"You crave it because you're terrified of what might happen to you if you deny him." Gail sighed. "I'm afraid he might kill you one day. Girl, you've got to get out of this situation."

"Well, actually . . . I met someone here the other day. And he's nice."

"Yeah? What brought this on?"

"It just happened. He was here, I was upset, so we talked. Anyway, Arlon knows I met this guy for coffee, and that's why he went ballistic on me. If I hadn't gone for coffee, none of that would have happened in the old store, and I wouldn't have decided to break up with him, so—"

"Nice. I kinda like him already."

"He's cute. Sweet."

"What are you waiting for?"

"I don't know. I think the guy's in a relationship. Might even be married for all I know."

"Well, there's always something, isn't there? But you went out with him anyway?"

"We had coffee twice, actually. Just coffee."

"What did he have to say about the artwork on your tit?"

"Just asked what *AJ* stood for. So I told him."

Just then an envelope came across the table. A client requested Gail Force and Babydoll for a public lesson in erotic asphyxiation. No penetration. Just choking.

They looked up from the envelope simultaneously, each knowing well who'd paid for their services.

"We can't," Margaux said.

"He's a member. We don't have a choice."

Gail took hold of the envelope, and Margaux followed her to the voyeur room, where patrons were already gathering to see the show.

Arlon was there, too, masked.

Margaux lay on the table.

"I want her tied," Arlon said.

Instantly, two pages came to the table and strapped her down.

Arlon stared down at her. "Is this going to be your last night in the cage?"

"I can't quit," Margaux said.

"You will."

"You're not in charge of me anymore."

"Excuse me? Who's in charge? Who paid for this room? Who labeled you?"

"I'm doing this for law school. Are you going to pay my tuition?"

"Answer only my questions. Is this your last night in the cage?"

"No."

"Who's in charge of you?" He placed his hands around Margaux's throat. "Tell me I'm in charge."

"No," Margaux managed. "There's someone else. I met someone else."

"You lied to me."

"No," she gasped. "It only just happened."

"Let up," Gail Force said.

But Arlon didn't loosen his grip.

"Enough!" Gail screamed.

Still, he didn't relent. "No one has you if I don't have you!" He spoke through gritted teeth.

Gail whipped his back. "Release! Release!"

The pages wrangled their way to the tableside.

Margaux gasped for breath.

"Show's over." A page whipped the curtains closed.

Margaux wheezed.

"You'll be banned from any special requests from now on," Gail said. *"Banned for life."* She turned to a page. "Run his code. Record the restriction in the computer."

Margaux coughed and held her neck, as if to prove it hadn't snapped.

Gail Force shoved him. "What were you thinking?"

"I was thinking she's a bad girl who doesn't do what she's told." He looked to Margaux. "Get dressed. We're going home."

Margaux began to shake her head, but Arlon leaned in close. "Do you know how easy it would've been for me to snap your neck? Do you honestly think I won't do it some night when you're begging for the rush, when you're aching for the thrill of it? Do you think I won't do it if I don't get my way?"

"I don't want you anymore."

"What makes you think it's your decision? I pay, you play."

Margaux pulled the wig from her head.

"Meet me outside," he said. "Five minutes."

She sobbed into her hands.

Arlon slammed the door.

"Honey." Gail placed a warm hand on her back. "Margaux, you can't keep doing this with this guy. He's unsafe. Unpredictable."

"You heard him." Margaux met her friend's gaze. "I've tried to keep him out, but he only gets angrier. I have to play by his rules until he gets bored."

"Or until he kills you. What about Richard?"

"He's paying, too, doing everything I ask, but it's taking too long. Every time Arlon comes for me, he pays. I can handle it. You'll see."

"And if you're wrong?"

"A girl like me . . . I don't have much of a choice."

Chapter 24

KIRSTEN

When Ian enters the house, I don't get up to greet him at the doorway for the first time since we married at age eighteen. I pour a glass of wine. I let him open the front hall closet, hear his heavy sigh when he must see the eight-by-ten glossy I've hung there, and I parlay the sip into a gulp.

Strewn about the kitchen are the bank statements with unusual transactions highlighted . . . and the occasional naughty photograph thrown in for good measure.

His steps down the center hallway are slow, calculated, as if he thinks that by taking his time, he can argue his way out of it all. His shoes crunch against the debris I've left there.

"Kirsten," he says when he sees me. "What are you doing? And with all this . . . what *is* this?"

"Frankly, I don't think *I'm* the one who has to explain anything."

He bites his lip. It's the same concentrated look he gets on his face when he's about to approach the bench and spin some statistic for a judge. "You have pictures of my cousin and his mistress hanging all over our house, and you don't want to explain?"

"That's not Doug in the pictures."

"Yes. It is."

"Do you think I'm stupid, Ian? That I can't tell my own husband even after a few sips of wine?"

"Firstborn of my mother's twin. It's not rocket science. We look alike."

He's holding one of the photographs, and he turns it sideways, as if from another angle, he can escape my recognizing who is in the image. "Well, if you've had a couple of glasses of wine, I guess that explains it. God, this could even be Patrick."

"I said *sips*, not glasses. And look at the tattoo, Ian."

"Yeah, well, Patrick got the firm's tattoo last summer, too. All of us have it, so . . ."

"You're saying I've been looking at saucy pictures of our son."

He grins. "*That* sure puts a different spin on things, doesn't it?"

"Don't you dare patronize me!" I leave my unfinished wine on the cocktail table and approach my husband, who is still pretending to be unaffected by my ambush. I shove him at the chest, but he's so firmly rooted that I don't even compromise his balance. "I've known your body since we were *fifteen years old*! How dare you suggest I'm acting irrationally and not thinking clearly?" I pound on his chest, tears flowing from my eyes. "How *dare* you! And the money! Twenty grand a month transferred out for the better part of a year! Who are you paying off?"

"Kirsten."

"Who knows what you've done with this girl? Who are you paying to keep quiet?"

"Kirsten!" He's got me by the wrists now. "Calm down. That isn't me in the pictures."

"It's your tattoo," I say.

"Doug has the same tattoo. We got them together in Cabo, remember? And listen, Patrick got it, too. In New York this past summer at Doug's bachelor party." He takes a deep breath, and I let it all sink in.

"We're the same build, my cousin and me. People have been confusing us since childhood. It's an honest mistake."

"Don't lie to me."

"You're drunk," he says, "and you're mistaken."

"I know I'm not mistaken." But I see that there's no way he'll admit to doing anything as reckless as being caught on film with his head between the thighs of a woman barely old enough to order herself a glass of champagne. I pull out of his embrace. "And I'm not drunk."

"I told you before." He unclips his watchband, slides it around his wrist, and refastens it. "I was covering for Doug, my best friend, my cousin, my business partner. I was his best man, and that's what you do when you realize someone's made a mistake that could jeopardize his entire future. He slipped up with this girl, and she refused to end the relationship. She's gone now because she couldn't live with the guilt of what she was doing, and that's the end of it. Donna doesn't have to know, and if you persist, you could ruin a lot of lives."

"That's a precise explanation, given you don't know if it was your son or your cousin sticking it to this girl. So who is it in these pictures? Is it Doug? Or Patrick? Pick a team."

"Like I told you the first time you mentioned this girl, it's Doug. What I'm saying, Kirstie, is that you're hinging your beliefs on pictures so unclear that I can't discern if the man in these images is forty-two or twenty-two."

"Then how do you explain the hush money? There's money missing from our account." I point to a statement. "Twenty grand here. Twenty grand there. All going to the same account across town."

"I told you, Kirstie. There have been some strange transactions. I don't *know* where that money is going."

"Stop lying to me. I know nothing leaves that account without one of us knowing about it. You really must think I'm an idiot. I found the pictures on the flash drive in your desk. Hence . . . all of this." I indicate the kitchen, where I've spread copies of the pictures on the island. "I saw the note demanding a meeting. Did you meet whoever sent it? You must have, because they didn't follow up on their threat to send me a copy of the pictures. Is that where the twenty K's been going?"

"I swear to you, Kirstie—"

"*Moving on.* Here's that other interesting charge. Over seven hundred dollars at a women's clinic."

"And *that's* why I changed the password." He takes a seat and folds his hands on the table. "But I figured it out. Patrick didn't want you to know. He and Becca had been careless, and—"

"Stop right there. That doesn't make sense."

"Believe me or don't. I'm telling you the truth. Patrick borrowed my card to pay for it."

"If it were true that Becca got pregnant, Patrick wouldn't need to go to you for help. I know you pay him far better than you pay most interns. And Becca has a full-time job." Discreetly, I FaceTime Quinn, keeping the sound on my phone turned all the way down so Ian can't hear the alert. "If Patrick and Becca wanted an abortion, they'd get one without going to you. Additionally, if it were true about Patrick, you wouldn't have first gone to Quinn, the more plausible of your two options, as she really would have had to ask for help if she found herself pregnant. You asked her to cover for you and lied to her about why she'd have to."

He stabs a finger at his phone; I assume he's texting one of the children with a pleading to keep the story straight. "I don't know what she told you—"

Quinn's face appears on my screen. She can hear us, but I've silenced her. I put my finger on the volume button so I can turn it up at just the right moment.

"—and I don't know why she'd lead you to believe such a thing, but I would never use our daughter like that."

And the moment is now.

"*Excuse* me?"

Ian startles when he hears Quinn's voice.

"Daddy, whatever you did, own up to it. Don't expect me to cover for your bullshit."

"Quinn, I already told your mother—"

"Here's the problem," my daughter says. "You think, somehow, that women are disposable and interchangeable. I don't know why you feel that way. Look at what Mom's done for you, and here you are, insulting her intelligence by thinking she'd believe such a crazy story. And she *is* intelligent, Dad. She didn't go to college, but not because she's not smart. She didn't go because she was busy holding together the mess the two of you made together. And A: if I were pregnant, I'd go to Mom for help. Not you. B: I know you have a problem with women, but here's a news flash. *I'm* a woman. Therefore, your asking me to cover up the fact that you obviously had a big oops with someone other than your wife, my mother, insults *my* intelligence."

"Quinn, be reasonable," Ian says. "Your mother knows what happened."

"Stop texting me what you want me to say!" Quinn rolls her eyes. "You okay, Mom?"

"Yes."

"Want me to come home tonight?"

"That's not necessary."

"I gotta go to class."

"Love you, Quinn," I say.

"Kiss, kiss. Love, love," she says.

I terminate the call. "You'll have some repairing to do there, obviously."

"I don't know why she's doing this," Ian says, still sticking to his story.

"And now, there's the matter that this girl is dead. I've got all these pictures. We've got a decent amount of money going out the door on a monthly basis. A pair of panties. Where do we see this going?"

"All of this is circumstantial, Kirstie. None of this would hold up in the court of law."

"We're not *in* the court of law, we're in our living room, and I'm asking you, for the sake of everything we've shared together, for everything we've created over the course of the past twenty-four years: come clean."

"I'm telling you the truth. I've answered all your questions." He reaches around me and picks up my wine. "You're creating drama where there isn't any." He drains the glass and sets it down. "I think Quinn and Patrick are right. I think you need to do something that makes you happy. Something satisfying to occupy you. We'll carve out time to make it happen. I'll take my own dry cleaning in from now on."

"Whatever will I do with the extra fifteen minutes per week?"

"You're a good mother." He reaches for me—I let him—and he brushes hair from my forehead, trails a finger down the side of my cheek. "Maybe . . . should we have another baby?"

"Are you kidding? Is that the only passion you think I harbor? Taking care of babies?"

"Come on, it'll be fun." He plants a hand on the counter on either side of me, fencing me in. "Something we'll do together. I'd be here to help this time. We were so young and stupid the first two times around. You were tired and overworked, and so was I. Money was always tight, and it was stressful, your folks checking out like they did, and living with my parents until I was out of law school. It could be a completely different experience this time."

"I don't want to do it again. I'm sorry you missed it, all of it, but I'm not going to have another baby for you so you can feel better about being there for *someone's* first steps."

"Again, I have to hear about how you did it all on your own?" He hangs his head, as if I've pulled all the energy out of him, and steps back. "I was out making money, Kirstie. Money to feed, house, and clothe all of you."

"That doesn't make you any better than me."

"Did I *say* that?" He washes his hands over his face. "Let's go away. Just the two of us. Maybe Greece. You've always wanted to go there. Doug owes me some time. What do you say?"

"Would it serve you well to leave the country right about now? While this girl's death is being investigated?" I pick up my wineglass and cross the room to the wine bar. I refill and sip.

"So this is what you needed me home for? I skipped a team dinner so you could toss these ridiculous accusations at me?"

"Dinner with a client? Or did you have an appointment with a certain detective from the Chicago Police Department?"

"All right." His cheeks turn a deeper shade of pink. "You need to stop checking up on me with my secretary! My schedule is *privileged.*"

"And now you're at phase two. Denial didn't work, so you're trying to get angry. Trying to scare me into shutting up, and I can't blame you because it's worked our entire lives. I've been at your feet for decades, and you don't think I can live without you because I've never been able to try!"

"Stop."

"Do you think I can't, Ian? *Watch me.*"

"I'm going to catch the end of the dinner. If it'll help you feel better, I'll ask my cousin to confirm everything I'm saying. Or, hell, go ahead and pass out before I get home. I don't care. But we're done with this discussion."

"That's how it always is with you. You decide when we're done, so you always get your way, so you always get the last word. But if you think you can bail on this discussion now . . . over my dead body." I squint at him. Take another sip. "I wouldn't put it past you to take that threat literally."

"I don't know what you're inferring, but—"

"Ian. You realize they're going to look at you for this girl's murder, don't you?"

"I don't . . ." He shoves his hands in his pockets and shakes his head, as if I've absolutely exhausted him, as if he's been trying to explain to me that two plus two equals four and I'm just not getting it. "No, Kirstie."

"Yes, Ian. They will."

"I didn't kill anyone." He slices the air horizontally with his hand. "*No one* killed her. She killed herself. And you know it. We watched the report on the news together."

"You don't know how her panties got into your suit coat. You don't know how your body and hers were photographed together. But you know she killed herself."

"You sound crazy when you talk like this."

"Crazy? Do you know there are charges on our statement to a boutique lingerie store in the city? And they sell the label on the panties I found in your jacket."

"You need to stop with the panties, already! I've already explained how they might have shown up in my coat."

"When are you going to realize, Ian, that I'm the only friend you've got? And you just burned a thousand bridges between us."

Silence itches at the air hanging between us. Finally, with his knuckles whitening as he grips the back of a chair, he says, "So what are you going to do? Leave?"

"I don't know what I'm going to do."

"We live in a no-fault state," he says. "I know the letter of the law, and I can keep this case in the courtroom for *years*. And the expense of it . . . I'm not sure Quinn would even be able to finish college. Do you really want to put our children through that? For something I didn't even do?"

"And here comes phase three: the threat to take me and the children out of this comfort zone. It's been the same thing our whole lives. We argue, you remind me of everything you do—financially—and tell me you can take it all away." The thought still nearly stops my heart after all these years, but I hold my head up. "If you'd do that to Quinn to spite me, you're not half the father I thought you were. But if you do, I'll find a way to pay her tuition without you."

"Ha!" Ian begins to laugh, but he shuts up the moment he sees the determination in my expression. "Good luck paying for college with a minimum-wage job."

"The thought of living in a two-bedroom apartment doesn't scare me anymore."

"Well." He shrugs a shoulder. "It'll be fun to watch you try."

"I don't think it's fun to watch anything from a prison cell." I gather the photos on the island and pick up my glass of wine. "Have a nice discussion with Lieutenant Decker. That's who you're *really* meeting with tonight, right? When I handed over the panties, he said he'd be calling you. And today must have been the day." I wink and walk out of the room.

THEN

Margaux

"You again." Margaux walked around the concerned third party, who was reading by porch light on the front step of Margaux's building, waiting for her when she dragged herself back from the Aquasphere. "Ever going to finish that book?"

"I can't help it. I'm distracted these days. I read a few pages, and I realize I have no idea what I've just read."

Margaux unlocked the door and held it open. "I think you should come inside."

"Only if you're comfortable with that."

"We should talk."

"I agree."

"In private."

"If that's what you want."

Margaux led her guest over the white hexagonal tile of the foyer and up two flights of stairs to her flat. Her hands trembled as she attempted to unlock her apartment door; she dropped the keys before managing to slide one into the lock in the door.

"Can I get you anything?" she asked. "A glass of water?"

"No, I can't imagine I'll be here too long."

"Would you like to sit down?"

"No, I'm okay. We can skip the cordiality and get right to it, if you wish."

"Fine." Margaux crossed her arms over her chest. "Would you like to start, or should I?"

"Go ahead."

"Do you want money? Is that why you're here?"

"If only it were that easy. If only that's what I cared about."

"What *do* you care about?"

"*You.* I'm here to take care of *you.*"

Margaux frowned and shook her head in disbelief. "But why?"

"Because we all deserve to be taken care of. Don't you think? Imagine how different this world would be if we banded together instead of divided and pitted ourselves against one another."

"He got mad. He could've killed me."

"What else is new? The way he treats you when you're intimate . . . like a whore. Like you're his prey."

Margaux stared out the window.

"I've seen what he does to you, and I've seen you react. It's not your choice anymore to do the things he wants you to do."

"He won't go away. The more I resist, the meaner he gets." Her eyes welled with tears. "But there's power to be had here, and I'm close. I feel it. I'm so close to having everything I've ever wanted!"

"Margaux, wait. What do you want? You want to rewind time, don't you? You want to be loved and not used. Right? You want to go back and stop good ole Granddad from putting his hands in your pants when you were too young to know you could stop him and still have a roof over your head. Goddammit, Margaux. Tell your story. People will listen to you. And walk away from this guy before it's too late."

"You don't understand. He's not the kind of guy I can just leave. He'll hunt me, do you understand?"

"That's what I mean."

"I went out with another guy."

"Good for you."

"This is what happened when Arlon found out." She peels the scarf from her neck to expose the bruises there. "But I can manage. He just loses control from time to time."

"Relationships aren't about control. They're give-and-take. They're two people teaming up to make it in this crazy world. He's no different than Akers. He wants to silence you, isolate you. Keep you for the same reason a cat will bat a mouse around before killing it: amusement. Whatever he's promised you . . . it's not sincere. It's to keep you under his thumb; it's to keep him in a position of power. If you want to take care of yourself, you have to stop seeing him. I know it. You know it."

Fat tears rolled down her cheeks, leaving rivulets of black mascara in their wake. "You want me to stop seeing him."

"I want *you* to want to stop seeing him. You're worth it, Margaux. Believe that you're worth it."

"You don't understand. I have nothing without him. It's like you said: at least he can pay my tuition. I just have to be patient. It'll happen. I just have to wait."

"And if he happens to squeeze too hard next time?"

"He won't."

"What if I told you I had an idea? A way to get what you want and then be free of Arlon Judson?"

She wiped a tear from her cheek. "I'm listening."

Chapter 25

Kirsten

I pretend to be asleep, but I hear Ian getting out of bed and stepping into pajama bottoms. I hear the scraping of his phone against the table-top as he pulls it from the nightstand.

He slips out of the room and into the hallway. I hear the brush of his bare feet against the hardwood floors, then on the stairs as he descends.

After a minute or so, I follow. I listen at the top of the stairs:

"I need you to tell her it was you," he's saying. "She's insisting it was me. She has these pictures . . . Listen, please. Please, Doug. She won't tell Donna. I promise you—your life won't change. I can't lose her, and she's one foot out the door. I know, I know. But I'm done with all that. I don't want her to go. I feel it for the first time since we were kids. You can't let this happen."

My fingertips tingle.

"The cop?"

He's pacing. I hear the creak of the wood floors under his feet.

"No, nothing to worry about. They're looking for Arlon."

He laughs.

"Yeah, Arlon Judson. Remember him?"

Pause.

"I know, right? Tell me about it. So I can count on you to admit this girl was your mistake?"

THEN

MARGAUX

The Akerses' house was colder than usual, and its museum-like quality, which had fascinated her during her childhood, offered more of an aura of impending doom than curiosity today.

She sat across from Richard in the large living room, where old maps hung on the wall alongside trophies of his hunting expeditions—deer heads, elk, and even the record Canadian moose from decades ago.

Margaux's gaze trailed across the room to where he sat in his favorite chair. His laptop was open on the side table, and he pretended to read while awaiting dinner. However, Margaux knew he was tracking sports scores behind Helen's back, calculating his wins and losses.

"I know you're having me followed."

He looked up. "Babydoll—"

"I know you're curious about what Arlon and I do, and I know you're paying someone to photograph me."

"I don't know what you mean."

"I met someone recently who brought all this to my attention."

"You've been played, my dear."

"Don't deny it. I know it's true. But I don't know why."

The alderman's eyes grew wide. "I don't know what you're talking about."

The third party said this would happen. Margaux had to stick to her guns. "Have you photographed me with every man I've been with? Or is it just Arlon?"

Silently, he nodded.

"Speak up, please. Every man?"

"Every man."

"You get off on watching me with other men?"

"I love you, babydoll. What am I supposed to do if you refuse to see me in that light?"

"I was a child."

"Still, it wasn't wrong. It was oh, so right."

"Do you think the voting public would think so? I know you've got your sights set on a higher office. Do you think that's going to work out, if I start talking?"

"But I'm repaying your trust. It's what you wanted."

She steeled herself and prepared to say what the concerned third party told her to say: "Well, now I want more. You want me to shut up about what happened between us? Then do something for me."

"Anything."

"I'd like to discuss a plan for the photos you're having taken of Arlon and me."

"The photos are just for me," the alderman said. "No one else sees them."

"Then I send this letter"—she pulled an envelope from her hand-bag—"to NBC Chicago. I tell all." She looked to the hallway, where she could see Helen seated on the tiny sofa there, paging through a magazine. "She'll be mortified, you know. The scandal, the press . . ."

"What do you have in mind?"

"I need you to follow these instructions." She handed over the envelope containing the letter. He'd find a few other instructions inside.

Chapter 26

Jessica

I'm drenched with rain by the time I get to the station. I wave to the desk sarge, who admits me, and I weave my way to Decker's cube, where he and Ollie are busy pointing fingers at index cards.

"Hey," I say. "What's the word?"

"The hair sample," Ollie says.

"What about it?"

"It's inconclusive."

I yank off my hoodie. "What does that mean?"

"In this case, specifically," Decker says, "the hair you pulled from the drain wasn't pulled from one head. Does your guy have roommates?"

"Not that I'm aware of."

"We're still going to test the hairs . . . just won't be able to tell which is Jack's unless you plucked one directly from his skull."

"I didn't."

"Well, thanks to your intel, we're able to track the leasing agreement of his apartment. It's owned by a corporation, so more than one person could use it." He massages his chin, which is bristly with a five o'clock shadow.

"Which corporation?"

"Barrett Enterprises. Ever hear of it?"

"No. Who owns the corporation?"

"We're working on that," Ollie says. "The company was incorporated in Nevada and shows virtually no income, has no shareholders of record, no contracts, no loans, and doesn't appear to be doing business in Illinois. So what that means is . . . the owner or owners want to stay anonymous."

"But for what purpose?" I ask. "Why go through all the trouble of incorporating a business if you aren't going to do any business?"

"We're hoping we'll know that when we learn who owns the damn thing," Decker says. "We're waiting for some paperwork to come in, but seeing as Nevada doesn't even have an information-sharing agreement in place with the IRS, you can imagine how quickly we expect to hear."

"Hmm." I lean against the wall. "How's the HOA of the apartment paid?"

"Money order."

"So, no bank information. You don't suppose . . ." I think for a second. "You said you couldn't find Jack in Chicago. He travels constantly. Maybe he's actually from Nevada."

"Devil's advocate," Decker says. "If he has the apartment for legitimate business purposes, why the secrecy with the corporation?"

"Because if I decided to fall hard for him, and he suddenly disappeared, I'd be able to track him home to wifey."

"Ah," Ollie says. "That's an angle."

"Yet more compelling," Decker says, "friends in central Illinois sent up a file on Arlon Judson. Same height and weight as your friend's husband."

"So he could be the one photographed with Margaux?"

"Well . . . if you'd guess what's on his right shoulder . . ."

"Infinity symbol?"

"No. *Nothing.* The guy's got a record. History of domestic battery when he was in his early twenties—"

"Wow."

"—but no tat, and he has an airtight alibi. Supposedly reformed now. Sober. Preacher at a church. His wife says they haven't spent a night apart since they were married seven years ago."

"Could she be lying?" I ask.

"With four kids in seven years?" Ollie asks. "I doubt it. They've been busy."

"I don't think he's our guy," Decker says.

My phone vibrates in my pocket.

It's a text from Jack.

He misses me.

Chapter 27

KIRSTEN

"Kirstie. How are you?"

I've been expecting Doug's call. "To be honest, Doug, I've been better. But now that I have you on the line, who do you recommend for family law? The best in the business."

"The best in the business would be Fordham, Lane, and Holloway. Your husband runs our divorce division."

"*Aside* from him. Who's his biggest rival? Who gives him the best run for his money?"

"I'm not going to answer that question before I say what I have to say."

"Top three."

"You don't need a family lawyer."

"Tell you what. I'll listen to what you have to say. But at the end of your spiel, you answer my question. Deal?"

He sighs. "Deal."

But the line holds only static, and he doesn't offer any information. I prompt him: "So you're calling to own up to knowing Margaux Stritch."

"I started seeing her right around the same time I met Donna. When I realized what Donna and I had, I ended it with the other girl, but I let it linger too long. Ian was telling you the truth. He's been covering for me."

"I appreciate your coming clean," I say. "Top three?"

"Ian loves you. You don't need a lawyer."

"Doug. Even if what you're telling me about this girl is true, there are other issues at play. I probably *don't* need a lawyer, but I think I ought to talk to one, don't you? Ian has already tried to scare me into staying. Don't you think I deserve to know my rights? Don't you think I should know what my options are, so I can decide for myself which risks to take and moves to make?"

"You don't need a lawyer."

"Mm-hmm." I think of the last night Ian and I spent together. Body to body. If only I could forget the rest, if only I could forget the woman in the periphery.

I need to talk to you, Ian.

Maybe Doug's tale and Ian's case might hold water in the court of law. Those obscure pictures might not be convincing to a jury. But I don't need a jury. I was there. I saw the way that young girl touched his arm, as if she'd touched it a thousand times before.

I can't make love with my husband without hearing her voice, without seeing her young body, without imagining her long limbs wrapped around him. There's no room for both of us in our marital bed, and even though she can no longer interfere, the ghost of her scent still lingers.

"Tragic," he says. "The way it all ended."

I fill the space between us with silence. It's an old lawyer's trick, but it's also served me well in motherhood. People don't like silence. They want to fill it so they don't have to endure it.

Finally, Doug clears his throat. "I'd say top three are Goldstein, Yates, and maybe . . . Trisham."

"Thank you."

"You won't tell Donna?"

"Of course not." I catch a tear on the tip of my finger. "Your secret is safe with me."

Chapter 28

JESSICA

"Thanks for the ride." I'm in the front seat of Decker's car, and it's still dumping rain by the buckets.

He pulls up to the cross street at my building, which is now directly viewable out the front windshield. The streets are practically barren—who in his right mind would be out in this weather?—but just as I'm about to get out of the car, I see a figure in front of my building.

Decker must see it, too, because he closes his fingers around my arm and nods in the direction of my residence.

I follow his gaze to the steps of my building, where a man is craning, appearing to look up at the bay window to his left—into my apartment.

Despite the newspaper tented over his head, his white button-down is stuck to his body like a second skin.

"I'll wait here," Decker says. "Don't let him up to your apartment."

I treat my companion to my best are-you-kidding-me expression. "Obviously." I yank my hood over my head. I don't have an umbrella, but it hardly matters. I'm heading straight from the street to the shower. I leap over puddles. As I draw nearer, I see a tattoo on the back of the visitor's right shoulder, visible now that, thanks to the rain, the color of his flesh bleeds through the fabric. I stop short.

It's an infinity symbol. Just like the one Decker's chasing down through the photos that showed up at Kirsten's place.

He turns around. "Hi. Are you Jessica by any chance?"

I look back at Decker's sedan. Hopefully he'll be able to read my mayday through the rain.

"I believe we have a mutual friend," he continues. "Would you mind inviting me up? This storm is—"

"Stop right there." I hold up a hand when he takes another step closer.

I hear the slamming of Decker's car door. He got the message, all right.

"Suit yourself. But I'll have to come back if we don't do this now, and if you don't mind, I have a busy schedule." He extends a hand. "Nice to meet you. I'm—"

"Interesting tattoo you have there," Decker says as he approaches. "Would you mind coming down to the station so I can ask you a few questions?"

"To be honest, I don't have time."

"You can make time, or I can arrest you on probable cause."

"Probable cause of what?"

"Arlon Judson, right?"

My visitor takes a few steps backward, and before I can so much as blink, he takes off running.

But his loafers betray him in this weather. When he slips, Decker's got my visitor in cuffs. "You have the right to remain silent . . ."

"Wait, wait," the cuffed man says.

"Anything you say can and will be used against you in a court of law." Decker leads him back to the car.

I follow a few steps behind.

"Check my wallet," he says. "Please. You'll see I'm not who you think I am. It's in my back pocket."

Decker slips the wallet out—I take it from where he sets it atop the roof of the car—as he shoves the perpetrator into the back seat.

I open the wallet. My jaw hits the floor when I see the name on the driver license. "Uh, Deck?"

He's calling the station: "I need a patrol car to transport a person of interest to CPD fourteen."

"You wanna know this guy's identity?" I ask.

"Don't need to know."

"He's not Arlon Judson."

"We know the Arlon Judson we're looking for is likely not really Arlon Judson. He took off when I mentioned the name. This guy's got a tattoo. Just happens to be the tattoo I've been looking for, too." Decker looks at me. "And here's where you go up to your apartment and let me do my job."

"It says here his name is Patrick," I say. "Patrick *Holloway*. I think he's Kirsten's son."

"Great."

"He lives on Oakley Street," I say. "And the label on the magazine in Jack's apartment said Oakley, remember?"

"Yep. He might know someone who lives at Jack's place."

"You mean he might know Arlon."

"I guess we'll find out sooner or later."

THEN

MARGAUX

Arlon was calling. Probably to apologize for losing his temper at the club. But she wasn't ready to hear it yet.

She declined the call.

A moment later, the doorbell was buzzing, too.

She peeked out the window, saw his car parked at the curb in a tow zone on Webster, and instantly, a numbness filtered through her system. He wasn't going to go away. He'd stay out there, pressing her buzzer, all night, and the longer she waited to acknowledge him, the more brutal his reception would be. Eventually, he'd come up—whether she admitted him or someone else in the building tired of hearing the buzzer—and he'd be furious. She'd learned from the night of the catsuit that he could be downright cruel when he was angry.

She had to stand up for herself, once and for all, put a stop to this fear.

She pressed the door intercom button. "Can I help you?"

"You're right." His voice came through the speaker. "It's your choice how you want to earn your money."

For a few seconds, she didn't move.

"But maybe there's another way. I have money, Margaux. Would you still perform underground if you didn't have to?"

The look she'd seen in his eyes when he'd closed his fingers around her throat would haunt her forever. He was going to kill her . . . honest-to-God *kill her*.

"Please. Let me come up. Let's talk. I have money. I can take care of you."

Against her better judgment, she admitted him.

She listened at the door as he climbed the steps. First one flight, then the second.

She jumped when he rapped on the door.

It was her last chance to come to her senses, to tell him to get lost.

But instead, she turned the dead bolt and opened the door.

He walked in.

He cupped her face in his hands and kissed her hard and long. "I love you," he said between kisses.

She was numb in his arms.

He led her, their bodies entwined and his tongue shoving against hers, to the window, where they'd first made love.

He held her against the sill, kissed her for a time as he tore at the small sash at her waist. Then he flipped her around to face the window, ripped open the zipper at her back, and slipped her dress down over her bare shoulders, his fingertips following the curves of her body along the way.

Her reflection in the window stared back at her.

She braced herself for whatever was about to come—a knife, a rope, another few hundred bills tossed at her feet, another ignored *black crow*.

He was on his knees behind her now.

She held her breath.

"Maggie?"

She froze.

"God, Maggie. Marry me."

"What?" She turned to find him genuflecting in front of her, a small box open in his hands, a ruby ring nestled on a bed of black velvet.

"Marry me."

"Arlon."

"Law school. We've talked about it, and I've decided: I'll foot the bill. All you have to do is save your performances for me. Stop seeing that other guy. And say yes."

"I can't—"

"We *can*. Do you love me?"

"I thought I did."

"That's all I need to know." He slid the ring onto her finger, got to his feet, and held her close.

She stared at the ring on her finger. He'd offered more than the rest of his life. He'd promised law school. Wheels started to turn in her head. There was a way to beat him at his own game.

She could take what he offered—tuition—and chew him up and spit him out on graduation day.

This ring was a momentum shift.

A passing of the upper hand.

This changed *everything*.

Now *she* was in charge.

Chapter 29

Kirsten

My phone is practically dancing on the countertop, vibrating with text alert after text alert.

It's Jessica:

Decker has your son.

He's been arrested.

In connection with Margaux.

"Oh my God," I say.

My fingers are trembling, but I manage to dial my husband's firm. Doug is head of the criminal division. He'll come. He'll help.

"Doug, it's Kirstie. Patrick has been arrested."

———

I'm seated at a table in a holding cell across from my son. Doug is with us and on his feet. Doug's being here means the recording devices have been turned off, as everything uttered between them is considered privileged information, but I keep looking at them to be sure. No blinking red lights. No widening of the lens as it focuses.

"Of course I submitted the DNA sample," Patrick says.

My heart sinks. I had a conversation with the detective yesterday. I gave up the red thong. I handed over the flash drive. I blabbed about the letter I found with it. The letter addressed to *Mr. Holloway*, which could just as soon reference my son as my husband. "You didn't."

For all the vacillating as to whether I could throw Ian to the wolves in the face of justice for this poor, dead girl, I would've agonized ten-thousand-fold over what to do had I known Patrick would be the one facing charges.

"They think I killed this girl," he says. "They'll run the sample, see it doesn't match, and that'll be the end of it."

"Patrick." Doug paces with arms crossed and a thumb under his chin. "You *never* do that without a warrant. You should know better."

"I *do* know that, Doug. But I don't have anything to hide. I know I didn't kill this girl, and I know I never slept with her, so what's the worst that could happen?"

"Our best shot is to get the sample suppressed."

"We won't need the shot," Patrick insists. "Because I. Didn't. Do. It."

I reach for my son's hand across the table. "You don't know what's about to happen. The police have a pair of underwear—"

"What?" Doug interjects. "How—"

I hold up a hand. "A pair of underwear your father has been insisting belongs to whichever girl you sneaked away with at Doug and Donna's wedding reception. That underwear will likely test positive for Margaux's DNA."

Patrick shrugs. "Well, I was with Becca at the wedding, and I didn't sneak off with anyone, so . . ."

"The police also have a flash drive full of pictures of a man with Margaux."

Doug: "Kirstie! You didn't."

"I didn't have a choice, Doug. I went to a friend with the pictures after I found them in Ian's desk drawer. She shared them with the police. I could have been obstructing justice if I hadn't met with the detective yesterday."

"He's your husband," Doug says. "They can't make you testify against your husband."

"Is there a law against testifying against your husband's cousin? Because Ian's insisting it's *you* in the pictures. And you confirmed as much when you called me. All three of you have the same tattoo, the tattoo that was featured prominently in the pictures."

Dumbfounded, Doug stares at me. "Kirstie."

"What was I supposed to do? All three of you were telling me I was reading too much into things, that we had nothing to do with this girl, nothing to hide. *What was I supposed to do?*"

"Nothing," Patrick says. "We *don't* have anything to hide."

I turn to Patrick. "Here's the trouble: you didn't kill this girl. You didn't sleep with her. But if your father did, your DNA just might be a close enough match to his to take you to trial."

"Do you think my father is capable of murder?"

"Maybe. Maybe not. But he probably slept with her."

"This again." Patrick rolls his eyes. "Mom, seriously. Dad wouldn't—"

"Is that right? I guess we'll see when your DNA comes back as a close match to traces of semen on the underwear. That'll be enough to get the ball rolling. They always suspect the significant other. *Always.*"

"Well, I'm not the significant other, so . . . they'll have to find someone else. Becca and I have been together for . . . jeez, six years now. No jury's going to believe a guy like me could do this."

"And you don't think your father could've, either. Yet your sister's heard you've been out with other women. There's a chance other people can testify the same. These girls you're out with . . . how do you think they'll feel when they see your face on the evening news? When they hear your defense is that you're in a long-term relationship with Becca, so you just couldn't possibly have done this? I'll tell you what they're going to do: they'll *crucify* you."

Patrick shrugs. "Circumstantial."

"So confident an attitude for a man about to take the heat for his lying, cheating father." I squeeze his hand. "I don't know if your DNA is going to differ enough from the samples. And women, whether or not you believe it, can be pretty damn powerful. Especially when they've been wronged."

"It'll be okay, Mom. Because Dad's DNA won't match, either. I promise."

"Do you even think he's going to submit a sample to clear you?" I ask.

"He won't have to. Because my sample won't match at all."

I feel sick. There's no talking to him. He's blinded by the light of his father's ego. And he just might have done something that can't be undone.

"Why'd you run?" Doug asks. "When the cop approached you, why'd you run if you're confident your dad didn't have anything to do with this dead girl?"

Patrick glances at me, then sighs.

"Why did you want to talk to Jessica Blythe?" Doug asks.

"I can't say in front of Mom."

"Now you want me to *leave* so you can share secrets?" Tears I've been keeping at bay threaten and crest in my eyes. "Patrick, look around you. *Look.* Is your father here? Is he here, owning up to everything he's done to get you out of here and home where you belong? No. But *I'm* here. I'm the one who's always been here, through thick and thin. Whatever you have to say, I can take it. Let me hear it."

My son shakes his head and looks back to Doug. "Not in front of Mom."

Chapter 30

JESSICA

Kirsten bursts out of the interrogation room where her son and her husband's cousin, the lawyer, still sit.

She looks like she's just seen a ghost, or at least as if she just narrowly escaped a dangerous situation and got out with her life.

Across the room, we meet in a deadlock stare.

My first instinct is to run to her, but then, there's something in her expression—hurt, dismay, with a touch of anger—that cements me where I stand.

An instant later, she softens and begins toward me.

"You want to get a drink?" I ask.

"Yeah. I really do."

A few minutes later, in the hole-in-the-wall nearest the station, I tell Kirsten what's frustrating me: "Decker can't find a Jack Wyatt in the system. He says it's an alias. The apartment Jack lives at is owned by some LLC—Barrett Enterprises."

"Barrett?"

"Yeah, you know it?"

She starts to deny it with a shake of her head.

But I'm on a roll: "It was incorporated in Nevada, which is a state that doesn't opt in to information sharing, and I can't get to who owns the damn company. So it's sort of like I've been dating an apparition. Decker found one Jack Wyatt in the right demographic but not in Chicago—from northwestern Indiana, actually. And it wasn't my Jack. And the things my Jack had up on his laptop: all about Margaux. *Including* the Instagram page of the one guy Margaux's family said we should be talking to—Arlon Judson."

"Arlon Judson?"

"Yeah. That's supposedly who Margaux was seeing when she died. Only when Decker found a guy with that name, it didn't add up. Plus, I think the guy was at Disney World with his family when she died. The pictures on his Instagram support the alibi."

"Maybe there's more than one Arlon."

"It's not a common name."

"No, I guess it's not."

"But Decker thinks it's a name your son might be using."

"Oh God." She drops her head into her hands for a moment, and I think I hear a muffled whimper before she takes a breath, looks up, and is composed again.

I feel like she knows something but isn't telling me. "So I guess I have to find Jack and get him talking."

"I think Ian knows more than he's telling, too," she says. "The other night, I overheard him talking to his cousin. The name Arlon Judson came up. They didn't say much about it, just that the cops were looking for him."

"But they know him?"

"I can't place the name, but I feel like I've heard it before. Listen, I don't know about you, but I'm tired of relying on men to get the job done. Jack Wyatt's not who he says he is; Arlon Judson isn't Arlon Judson. Christ, even my own son won't trust me with information. Why was he at your place?"

"I have no idea. I swear to God, Kirsten. I'd never seen him before that moment."

"And my husband! We all know who's in those pictures. We all know it isn't Patrick. So, where's Ian? Where is he when his son is about to take the fall? No, I'm done waiting for men to figure things out. With my son's future hanging in the balance, I'd rather rely on a woman, wouldn't you?"

She makes a good point.

"In order to get Patrick out of this mess," she continues, "we have to find the one person who may have seen Margaux and Arlon—the Arlon she was involved with—together. We have to find Gail Force. She has to tell us what really happened."

"I'm already on it. But to be honest, the culture underground is tight-knit. If Gail doesn't want to be found, she won't be found. And she's sure as hell not going to comment on a murder investigation."

"You know . . ." Kirsten reaches for a cocktail napkin and begins to jot notes on it. "My husband's cousin recently married someone who used to bartend upstairs at the Aquasphere. Her name's Donna, and I'm pretty sure she knew Margaux. I've tried to get her talking, but she won't budge. Maybe she'll talk to you. Or Decker, if she feels she doesn't have a choice." She shoves the napkin toward me.

On it is the bartender's full name and a phone number.

I raise my glass. "I'm on it."

She touches hers to mine. "Slainte."

Chapter 31

KIRSTEN

It's late by the time Ian walks in the door. I'm sitting in the dark, staring into a fire in the fireplace.

"Patrick's been arrested," I tell him, as if I hadn't sent the news via text a hundred times since Jessie Blythe and I shared a pitcher of sangria at the Corner Bar.

"I bailed him out," Ian says. "He's home now."

"Great, but for how long?"

"For always. He has no ties to that girl and, soon, the police will realize it."

"You can expedite the process," I tell him. "Submit a sample to clear him."

Ian leans against the mantel, his sport coat flung over his shoulder. He's backlit, so I can't read his expression, but he says, "They've got nothing on him. You need to relax."

"He submitted a DNA sample."

"He wouldn't." Ian very nearly laughs at the prospect, as if I'm bluffing and he sees through me. "He knows better."

"Regardless, he was certain it would turn up negative, so he gave them what they wanted."

"He wouldn't." There's a strain in his voice this time. He clears his throat.

"He was certain," I say. "But talking with you now, I can see you're not so sure."

"Kirstie."

"Do you have something to tell me?"

"I can't believe he'd do that—"

"So you do have something to tell me."

"—but not because there's any chance of the DNA matching."

"Promise me. If this goes any deeper, you'll come clean. For the sake of our son's future."

"Patrick got himself into this mess," Ian says. "He'll have to dig his way out."

"Did he get himself into it? Why was he at Jessica Blythe's house?"

"Whose house?"

"Jessica Blythe. She's a Chicago firefighter."

"And how do *you* know a firefighter?" Ian chuckles and takes a step closer, and another, and another, until he's leaning over me. He smells of musky cologne and some antiseptic liquor. Scotch, maybe. Or whiskey. "You need to let this go. Everything will be fine if you let it go." He presses a hard, wet kiss to my lips.

"Do the right thing," I say. "So many lives are already affected."

"Everything will be fine," he says. "Take a pill tonight. Get some sleep."

"I already did," I hedge.

"Good." He pats my head. "I'm heading back to the office. With all the extra drama, getting your call about Patrick, I didn't get much work done today."

"Staying downtown?"

"Probably. Unless . . . will you be okay?"

"I'll be fine."

It's probably better that he goes. I can't stand to even look at him right now.

Chapter 32

Jessica

I peruse Donna Fordham's Facebook page. She's one of those chronic posters with virtually zero privacy settings turned on. Her latest update: Hanging till last call. She's posing with a few girlfriends at a bar I frequent.

I text Decker: Stopping in at the River Shannon before my shift. Care to join?

I don't wait for his reply—it could take hours for him to even open my text—before running a quick gloss over my lips and heading out.

In the cab along the way, I keep tabs on Donna's page, lest she and her friends opt to leave before last call, but as luck would have it, they're still there by the time I arrive.

I pay my cover, enter past a lazy Labrador curled at someone's feet, and slide inconspicuously into a booth.

Donna and her friends are playing the enormous Jenga near the rear of the place, and I observe for a while, determining the best way to infiltrate.

I turn around only once, to order a club soda, straight, because I have to be at the station soon, but when I turn back, I have to stifle my gasp.

Jack Wyatt is suddenly here, pulling Donna by the elbow, away from her friends and *closer to me*. I tuck myself deeper into the booth and listen.

"Are we good?" he asks.

"We're good," she says.

"Wouldn't want your husband to know our little secret, would we?"

"I don't think that would be good for either of us."

"Okay, then. As long as we understand each other."

"It's crystal clear."

He turns. He's coming right for me.

I put my head down. Hopefully he'll pass me by, but if he doesn't, maybe it will look like I'm merely busy on my phone.

"Wait." The click of Donna's heels tells me she's rushing to catch up with him. They stop a few inches past my booth. I have a clear shot.

He places a hand on the small of her back and pulls her in close.

I aim my phone at them and snap a picture.

"Did you . . . you didn't have anything to do with *you know*, did you?"

"Don't be ridiculous," he says. "As far as we're both concerned, we never met her."

We. I wonder if they met her at the same time. In which case, I wonder . . .

Gail Force worked at Aquasphere Underground, as did, allegedly, Margaux. Donna tended bar upstairs. If Jack frequented the place . . . and they're keeping something from Donna's husband . . . I wonder if they know Gail Force or where to find her.

"Never met her," Donna repeats.

"Keep it that way."

I sink lower in the booth as he passes and exits the premises.

Donna lowers herself to the nearest chair, rests her head in her hands, and lets out a long sigh.

I inch my way out of the booth. "Excuse me."

She looks up.

"How do you know Jack?"

"Who?"

"Jack Wyatt."

She looks over her shoulder at the place he not long ago occupied.

"It's just that he told me he was out of town," I say, "and well . . . here he is, talking to you, so . . ."

"Ah. You're the new victim."

Victim?

"We're involved, yes," I say.

"Honey." Donna stands and makes a move to return to her friends. "Run."

"Do you know Gail Force?"

She stops and slowly turns toward me. "Why?"

"You do." But I know she's not going to admit it. I need a reason to keep her here, talking. "It would be a shame if your husband, *Doug Fordham*, learned you're secretly meeting with other men. I'd hate to interfere, but . . ." I call up the picture I took of the two of them and afford her a quick view. "This doesn't exactly look innocent, now does it?"

Her eyes are wide. "Look, I don't want any trouble, but—"

"Neither do I. I'm interested in securing justice for Margaux Claire Stritch, and as a woman, in a city where crimes against us abound, I'd think you'd want the same."

"I do, but I can't get involved. I'm sorry."

I check the time. "Actually, I have to get going. I have to work. But I know how to find you. Where you live, where your husband works"—at least I hope Kirsten knows these things—"so in the interest of keeping all this under wraps, lunch tomorrow? We could meet here, at the River Shannon."

"I don't think so. But good luck." She turns away.

"I'm the one who cut her down, you know. That changes someone."

She stops and looks at me over her shoulder.

"I'm just trying to understand," I say. "And I think you can help with that."

"No cops, okay?"

"No cops." Three minutes later, I'm on my way to the firehouse.

I text Kirsten: River Shannon tomorrow at noon.

Chapter 33

Kirsten

I'm far too old to be in this bar, but I walk into a warm, welcoming atmosphere. A quick scan of the place tells me Jessica hasn't yet arrived. That figures. I'm nearly ten minutes early. I didn't want to risk being late, and I didn't know if I'd readily find parking downtown, so here I am.

There's an open seat at the bar, sandwiched between a young couple engaged in an extremely close conversation and a group of frat-boy types busy milling around the stools they used to occupy and high-fiving one another over any number of sporting events displayed on the many widescreen televisions in this place. I squeeze my way into the tiny space and consider, too late, that I may have stolen a seat from one of the frat boys, who turns to me the moment I sit, as if he somehow senses my presence.

"Hey."

"Hi." I afford him a glance, but it's quickly diverted by the ball of fur in his arms. It's a puppy. A beautiful, blue-eyed Siberian husky no larger than a watermelon. "Oh my God." My hand goes to my heart. He's adorable.

"You want to hold him?"

"Oh . . . no. That's all right. Beautiful dog."

"He's one of twelve."

"Yeah?"

"We rescued Mama from a puppy mill." Frat boy spills the puppy into my arms. "They all need homes. Think about it."

I stare eye to eye at the dog. "I've never really—"

"He likes you."

For a moment, I'm practically mesmerized by the cool blue eyes staring back at me. Could I . . . ? *Should* I?

"Maybe someday." I hand the dog back to the man-boy peddling him. "Ian would absolutely kill me if I came home with—"

I shut up.

What could my husband say about it if I did decide to adopt a dog? I'd train the dog, clean up after the dog, take it to the vet . . .

It's true we've never had a pet, and it's also true that's because Ian never wanted to deal with the hair, the responsibility, the plain thought of it traipsing through our home.

"If you change your mind . . . they're at Have a Heart Rescue. It's our philanthropy."

"Have a Heart. Got it."

He treats me to a stare so long that the hair on the back of my neck pricks to attention. "How about a drink then?"

"I'm fine."

"I know. I'm wondering if you want a drink." He grins.

Is he *hitting* on me?

"Kirsten. Hi."

I turn to see Jessica is suddenly next to me, removing her coat. She leans in. "Let the guy buy you a drink."

"How's the chardonnay here?" I whisper.

"I don't even know if they know that word in this bar," she whispers back. Then to the boy with the dog, whom she's expertly managed to displace a foot or so as she squeezes between us: "She'll have a Goose Island 312."

"And you?"

"I'll have the same. Thanks."

"I don't drink beer," I tell her.

"You'll like this one."

"So what's going on?" I ask.

"Well . . . for starters, Jack knows Donna Fordham."

"Your Jack?" My Goose Island arrives. I take a sip. Not bad.

"Furthermore, I think she knows something about him and Margaux. I haven't gone to Decker yet with the possibility. Haven't been able to nail him down the past day or so."

I chew on this for a few seconds. "You know, come to think of it, she ran the second I mentioned Margaux. She couldn't get away from me fast enough."

"She doesn't want anything to do with the case, that's for sure. Jack's got something on her, and I'm pretty sure that's why she's keeping quiet." Jessica is scrolling on her phone. "She looked almost scared when she talked to him last night. Look."

Just as Jessica is about to allow me a look at the phone screen, she looks past my shoulder at someone behind me. "Donna. Wait."

My husband's cousin's bride is hightailing it out the door as soon as she walks in.

Chapter 34

JESSICA

"Wait." I meet up with Donna on the sunny sidewalk outside the River. "Why'd you run?"

"I can't do this," Donna says. "She's *family*. If you tell her I'm involved with *Jack*—"

"She doesn't have to know any of that."

"But she will. She'll figure it out. My marriage will be over."

"Her son was arrested, and she wants your help finding Gail Force so she can clear her son's name. That's all."

"Why Gail?"

"Because of the quote in the paper. About why Margaux was dancing at the Aquasphere. We think Gail can identify the man who was in a relationship with Margaux."

She brings her hand to her mouth and starts to gnaw on a thumbnail.

"Do you know where to find Gail?" I ask.

"Well, I mean . . . sort of, I guess. *Maybe.*"

"Come back inside. Let's talk. Come on. Cute frat boys are buying our beers."

She takes a deep breath, and after a moment, she goes back inside with me.

"Hi," Kirsten says.

"Hi," Donna says.

"I trust you got to where you were going on time the other day," Kirsten says.

"Pardon?"

"You sprinted up the street last time I saw you."

"Yeah. Sorry about that. It's just . . ." She sighs. "With what happened to Margaux . . . I was in shock, I think."

For a minute or so, the three of us sit rather uncomfortably. I break the ice:

"I'm just going to come out and ask: Arlon Judson. Do you know who he is?"

"Yeah," Donna says into her mug of beer, which just arrived, courtesy of Delta Chi.

"Kirstie says your husbands mentioned his name the other night. And the Akerses say she was dating him," I say. "Is that true? Did you see them together at the bar?"

Donna nods. "I warned her off him the first day they met."

"Why?" Kirsten asks.

"I don't know . . . You know when a guy's just too aggressive? I'd seen it happen. He was pushy and had trouble taking no for an answer. Margaux seemed quiet. *Sad*, really. I figured the last thing she needed was a jerk pressuring her to go downstairs."

"Arlon Judson's married," I say. "The Arlon Judson we found, anyway, but we've ruled him out. It's not a common name, so we're puzzled—"

"No one uses his real name underground. Someone probably made it up, or fantasized about having control of someone else's identity. Someone they aspire to be, maybe. One guy there goes as Thomas Jefferson—and dresses like him, too. People choose aliases for weird reasons."

I text Decker: See if the Jack Wyatt you located and the Arlon Judson you've already ruled out have any overlap in their histories. Could be someone at the Underground is using both names. I remember what my research about the club taught me: someone who'd been kicked out could just obtain a new bar code.

"Do you know if Arlon Judson has a tattoo on his right shoulder blade?" I ask. "An infinity symbol?"

Donna nods. "Without a doubt."

"So you've been involved with him?" Kirsten asks.

"That's irrelevant," Donna says.

"How could you have seen his tattoo if you only served him drinks?" Kirsten persists.

"Because." Donna sighs. "Here's some inside information for you, but you didn't hear it from me, got it? I'm breaking code by talking about it. *Every* member of the Underground has the opportunity to be tattooed with the seal, and Judson was definitely the type to ink up. I mean, the guy would've been branded if the club offered it."

"Wait. Seal?" I ask.

"The sideways figure eight." Donna digs in her purse for a pen and, in absence of anything else to draw on, demonstrates on a coaster. She scribbles the word *Aquasphere*. "It's the upstroke of the E at the end of Aquasphere." She draws a curve up and extends it back to the left. "And the downstroke of the P." She draws down and to the left and loops up meet the first line. "One of the rooms downstairs . . . it's a body-art studio."

"So you've been downstairs," I say. "To the Underground."

"Would you be able to work there and *not* venture downstairs upon occasion? Just out of curiosity?"

"Wait a minute." Kirsten flips through photos on her phone. "Are you saying *this* is an Aquasphere Underground tattoo? And not the logo of Fordham, Holloway, and Lane?" She slides her phone across the table to Donna, who studies the photo.

"That's what I'm saying."

"So our suspect pool just increased by hundreds," I say.

"Okay." Kirsten closes her eyes for a long breath. "I need you to look at the man in the pictures, Donna. Look closely."

Donna picks up the phone. Zooms in. Flips from image to image.

"Can you rule out that this is your husband?" Kirsten asks. "Ian says it's Doug."

"Hmm." Donna's brow knits. "I don't think so."

"How sure are you?" I ask.

"About two hundred percent. Doug has a mole near the tip of the tattoo. Right about there." Donna points to the screen. "This guy doesn't have one."

"Okay." Kirsten turns to me. "That means it's Ian. He says it also could be Patrick, and since the cops picked him up . . . I thought, you know . . . maybe."

"It could be *anyone*." Donna hands the phone back to Kirsten. "Why are you torturing yourself? You can hardly see the guy's face."

"That's what Ian said," Kirsten says. "But the pictures were sent to *Ian*, so odds are, it's him."

"Or someone wants him to think it's him," I say.

This means that the man in the picture could be anyone else at the club. Perhaps good news for Kirsten, but it doesn't bode well for Deck's investigation. "Could it be anyone else in particular at the club?" I ask. And, because I'm fishing for information about my would-be boyfriend, I add, "Could it be, say, Jack Wyatt?"

Donna trades glances between Kirsten and me. "It could be. Maybe. Good chance that it is."

"Gail Force would know for sure, wouldn't you think?" I ask. "It'd be helpful to speak with her."

"I'm not sure she exists anymore," Donna says. "She hasn't been to the club in a long time."

"Do you know how we might find her?"

"Actually . . ." After a minute, Donna looks up. "You already did."

It takes a moment for the message to register, but when it does, it hits like a tidal wave. "*You're* Gail Force?"

Donna looks at Kirsten, then quickly looks away. "I used to be. Listen, no one starts out in life wanting to make money that way. I started bartending there. That's it. But there's not enough money in slinging drafts, so I started working both circuits. Double the shifts, quadruple the money. I wanted to be a party planner, I'll have you know. The plan was always to go back to school once I had enough saved."

Kirsten reaches across the table and squeezes Donna's hand. "No one's judging you. I understand. But I need you to talk to the police. This is my son's future we're playing with."

"You don't get it: I'm finally in a position to *do something* with my life. Doug and I are comfortable. There's a chance he'll leave me if he learns what I really did at the Aquasphere. He knows I tended bar, but he doesn't know about the other stuff."

"That's a double standard if I ever heard one," Kirsten says. "Didn't they kick off Doug's bachelor party at that club? And if he has the tattoo, that means he was probably part of the culture at one point, too."

"Not necessarily," Donna says. "I don't know why *your* husband got that tattoo, but *mine* got it as a tribute to the firm he established."

"Don't be naive."

"I'm sorry, Kirsten, but Doug's Doug, and Ian's Ian."

An uncomfortable lull of silence hits us.

"I have an idea," I say. "What if I could guarantee your anonymity?"

"My husband's a defense attorney," Donna says. "Do you think I haven't wondered about that possibility? Anonymous information is inadmissible."

"We couldn't use your testimony in court, in that case, but Decker is a brilliant detective. He needs something—*someone*—to give this investigation the teeth it needs. It'll bite on its own."

Chapter 35

KIRSTEN

Ian's a good lawyer. He can argue his way out of anything.

I wonder how he'll argue his way out of my asking him to leave.

Considering the fact that my days are filled with inquiries about my husband and sex clubs and dominatrices, this should be easy. However, when you've spent your life with someone, when you've built your life around his, naturally, it's terrifying to open the door to change.

But I want things to change. *Need* them to, if I expect to hold my head high in front of my children, if I expect Quinn and Patrick to strive for a marriage or partnership stronger than the example their father and I have set.

I wrap a page of *Chicago Tribune* around another framed photograph of Ian and our son and slide it into one of many boxes I'm packing.

A sense of guilt filters through me, but I shoo it away like an annoying housefly. It's not as if Ian doesn't have the firm apartment at his disposal. But I'm removing him from our home. I may as well take an eraser to the past quarter century of my life, as if I'm saying *scratch that, it was a mistake, let's start again.*

Don't get me wrong. He deserves the ousting. That's not what I'm mourning, here.

He did what he did, and there are consequences. But that doesn't mean this is fair.

I played by the rules. I was a good wife. I cooked, I cleaned, I took care of babies at all hours of the night. I supported my husband's career. I perched myself on his arm whenever he needed an ornament. For the love of all that's holy, I'm packing his bags. I'm rolling his socks, polishing all his shoes, and I've even arranged for delivery of his wardrobe downtown. No one can accuse me of not doing what I'm supposed to do. I've held up my end of the bargain.

Ian may deserve to be kicked out, but I don't deserve to be left alone after all the hard hours I put in, after I endured the sacrifice that comes with being an at-home mother, a homemaker.

And he's right. He can string a divorce case over the course of years. He can wear me down, starve me out. He can squirrel away assets while filing continuance after continuance. I could find myself temping at one of those large corporations—nameless, replaceable, and earning a dime over minimum wage when this is all over.

Do I want to put myself in that position? No one wants to take a chance on a woman pushing forty without a single job on her résumé. I have no health insurance without Ian's corporate policy, no retirement fund, no skill set. Nothing.

My life's work amounts to two people about to forge their way into the real world—one of them under suspicion of murder—and while I'm proud of what I've done to help make them who they are, that pride will scarcely keep me fed until my dying days.

And, God, I can't relax.

Patrick's future is in question until I can convince Ian to come clean and admit it was he who had the affair with Margaux.

———

I don't hear Ian come in so much as I sense that he's suddenly in the room with me.

I've just gotten out of the shower. I'm bent at the waist, drying my hair upside down, and wearing the black satin robe Ian and the kids bought me for Mother's Day some years ago.

He's standing behind me.

The heat of his hands permeates through the satin.

I straighten and turn off my hair dryer and find his gaze locked on mine in the reflection of the mirror.

He tugs on the sash of the robe, and soon those hands are traveling over my bare belly, navigating the curves and swells with the expertise that comes from years of exploring the same terrain.

His mouth is at my neck.

"Ian. Wait."

"Shh." He guides me out of the en suite bathroom, to our bed, onto which he coaxes me under the persuasion of kisses and his touch.

I look him in the eye and read his unspoken message, a silent dare to wipe the slate clean and start again. But first . . . repent.

His expression tells me he is focused on claiming what he thinks he's due, what he assumes is his for the taking and always will be.

My hands go to his fly, first only mechanically—it's what he expects because it's what I've done for years, and I'm going through the motions—but once I release the buckle of his belt, a sense of calm filters through me for the first time today. He wants me? I want a little something from him, too. A reckless hunger drives me to tear at the button, the zipper.

And I can't get him inside me fast enough.

He pins my wrists over my head with one hand and kisses me, open lipped, open eyed, as if he needs to keep a close watch on me. He's assessing me, waiting for some cue, waiting to know: Did I buy Doug's confession? Is all copacetic and business as usual?

He presses a palm up the side of my body, over a fleshy hip and the side of a breast. He backs off, as if studying me—a last look, perhaps—and draws his fingertips over my neck.

"Do you want to do it?" I ask. "Do to me what you did to her?"

His lips smash into mine, and it's all over but the orgasm.

For a few minutes, we wrestle in the moment, and the anger, the love, the mistrust . . . it all flows together for one heated tryst in a bed that's served us well for over two decades.

When he's finished, we lie there for a minute.

I hear her voice in my head: *I need to talk to you, Ian.*

I stare at the window but see only the silhouette of her dress in the flowing fabric of the draperies.

I need to talk to you, Ian. Ian. Ian.

I climb out of bed.

"Where you going?" he asks.

I begin to dress. "Out."

"Out where?" There's a trace of laughter in his words. "Kirstie, come on. Come back to bed."

"I'll be back," I tell him. "There's just something I have to do first."

Chapter 36

JESSICA

After a lot of convincing, Donna Fordham agrees to come to the station with me for a conversation with Decker. I was supposed to leave the moment I delivered the mysterious and elusive Gail Force, but Ollie opened a door for me, and I slipped behind the two-way mirror to witness the interrogation.

"I need to be disguised," Donna insists. "My voice, my face. Or I'm not talking."

"You don't work there anymore," Decker says.

"No," Donna says.

"So what's the problem with talking? With telling me what really happened over there?"

"First of all, there's my husband's career," Donna says, "which might take a hit if my alter ego goes public. Second, the people who can afford to go to a place like the Underground? They're *powerful people*, okay? Politicians. People with mafia ties. People who value their privacy and would stop at nothing if that privacy were compromised. These people can hire a hit and wouldn't think twice before doing it. So I'll talk, but everything's off the record."

"Want to tell me your name?"

Donna looks at Decker. "No."

"Okay, I'll revise. Are you the dominatrix known as Gail Force?"

"Yes."

"Are you the Gail Force referenced in this article dated the day after Margaux's passing?"

"I don't know why I agreed to come." She shakes her head. "I can't do this."

"If you're so afraid, why did you comment publicly? To a *reporter*?"

"I thought it owed it to Margaux to set the record straight about who and what she was. And I didn't talk to a reporter. I posted the comment as Gail Force in the Aquasphere Underground chat room, and someone must have lifted it from there. I wouldn't talk to a reporter. I'm not an idiot."

"But you were acquainted with Margaux Claire Stritch?"

"Yes."

"Can you describe your relationship?"

"For a time, in certain circles . . ." Tears rim her eyes. "She was my best friend at the club."

Decker takes the photographs with which Kirsten supplied us and lays them on the table. "Do you recognize this man?"

"Do I recognize the back of his head, you mean? I recognize the tattoo. And that's Margaux, so . . ."

"Is this the Arlon Judson the Akerses referred to?"

"I think it must be. She wasn't sleeping around, so it must be Arlon."

"Being Margaux's best friend, had you ever observed the two of them together?"

"First, you have to understand: What happens in the Underground? It stays there. Margaux and I . . . we wouldn't have gone out to lunch together, or shopping together. We didn't double-date, and I don't know where she lived, what her favorite food was . . . We weren't the Hallmark version of BFFs. We were there for each other at work. I had her back, you know? *Someone* had to have it. That said, I more than observed. I coached them in the Party of Three room."

"You were present during intimate interactions."

"Once at the club, yes."

"Can you describe their relationship in that instance?"

"He was controlling, which was the whole point. But he took things too far. It was my last private party, when he . . ." She stares off into a corner.

"What happened?" Decker presses.

"He almost killed her. I tried to make him stop, but he wouldn't let up. No matter what I said, no matter how hard I hit him . . . I saw the look on his face. He wanted to kill her. I quit the next day."

"This guy here?" Decker stabs a finger against a photograph.

"I think so. If I could see his face, I'd know for sure, but . . . I think so."

"This is Arlon Judson?"

"That was the name he went by at the club, yes. But no one uses their real name at the club."

"It's an alias."

"Yes."

"Do you know any other names he goes by?"

She swallows hard. "If you can identify this man, you've got someone capable of killing her."

Next, Decker slaps down a picture of Kirsten's son, Patrick. "I know you recently married into this kid's family, so forgive the discomfort I'm sure this causes: Have you ever seen Patrick Holloway at the Aquasphere?"

"Yes. Yes, I have."

"Ever see him with Margaux?"

"No."

Decker glances at the mirror and somehow manages to dart a gaze right into my eyes. "How about Jack Wyatt?"

Donna closes her eyes for a moment. "Look. *Lots* of men went to the club. *Lots* of men got the tattoo. But if you're looking for someone based on the name he used underground, you may as well be looking for a ghost. I restricted Arlon Judson's membership that night, but if he had the means, he could come back with full privileges, and maybe he has. Maybe he's now Jack Wyatt. But you'll have to ask someone else."

"Because there are too many powerful people," Decker says, "too many people who can ruin you—can ruin your marriage—if you talk."

For a breath, with her head hanging, she doesn't say anything. But when she looks up, she squares her shoulders and says, "You want to know what happened at Margaux's place the night she died. Well, so do I. I wish I knew."

THEN

MARGAUX

Margaux spied the concerned third party reading on a bench near the chessboard tables in a park in Logan Square. She took a close seat and stared straight ahead as she began a conversation. "I thought I'd find you here."

"How did you know I'd be here?"

"I saw you here last week. Where've you been?"

Margaux's acquaintance flipped a page in the book. "I have other things to do than meddle in your business, you know."

Margaux tightened the sash of a silver raincoat around her waist and adjusted the gauzy red scarf wrapped around her neck.

"Is that scarf hiding a bruise on your neck?"

"Listen, I didn't come for a lecture. I got what you wanted." Margaux tapped the arrow on the screen, and a video began to roll.

The camera was panned upward, as if her phone was set on a table unassumingly, or maybe held in her lap, and centered in the frame, if even crookedly, was the alderman, Everyone's Granddad Akers, explaining:

"I didn't groom you, Margaux. I loved you. I waited until you were old enough to give you what you wanted—what we both wanted—and that's

no crime. We were special, you and I. Still can be. Still will be, once you stop being so angry about it."

"*I'm angry because I know better now. You used me. All you cared about was getting what you wanted, and once you got it, you decided to stay with Helen.*"

"*In my profession, I had no choice, but if I had a choice to make, it'd be you.*"

"*What about the others?*" Margaux asks. "*Did you say the same things to them?*"

"*The others were . . . no. They needed teaching, had some growing up to do. Not like you. You came to me ready.*"

"*Do you remember what I said to you that night? When you began to undress me?*"

The alderman sighed. "*I know what you said. But I also know what you meant.*"

"*I said no. I said I wasn't ready. Do you remember what you said to me?*"

"*I told you I knew what was best for you.*"

"*And then you covered my mouth and did what you wanted to do.*"

The concerned third party reached over and stopped the recording. "That must have been terrible."

"There's more."

"It's okay. I don't need to hear it. I've heard enough. You'll forward it to me?"

"I already did."

"And you told the alderman what to do? And when?"

"Yes."

"He'll do it?"

"Does he have a choice?" Margaux draped a flyaway tendril behind her ear, at which point her companion noticed the ruby on the fourth finger on her left hand.

"I see you haven't broken up yet. Easier said than done?"

"Things have become more complicated."

"Is that right?"

She shifts next to the concerned third party. "I'm so sorry to disappoint you, but I'm pregnant." Her eyes reddened with tears. "We've been careful. *Almost* all the time, but . . . it happens, I guess."

"How does this fit into law school?"

"I don't need a lecture. I feel stupid enough—"

"How does the daddy feel about it?"

"Arlon doesn't know yet. But he said he'd pay my tuition, so . . ."

"You really believe that?"

"He promised me. The way I see it, it's insurance. If your plan doesn't work with Richard, Arlon will have to support the baby."

"Sweetheart. Child support won't pay your expenses, your tuition, *and* day care. What are you going to do about the baby while you're at school? Surely, given the circumstances, you don't want to rely on the Akerses to babysit while you're studying for the LSATs. You honestly don't think Mr. Wonderful will be there with you, do you? It's a big job, raising a baby on your own, and a man like that, with his circumstances . . . he'll be gone the second you tell him."

Margaux sighed. A whimper slipped out with the breath.

"He's going to leave you alone and destitute," her acquaintance said, "and that's why this plan with Akers is so important."

"But Arlon gave me a ring. He asked me to marry him." She straightens the ruby ring.

"I see that. Very elegant."

"Thank you."

"Congratulations. On both accounts."

"Thank you. Don't you think this is a sign? That things don't have to be this way? He's changing, I think, but even if he isn't, I have the upper hand now."

"I hope your dreams come true," the third party said. "But consider the probability. The odds are stacked against you."

"I'll hire a nanny with the money Granddad will pay to keep this story out of the papers. Arlon's paying my tuition."

"*Arlon* will help pay for an abortion. Seeing you to the clinic . . . that's about the extent of the man's capabilities. If you have this baby, if you keep it, however valiant and brave a decision it will be, you'll find yourself alone, filling the shoes of both mother and father."

"But I think he's changing. The last time we were together, he was softer, somehow."

"That same softness landed you with a bruise on your neck, with a carving on your chest."

"I know how Arlon feels about me. He's rough sometimes, but usually only when I deserve it. If I rationalize it, I can get what I want."

"Honey. Arlon isn't even his name."

For a moment or two, Margaux stewed in the accusation.

The stranger stood. "There's a wedding this weekend at the Columbus Park Refectory. A young bride and a man far too old to be her husband. Why don't you drop in and see for yourself if you don't believe me?"

"He's lying to me? About even his name?"

"You would know better than me. You told me the first day we met: You're the only one who matters, remember?"

Chapter 37

KIRSTEN

I enter the fourteenth district police station and approach the counter, where there's an uninterested officer of some rank refusing to look at me.

"Excuse me," I say. "I'd like to speak with Detective Decker—"

He raises a finger.

I shut up.

But after several seconds of his scribbling notes on a scrap of paper and turning to speak and chuckle with a colleague who's walking past, I clear my throat. "It's important, gentlemen, that I speak with the detective. It's time sensitive."

"He's in interrogation." Officer Crabass points to a bench. "Have a seat. I'll let him know you're here, Miss . . ."

"Holloway. Kirsten Holloway. I was in once before. You arrested my son last night."

"Here to post bail?"

"No. He's already out on bail. I just need to talk to—"

"Have a seat."

I wring my hands in my lap as I deliberate for minutes upon minutes. It would be easy to walk right out that door. No harm, no foul. I already gave them plenty to go on—the panties, the pictures, the cryptic message that hints at blackmail.

But Patrick already gave them plenty, too, and I just can't play with his liberty.

I stay put.

Watch the minutes tick away like hours.

And finally, the detective appears and waves me back to a conference room.

"Sorry about the wait. What can I do for you today?"

"Let me explain." I remove a scarf from my neck to reveal the marks about to bloom there. "No one's going to allow my kid to take the fall for this."

———

Hours later, I return to Ian in the black of night and slip between the covers as if I were never gone.

Ian stirs, however, and gets out of bed.

I stare at his bare, white ass, practically glowing in the dark of the room. He stands at the window overlooking our acreage.

My body is practically electric right now, satisfied and worked over properly.

This was the last time.

My husband doesn't know it, but he will never again know my body the way he knew it tonight.

"Kirstie," he whispers. "I love you. You've got to believe that, don't you?"

"I don't know what to believe," I whisper back. "But I packed your things and sent them to your apartment in the city. I need you to go in the morning."

"Kirstie—"

"It's not up for discussion. You'll go in the morning."

Chapter 38

JESSICA

"Code sixteen, code sixteen." The sirens are blaring throughout the firehouse. "Fire in progress at oh-four-one-three Western."

I strap on the last of my gear and pile into the ladder truck.

At least the last two hours of the shift will be action packed. Still, I can think of better ways to spend my time at four in the morning.

"All units, all units," the dispatch comes in through the radio.

"Four thirteen Western," I say. "That's the Aquasphere."

We're briefed along the way with what we know, but stories often change by the time we get there. Club closed for the night at three. No patrons inside. Last of the crew left half an hour ago. Presumed electrical fire. Old building, old wiring.

"My ass," the battalion chief says. "Someone didn't want that place standing anymore. Someone wanted the secrets burned along with it."

He might be right about that, considering all the media attention on Margaux's case, the allegations that she worked at the place of ill repute now in cinders, and not to mention the rumors running rampant about Everyone's Granddad Akers, his gambling debts, and his taste for the kinky.

By the time we arrive, the old church is ablaze. Flames shoot out from the underground entrance and lick the old stone walls.

I fight the fire on a line with a hose, and when the entire place is doused and the hullabaloo dies down, I breathe in the stench of the burn.

We walk through the debris like through a museum of what once was. Skeletons of cages and tables abound. Stages and stations and tiny rooms.

When I emerge from the building, I see him standing amid a crowd of onlookers on the corner across the street: Jack Wyatt.

For the past few days, ever since I spied on him and the girl who turned out to be Gail Force, I've been ignoring his calls and leaving his texts unanswered.

A moment after making eye contact—his stare is piercing and unrelenting—he disappears in the crowd.

Maybe he's not interested in seeing me, either, which is just as well. Or maybe he's caught on that I know he knows something about Margaux and he's here to check up on me. What a chilling thought.

I should share it with Decker.

No sooner than he pops into my head do I see him. Arms crossed, squinting at a floodlit area, gnawing on a wad of pink gum—and likely on a theory as to how the fire started.

We make eye contact.

He gives me a nod.

I nod in return.

It was a good night. No one died, not even all of the Aquasphere. We even managed to keep the fire contained to the tawdry section of the building; most of the original worship gallery half a story above street level was spared.

But after a call like that, no way in hell am I falling asleep. My entire body is humming with adrenaline. And the sun's just coming up.

———

"Hold up your hair." Decker fastens a necklace around my neck.

"What's this?" I touch the pendant and see it's the ruby necklace Jack Wyatt gave me on our sushi date.

"We couldn't lift any prints off it. I mean, none other than *yours*, so I thought I'd bring it back to you."

"I don't know if I should wear it, considering—"

"Why not? It's a nice necklace. You're a beautiful girl. You deserve nice things."

"Deck . . ." If I were any other girl, with any other man, I might have melted onto his lips.

"I probably owe you an apology," Decker says. "Based on recent findings, it seems your boy wasn't our man after all."

"Huh?" I'm exhausted after our aerobic romp, and until two seconds ago, all I wanted to do was sleep. My hair is still damp from the shower we shared, and my clothing is a rumpled mess in the corner of the room. The scene is so very domestic that it could either comfort or terrify me, depending on the day, hour, or minute.

"Whoever Jack Wyatt is, he probably wasn't fucking around with the deceased. I'm sorry if I made you feel like he was lying to you."

"He sure as hell wasn't telling me the whole truth."

"True. But we got the prelim results back from our DNA swab on the Holloway kid." Decker persuades me to look at him with a warm finger under my chin.

"And?"

"He has biological similarities to Margaux's baby. They're related."

"Oh no." Kirsten's going to fall apart. "Father-child related? So you're looking at him for Margaux's murder?"

"Would be crazy not to."

"But that doesn't necessarily one hundred percent clear Jack. I mean, that magazine was addressed to someone on Oakley, and Holloway lives on Oakley."

"Could be a coincidence. We'll know soon enough." He grins. "I'm close, Jessie. I feel it."

Chapter 39

KIRSTEN

"I don't understand how this could happen." Patrick's head is in his hands. He's seated at my kitchen table. "I've never been with her. I swear to God. So how does my DNA hit as a possible match? To a friggin' *embryo*?"

My heart has been in panic mode since the lieutenant called with the news less than an hour ago: Margaux was pregnant when she died, and the embryo's DNA is similar to my son's. I take a deep breath. I have to be strong. I have to remain calm for my son. "It's time to face the truth, Patrick." I slide a mug of coffee across the table toward him. "It's what I've been telling you since this whole thing began: your father has secrets."

"But . . . it doesn't make sense. Quinn said something fishy was going on. I looked into it. I didn't find anything, Mom. I mean, *nothing* about this girl pointed to Dad, and I'm a good researcher."

"Maybe your father's just a better liar. Maybe he covered his tracks too well."

"Does he know this girl was pregnant when she died?"

"I don't know. We're not speaking much these days. You might want to ask him."

"I have."

"Let me guess. He denied it."

"Not exactly. But he didn't admit it, I'll tell you that much."

"How did he react?"

"I don't know how to describe it . . . at least not to *you*. Smug, maybe. Not how I thought he'd be."

A feeling like a pebble dropping from throat to gut itches at me. It's the same feeling I got when I overheard Patrick, at age eight, explain to Quinn that Santa Claus was really Mommy and Daddy . . . the feeling that the jig is up, but I want him to keep on believing. Just a little while longer.

"You have to understand. I never would have submitted that sample if I thought in a million years it would hit. *Never.*"

"I know."

"And now . . . now I know the truth about what he did. What are you going to do?"

"I don't want to think about that right now. First, we have to clear your name."

"God, Mom. I can't go down for this." Finally, my son raises his head and takes a sip of coffee. "I just can't. And if I report my alibi, Becca's gonna be *pissed*. Do you know where I was that night? What I was doing?"

I sip from my mug. "Hmm?"

"I went to that club. To the underground place that just burned down."

"Patrick." I sigh and take another sip. "It's better to have a pissed-off girlfriend than a felony murder conviction. Come clean with Becca and make some changes if you want to pursue a life with her." I reach for his hand.

He grips mine—tightly.

"And if you don't want to pursue a life with her, be kind. Communicate and walk away. She deserves that much." I think for a minute. "Patrick. Quinn said you'd been out with other girls."

He draws in a long inhale. "Quinn should mind her own business."

"This girl who died . . . was she one of them?"

He stares at me, silent.

"Patrick?"

"I don't cheat on Becca."

"If you were seeing this girl, no one is going to believe you weren't sleeping with her. Given you've told the police you were at the Aquasphere the night she died, given they suspect she worked there, and your DNA matches . . . Do you have something to tell me?"

He shakes his head.

"Patrick."

"Unless they find a more likely suspect, I'm fucked."

"I've done what I can," I say. "You know I'll do everything in my power to help you. You'll see."

"How? Mom, seriously, you can't write a note explaining that I'm incapable like you did when my ninth-grade biology teacher accused me of copying my lab work. This is a big deal."

"Yes, it is."

"Do you think, if Dad submitted a sample, his would be a better match?"

"Patrick, it would be suicide, but—"

"Even if it means saving me? My future?"

"I hope he will. And I hope it does."

———

For a little over two weeks now, I've come home to an empty house. No one to cook for or clean up after. Just me, my FaceTime with Quinn, my firstborn's worry about his government-issue anklet and house arrest, and a fire in the fireplace. Tonight, I'm sipping a glass of chardonnay.

Patrick's pretrial hearing is coming up.

I've already done all I can do to redirect the investigation. I went to the station and offered what information I could to clear my son's name. I declined pressing charges for the mark my husband left on my neck that night despite Detective Decker's urging otherwise; it was consensual that night. I practically dared him to do it. But my point was made: Ian is capable of wrapping his hands around a woman's neck. I have to be patient and trust in the system. But I know more than one case has been botched because of lazy prosecutors. Or the public gets antsy and demands resolution. And the next thing you know, an innocent man is in prison.

The writing is on the wall: this is exactly what's going to happen with Margaux's case. She's become a media darling posthumously. The Akerses are stirring up buzz that the CPD is inept and can't solve the case, and the public, especially after the fire broke out at the club, wants the case closed so they can feel safer in the city at night. None of them realize that a quick wrap of this case could mean snuffing out my son's liberty.

I stare out over the grounds of the Giardino Segreto, seeking the serenity Ian promised me when we moved out here. There's movement in the shadows at the tree line, just before the marshland. Probably a coyote, or maybe even a deer. I still look for the one I hit weeks ago. I consider her fawns, whether they're still alive out there, or if they've fallen prey to some force of nature.

Because that's what's going to happen to my son if things don't fall in line.

A sense of loneliness filters in as I acknowledge the possibility. A deep, dark cavern full of unrealized dreams. If Patrick goes down for this, what does that say about me, his mother?

"Kirstie."

I jump when I hear Ian's voice behind me.

I take a step back when I see the cold, angry look in his eyes. I cover my heart, which is suddenly beating at Mach ten. "You're early."

It's true I invited him tonight, but I wasn't expecting him for half an hour or so.

He tosses his keys to the cocktail table and sinks to the sofa. "I've given you space, Kirstie. I've been gone long enough. I'm moving back in."

"I'm not sure that's for you to decide."

"Oh, I'm pretty sure it is. I live here. I make your life possible. So let's have it out. I'd like to be in bed by midnight."

"I know what you've done, you know." I lean against the window-sill. A frigid breeze breaks through the old panes.

He stares at me.

"Do you know there's a real possibility Patrick will be brought to trial for this girl's murder? You know it will be hard to refute his DNA match. But one thing's for sure. If you own up to what really happened, Patrick still has a future."

"I don't know what happened."

"He's our *son*. Will you hold so fast to your lies and deceit that you won't even tell the truth to save our son?"

"Kirstie, I—"

"Let me see if I can spot this one. You throw your money around a little bit. You get to be someone else for the course of a night, maybe even the course of a relationship, with some young girl who probably isn't interested in going the distance, someone who, so very unlike me, wants to make a priority of her future, of her career. Someone who grew up in the age of the internet, desensitized by the vast array of options out there, someone who'll do scandalous things with you in the dead of night. Someone who isn't the old bag who tied you down in your prime. You let the relationship run its course, eventually stop paying attention when you're bored, or when some other girl catches your eye. And should she ever want to reach out and find you again, you're a ghost. Because you never existed in the first place. They can't find you because they don't know the real places to look, and eventually, they forget they're looking for you at all. You're a figment of someone's imagination. And that's the way you like it."

"Okay, enough."

I raise a brow. "Excuse me? *You're* telling *me* you've had enough? You're not even supposed to be here until six. You now live in Lincoln Park."

"We're dealing with something a little more serious than your anxious episodes, so let's dial it back. You don't understand, Kirstie. You can't possibly fathom the amount of pressure I'm under all the time to provide. The sacrifice . . ." He shakes his head, pinches the bridge of his nose. "The repeated sacrifice."

"You think I don't understand sacrifice, Ian? Which one of us went to college and earned a degree? *You* did. Because I was delivering our firstborn child during what would have been a final exam for my first college course. Which one of us has a career?"

"I've worked damn hard to get where I am."

"*You* were gifted the opportunity to follow your dreams, to become what you were meant to become. Since you were a boy, you and your cousin dreamed about heading your own firm, following in your uncle's footsteps, and damn it if you didn't do it!"

"I've worked damn hard to get my name on that door, so don't you condescend to tell me it was a gift—"

"It *was* a gift, Ian. A gift from me. I afforded you the time, the energy, and the space to work hard. Do you think you would've made partner if you'd been up all hours of the night breastfeeding babies until your nipples bled? Rocking colicky kids until you may as well have been a zombie? Canceling your days' agendas when one of them got sick on the bus ride to school? Do you think you would've gotten as far as you have without my ironing your goddamned shirts? Without my wearing cheap drugstore slides so we could afford to outfit you in your lawyerly best before the money started to come? And don't get me started on your three-hundred-dollar lunches while I was eating peanut butter and jelly. You want to talk about sacrifice?"

"Don't I get any credit for what I've provided? You have a four-thousand-square-foot house, standing manicure appointments at the salon, a credit card at your disposal. I work so you don't have to."

"I work harder than you've ever realized."

"We can afford anything you want—"

"I don't want anything, Ian. I wanted you. I wanted our family. I didn't want nice things that you could bank as *credit* to pay me off once I caught you with your pants down."

Even now, after I've reminded him of my contributions to our family, he shakes his head in disgust, as if he can't believe that I dared to suggest I'm just as important as he. But then he mutters, probably because he knows he needs an ally right about now, "I know what you do is important."

It doesn't sound sincere, or even believable.

"Ian."

Now with his back to me, he stands in front of the fire and slides his hands into his pockets.

"This girl is dead," I remind him.

His head bobs.

"You're the last person to see her alive."

I watch him closely to register his reaction, but he plays his cards close to the vest. He runs a finger along the edge of the mantel, then whisks away the dust gathered on his fingertip.

"Ian? Is there something you need to tell me? Do you know what happened to her?"

Silence.

"Is your semen going to match the semen found in the threads of that red thong? Is your grip going to match the marks on her neck? Is your DNA going to match that of her embryo?"

He spins toward me. "Embryo?"

I raise a brow.

He tries again: "You said *embryo*."

"She was pregnant when she died, Ian."

He looks shocked.

"Patrick's sample matches," I say. "Which means yours probably will, too. Am I right?"

He stands stoic, refusing to crumple. "I don't know. And no one ever will. In order to compel a sample from me, they'll need a warrant. And in order to get that, they need something concrete to show that Margaux and I might have interacted."

"What they have is concrete enough to center on Patrick, isn't it? Don't you get it? He could go to trial! Juries have convicted on less."

"Justice will prevail. If he didn't do anything wrong, he has nothing to worry about."

"If it all came down to it, Ian, would you sacrifice your image, your practice, your life for one of our children?"

"If it . . . Kirstie. Honestly, the questions you ask."

"That's the difference between you and me. You think you're too important, don't you? That's what happens when you've grown up thinking you're God's gift. You don't love anyone, Ian, but yourself."

"I don't, huh? I suppose that's why I bought you this enormous house when you couldn't keep it together in Evanston."

"We both know the real reason we bought this house."

He pauses to gauge my comment, and I say, "Whatever you do, you do because it serves you well."

He grits his teeth. "I could strangle you."

"You loved to leave your marks on me," I continue. "Our little secret, right? So when I felt the ache of my bruised inner thighs, I'd remember what it felt like to be with you the night before."

"You liked it," he says.

"You *hurt* me, Ian. And I know that now. You've been in control of me since the night you stole my virginity on Oak Street Beach."

"Stole?"

"That's the way I remember it. I was enamored with you. It was happening before I knew we'd decided to do it. And it hurt. But I thought I loved you, so I let it happen."

He's staring into the fire.

"It was a different era, Ian. Before women knew we could speak out against the most popular boys in school. Before we were educated. Before anyone would do anything about it if things went too far, further than a girl was ready to go. If we knew our perpetrators—if we loved them—we assumed we got what we deserved. Furthermore, we assumed that we'd subliminally asked for it, even if we'd never wanted it to begin with. And then I was too ashamed not to continue seeing you. I had to make it worth it, you see. I had to go the distance with you. I couldn't lose you, because if I did, my worst fears would have been realized—I would have been exactly what you thought I was back then. Easy. Disposable. Unimportant."

"I love you, Kirstie. Always have. I wouldn't have thought . . . I wouldn't have done what you're saying I did. You're angry with me. You're revising history to justify that anger now."

"It's not like it happened only once. Our first night out after Quinn was born . . . with the rope, and the hook . . ."

"That was *hot*. You wanted it."

"Someone who wants it isn't bawling her eyes out. You delve into these fantasies, and you can't stop. You feel powerful. You're addicted to the rush, and you don't even care that you're hurting people. You throw us away when you're finished. Roll over, leave the room . . . And you know what? For a while, I felt special. That you had to go to such great lengths to have me, that you wanted me so fiercely that you'd take me, if even against my will. There's prestige in that, Ian . . . until I realized it wasn't exclusive to me. Until I realized you feel that way around every attractive woman you meet."

"It's not true."

"If you love me, you'll tell me about the money that's missing. If you love me, you'll explain it all. If you love your family, your son, you'll come clean."

"I have nothing to come clean about!"

The doorbell sounds.

"Expecting company?" Ian asks.

"As a matter of fact, yes."

"Since when do you have a full social calendar?"

"Just tonight."

He follows me to the front door, where I greet Detectives Decker and Oliver.

"Gentlemen," I say. "Good evening."

"Mrs. Holloway," Decker says. "I have a warrant here."

"Come in."

"Warrant?" Ian asks.

"Ian Holloway, you're under arrest for the murder of Margaux Claire Stritch. You have the right to remain silent—"

"What's your probable cause?"

"We'll get to that at the station, Counselor."

"Whatever it is, it won't stick."

"Probably not. DNA evidence is hardly reliable."

"DNA? How?"

Realization dawns.

The last time we had sex, I'd practically taunted him.

He wrapped his hands around my neck and did to me what we all suspect he did to Margaux.

And he left me—like Margaux—with plenty of DNA to pass off to the police force for analysis.

"That's where you went the night after?" he asks. "The cop shop?"

I raise a brow. "They would have been here sooner, but it takes a while to process the samples."

"I didn't kill her," Ian says through gritted teeth and a dagger of a stare. "All you've done is prove that you weren't woman enough to keep me."

"Time will tell," I say. "And what was it you said? Justice will prevail."

"By the way." Oliver hands over a five-by-seven padded manila envelope, not unlike the one in which I found the flash drive of pictures. "This was on your doorstep."

THEN

Margaux

Margaux entered the conservatory and observed the wedding from a distance. As she ventured closer, she caught the glance of the concerned third party, who raised a brow, as if to say *what did I tell you?*

The third party was right.

Arlon Judson was not going to leave his family. Not even for the embryonic cells rapidly dividing and developing inside her.

And Arlon Judson was not his name.

Best man Ian Holloway took the microphone and told stories about his cousin and a woman she thought was her friend—Donna, a.k.a. Gail Force from the club—who hadn't even bothered to tell her she was getting married, let alone to a man who was cousin to Arlon, the man she both loved and feared, craved and abhorred.

It seemed she, Margaux Claire Stritch, was unimportant, merely a caricature, a punch line at the end of a bad joke.

Maybe it's time she had the last laugh.

She strolled into the ballroom and smiled at the family surrounding the man she'd fallen in love with, the man she'd opened her very soul to, the man she'd trusted even when warning signals went off in her head—when his hands were around her neck, when pain became part of pleasure to the point she feared she might never breathe again.

"Excuse me." She touched his arm. It seemed the natural thing to do. "I need to talk to you, *Ian*."

The look of surprise on his face quickly morphed to a controlled expression. He never let his surprise show. "Of course." He dropped his napkin next to his plate, stood—"excuse me"—and began to walk.

"Who is that?" she heard a young woman who must be his daughter ask.

"I don't know," the wife said.

Ian led her to a barren corridor, staying just a few steps ahead of her, not daring to look over his shoulder. To any bystander, it would appear she was following him, a perfect stranger coincidentally walking the same path. But the moment he knew they were alone, he took her by the elbow—hard.

He whipped her around, and her back slammed into the wall. "What are you doing here?"

"You're *married*."

"You have two minutes, and the time's already ticking."

"I have something to tell you, Ian." Tears clouded her vision, but even through the mascara burning her eyes, she saw the set of his jaw.

His brows came together in a stern expression. "Tick tock."

"I'm pregnant."

"If I had a dollar for every time some girl tried that trick . . . my *family* is here. Do you know what you nearly did back there?"

"But I didn't know you were married. I didn't know you had a family. Arlon, you lied—"

"I'm supposed to believe you're pregnant? When we've taken precautions?"

"Not every time."

"Nearly every time, and the news is rather convenient, don't you think? Tonight? Of all nights? You could've broken the news tomorrow, when it wouldn't have made a scene, but the fact that you chose tonight . . . well, I wouldn't be surprised if it was all a lie."

"Here . . . wait. I can prove it." She opened her clutch and produced a positive early pregnancy test. "I took about ten of these." She smiled. "This one, I took this morning."

He looked at the stick, pinched his eyes shut, and hung his head, as if in defeat.

His grip on her eased. "Maggie." His expression softened, and he took the test from her grasp. "How can you be sure it's mine? With what you do at that club—"

"It's *yours.*"

"Do you expect me to believe you know that for sure? You slut around town—"

"I haven't been with anyone else. I know it's yours."

"It's still early."

"Yes. About six or seven weeks. But there's no reason to think I won't carry to term." She took his hand and pressed it to her abdomen. "It's a boy, Arlon. I'm sure of it."

"Seven weeks?"

"Or six. It's hard to say exactly when—"

"First trimester."

"Yes."

"Then you can still get rid of it."

"Arlon!"

He pulled his hand from her middle and tossed the stick into a nearby trash can. "Get rid of it!"

"You're a father. How can you say that? Imagine if your wife had aborted your son. There's a real, live being growing inside me, and even though it's too soon to tell what he'll look like, there's a DNA map already determining the color of his eyes, the shape of his smile. It's the magical combustion of you and me. *Our baby.*"

"Get. Rid. Of it."

"I don't *want* to get rid of it."

"Maggie." He leaned his forehead to hers. "Please understand. The timing couldn't be worse."

"I know. I'm about to go to grad school . . . that is, if you're still willing to help me finance it. This isn't convenient timing for me, either, but if we're patient—"

"No." He backed off, opened his wallet, and pulled out a credit card. "I'll pay for the abortion. But then we have to cool it for a while." He pressed the card into her hand. "She can *ruin* me in court, do you understand? Even though we live in a no-fault state, conduct makes a difference. It's not supposed to, but it does. And I loved her once. Still do, when I let myself. I'll leave her—I'm already working on managing the assets—but I can't leave her for you. Not this way."

"I don't want an abortion, Arlon. I want to have this baby."

"Go to the Grand Avenue Women's Clinic. It's not far from your place."

"No."

"I'll be watching the statement. You won't see me until I see the charge for the procedure come through. And if you don't do it, you'll never see me again."

"But this is our baby." She grabbed his hand and held it tight to her abdomen again. "Life. We created it together. You love me. Please. Let's talk about this."

"You're pregnant."

"Yes."

A throaty groan escaped him, and he began to gather the skirt of her dress in his hands. "You're *already* pregnant."

He spun her toward the wall.

"Arlon—"

And, with one strong arm, held her there.

"Wait," she said. "Please, wait."

He pulled her panties aside to allow him access, and in an instant, he had her dress up at her waist, his zipper down.

"Don't." Her whisper fell on deaf ears.

He positioned himself.

Her cheek scraped against the wall with the momentum of his first powerful thrust. "Arlon. Wait."

But he was already rutting on her from behind, one hand gripping her waist, the other palming her head, holding her captive against the wall.

She closed her eyes, but the tears still came, burning hot rivers down her cheeks. Her head ached where he held it, and with every repeated pierce into her body, he may as well have torn at the flesh between her thighs.

"Stop," she managed to whisper.

"This is what you want," he said through gritted teeth. "For the rest of your life."

Not like this, she tried to say. But all that came out was "Please."

It took only a few angry thrusts for him to finish.

He slapped her on the ass, as if punctuating the power he held over her.

She let out a whimper.

He tucked his cock back into his pants.

She muffled a sob and sank to the floor, her head in her hands. "You love me." She braved a last look at him. "Tell me at least that much is true. You do, don't you?"

He snapped his fingers and offered his hand, palm up.

Just as she was about to take his hand and get to her feet, he spoke again:

"Give me the ring."

"What?"

"The ring. Now. I shouldn't have given it to you. You think I can't tell when a girl's trying to trap me?"

"I'm not—"

"The ring!" He forced her to her feet with a rough yank on her arm. "Give me the ring."

"Okay." She began to twist at it. "Okay."

She tugged and wrung at her finger until the ring came free. She pressed the ring into his hand.

He leaned in close.

She smelled the bourbon on his breath.

"I live with entrapment every day of my life," he hissed. "Every fucking day."

"I'm sorry," she said. "But I can't do what you want me to do."

"Get it done," he said over his shoulder, zipping up as he walked away.

The proof of what had happened dripped down her inner thighs and pooled in the hammock of the red thong and in the folds of fabric of her formal dress. She dropped her face in her hands and sobbed until she had no more tears to cry.

Chapter 40

Jessica

"Jessie? Are you on shift today?"

"Kirsten?" I put a hand to my ear to block out the noise of my four-year-old niece's birthday party. "Are you okay?"

"I'm . . . listen, I'm heading to the fourteenth district police station, and I'm wondering if you can meet me there."

"Yeah, I . . . can it wait a few minutes? Ellie's about to open presents."

"Of course. I'm still a ways out. Coming from Mettawa."

"Sure." I wait for her to elaborate. When she doesn't, I say, "Is something going on?"

"They just came for Ian."

"Oh." She seems oddly calm for a woman whose husband was just brought in on suspicion of homicide.

"Will you come?"

"I'll be there as soon as I can."

I hug my niece—"Happy birthday, Ellie"—and kiss my brother on the cheek.

"On call?" he asks.

"Not exactly. A friend of mine's heading to the station and needs support."

"Auntie Jessica's blowing us off for another guy on the job."

"Actually, it's a *girl*friend."

"You don't have women friends."

"Not usually. But I do now."

———

Kirsten's already there by the time I arrive. She's casually texting, or maybe playing a game, on her phone in the lobby.

As if I'm equipped with a homing beacon, she looks up at me the moment I cross the threshold.

"They just took him back," she says. "This guy"—she indicates the desk sergeant—"won't let me back to see him."

"Not until he's processed," the sarge says. "Then you can post bail."

"I don't want to take him home," Kirsten says. "I've been trying to keep him at the place in Lincoln Park."

"Lincoln Park?" I ask. "Jack lives in Lincoln Park."

"I want to talk to the detective," Kirsten says.

"What do you say, Sarge?" I say. "I'll buy you a beer next time I see you out."

"You know this girl, Jess?" the sarge asks.

"I do."

"All right. I'll get Decker for you."

Minutes later we're in a cold conference room waiting for Decker. When he finally comes in, with a thick file tucked under his arm, he's twisting open the waxy packaging of a hunk of Dubble Bubble.

"Ladies. What can I do for you?"

"I want to know what's happening. If you have enough to drop the charges against my son. I'd like to get that band off his ankle and put him back on track as soon as possible."

"Here's the deal with father-son DNA. It's a little trickier to determine who's the father of the girl's baby. Sons sometimes come up as a false positive."

"But you have Ian's DNA, too. With Margaux's, you should be able to tell beyond a shadow of doubt who fathered that child."

"I'm told it's trickier, that's all, but we fingerprinted your husband, so hopefully we'll hit on a match to prove he was in Margaux's apartment shortly before she died. It would be helpful if your son could come up with a reliable alibi. Short of resurrecting the Aquasphere Underground and waiting for someone to exit and admit to seeing him there that night—"

"That's where he said he was." Kirsten looks as if her hopes are about to be dashed away. "Like father, like son."

"Don't say anything more." A man in a suit bursts into the room.

My jaw practically hits the floor. I don't know him, but I feel like I do.

"Doug." Kirsten stands. "I'm just trying to figure out—"

"Kirstie, you retained me to represent your son, and Ian just retained me in this matter, and as your family's counsel, I'm here to tell you not to answer any of the detective's questions."

"I'm not," she says. "He's answering mine."

"Excuse me," I say. "You're the *cousin*? The lawyer?"

Doug Fordham turns to me, as if he just now realized I was in the room.

"Doug, Jessica. Jessica, Doug," Kirsten says by way of introduction. "Doug is Ian's cousin and lawyer. Jessica's a friend of mine."

"Nice to meet you," Doug says. Then he turns to Kirsten. "Why is a friend of yours in on this discussion? None of this is privileged, you understand. She can testify to what she hears."

"Wouldn't that be hearsay?" Kirsten asks.

I'm still staring at the lawyer, who says to me, "Will you excuse us, please?" And then to Decker: "You too."

"Wait, wait," I say.

Decker's already halfway out the door. "Jessie?"

"But . . . I just . . ." I swallow hard over a dry lump in my throat.

"We'll talk in a minute," Kirsten says.

I follow Decker out of the conference room.

My fingertips are tingling, but the rest of me feels numb. "Deck?"

He turns to me. "Whoa. You all right?"

"He looks like Jack."

"What?"

"The lawyer."

"You're saying the lawyer is Jack Wyatt? The Jack Wyatt I can't find?"

"No, I'm saying the resemblance is uncanny. Do you have Ian Holloway's mug shot printed?"

"Why?"

"I want to see a picture of him."

"You can see *him*, if you want. I've got him in interrogation three."

I head toward the interrogation hallway.

"Jessie—"

I pick up my pace. "Where's number three?"

"Ollie just came out of it."

I beeline toward the door, with Decker quick at my heels.

I burst into the room.

And there, in cuffs, seated at an industrial folding table, is the man I know as Jack Wyatt.

Suddenly, it all makes sense. The odd schedule. The windows open on his laptop during our last breakfast. The necklace matching the ring he gave Margaux—I touch it now—all part of a set. And Patrick showing up to talk to me. Maybe, because Kirsten kept insisting Ian was hiding something, Patrick followed clues his father left behind. And those clues led him to my apartment.

The color drains from Ian Holloway's face. "Jessica. What are you doing here?"

"I just came to say hello . . . *Ian*."

Chapter 41

KIRSTEN

"You don't believe he did this, do you?" My husband's cousin paces in a ten-by-ten conference room at the CPD fourteenth district building.

"I don't know if he did it or not, Doug."

"What do you mean, you don't know? He's your *husband*, Kirstie. You've been together since you were kids. If you don't believe his story, how is anyone else going to get on board? Do you hear what I'm getting at?"

"You want me to get on board. I understand that. But I can't *lie*. They asked if I could account for my husband's whereabouts on the night this poor girl died. I can't. He wasn't home. He was supposed to be working through some case file at the office that night, and he came home later than usual. That's what his text messages will prove, and that's what I've gone on record as knowing. So if you want to get him out of this, *you* can vouch for him."

"I was still on my honeymoon that night, Kirstie."

"That's right. You were."

"I can't vouch for his whereabouts." He shoves his hands through his hair. "From now on, just say you can't recall. You don't remember. It's not our job to make their case." He takes another lap around the conference table. "I want you to know we're going to beat this. The evidence is strongly circumstantial. So his block letters match the suicide note. So it looks like the name on the note was forged. They'll probably find his prints all over her apartment. Of course they will. He had an affair with her. We'll admit that. But they can't prove he attempted to sign her name on the suicide note, let alone that he killed her. Christ, they don't even have a solid motive. He'll be home with you before you know it."

"Why did you lie for him?" I ask.

"What?"

"About this girl. You were willing to jeopardize your marriage to protect him. I could've gone to Donna with what you told me, and it obviously wasn't true."

"On some level, I knew you wouldn't believe me. We have a strong basis of trust, Donna and me, and while she wouldn't have approved of what I did for Ian, she would've understood."

"You don't know what kind of guy you're protecting. He's not the same man he used to be. You need to know that there's a possibility—a real, fathomable possibility—that he didn't want Margaux around. You say they don't have a motive. But if she was pregnant, if she came to the wedding threatening to tell me . . ."

"You don't know for certain he did this. And you're forgetting I'm probably the one guy on this planet who knows your husband just as well as you do."

"I don't think you do." I open my shoulder bag and pull out the envelope Detective Oliver found on my doorstep this evening. "Someone mailed this to Ian. I found another a while back—the one I told you about—with a note that looked suspiciously like an attempt at blackmail. I suspect it came from whomever he's been paying twenty grand a month."

"*Twenty grand?*" Doug hangs his head and sighs. When he again looks up, he gives his head a slight shake. "Are you fucking kidding me?"

"I wish I were."

"He didn't mention it to me."

"I'm not surprised, given what's on this drive." I spill the contents of the envelope into Doug's waiting hand. "Listen, I don't want to think this implicates Ian. I don't want to think he's capable of taking this girl's life, but considering things I've recently learned . . ." I sigh. "Point-blank, if he had anything to do with Margaux's death, he should answer for it."

He unfolds the note first and reads:

> Mr. Holloway,
> Due to the passing of MCS, consider your initial debt
> paid in full. As promised, see enclosed.
> Thank you for your contributions to a noble cause.

The note is, like the previous one, typewritten and unsigned.

"Hmm." Doug frowns. "Let's have a look, shall we?" He pulls a laptop from his briefcase, boots it up, and plugs in the flash drive.

I should warn him about what he's going to see. I really should.

He crosses his arms over his chest as the files load. He clicks on one and gasps when the image materializes on the screen.

"I'm sorry," I say.

"That's Donna."

So much for a strong basis of trust.

"Yes. Your wife. With my husband."

"What is she wearing?"

She's clad in black leather with cutouts in all the right spots.

"This is the firm's condo." He looks at me over his shoulder.

I nod.

"How long have you known about this?"

"I just got the package today. The first flash drive I found contained pictures of Margaux and Ian. It was obviously a blackmail threat to keep the affair with Margaux from me. But this one, the pictures of Ian and Donna and the note about MCS being dead . . . I think Ian was paying whoever sent it to keep the affair with Donna a secret from *Margaux*."

For what seems like an eternity, he stares at me, as if challenging me to back down, or maybe willing me not to know what we both now know.

"So who sent the note?" Doug asks. "Who sent these pictures?"

"Who's in a load of debt?" I ask. "Who's being investigated for misuse of public funds? Who would know enough about all of this to ensure funds could be repaid while protecting Margaux from the fact that her boyfriend is a serial cheater?"

"The alderman."

"That's right. That's what I'm thinking, too. I know the account number where the money is wired. It'll be up to the cops to determine whose account it is for sure, but I'm pretty convinced it's the alderman's. And if he's blackmailing Ian, couldn't that be motive for Ian to kill Margaux?"

"He wanted to start fresh," Doug says. "He told me he was done with all this, that he wanted to recommit to you."

"How can you believe that, considering these pictures of my husband with your wife?"

"Ian . . . Ian introduced Donna and me."

"I didn't know that. I thought you all met at the same time."

"It was at a bar after a company dinner. He knew her. Which means this could have happened between them before me."

"Could have. I suppose it's a valid theory, but is it probable?"

"It doesn't matter. All that matters is that it's *possible*. That's what I say to juries every day. If I can get a jury believing in a possibility, the verdict of not guilty is nearly in before the judge retires to chambers."

"Even if the guy you're defending is guiltier than sin? Doug, this is your *wife*. Your wife slept with my husband."

"I have to think it was before. It's the only way to keep them both. I have to suspend disbelief."

"Okay. I understand that. I understand it and support it if that's what you want."

"Christ." For what feels like an eternity, he stares at me.

But I won't back down. I won't blink.

"What do you want me to do, Kirstie? Not defend him? Let him thrash around until he drowns himself? With my help, he's going to get off. This case is riddled with holes. The prosecution's got their work cut out for them, that's for sure. Ian's done some things he isn't proud of, but that doesn't mean he's capable of murder."

"Whether or not he's capable, it looks bad. He was paying someone twenty grand a month . . . it's a wonder we're able to pay our bills. Don't you think there might be motive there? He has a lot to hide. The police are going to agree."

I stare at him, long and unrelenting, until he finally nods.

"If Ian did this, he should answer for it," I repeat. "He should take the heat off Patrick, and he should answer for it."

THEN

MARGAUX

Margaux, in a stunning red dress, exited out into the gardens at the Refectory. She was one of only two wedding guests on this side of the park, as everyone else was likely on the dance floor.

"You were right." Margaux lowered her body to a long, golden-toned bench. "About everything. His intentions, his image, his dark side. You were right about everything. He only wants what serves his ego."

"I wish I were wrong about him." The concerned third party took a seat next to Margaux.

The lights from the lampposts filtered down through the canopy of vines and raced through the golden strands of Margaux's hair. She rubbed her right cheek, which was starting to ripen with color.

"Did he hit you?"

Margaux wrung her hands in her lap, twisting a scrap of red satin and lace. Panties.

She met her companion in a knowing glance.

Much worse than a fist to the face occurred between her and Arlon tonight.

"Tell me what happened tonight, Margaux."

"You know what happened. It's everything you *said* would happen."

"You should report this."

Margaux shook her head. "You know who I am, what I do for a living. Do you honestly think they'll care?"

"The world is changing. Everyone deserves a right to say no."

"Or I can just get on with it." She opened her grasp and revealed a credit card, with End-all-be-all's given name on it, resting alongside the panties. "He gave me enough to kill our baby. No more, no less. And if I report it, the press will know about the abortion, too. I don't know if I can do it."

"You don't have to. You do what *you* want to do, what *you* think is best."

"I can't believe I'm in this mess." Although she kept a tight grip on the Visa, she abandoned the underwear in her lap when she wiped away a tear.

"You should be on your way home," the third party said. "His family is here. He might deserve the exposure, but his family doesn't. Not here, not tonight."

The panties slipped to the garden path when she stood.

Her shoulders trembled with her sob, and before she knew it, she was resting her head on the stranger's shoulder, crying. Maybe *stranger* was no longer appropriate. Maybe they were friends.

"Hit him the right way," the third party suggested. "You have his credit card, his real name. Whatever you decide to do about the baby is your business. But report what he did to you—to your body—tonight."

"It's nothing I haven't let him do before, nothing I haven't willingly participated in. Who'll believe me? Who'll believe that he nearly squeezes the life out of me every time? And that it usually turns me on?"

"Your cheek is bruising. Other parts of you will bruise, too. There's evidence. Don't let him get away with this."

She pulled back and stared at her friend, eye to eye. "Why do you care?"

"I told you. Everyone deserves kindness and caring. Do you have cab fare?"

She nodded and smeared a tear and streak of mascara like the tail of a comet across her cheek.

"Go then. Go directly to the police station. Tell them what he did to you tonight. Practice. Say the words. Use his real name."

"Ian Holloway assaulted me tonight."

"Say it again. The more often you say it, the easier it's going to be when you file an official report."

Margaux repeated it a few more times before turning away.

The clicking of her heels against the flagstone path echoed like a clock counting down to doom.

———

The third party crouched to the ground and retrieved the panties and returned to the reception hall.

Ian's jacket hung on the back of his chair, and if Ian was on the dance floor, doing the hokey pokey, he was far too drunk to dig through his pockets for keys. He'd take an Uber back to the hotel like everyone else. And it was a warm night; he likely wouldn't be putting the jacket on again for the duration of the party.

No one was looking. No one would notice someone shoving a pair of panties into the inside pocket of the jacket.

Sooner or later, the panties would be found.

He would be exposed.

This time, he wouldn't get away with it.

Chapter 42

KIRSTEN

The last time we were in the same room was for Doug and Donna's wedding. Now we're in the great room at the house in Mettawa, where we share not a single memory. Yet here we are, discussing my upcoming meeting with the Chicago detective. This moment is going to be forever cemented into all our minds.

Instead of *remember that one Christmas when . . .* , we'll be referencing *the time Dad was arrested for murder.*

"They're looking to see if Ian has an alibi," Doug says, "if his story holds water. Anything you can do to help establish that alibi will help. But remember, they're counting on your being bitter and vengeful. They want you to play the role of the disgruntled wife. Stay strong. Poised. They're going to try to trip you up, so if you're not sure about something, say you don't recall."

"Tell the truth." Ian winks at me from across the living room. "Establish my alibi, baby."

For a moment too long, I harden my gaze on him. It doesn't occur to him that asking his wife to cover for him for the night his girlfriend died mysteriously just might be too much to ask of anyone. And I'm sort of astounded that he thinks, even while he's sleeping in the corporate apartment downtown, that I'd stop at nothing to protect him, if only to put on a happy face in front of our children.

"But you can't *lie*, Mom." Quinn wrings her hands. "Even to save Dad's life. If they catch you lying, it'll be worse. And, I might add, maybe Dad shouldn't have done what he did with this woman." She glares at her father. "I can't believe you'd do this to Mom."

"I don't even know why we're worried about it," Patrick says. "We both know Dad didn't kill this girl, Quinny."

"Whether or not he killed anyone, he's still in the wrong," Quinn insists.

"Wait a minute, Quinn," Ian says. "You're passing judgment on something you know very little about."

She points her finger at her father. "You. Are. Wrong. Dad, knowing you've been involved with this young, trusting woman . . . the position you put her in, the lies you told her to get what you wanted from her until you were bored with her . . . it's insulting. Unforgivable."

"Quinn," Ian says. "You don't understand what's really happened here—"

"Dad, I'm a woman. If you see fit to treat one of us this way, you're saying it's acceptable to treat *all* of us that way. How would you feel if someone treated *me* that way? Or Grandma? So why would you do this to Mom?"

"This is about Dad's not being a murderer. It isn't a feminist issue," Patrick says with a roll of his eyes.

Quinn rolls hers in response. "Of course it isn't, coming from the white, privileged man."

"But he didn't kill her," Patrick says. "That's the point I'm making."

"We don't know that," I say.

"Jeez, Mom!" Patrick says.

"You know what?" Quinn stands. "A woman is dead, for God's sake, and all you care about is saving Dad's skin. As I understand it, you might want to think about saving your own."

"Quinn." Ian makes a move toward her.

"Stop right there," our daughter says. "Let's get something straight. I'm here for my mother, got it? I'm not here to support you."

Ian looks to me. "Are you going to let her talk to me that way?"

"Yes." I nod, in case he didn't hear my words. "I think I am."

Patrick, feigning casual aloofness, pops his knuckles, which he hasn't done since middle school. He's chewing his lip the same way he did the first day of high school, as if he's afraid but doesn't want me to know it. And for a moment, I can't help seeing him the way I saw him as a child. My baby boy. The reason his father and I are here today. We both loved him enough to give forever a shot.

"Everything's circumstantial," Doug redirects. "I'm not worried about it, but at the end of the day, sealing up an alibi can only help us sleep more soundly."

If the case against Ian is as flimsy as Doug says, this could all come crashing down on Patrick.

"If I hadn't given that sample, we wouldn't be here," Patrick says.

"They have the tattoo, and they have the semen. The tattoo is inconsequential. I can argue our way out of that, considering the Aquasphere brand. It doesn't prove anything. But Patrick, your DNA matching the embryo's actually helps your father. It puts doubt into the jury's mind. Someone closer to Margaux's age . . . it's plausible."

"Absolutely not," I say. "You will not throw my son under the bus—"

"Kirstie, it's okay," Doug interjects. "The case won't hold water even if the prosecution attempts to try it, because there's nothing to back it up."

"It certainly is *not* okay. It's not an option," I say to Patrick, "and we're not here because of you. We're here because your father screwed the wrong girl!"

"They'll believe it was you," Ian says to our son.

"They'll believe I was having an affair with her," Patrick says. "We're the same age. It makes sense."

"Patrick, no," I say. "Maybe that gets your dad out of hot water, but it puts you back *into* it."

"I haven't seen the pictures," he continues, as if I never said a word. "But from what I understand, they're obscure. Can they pass for me? Like, fake-ID pass?"

"For a minute, I thought it *was* you in the pictures," Ian jokes.

I shoot him a glare.

"Mom, this is about saving Dad from a bogus murder charge. We'll deal with the girl later. Right now, we have to stick with what's important. We have to get him out of this mess. The tattoo matches," Patrick says. "The build matches, right?"

"Yes, it does. I've been keeping myself in shape," Ian says. "It's important."

"Dad and I wear the same size suit," Patrick says. "Which is why I probably borrowed his jacket that night."

"You didn't borrow his jacket that night!" I scream. "You didn't, not once, take his coat from the back of that chair!"

I get to my feet amid the silence ringing in my ears.

I look around the room at my family, all staring at me, agape, and my husband's cousin–slash–best friend–slash–law partner–slash–lawyer. "It's not happening," I tell Doug. "Find another way. You leave Patrick out of this."

No one says a word in response.

Finally, Quinn pipes in: "Are you going to tell them, Patrick? Or should I?"

"What?" I spin toward my daughter.

"I went out with her," Patrick says. "I met her at the club. I took her out. Twice."

"Oh my God," I say.

"But I didn't sleep with her. It was just coffee. Then one night she called me when this asshole left her destitute in a bad neighborhood, and we had dinner."

"You had dinner with this girl?" Ian asks.

"Nothing happened," Patrick says with a shrug. "I thought she could use a friend."

"Then I guess we play the Arlon Judson card," Doug says.

"Yeah. That's the guy she was dating," Patrick interjects. "She told me all about him."

"The police are looking for Arlon Judson," Doug continues. "We admit to Ian's affair, we tell the jury all about it before the prosecution has a chance, but center on the theory that Judson was irate when he learned of it. Boom. Motive."

I sigh and roll my eyes. "Glad you've got it all figured out." I walk to the kitchen, retrieve my Louis and my keys.

"Wait!" Doug says. "I should accompany you. I'll be there to coach you through the questions."

"I'll be fine on my own." I shoot another dagger of a stare in my husband's direction. "I'm just going to stick to the truth."

Ian keeps a stupid smile plastered to his face, but I see his Adam's apple bob in his throat.

I hold his gaze. *That's right,* I say without making a sound. *How confident are you in my loyalty?*

I head to the station.

THEN

Margaux

"I'm looking for Babydoll."

"You found her." Margaux turned toward the man waiting outside the dressing room at the Aquasphere Underground. "Patrick." He wore a navy-blue suit, tasseled loafers, and a striped tie.

"Maybe you want to take a break?" he asked.

"You want to know what I want? I want a decent guy for once. I want to be treated with dignity and respect."

"How about another dinner sometime?"

"This . . ." She indicated from top to toe. "This is all an act. This isn't who I am. Underneath, I'm just a jeans-and-cute-top kind of girl. I binge-watch *Friends*. I deal with the life that landed in my lap."

"I know. I'm not asking for romantic reasons, anyway. We're accepted at the same law school. I thought, you know . . . if you decided to go to Loyola . . ."

"Well, lots of girls were accepted there, so . . . why me?"

"To be honest—"

"Yes, please be honest."

"You're too good for this place. And this guy you're dating . . . his name's Arlon, right?"

"Yes."

"You're too good for him, too. You're sure you're okay?"

"I will be."

"Well, I'll be around, so . . . if you need anything . . ."

"Thanks."

"You shouldn't put up with Arlon's bullshit."

"I wish I'd met you first."

"No, you don't. I have a girlfriend."

"Ohhhkay." That made things even more confusing. "I'd get it if you were trying to get into my pants, but . . . why are you here, if you have a girlfriend?"

"I told you. You look like you could use a friend."

"Well, if you ever lose the girlfriend, give me a call."

"You'll be the first I call." He winked and walked away.

Chapter 43

Kirsten

"Thanks for meeting with me," Detective Decker says.

"Of course." I take a seat in yet another conference room. "What can I do for you?"

"For starters: I need help understanding who these guys are. Arlon Judson. Jack Wyatt."

"Why? What difference does it make?"

"We get only one chance to prosecute someone. One shot before we weaken any subsequent chances to serve justice on Margaux's behalf. I want this case as airtight as possible before I pass it off to the prosecutors," Decker says.

"It isn't tight now? With the DNA?"

"It could be better. Obviously, your husband had been with this girl. He's admitted that, but infidelity isn't murder. Any defense attorney worth his salt can cast a shadow of doubt. The way this case reads, Margaux was involved with Arlon Judson but carrying Ian Holloway's baby. It reads like she had two boyfriends, and even Gail Force has admitted that Margaux talked about seeing someone else while she was dating Arlon. *Arlon Judson* may have had as much motive, if not more, than your husband to kill her. And *Arlon Judson* is a ghost."

"I see."

"Margaux didn't post a single picture of the guy on her social media pages, but Helen Akers insists they were together. But she never met him, so as far as an identification goes—"

"You can't do it." I finish his thought for him. "It's a hole in the case."

"So far, yes. My theory is that Arlon and Ian are the same person, and I could use your help proving it, but I'm guessing you don't want to do that even if you could."

I think for a second.

"We have two known aliases in the Underground," Decker says. "I found a Jack Wyatt, roughly the same age as Ian."

"Jessica's boyfriend."

"Right. Only last time Jessica was here . . . spoken to her lately?"

I shake my head. "She must be busy. She hasn't taken my calls."

"She saw your husband here the night of his arrest. She attests to the fact that Wyatt and Ian are one and the same."

My heart quickens, and my fingertips go numb. "She's been seeing my husband?"

"She's been seeing *Jack Wyatt*. And Wyatt's apartment . . . ," the cop continues. "Venture a guess as to the address?"

"I'm guessing it's in Lincoln Park? Fordham, Holloway, and Lane's corporate apartment?"

"Bingo. So all signs point to Ian Holloway and Jack Wyatt being one and the same. It proves your husband used aliases, but we still need to connect him to Arlon Judson."

"I see." If this detective is able to do such a thing, Doug's backup alternate scenario is as good as gone, which means they'll use Patrick as a distraction. The only way my son is safe from suspicion is if this cop seals up his case against Ian, airtight.

Decker continues, "According to Gail Force, members of the Underground choose aliases for a reason. Pretending to be someone else is one of them. And I found an Arlon Judson, who's forty-two. But he's never heard of Jack Wyatt. I'm looking for a connection, but their lives don't overlap."

"With each other's. But what about with Ian's?" I wait a second for the cop to react. When he doesn't, I continue. "A Jack Wyatt beat out Ian for a fellowship in college—at Northwestern. He *still bitches about it.* But Arlon Judson . . . I don't know him. I overheard Ian say his name a few weeks back when he was talking to his cousin, but I don't know who he is."

"Let me enlighten you. He used to practice family law but was disbarred. Something about a domestic battery charge and mayhem."

"Maybe Ian knows him, then. You should ask him."

"We have." The detective leans back in his chair and stares me down.

I sigh. If Ian is responsible for Margaux's death, he deserves what's coming. If he isn't, this isn't going to help his case. Still, better him than Patrick. "Ian said the name. I'm one hundred percent certain. Maybe Ian meets girls, he's a jerk, and then all the girls are left thinking *Arlon Judson*'s an asshole. Or *Jack Wyatt*'s an asshole."

"That's helpful. Thanks."

"Anything to keep this spotlight away from my son."

Decker pours another sugar into his coffee. "Everything you know, please tell me. You never know how it might help."

"In that vein, you also might want to have another chat with Gail Force," I say. "I think she knows more than she's telling. I think she's scared."

"Will do."

"So the theory is Jack Wyatt is Ian." I bite my lip.

"Appears so. Sorry to say."

"How's Jessica handling the news?"

"Hanging in there. Probably more worried about what's going through *your* head."

"I should call her."

"She'd appreciate that."

"So where does that leave my son?"

"When we ran Ian's prints through the system, it was like fireworks went off for miles with all the hits. All over Margaux's apartment—on the money left on her counter, in her bathroom, on the vase found half-filled with water in her sink. On a knife there, too. We know Ian was at the apartment—likely the night she died."

"So why are you looking at Patrick at all?"

"Because circumstantial evidence won't convict. I need to look at everyone if I expect justice to run its due course. And that includes looking at your son."

"Patrick didn't have anything to do with this."

"Can we go over it one more time: How did you learn of the affair?"

"I suspected it after I found a pair of panties—a red thong—in the dry cleaning."

"And when was this?"

"Oh, I think the day Margaux died, but they were in his suit coat for weeks before I found them."

Decker nods. "Mm-hmm. And how do you know that?"

"It was the suit he wore to his cousin's wedding."

Decker nods. Says *uh-huh* at intervals. I get the feeling he's going through the motions. He wants me to admit something spectacular, something he doesn't already know. Little does he realize my whole life revolves around dry cleaning and errands and household chores. If he was looking for fireworks, he called in the wrong gal.

Finally: "Can you account for your husband's whereabouts the night of Miss Stritch's death?" He states the date, the time.

"He texted and said he would be late, that he had some work to finish at the office."

"Was that usual? Did he do that often?"

"Lieutenant, my husband is a lawyer. That means that even when he's home, he's working. It's very common for him to stay late to work on a case, especially if a court date is looming."

"What time did he come home that night?"

I pause. Take a deep breath. "I was tired. I wasn't feeling all that well. I turned on a movie and lay down on the sofa."

"Did you speak to him when he came home?"

"I did."

"Did he appear disheveled? Nervous? Anything out of the ordinary?"

I shake my head. "He came home with a bottle of red wine that night. And roses."

"That's out of the ordinary?"

"We've been married for twenty-two years. Together for three before that. Not unusual. Just not an everyday occurrence."

But, now that I think about it, I should have questioned it. When we got together, we were very young and very broke. Ian's idea of sending flowers was leading one of our kids into the kitchen with a fistful of dandelions. I buy flowers. Ian doesn't.

"About the wine and roses . . . his lawyer provided us with proof of credit card activity to support what you're saying. He bought the wine around seven, then the roses at seven fifteen. Did he come home shortly thereafter?"

I think for a moment. If I concur, I establish Ian's alibi. But I honestly don't think he came home that early. And if he harmed Margaux, I can't cover for him. "I don't think so," I finally say. "But I can't be sure. I took a pill."

"Mrs. Holloway, your husband's DNA matches that of tissue extracted from Margaux's uterus. Does that sound like a man who's worthy of your protection?"

"I'm not protecting him. I really don't know."

"One more time: Was your husband with Margaux Stritch the night of her death?"

"Possibly."

"Did he ever mention the name Maggie?"

"No."

"Did your son?"

"My son?"

"We have enough of a match to continue looking at him, too. And Ian's told us the thong belonged to whomever Patrick disappeared with that night."

"He said that? Actually went on record and *said* that?"

"The night we arrested him."

It's happening. Doug and Ian have already put the pieces in place. They're already pushing my son into moving traffic.

"But that didn't happen."

"Your son didn't disappear for a time the night of the wedding?"

"He went out for a cigar—"

"Alone?"

"Yes, but he didn't take the jacket."

"You're sure?"

"*Positive.*"

"You know what your husband's lawyer's going to say, right? That you're unreliable. That you're angry about the affair and you want to save your son's skin, so you're not remembering things clearly."

"That's a crock."

The detective shrugs. "You have anything definitive that puts your husband *at that apartment* the night she died?"

"Here's what I know: his father came home with wine and roses the night Margaux died . . ."

I review it in my mind. I lay down on the sofa with a fire going. Ian came home with wine and roses. I heard him come in, but I was only half-awake and groggy from the antianxiety meds. He woke me with a kiss and a glass of wine. He'd changed from his daily attire to a pair of track pants and a T-shirt.

Realization dawns. I've been missing something all along. It's the dry cleaning. There's proof in the dry cleaning.

"Let's get back to the underwear," the detective suggests.

I rise from my chair and pace. I'm sick of talking about the thong. Every time he mentions it, it's like he wants to remind me what went on behind my back. "Tell me you're not hinging this case on the underwear. I'm positive it was hers, but I'm also one hundred percent sure it was in that pocket for at least twenty days. They weren't on her body the night she died."

"Am I overlooking something?"

"She showed up at the wedding, all right? He took her aside. They were gone for a few minutes. And you're telling me they were going to have a baby, and there were panties in the pocket. *Of course* they're Margaux's panties. But they don't do anything but prove the affair happened, and maybe that they had sex right there at the wedding, but that doesn't help you determine what happened the night she died."

I stop walking. "He'd been after me for weeks to get that suit to the cleaner's. He claims he didn't know how the underwear got into the pocket, and honestly, why would he hound me to drop the suit off if he knew there was evidence of an affair in the pocket?"

"Maybe he forgot the underwear was there."

"Or maybe he really didn't know." Pieces of the puzzle fall effortlessly into place in my mind now. He wanted me to take in the dry cleaning. But it really wasn't about the Brooks Brothers suit. He knew that if I were going to the cleaner's, I would bring everything that had to go. The urgency, I realize, was about the shirt he'd worn the day Margaux died. He'd spilled some wine on the collar.

Spilled wine.

That's what he said.

But he'd changed before he opened the bottle.

And even if he didn't, even if he somehow changed *after* opening it, how would he splash wine on his *collar*? And the girl at the cleaner's said someone had tried to lift the stain at home. When had he ever attempted to get a stain out on his own before? If it were wine, as he said, he wouldn't have tried to hide it.

Decker challenges me with a stare.

Finally, I break the silence. "Lieutenant, I'm here for you to see if I can establish an alibi for my husband, is that right?"

He gives me a nod.

"I can't help you any more than I have already. I'm sorry, but I just don't remember what time he came home. I remember that I heard him come in. I remember he'd changed before joining me in front of the fire because there was a stain on his shirt. But I don't know what time it was. It was weeks ago."

He stands, and we're eye to eye. "I'll walk you out. You'll call if you remember something?"

"I can scarcely remember anything these days. Can't even remember to pick up my dry cleaning, what with everything going on." I riffle through my purse and produce my keys. My pink pickup slip from the dry cleaner's sticks to the keys and floats to the table. I glance at it purposefully, then meet Decker's gaze.

Hesitantly, his fingers go to the slip.

I nod. *That's right. Take it.*

"I remember the shirt was white with gray pinstripes. The stain was on the collar. On the left. If I think of anything else, I'll call you."

"Thank you."

We exit the room and walk side by side.

"Can you tell me: How did this girl die?" I ask. "Was it by hanging, as the initial news reports said? Or is something bigger going on?"

"I'm afraid we have to hold back some details during an active investigation."

I want to know if she had any open wounds.

That spot on his shirt? I'm pretty sure it's Margaux's blood.

And I just gave Decker the ticket to test whatever's left in the threads of the fabric.

Chapter 44

KIRSTEN

"Patrick and Quinn are staying the night," Ian says when I return from the station. He's a little drunk, judging by the slight slur in his words, his heavy eyelids.

I look to the open bottle of wine on the island, next to an empty one.

"Do you mind if I stay, too?" he asks.

"Well, you probably shouldn't drive." I pull the scarf from my neck and begin to unbutton my coat.

"Let's hit the hay, then. I'm beat."

"And the sofa's quite comfortable." I smile at Ian's exasperated sigh, pour myself a glass of wine, and take a seat at the kitchen island. "What, like I'm going to let you back into my bed? After you nearly brought a child into this world with another woman?"

"She said she had an abortion." Ian pulls up a counter stool across the expanse of the island so we're across from one another. "Is this okay? We can talk about this?"

I indicate the stool with an open palm. "I suppose better late than never."

"You saw the charge yourself." He takes a seat. "Do you suppose the police are bluffing?"

"You wanted me to get an abortion, too," I say. "When I was pregnant with Patrick."

"Do I have to hear about this for all of eternity? I was eighteen, Kirstie." Ian worries at a callus on his right forefinger with his thumb. "I didn't think I could take care of myself, let alone a wife and a baby."

"Well, you're not eighteen now. And not too long ago, you suggested *we* have another baby. Was that because of what happened with Margaux?"

"Tragic." He dabs at his eyes.

Is he fighting tears? For the first time, I realize he may be mourning her death, or her baby's. She was part of his life, after all. Or maybe it's a show of remorse for what he's done to our family by crossing the line with this girl. "Were you trying to replace what was lost?"

"There's no comparison. You're my *wife*. We have a family. I couldn't see what was happening with Margaux as fatherhood. I just didn't see her baby as mine, and honestly, I figured she was sleeping around. I didn't know the kid was mine."

"It's always someone else's." I roll my eyes.

"It would've been different with us. Kirsten, it always was."

"Margaux's pregnancy was terminated, just like you wanted. One way or another. It just didn't happen at the clinic."

"She had an appointment. She was going to do it. I thought she had. She paid for it—as you've already discovered—with my credit card. And I told her . . ." He hiccups, as if he's holding back tears. "I told her if she did it, we could continue to see each other. But I didn't mean it. I just wanted to say something she'd believe. Something that would persuade her to do it. And then that night . . . the night she died, I was going to tell her I'd changed my mind, that I didn't think it was a good idea to stay involved. I went there early, before she was usually home. I was writing a note to tell her it was over."

"Did you arrive at that conclusion because you'd begun to see Jessica Blythe on the side? It must have been terribly difficult to juggle all three of us."

"All right." He gnaws on his lower lip and stares at the countertop. "How do you know Jessica?"

"We met by chance. Care to explain how all that started, too?"

"That's beside the point. I wanted to end it with Margaux because it was the right thing to do."

"Yet you took her to bed one last time."

"It just happened. Don't you think I wish I could take it back? And the whole time, she kept begging me to squeeze. Just a little tighter, just a little longer. It's almost as if . . . It's like she *wanted* me to leave marks on her neck. I think she planned it. I think it was the ultimate revenge. I left marks. She staged her suicide to make it look like I killed her."

I blink tears away. "That poor girl."

"Poor girl? She's trying to ruin me from the grave."

It's silent; I consider the possibility of what he's saying. Do I believe more in the vindictive nature of a woman scorned and at the end of her rope? Or do I believe my husband, who is obviously capable of emotional torment, could kill?

"Ian, do you regret it? The life you've had with me? If you were done staying faithful to me, if you were ready to move on and have affairs with other women, *relationships*, even, I wouldn't have liked it. But it would've been better, more dignified, if you would've left me."

"Honey, don't you know? I did it because I *couldn't* leave you. I don't know life without you. You've taken care of me for so long."

"You should have left me."

"Never."

I take another sip of wine.

"Twenty grand a month," I say. "This secret you've been keeping has cost us twenty grand a month. Do you know what I could have done with that kind of money? I could've gone back to school. Or there are these workshops in Door County for artists."

"Well, I did try to foster your love of art," Ian says. "I stocked you up on canvas and brushes, and—"

"For the last time, I took a painting class in high school, Ian. I wasn't good at it, I didn't like it, and it wasn't my chosen medium. Painting is *not* my passion."

"Well, whatever. I didn't have a choice but to pay the demand. He was going to expose me."

"The alderman?"

"I assume so. Someone followed me to our place in Evanston once, but it didn't happen again, so I thought it was a coincidence—until the letter showed up, asking for money. And it wasn't just *you* who would've been hurt, so—"

"You're talking about Patrick."

"Mm-hmm."

"Quinn."

"Of course."

"And Doug and Donna?"

He fixes me with a stare, feeling me out, seeing what I know.

"The package Detective Oliver found on our front porch the night you were arrested . . . Wager a guess as to what was inside?"

His jaw descends a fraction of an inch or so, then he clenches up. But I don't back down.

"Kirstie."

"Ian."

"Did you go to Doug with it? Does he know?"

"He hasn't confronted you?"

Ian shakes his head.

"Why don't you tell me how it happened?"

"You put a stop to the choking. You were afraid I wouldn't be able to stop one day. I tried, Kirstie. And then I found the Aquasphere. We went there, remember, with Fiona and Dave before the Hawks game, and . . . that's when I found Donna. She was a choking coach, someone to teach me how to do it the right way so I wouldn't hurt anyone, so I wouldn't hurt *you* anymore. It was strictly business at first. But it just happened one night. I couldn't stop myself."

"Was it consensual? Or do we have to worry about Donna filing charges against you, too?"

"Please." He waves the idea away. "She wouldn't dare. She can't afford the exposure."

I close my eyes and inhale a deep, cleansing breath. He didn't exactly answer my question. "And the blackmail?"

"Margaux said the alderman had her followed, that he had a twisted obsession with her. He took pictures, must have hired someone to follow me home and found out I was married. It was months after I started seeing her that he sent a flash drive to our place in Evanston with demands. It was right around the time you had your episode. I couldn't come clean with you then. What choice did I have but to pay? And then later . . ." Ian sighs. "He caught me during a session with Donna, and I guess he saw the opportunity to squeeze even more out of me. He threatened to go to Margaux. I figured if she knew about Donna, Margaux would come find you out of spite, and maybe even contact Doug. He and Donna had just started seeing each other, so I paid those demands, too."

"This doesn't look good," I tell him. "You have motive."

"I didn't kill her."

"Well, you did plenty. And we have to talk about protecting assets, here. If you're put away, I need a sense of security. Quinn has to finish school. I'll have to pay the bills, and as you've aptly indicated more than once since this whole thing began, I'm not all that marketable in the workforce."

"Maybe you should've thought of that before you offered up my DNA."

"Maybe *you* should've thought of it before your screwing around put our son under that cop's suspicion."

"You know . . ." Ian fiddles with the band of his watch. "I want a fresh start. We have to forgive each other if we're going to get past this."

"I think we should divorce."

"Divorce?" He bursts out of his chair.

"I think it's the only surefire way to protect our assets, to ensure our children get the leg up they deserve."

"Kirstie." He rounds the island and drops to his knees in front of me, his hands grasping mine. "I came home with flowers and wine to surprise you that night."

"You did. I remember."

"That's right, I did. And the time stamps on the credit card statements will prove I did it before Margaux died. It'll be my alibi. They'll determine she died after I was already home. We can put all this behind us and start again, start fresh."

"Wait. Let me get this straight. You stopped for wine and roses *before* you went to Margaux's place? Why did you stop for wine and roses if you were only going to break it off with her?"

"I was going to bring them to you. You have to believe me."

"If that's true, you would have bought the flowers closer to home. You would have bought a chardonnay because you know I prefer white. But you bought a merlot."

"You're reading too much into it. I just felt like a red that night."

"Ian, you bought those gifts for Margaux. Because you thought she had the abortion. You went there that night to make amends."

His lips press into a thin white line, and he tightens his grip on my hands.

I put the pieces together: he told her he'd continue to see her if she terminated the pregnancy. He told me he was working late. He bought wine and roses . . .

"I was coming home to you. I swear it. I was ready to recommit. If you back me up, I have my alibi."

"Oh my God," I whisper. I meet his gaze, tears pricking the corners of my eyes. I think of our children, of the long stretch of their lives ahead of us and the funds necessary for them to have all they deserve to have. After their lean early years.

"It's brilliant," he says again. "It's the only way."

"It *is* brilliant."

"Yeah?"

I nod. "Yes, Ian. It's brilliant. You just want me to tell the truth."

"That's my girl." He cups my chin in his warm hand. "The *truth*."

I lean close.

My lips touch his ear.

"I already did. Good night, Mr. Judson."

THEN

MARGAUX

It had been a long couple of days since the wedding. Reparation of the heart was tricky business, and while all she really wanted to do was sleep, there were arrangements to be made. Clinics to visit. Research to be conducted. Futures to be planned, and reports to be filed.

The rain wasn't helping. Everything in the city was more difficult in the rain. It was as if the city, herself, were weeping for what never would be.

Goodbye, boyfriend.

Goodbye, baby.

At least, thanks to the third party's plan, law school was still on the horizon. Thus far, the alderman had already replaced a good portion of what he'd lost.

Margaux slipped off her shoes at the door and hung her raincoat to drip dry on the old mosaic tile floor in the foyer.

She'd manage. She'd come through worse: losing her parents at an early age, growing up with stuffy, old, judgmental Helen and her husband, the child molester with a gambling problem . . .

"Hello, gorgeous."

She let out a yelp when she heard the voice across the loft, and covered her mouth to muffle it when she realized she knew the man leaning over the countertop in her kitchen. The man she'd known until recently as Arlon had a pencil in hand, its tip pressed to a pad of paper. He dropped the pencil. "You're home early. And damn. Great dress."

She wrapped her arms around her middle, as if she could hide her body from the man who knew it best. "What are you doing here?" She nodded toward the bundle of red roses on the countertop, alongside the bottle of red wine. "After the things you said to me . . . after what you *did* to me at Columbus Park—"

"Wait a minute, Maggie. What *I* did to *you*? You practically ambushed me. I was perfectly clear when we began this relationship: there were going to be times you couldn't be with me, times I'd be unreachable."

"Because of your career, not because you had a whole other identity, a secret wife, and children you conveniently forgot to tell me about!"

"You're confused."

"I'm not confused about what you did to me in that hallway, Arlon."

"I didn't do anything to you we hadn't done a hundred times before."

"Against my will that time."

"Wait. Let's put this in perspective a second."

"How do you think your wife would feel—your *daughter*—if she'd seen what you did to me?"

"Stop talking about my wife and my daughter. They're none of your business."

"What do you think the police would have to say about it?"

"Let's not get carried away. The police?"

"I've been to the station. I talked with a sergeant there."

"You didn't."

He didn't have to know she'd chickened out before filing a report. In the end, the threat of exposure was just too much for her to bear. But she could still do it. She *would*, as a matter of fact. First thing in the morning. She raised her chin. "I did."

"You told them my name? My real name?"

"What's with the flowers and wine, Arlon?"

"Cat's out of the bag. You can call me Ian."

"Ian." She rolled her eyes, crossed her arms over her chest, and warded off a shiver. "Why did you lie to me about your name?"

"I didn't know what you and I were going to mean to each other. Of course I would do things differently, had I known."

"Let's talk about your domestic situation."

"I'd rather not."

"She's pretty. She looks sweet. And if I have to make a judgment on it all, the two of you look happy. I don't want to ruin that."

"I make it work until I don't have to anymore. I told you this at the wedding."

"No. You basically told me to get lost at the wedding."

"What did you expect? My children were there. I was angry."

"That's right." She massaged her temple and let out a sigh. "You have children."

"They're old enough to handle a divorce now. I'm leaving her. But the groundwork isn't set yet. You have to understand, baby."

"I *understand* that if I didn't have an abortion, I'd never see you again."

"I saw the charge from the clinic come through. It's done?"

She'd paid the fee, yes. But at the last minute, she couldn't go through with it. She left before she popped the Valium they'd given her.

Her eyes welled with tears.

And here he was, ready to use her all over again, talking about a future that would never come to pass, a future the third party had sworn would be unnecessary, as long as Akers played ball and did what he swore he'd do.

"That makes you happy? To think of killing our baby?"

"Oh, honey." He crossed the room, his footsteps echoing in his wake, and despite her flinch, he took her into his arms, holding her back to his chest. "It wasn't the right time for us. But like I said before: you're young. We have all the time in the world. Give me time to end it with Kirstie." He nuzzled her neck. "I have to protect my assets—the assets we'll share—before I leave her. We'll be comfortable that way."

"And what happens when you get tired of me? When you start slinking around town with someone else? Do you do the same thing to me? Hide money from me so you don't have to share your earnings, when I've been home with the kids? And then I'm kicked to the curb like you're doing to her right now?"

"Don't you get it? I never *chose* Kirstie. I was roped in the same way you tried to rope me in the other night. She's never worked a day in her life. Hell, I'd be lucky to get away with a sixty-forty split the way this state's run. I've worked hard to get where I am."

"And she hasn't?"

"Not this hard. She doesn't know what we have. She won't know what half is, so she doesn't know what she's due. If you give me time, I'll be able to move some assets around so her lawyer won't find it."

She caressed the fourth finger on his left hand. He never wore a wedding band. If he had, she might not have found herself in this situation.

"Do you love me?"

"That's entirely beside the point." He kissed the space between her neck and her shoulder.

"You can't even say it."

"I shouldn't have to."

She read between the lines: if he didn't say it now, she couldn't hold him to it later. Just like Richard, he'd groomed her to be what he wanted her to be, at first waxing the love on thick and then slowly letting it thin out until it was so watered down with anger and resentment . . . and control. And over the past few months, the third party had helped her realize that Ian Holloway/Arlon Judson had never loved her—he'd never loved *anyone*—the way he loved himself.

"I should put those roses in water." She freed herself from his arms and took a few steps in the opposite direction—breathing room—toward the kitchen, where he'd dropped the roses in a bundle on the countertop.

"You just have to be patient," Ian said. "I'll make it worth your while."

"You know, I used to think you were the best thing that ever happened to me, but now I think you might be the worst. You're evil. You say I'm special. That you love me. How many of us do you love? Just me? It's always been me? Except when there was Donna. And except for that little trek you took to Lincoln Park when you met the firefighter."

"You followed me?"

"I had to know how you did it. You were lying, and I fell for it, and I never want to fall for it again. And I sure as hell don't want to be your wife someday, if all you're going to do is leave me later, destitute, for someone else down the line the way you're planning to leave your wife now."

"My wife." He sighed heavily. "You know my name. You know my firm. It wouldn't be too difficult to track her down for a conversation."

"It sure wouldn't be."

"So . . . what's it going to take, Margaux? Law school tuition? A prettier ring? What's it going to take to keep you quiet? To keep Kirsten and my kids out of the equation?"

"You think I want money?"

"Akers is already bleeding me dry—"

She raised a brow. "Bleeding you dry?"

"That's right. He knew a long time ago what you just learned at the wedding, and he's been demanding payment for his silence ever since. So if you want cash, talk to the alderman."

She already had spoken to the alderman, at the third party's behest. She already had Ian's money. But suddenly, it wasn't enough.

"I don't want money." She smiled. "Baby, I want to ruin you."

Chapter 45

JESSICA

For at least the eleventh time today, I decline Kirsten's call and return to Decker's sofa with a bowl of popcorn.

"So I was browsing through some old cases online," I say. "There's a cold case in town. Dates back twenty years. Victim was strangled."

"No," Decker says. "This guy's not a serial killer."

"He bruised my neck. He bruised his wife's."

"He's into choking. It's erotic."

"You think choking is erotic?"

"*I* don't." He hands me a beer. "*People* do."

I raise a brow. "I get why a guy might be into it. Complete control. But complete surrender for the girl?"

"The orgasm, supposedly, is godly."

I imagine not being able to breathe, how close Ian came to doing that to me. "I'm not convinced, but to each his own."

"Well, I can imagine with your history, you know . . . with what happened to you when you were a kid—"

"Stop."

"I'm just saying maybe it explains why you prefer to have a firm grasp of control in the sack."

He has a point, but that doesn't mean I want to discuss it to death. "Not everything is about the past."

Deck clears his throat, takes the hint, and gets back to the case: "So, choking. The trouble is that it's all too easy to actually kill someone while doing it. Some people even hire a master or dominatrix to observe and teach them."

"Gail Force."

"Right. There's a whole subculture of people who are into these things."

"And that's why Margaux is dead."

"Not saying that's why, but it sure didn't help her live longer."

"Theory one: Margaux killed herself after a sexual encounter with this guy. Two: he accidentally killed her during sex. Three: he pursued her strictly for the purpose of killing her during sex. Think about it."

"Well, there's a reason the Aquasphere Underground burned down, and I'd say it sure as hell wasn't an accident. Whether it had to do with Margaux or not . . . it's just too coincidental to assume it didn't."

"Who do you think set the fire?" I ask.

"Suspect number one: Alderman Akers, or someone who works for him. With all the media attention about Margaux working there, and the press about the Holloway boy's arrest because of the tattoo being consistent with the Aquasphere logo, it's just too risky to leave it standing."

"But it was an anonymous cash business."

"With video cameras everywhere."

"Ah."

"Which brings me to the second and final person of interest on my list: Ian Holloway. If the club was subpoenaed, the establishment could have turned up some pretty damaging video feed of the accused—if, that is, Holloway is indeed Judson—and the deceased."

"I suppose so." I nibble my lip for a second. "He was there the night of the fire."

Decker raises a brow.

"Just standing there, staring at me from across the street. At the time, I thought he wanted a glimpse of me. We hadn't talked since he caught me snooping through his laptop."

"Mm-hmm."

"Or maybe he was just like all the others gathering around the place to watch it burn. And at the time, I didn't know someone had set fire to the club, either. They suspected the fire was electrical."

"We need something to stick," Decker says. "And soon. I need something more than circumstantial evidence against this guy or he's gonna walk."

My phone buzzes with a voice mail alert. Kirsten left a message.

"Why don't you call her back?" Decker suggests. "Obviously, she wants to talk to you."

"Are you kidding? She probably wants to ream me. I was *dating* her *husband*."

"You didn't know that. C'mon. She's a reasonable—"

"I don't think I can ever face her again."

"So you're just going to never speak to her again? Walk out in the middle of a conference, and that's it?"

I shrug. "Maybe."

"Jessie. That's not like you."

"No." I sip my beer. "It's not."

"Can I say something?" Deck asks.

I get the distinct feeling that he's going to say it whether or not I want him to.

"It doesn't take Freud to know you don't trust women. Probably because of what your mother did . . . not believing you when you told her what happened."

"That's not why—"

"Maybe not. I just think maybe some closure . . . maybe it'd help. Regardless of whether you ever want to talk to Kirsten Holloway again. Can't hurt, that's for sure."

"Guess not."

"Can I help?"

I slowly shake my head. You can smash a vase, apologize to it for breaking it, and you can even glue it back together. Maybe it even holds water again, but no matter what you do, its fractures will always be there. "Not unless you build a time machine." I try to smile. "Really, Deck. I'm okay."

He hands me my phone. "Then call her back."

No sooner than my phone hits my palm does it ring. I glance at the caller ID, expecting to again see Kirsten's name illuminated in the screen, but the name there practically drops my jaw.

Decker and I simultaneously look up at each other.

"Answer it," he says.

Chapter 46

Kirsten

"You don't get it, Doug." I'm in the kitchen in the firm's apartment in Lincoln Park. I ventured to the city today to review with Doug the half ream of paper that is the first draft of my divorce settlement. Ian is in one of the bedrooms down the hall while his lawyer tries to convince me not to file for divorce.

"The case against him is wafer thin, you know," Doug says. "Soon you can put this behind you and carry on as if nothing happened. Divorce is extreme."

"I think it's tighter than wafer thin, don't you? Considering the DNA, the money—"

Doug shakes his head. "They're playing a game of smoke and mirrors. I'm not worried about it. We'll admit to the affair, even to the alias, but at the end of the day, Ian is a respected, upstanding citizen. And the money? It's all been filtered into the alderman's campaign fund. There's no crime against donating."

"What about the letter? The pictures?"

"No way to trace them to the alderman, and the quality of the images is quite poor. I'm not worried about that, either."

"And the alias?"

"*Alleged.* No one at the Aquasphere has come forward to testify that Ian is the same Arlon Judson the police are looking for, but even if they did, what would it prove? That Ian had an affair?"

"What does Donna have to say about it?"

"Nothing." Doug slices the air with a hand. "She'll be happy to put all this behind her."

"So he's just going to get away with it. Get away with *everything* he's done."

"He's made mistakes. But there's no concrete evidence of a crime against him." Doug slides his hands into his pockets. "Kirstie, let this run its course, and then, if you're still feeling this way, *then* we'll discuss the divorce."

"You don't get it. Whether or not he's convicted, I can't keep doing this. All the secrecy, all the deception. Do you know what it feels like to learn your entire life is a lie?" I pause for a moment to gauge his reaction. "As if everything you're proud of is a mask and the reality behind it is a mess?"

But he remains in the same position, unaffected.

"What am I saying?" I mutter. "Of course you know what that feels like. You're a victim, too."

"I'm *not* a victim, and as a matter of fact, I'd like to limit the use of that word. The fewer *victims* here, the better."

"If you have a conversation with your wife, I think you'll feel differently. You don't even know what happened between them. There's a reason the four of us don't get together, and I tell you, it's not because I had an emotional breakdown when Quinn moved out of the house."

His brow knits.

"Your wife knows things. And with what she knows . . . the prosecution can bury him."

"Not if we stand by him and combat the picture the prosecution is going to be painting."

I cross my arms over my chest. "Doug, I have to protect the children. Financially speaking."

"But a divorce in the midst of this won't look good."

"I don't think I can afford to care how it looks. It's high time my husband realizes there are consequences for his actions. How long has he been getting away with this? And with how many women? You, of all people, should want *at least* a sense of penance."

"Were you happy, Kirstie?" Ian's question comes from behind me.

So much for my request for a few minutes alone with Doug. I turn and face my husband.

"Did our marriage fulfill you?" Ian asks.

"I was dedicated," I tell him *and* his cousin, both of whom seem to need a reminder that marriage is supposed to be faithful. "Dedicated. No one ever promised me fulfillment."

"If you don't expect it, maybe you should at least want it, then," Ian says.

"I do. And that's why I want a divorce."

"You can't expect me to be anything more than human. I've made mistakes."

"Well, I can expect you to be decent, can't I?" I check the time. "I gotta go. I'm going to be late."

"Late for what?"

"I have plans."

"Plans where?" Ian wants to know. "Plans with whom?"

When Jessica finally called me back, we compared notes. We're getting together to put a plan into action. Doug wants me to be a team player. I am. I'm just playing for another team today.

I push away from the counter—"The girls"—and I head toward the door.

THEN

Margaux

"You'll *ruin* me?" Ian asked. He picked up a knife and began to cut the foil off the bottle of wine. "Is that a threat?"

She wished she hadn't said that. Now she was going to have to answer for it.

Margaux cleared her throat and placed a vase beneath the faucet. "Take it for what you will."

"All right. You've made your point. Let's have a glass of wine."

"I prefer to think of it as a reminder: I, too, hold a lot of cards in my hands." Just as she was about to yank the protective plastic sleeve from the stems of the roses, a thorn ripped at her flesh.

Blood bloomed at the tip of her finger. She swore and shoved her finger in her mouth to stop the bleeding.

The note he'd been writing when she walked in caught her eye: I'M SORRY. I CAN'T DO THIS ANYMORE.

He'd come for closure. To break it off with her. He thought she'd gone through with the abortion, yet still, he was going to end it. And worse yet, he didn't have to balls to own up to it! How relieved he must have been to arrive at an empty flat. How cowardly he was to have considered ending it all in a *note*! Here he was, sweet-talking her, telling her everything she wanted to hear when he was only going to disappear in the morning.

It was all bullshit. He was *never* going to leave Kirsten. And that was just fine—she didn't want him anymore after all she'd learned. But that didn't mean she could stop loving him. The heart was not as logical as the head. Yet the fact that he thought he was so good at what he did, that she was stupid enough to sink into the quicksand he was pouring on so thick, that she wouldn't notice . . .

And what about the next poor girl down the line? Someone who didn't have a sleazy alderman for a guardian? Someone who wouldn't even be left with the blackmail money after Ian abandoned her?

"Arlon—"

But he'd already forgotten the wine. He was already sidled up next to her, groaning and pressing his hard body to hers, muttering about how watching her suck on something, anything, was *such a turn-on*. His hands were at her bare thighs. His mouth was at her neck.

"I love a bare ass," he said on a breath and hooked a finger into her thong.

He shoved the undergarment down past her hips.

It was Richard all over again.

This was all she meant to him. She wasn't special. He didn't love her. He needed someone to control with ropes and belts and whips in the bedroom. He needed someone who would surrender under his touch, his squeeze, his threat to snuff the life out of her.

Tears rolled silently down her cheeks.

He slapped her on the thigh. Hard. "Bad girl."

She didn't have to look to know he'd left a palm-shaped welt on her body.

"Not like this," she whispered.

Instantly, he took a step back, perhaps to prove that he was in control, that he always was in control—of his actions, of her, of every situation—especially in the abandoned hall at his cousin's wedding reception.

She spun around and faced him and closed her hands around his neck.

"You want to treat me like a whore?" She tightened her grip. "Pay me."

"You want to play rough." Ian pried Margaux's hands from his neck. "How rough?"

She grabbed him by the collar of his shirt and pulled him close. "As rough as you go. I want to feel how much you hate me."

"Yeah?" He gave her a little shove.

She stumbled but caught herself against the countertop. "I want to feel the way you think of me."

"You want to feel like nothing?"

"I am what you make me."

"If you're a fucking whore, I've certainly made you that."

"Pay me first."

He was slightly out of breath, his hair was rumpled, and she'd left a spot of blood on the collar of his shirt.

She smiled to herself at the sight of it. Proof that he was here, that he was with her. *That's good.*

He reached for her again, but she only slithered farther away.

"Fine." He pulled his wallet from his pocket and fished out a few hundreds, which he tossed next to the roses. "You want to play that game?"

"I may as well get *something* out of it. And if you want the works tonight, I'm going to need everything in your wallet."

"Small price to pay." He dropped the remaining contents of his wallet on the bills already stacked there. "And I can afford it."

Chapter 47

Jessica

"Jessie?"

I look up from my laptop at Decker.

It's too late to hide what I've been researching—my mother.

He grins. "Who would've thought Jessica Blythe would actually take my advice?"

"Make a big deal out of it, and I'll punch you."

"I wouldn't dare."

No one in our family has seen my mother in nearly fourteen years, and I haven't talked to her since she told me I must have wanted what Dan Grapplin did to me all those years ago. And despite what Decker thinks, I don't need to talk to her ever again. But I want to know if she's still alive—or dead. I want to know that she's no longer with that monster.

"You'll be here when I get back?"

"I mean, I'm going to meet Kirsten out, but it'll be only for a few hours."

"You let me know how it goes."

"Yeah." For a second, I concentrate on the facts of Margaux's case, and all the pieces of the puzzle. "Deck?"

"Hmm?"

"What are the odds Holloway's going down for this?"

"Not great, to be honest. We've got good theories, bits and pieces of things that make sense. But he's got a good lawyer. We need glue to hold it all together."

"I'll give you my full report after."

"You're coming back, then?"

I can't stop the smile threatening to bloom on my face. This isn't like Decker . . . isn't like *us*. Where's the guy who walks out the door after two days in bed and disappears for a week or so? "Do you want me to come back?"

"Hey." He leans toward me.

"Hi," I say.

"Of course I want you to." His eyes—a gray shade of green . . . have they always been?—seem smokier somehow, and I can't help it. I want to fall back into what we used to be. Maybe it was a merry-go-round, maybe we'll never go the distance, but what Decker and I shared was fun. Being with him was easy.

"I should probably go home and water my plant," I say. "Maybe grab a change of clothes."

"Oh. Okay."

"But you could swing by after your shift if you want."

"It's a plan." His lips brush against mine. "You always believed I was onto something, and damn it if I'm not right on the cusp of wrapping this case. I owe it, in great part, to you."

"Just remember us little people when you're neck-deep in a promotion. New title, new responsibilities, new minions. New life."

"You, my friend, are unforgettable."

"Okay." I roll my eyes. "What do you want?"

"What happened to you when you were younger . . ."

"Yeah."

"We don't have to talk about it if you don't want to."

I'd rather not. I shrug. "I'm okay."

"I couldn't sleep last night, and not that I don't have plenty to keep me busy with the Stritch case, but after our conversation . . ." He places a file in my hands.

I open it and see my worst nightmare staring at me. My heart starts banging in my chest.

"Dan Grapplin's been in and out of prison for the past ten years," Decker says. "He's on the registry for sex offenders."

"Oh." Guilt bottoms out in my gut. I wasn't the only one. "To think that if I'd spoken up—"

"You *did*. Your mother made you feel like it was all your fault."

"I could've said something to my brothers, to my father. Maybe Grapplin wouldn't have had the chance to offend again if I'd made more of an effort."

"Considering your mother's reaction, it's no wonder you kept your mouth shut."

"Still. I should've been stronger."

"You were a kid. You were as strong as you were supposed to be at the time. But now you're an adult. What are you going to do about this now?"

"What *can* I do? It was so long ago."

"Statute of limitations for something like this expires ten years past the victim's eighteenth birthday." His hand comes to my cheek for a few seconds. "You let me know if you want to do something about it."

Silently, I nod.

"You think about it. You let me know."

"Yes," I say. "Do something."

THEN

MARGAUX

He tossed the rope over the rafters and bound her by each of her wrists, then by each of her ankles. Like an animal spread to be quartered, her arms and legs stretched and ached, and the rope burned against her skin every time she shifted, and the floor bit into her back.

Her chest heaved with tears, but it only revved him up higher to see her in such a state. He attributed her tears to the pain, the humiliation.

But she was crying for her own stupidity, for her willingness to fall for such a monster.

He had to pay. It was the only way.

"Tell me you're sorry," he said.

She knew what she was supposed to say, what he expected her to do, but if she was going to exact revenge, this had to go just *so*.

"Over my dead body."

"You should be a good girl," he whispered.

He spoke too quietly. The neighbors needed to hear him if they were going to rouse any suspicion. And she wanted people to hear. She wanted people to notice *for once*. Notice, the way Helen Akers never had, when her respected husband ogled their adopted daughter, watched her undress, slid his hand up her inner thigh under the dinner table. Notice, the way no one ever had since her parents and sisters had been killed in that car wreck. Only she had been spared, but for what? For a lifetime of usurpation?

And because Ian was the reason she was once again spiraling downward, he was the reason she felt so used and abused, he needed to be held accountable for what he was doing, what he'd done, what he'd do over and over again, once he walked away from her for the very last time. He'd been getting away with it long enough.

It was time to stop him.

She'd be the sacrifice necessary to save all his future victims.

"Do you think I don't know what you are?" she screamed at him.

He narrowed his gaze. "Don't speak unless spoken to."

"Do you think I don't know that once you walk out that door, I'll never see you again? Do you think you can get away with it? I'll scream the truth until my throat is raw! You'll never do this to another girl again."

"How dare you."

"Never."

"Do I need to tape your mouth shut?" he roared.

"I'll say what I damn well please."

"Since when?" His jaw set, he climbed between her thighs.

Her eyes widened with fear. She'd never seen him look so angry before.

He tore at the zipper on his pants. "Remember: I paid you in advance."

She raised her chin in defiance, knowing it would lengthen her neck, knowing he wouldn't be able to resist placing his hands just so . . .

Chapter 48

KIRSTEN

A woman in a navy-blue pantsuit, with a graying chin-length bob, rises from her table at the rear of the room when I enter the River Shannon. She looks even more out of place in this bar than I do.

A cute corgi paws at me as I make my way inside. I stop to say hello to the dog, then continue toward the back of the room, to my fellow misfit. I extend a hand. "I'm Kirsten Holloway."

She looks like she just ate a lemon, which tells me she recognizes my last name. She shakes my hand. "Helen Akers."

"Yes, I recognize you from the news." I don't know why she's here, only that Jessica said she'd invited her—*she knows something big,* Jessica had said—so she somehow fits into this strange puzzle.

Helen resumes her seat, and together we wait.

"It's turning colder by the day," I offer.

She purses her lips and nods but doesn't say anything in return. Ohhhkay.

So she's not one for small talk.

"I was sorry to hear about Margaux."

She nods. "Thank you."

I suppose her icy demeanor is no surprise, considering my husband and my son are the focus of her daughter's murder investigation. Together, we sit, silent, save her occasional sniff or clearing of her throat.

I'm absolutely relieved when I see Donna walk in the door and thrilled when, thirty seconds later, Jessica appears.

I close my eyes in a silent prayer of thanks. We're all here. It means we share a common interest and are open to the possibility of working together.

I get right down to business:

"I know we're an unlikely band of soldiers, and at first glance, we don't have all that much in common. But I think we can work together for the better good. Why do we women still find ourselves in Margaux's position? Being victimized, objectified?"

Jessica and Helen share a look.

Donna sighs and begins to shake her head in what I can only describe as predetermined defeat.

But I don't give her a chance to resign just yet. "They—and by *they*, I mean the men in charge—know what they're doing. They're pitting us against each other, distracting us from the real issue at hand. Donna, you're keeping a secret about something that happened between you and my husband."

"At the time, I didn't *know* he was your husband, and Doug wasn't even *my* husband at the time."

"I'm not talking about the affair itself. I'm talking about how it happened."

"It wasn't an affair, but . . ." Donna's head hangs low for a split second before she raises her chin. "It doesn't matter."

"It wasn't your decision, was it?" I ask. "He'd been dabbling in choking. For years, he'd scare the hell out of me every time he did it. I put a stop to it, showed him proof that sometimes it goes too far, and I drew a line. I told him there were people who could tutor him, but you know Ian. He doesn't need anyone to teach him anything. Most of all anything like *that*. Reluctantly, he agreed to stop. And then we had drinks with another couple before a Blackhawks game at the Aquasphere. We didn't go downstairs, just stayed upstairs in the church, but the bar was an unlikely choice. I didn't know why we stopped for drinks so far from the United Center. But he recently admitted he took us there for a reason. I think he'd heard of the Underground, and I think he was doing research of his own. I think he met you there, looking for a coach. I think he hired you to teach him the safe way to do it, and things got out of hand."

Tears rim Donna's eyes, but she shakes her head. "It doesn't matter. I'm okay now."

"But I'm right, aren't I?" I ask. "He lost control with you. He did things you didn't want to do."

Jessica reaches for Donna's hand. "Is that how it happened?"

"He paid me." Donna sniffles. "Who'd believe I drew a line and he crossed it? Who'd believe I didn't want it? Especially now that I'm married to a man who looks an awful lot like him. I mean, honestly, *no one* is going to believe me."

"I'd believe you," Jessica says.

"Me too," Helen says.

I spin toward her and smile. The toughest nut on the tree just cracked.

"Your testimony," Helen says. "It goes to show a pattern."

"Testimony?" Donna says. "Like in court? *No.*"

"My husband makes a habit of losing control and hurting women," I say. "And this time it cost a young woman her life. The jury should hear about it."

"No way," Donna says. "I can't—"

"What if I said he did the same thing to me when we were kids?" I say. "What if I told you I rationalized it the same way you did?"

"The same way I did," Jessica adds. "There's always a way to tell yourself it was your fault."

Donna looks down at the table again.

Jessica and I share a look. "It's important for you to testify," she says to Donna. "Your testimony can solidify who Arlon Judson really is."

Donna snaps back to attention. "Count me out. If I claim Arlon Judson is really Ian Holloway, do you know what happens to my marriage? And it's a flimsy theory. All they have to do to counter is ask me if Arlon Judson was masked at the club, if there is any paperwork tying the name to Ian. I overheard Doug talking about it. It won't *matter* if I testify."

"It's a lot to ask, I know," I say. "We're all protecting ourselves and avoiding each other because that's the way he wants it to be. Our stories alone leave gaps in the truth. But together, we get to the bottom of this. Together, we leave no questions unanswered. For example: I know there is money transferred from our account. If our theory is correct, Helen, your husband received that money as sizable campaign donations. If we can prove that money was demanded, rather than donated, it will help to establish motive. I know you probably don't want your finances examined with everything else going on right now, but—"

"I might have protested yesterday," Helen says. "But something interesting came in the mail." She pulls from her purse a padded envelope. "I don't know who sent it, but it's a letter Margaux wrote months ago, addressed to NBC Chicago, detailing everything she's endured at the hands of my husband."

My heart plummets. That poor girl had been through so much.

"She'd made allegations before. She told a family friend, and I had to pay that friend to keep quiet about it. I assumed she'd lied. But this time . . ." Helen whimpers. "A video file, one Margaux had obviously recorded secretly, was mailed to my home on a thumb drive. It was a full confession of what Richard had done. To Margaux. To the other girls we took in through Catholic Charities over the years. I called Miss Blythe immediately."

Jessica nods. "And that's when I called Kirsten."

"Who sent the video?" Donna asks.

"I don't know. It came with this explanation."

I glance at the small card, which is typewritten: THOUGHT YOU'D FIND THIS INTERESTING.—A CONCERNED THIRD PARTY.

"I've been in contact with many of the girls," Helen says, "and we'll be pressing charges. Everything she always said was true, and I never believed her.

"I've just about had it with men having their way," she continues. "I was once a respected journalist in this town. I resigned to run my husband's campaign, and this is the thanks I get. *This*—" She pumps her fist, still gripping the envelope, into the air. "This is the legacy I'm leaving. Well, no, thank you. My life's work is worth more than the levels my husband has fallen to. And that campaign fund? It's a front. It launders his winnings and losses, and I can prove that, too. I know everywhere those funds go. A good chunk of which went back to Margaux, to the trust Richard borrowed from to bet on that damn horse."

"Hallelujah," Jessica whispers.

"The alderman can't get away with what he did to Margaux," I say. "And neither can Ian."

"He's not counting on our sticking together," Jessica says. "He's counting on our tiptoeing around each other. So instead of turning our claws on each other, we can stand united."

Donna meets my gaze and offers a weak nod.

"Sounds satisfying, doesn't it?" I ask.

"I still have media connections," Helen says. "People who will help us tell our story."

Jessica puts her hand out, hovering palm down. "Justice for Margaux."

I place my hand in the center of the table, too.
Then Helen.
And finally, Donna joins us. "For women everywhere."
Together, I don't see how we can lose.

THEN

MARGAUX

When he was finished, he collapsed atop her.

Their bodies still joined, her arms and legs still tethered—numb, aching, bruising.

He kissed her softly on the neck, where so recently he'd squeezed until she could barely breathe.

He loosened the ropes.

She sighed in relief as blood flow returned to her aching arms and legs. Her fingertips tingled.

Tears curbed around her ears.

"The note you were writing . . . It's over, isn't it? We're done?"

He nodded. "We have to be. I shouldn't have let it come this far." He stood and retrieved his pants from where he'd flung them.

"I was going to have your baby."

"It's just as well you aborted it." He stepped into his trousers and zipped up. "Clean break, all right? Let's make it like I was never here. You'll recover. You all do."

"You said I was special. That you loved me. You carved my skin with your initials."

"The funny thing is, Margaux, that you *are* special and I *did* love you." He shoved an arm into his shirt. "But it has to be over now."

"It wasn't over until you had your way one last time."

"Call it saying goodbye." While his words sent a message she might have appreciated, the smirk on his face sent another—it was a taunting, boastful sneer, and it told her she'd fallen into one last trap.

"What about the things you promised me? Our forever plans? My tuition?"

"Sorry, babe. I can't make it happen."

"You think you're so smart," she said. "So sly. You don't think you've been making it happen for months now?" One corner of her lips turned up in a satisfied grin, but half a breath later, the smile again dissipated, and she coughed over tears.

The truth hit him like a bolt of lightning. "You! You're behind it? You and Akers—you knew he was blackmailing me?"

"Does that make you angry, Mr. Holloway? That I'd dare to take charge and secure my own future? What choice did I have?"

"I'll expose you."

"Not without exposing yourself, you won't. How does it feel to be used the way you used me?"

He came at her then, and took her by the throat.

He squeezed. Squeezed harder. Squeezed harder still.

"Do it," she eked out. "End it all right here. It's the only way you'll truly be rid of me."

Chapter 49

JESSICA

I'm in the middle of a chick flick and greasy Chinese when my doorbell rings.

I glance at the clock. Too early to be Decker.

I'm not expecting anyone, but considering what happened the last time I ignored an unannounced visitor, I go to my intercom. "Yeah?"

"Miss Blythe? Do you have a minute? It's Patrick Holloway."

For a moment, I don't do or say anything.

A million scenarios dart through my mind. Maybe we've got it wrong. Maybe Patrick's DNA was a close match for a good reason. Maybe it wasn't Ian at all.

"If you don't want me to come up," he says, "we can meet at the River, or something. I just thought you deserved an explanation."

"I'll be right down." I throw on a pair of leggings and toss one of Decker's flannels over my tank top. I cover my hair with a backward Sox hat and shove my feet into Uggs.

When I open the door at the street level, Patrick is seated on the front stoop. He's built like his father—with a muscled frame. When he looks over his shoulder, however, and smiles, I see shades of his mother. He stands and extends a hand. "Thanks for seeing me."

I don't doubt he'll do well in a courtroom someday. His easy demeanor, and casual good looks, will serve him well in front of a jury.

"C'mon," I say. "Let's get a drink."

We begin to walk toward my favorite neighborhood bar.

His hands are deep in the pockets of his coat. Finally, he breaks the silence. "You've been a great source of support for my mom."

"Your mother is stronger than you think she is."

"Yeah, I suppose that's true." For a few measures, he doesn't say anything. Then suddenly: "I'll bet you're wondering why I came to see you that day."

"I've wondered."

He nodded. "About six months ago, my mother had what the doctors called an episode—she became hysterical for seemingly no reason. Mom said it was because my sister had just moved out, and she had trouble dealing with an empty house. My sister didn't buy it. She was convinced something else had set Mom off—that our father was too flirty with a neighborhood woman at a party—and Quinn thought our father may have taken things too far. I couldn't see it, but then I borrowed his car one day and found a log of addresses in his GPS. He'd been to the Aquasphere. *A lot.* He'd been all over Bucktown, to an apartment near Leavitt and Webster."

"Margaux's place."

"And your address was in his GPS, too. When I followed up on Margaux, she said she was involved with a guy named Arlon Judson. I thought that was the end of it. And I thought for sure you'd deny knowing my father, too."

"Yeah. But I would've recognized the last name. I already knew your mother at that point."

"I guess you did."

We enter the bar, which is slow tonight.

Patrick buys me a beer.

"Are you going to testify against my father?"

"If they call me, yes."

He nods and takes a sip of his beer.

It's my turn to ask a question: "Do you think your father killed her?"

"Little by little, until she couldn't take it anymore. One way or another, he's responsible. Take my father out of the equation, and Margaux Stritch is still alive."

"I have to agree."

"The day I was arrested, I told Doug about meeting Margaux. I told him about why I went to your place, too. But I couldn't say it in front of my mom. I feel like such an asshole. There I was, thinking she was too frail to hear it all, and she's the one who forced the truth to come out."

"She's quite a lady. You should tell her you appreciate her."

He downs the rest of his drink. "You okay to head back on your own, or . . . ?"

"Yeah, I'll be all right."

"Thanks for being there for my mother."

"I think she's there for me as much as I am for her."

"One more thing. I notice you wear a ruby necklace." He pulls a small box from his pocket. "I think this was probably supposed to be yours."

I open the box. Margaux's ruby ring stares up at me.

"I saw your necklace the day I was arrested, and I found this in the glove box of my dad's car. He probably bought it for you, and after all you've been through, I think you should have it."

"Patrick." I look up from the ring. "This was Margaux's. The police have been looking for it."

THEN

Margaux

She went limp, and instantly, he released his hold on her neck.

"Margaux?"

She didn't answer.

"Margaux! Fuck!" He screamed under his breath. "What the fuck did I do?"

He pressed two fingers to her wrist. "Thank God. A pulse."

Quickly, he finished dressing, grabbed the roses and the wine, and left.

Like he'd never been there.

Chapter 50

KIRSTEN

"Doug says I should take the plea," Ian says. "Manslaughter."

"Maybe you should," I say.

"And open myself up to a wrongful death suit?" Ian says. "Hell no."

"I hate to tell you this, but you're probably looking at one of those, anyway."

"I'll take my chances."

"Entirely up to you."

"Not really," he says. "This involves you, too."

"I want a divorce," I remind him.

"What? This again?" Ian turns toward me. "If we divorce now, they can call you as a witness."

"Let them call me! I don't know anything, anyway! If we don't divorce now," I explain, "a civil suit can take away everything we own, and we have children and expenses, and I'm entitled to my half. You can lose your half, or spend it all on other women or legal fees if you want. I'm done."

"Kirstie." Ian looks dumbfounded, as if he didn't know this was coming.

"Let's walk through the evidence against you, shall we?" I pour myself a glass of chardonnay. "We have the embryo—yours. We have the handwriting on the suicide note—also yours. We have fingerprints on the cash on the counter—ditto. Blood on your shirt, which you tried to conceal—is that Margaux's, too? Your prints on a knife in her kitchen. A cut on her cheek with a blade similar to the one in said knife. Underwear in your pocket—Margaux's. Money gone from our accounts. By. The. Boatload. We have a note dropped to a neighbor hinting that Margaux knew something bad was going to happen to her. Another neighbor witnessing an argument between you two. Pictures on flash drives. Your cousin's wife and a headstrong firefighter who figured you out, and they're all going to testify against you. Am I missing anything else? The state's attorneys don't *need* to call me, because they can call any of these women to testify as to your choking fetish."

"We have a medical expert who says the bruising on her neck occurred at least an hour before death. His testimony proves suicide."

"And the state's medical expert disputes that."

"And a specialist who can testify the chair tipped over in accordance with suicide—studies about her body weight, and the way the chair would have fallen are consistent with what they found at Margaux's apartment."

"And I'm sure the state can find someone who says the scene was staged. You're flipping a coin, Ian. Take the plea."

"But she was alive when I left. She had a pulse. She'd passed out, but she was breathing. Even if she somehow died after I left, I'd take the plea. But she was *hanging*. I didn't hang her. I didn't stage the chair or sign the note."

"But you were there. A plea's not a bad idea."

"The sexual nature of this case, Kirstie, the felony homicide . . . if I take the plea, I'm disbarred," Ian says. "It's called moral turpitude. It's an immediate disbarment."

"Well, how's that for poetic justice?" I sip my wine. "Both of us, starting over at age forty."

"We're not getting divorced," Ian says.

"I already have the papers drawn up." I pull them from the drawer where I stashed them earlier. "Doug gave me the name of a good lawyer, so—"

"But we can beat a civil case. The evidence is highly circumstantial."

"Yeah. But where are you going to find a jury to acquit? You're the most hated man in Chicago right now. Ask Doug: if you go to trial, they're going to convict."

"Not if we establish doubt. We have to play the Patrick card to establish doubt. I know we don't want to, Kirstie, but—"

"Stop." I close my eyes and gather every breath of patience I can find. "Sign the papers. I want sixty-five percent of everything. My lawyer tells me this is a textbook maintenance case, but I don't have confidence in your ability to pay me maintenance. Buy me out of the firm, and as part of the settlement on the business front, I want sole ownership of Barrett Enterprises."

"Barrett?" Ian begins to flip through the terms of the divorce.

I grin. "I have a good lawyer. He found a lot of assets I didn't know about. You established a company in Nevada. Very tricky. You established it in my name—my maiden name. Trickier still. Since it's already mine, I want it. Along with the house in Tahoe, which of course I'm going to sell. But the firm is marital property," I tell him. "And I'm entitled to a percentage of your shares. I want two point five million."

"Two point five." Ian chuckles. "You're out of your mind."

"I'm actually entitled to three. Doug sent the net worth of the practice, and together, he and my lawyer find two point five more than fair, considering I'll be footing the bill for the rest of Quinn's studies."

"Doug wouldn't do that."

"Maybe you shouldn't have taken liberties with his wife. Just saying." I toss a pen to the half ream of paper on the table in front of my soon-to-be ex-husband.

"Buy something nice for yourself," he says as he signs.

"I will."

I'm thinking of heading to Have a Heart Rescue . . . for a husky pup.

THEN

Margaux

She came to with a gasp and a headache that just wouldn't quit.

And her throat hurt, inside and out.

The rope still dangled from the rafters above.

The underwear he'd torn from her body still lay, discarded, on the floor.

And, adding insult to injury, the wine and roses were gone, but the pile of cash remained.

Maybe he thought she was dead. And he left her.

He'd gotten his way after all. The joke was still on her.

But the day wasn't over yet.

Margaux trod past the rope, to the bathroom.

A mark was already forming on her neck.

He'd been extra rough with her. She wondered . . . would things have been different had he known she still carried his child? Had he wanted the child, would he have been loving and gentle with her?

She walked back to the scene, which he'd left untouched, then circled around to the kitchen. She fixed her gaze on the note he'd been writing when she walked in.

Well. It just about said it all, didn't it?

I'M SORRY. I JUST CAN'T DO THIS ANYMORE.

She picked up the pencil and began to sign her name. Halfway through the *M*, she stopped. Was she being silly and dramatic about this whole thing?

She pressed the pencil back to the *M* and continued to write: *M-A . . .*

She paused again, brought a fist to her lips, and sobbed. She then pressed the tip of the pencil back to the paper, about to scrawl an *R*, but thought better of it and formed a *G*. He should know he was the reason she was doing what she was about to do, and no one but he called her Maggie.

But should she do it at all?

There were plenty of reasons to go through with it, but were there any reasons not to?

What did she have to live for?

Everything that mattered was gone.

She wrote another *G*, then paused.

Not everything. There was her baby.

But what kind of life could she provide for a child? She looked around the apartment. Where would she even *put* a child in this place?

And then there was the heart of the matter: no matter how or where the child grew up, he'd have *her* as a mother. A few hours ago, she'd intended to terminate the pregnancy. She was an unemployed practitioner of deviant acts in the sack. A slut, as Ian often reminded her. A pushover. She was an orphan. Friendless. Put here on this earth to be used by even the man who'd adopted her years ago.

She brought a fingertip to the raised flesh on her right breast, where Ian had carved his fake initials. Branded a fool.

She finished the signature with a flourish. Signed *Maggie*.

Then she wrote another note to her neighbor downstairs: *If anything happens to me, tell them it wasn't an accident.*

She picked up the panties Ian had torn from her body and tossed them into the trash. She threw on a dress and took the trash outside. At the last second, she hurled the bag over the fence, and it landed in a neighboring dumpster. That way, if the authorities found it, it would look like someone had deliberately tried to hide it. On her way back up to her apartment, she slipped the note under the neighbor's door.

She then climbed the stairs and entered her apartment for the last time. She didn't bother to lock the door behind her. She'd save them the trouble of taking an ax to it.

She pulled off the dress, so they'd find her in the nightie Ian bought for her, and reapplied her lipstick.

One last look in the mirror. She touched the scar on her cheek.

She thought of her mother, her father. Her sisters, Chelsey and Kendall.

"I'm coming home," she whispered a moment before slashing at the scar with the knife Ian had used to cut the foil from a bottle of wine he'd never opened.

The end of the rope that used to bind her limbs became a loop, and she placed it around her neck.

They'd suspect him, considering the evidence:

His handwriting on the suicide note.

The name she'd signed on it.

And there were witnesses, people who saw them together at Aquasphere, and the concerned third party. The neighbor downstairs, who could testify to hearing her screams. Her friend, the recently married Donna Fordham.

There was the crust of his ejaculate on her inner thighs.

His baby in her uterus.

Marks on her neck that surely could be matched to his fingers, his thumbs.

And his fingerprints on the knife she'd just used to slash at her cheek.

He'd go down for this.

The police were smart. They'd find him.

The moment she stepped off the chair, she caught sight of a red brassiere flung to the corner of the room in the midst of his passion, but it was too late to pick it up.

The world went black.

Chapter 51

KIRSTEN

Helen's article—Justice for Margaux—went to print this morning on the front page of the *Trib*, the very morning arguments closed in the *State of Illinois v. Ian Holloway*.

The alderman is being arraigned down the hall, but Helen isn't present in his courtroom. The charges against him range from arson—one of his cronies will testify to torching the Aquasphere to conceal the alderman's history there—to child molestation to extortion.

Once Helen and I started working together, we confirmed that the twenty grand per month had been deposited into the alderman's campaign fund. From there, it was transferred into various accounts—one of which was established in Margaux's name. It seems he was reimbursing Margaux's tuition fund all along.

Helen and Richard Akers offered to return the money to me, but I opted for another, more philanthropic recourse. "The money will go to the Margaux Stritch memorial scholarship," I tell Ian. We're in a conference room at the courthouse, awaiting the jury's decision, and although our divorce was uncontested and final last week, I'm here anyway. I'm not here for him; rather, I'm here to ensure justice is served.

Furthermore, this could very well be the last time we speak without Big Brother listening in on the line.

"I might need the money Akers extorted for an appeal," Ian says.

I shrug. "Oh, well. I think it's put to better use this way. You have thirty-five percent of our marital estate, should you need an appeal."

"Did you take a pill this morning?"

"Why?" I pull my feet up under me and lean back in the chair I'm occupying and flip through my Pinterest boards on my phone.

"Why? Because Quinn tells you she's leaving for school early, and you have a psychotic episode. I could be put away for a good, long time, and you're about to take a nap. What gives?"

"First of all, my *episode*? It wasn't about Quinn going to college. I lost my mind because I'd learned a few things I didn't care to know. See, one morning the previous week, a package arrived at the house. Enclosed was a flash drive."

"Oh, Christ. You're not actually hinging this belief on the alderman's accusation—"

"Do you want to talk? Or do you want me to explain? You can't have it both ways."

Ian throws his hands in the air.

I continue, "I didn't plug in the drive. I wasn't ready to face it. I didn't see what was on it until I rediscovered it in your *Hustler* after Margaux died. But I started following you and learned you had a girlfriend. One night, I followed you into a bad neighborhood. You called her a whore, and you fucked her up against a wall—very violently."

Ian looks pale. "You're mistaken." He fiddles with the band on his watch. "It couldn't have been me."

"It brought back memories of Oak Street Beach, what you did to me there, and I couldn't sleep that night. I didn't know what to do, and then, at the farmers market, it all crashed down on me. There I was, pretending everything was fine, and Fiona was babbling about everything coming to an end, and I lost it. My life was a lie."

"You don't know what you saw."

"And then you suggested a move to the country. To the Secret Garden. Very aptly named home, don't you think, considering the multitude of secrets you were keeping? But the move, I've recently figured out, wasn't really to give me space or a fresh start. It was because your cousin decided to marry a girl you'd been involved with, and they were living down the street in Evanston. You needed to distance me from her because you assumed she'd tell me everything. And you know what? She did anyway. It just took Margaux's death to get her talking."

"You can't believe everything—"

"It wasn't until I started hearing the name of your archrival from the past—Jack Wyatt—that I realized this thing was bigger than you and some young girl you'd met and hooked unaware. It wasn't about the number of other women you'd flirted with over the years and even screwed when you thought I wasn't looking—yes, I suspected it was happening all along."

"I'm sorry." He hangs his head. "But it's all in the past."

"But if you want to know the last straw, it was when I saw her face on the news. Margaux was dead, and even if you didn't kill her, it was your fault. I started thinking about all the other women you'd ruined, all the women who were fragments of what they used to be . . . because of *you*. I knew then and there: you deserved to pay. But I had to be patient about it. Had to play my cards close to my chest. You had to keep thinking I was clueless if I was going to hem you in so tightly you wouldn't be able to wiggle out of it."

"Kirstie, I love you."

"You're still stuck in a world where you have to prove your strength because you're not quite good enough for first place. Stuck in a world where you take a girl when she's not ready instead of taking your time because what if she's never ready? Stuck in a world where you're just a scared kid staring at a positive pregnancy test."

"You're exaggerating things." He flips his watch around his wrist again.

"And then, when I call you on it, you tell me I'm imagining things. You tell me I need a sedative. You lie through your teeth, and you want to know how I know that? Every time you tell a lie, you play with the band of your watch."

He snaps his hand away.

Doug peeks in. "Verdict."

"Do you feel better now?" I ask. "Knowing I know everything? Knowing you're not nearly as mysterious as you seem to think you are?"

"Kirstie?" He reaches for me, but I don't fold. "You can't believe I'd actually kill someone. Could you?"

"It doesn't matter if you did it or not. You deserve whatever punishment they give you."

I walk back into the courtroom and slip into a row in the back. We form a chain, grasping hands: Donna, me, Jessica, and standing in for Margaux, Helen.

"All rise." We stand as a united front.

Quinn and Patrick didn't come, and it's just as well.

Not a single jury member looks at my ex-husband as they file in.

But we, the four of us, those he'd hurt and stolen dignity from, stare him down when he looks at us over his shoulder.

His one fatal flaw: he never dreamed we'd band together.

He thought what he could offer us was more than what we'd offer each other.

The verdict: guilty.

The women on either side of me squeeze my hands.

I squeeze back.

Chapter 52

KIRSTEN

"If I have to take a few years off before continuing my education," Quinn says via FaceTime, "I don't mind."

"Absolutely not." I'm walking Brady, my new husky pup, who's growing way too fast for his own good, through the woods today.

"Are you honestly going to stay in that big, empty house?"

"It's growing on me."

"But that house was Dad's decision."

"I'm renovating."

"That must cost a lot, too. I want you to be able to go Door County, Mom. I want you to be able to do something for you, after all you've been through."

"I'm doing plenty for me. Don't worry about your tuition," I tell her. "Your father and I had saved quite a bit, you know, and one of the reasons he agreed to a quick split was to protect our assets for your education."

"That's your money, and you have far less earning power left than I do."

"Thanks, kid. But I'm not exactly ancient, you know."

And I know I came away with slightly more than my fair share of the nest egg. When Ian's time is served, he'll be searching for a new career. He'll start from ground zero in planning for his retirement, too.

It's only fair. I have to start there, and I *didn't* commit a crime of moral turpitude. All I did was raise good people and believe in the man who helped me conceive them.

"Mom?" My daughter looks really sad. "Why did he do this? To all of us?"

Someday, maybe, I'll tell my daughter it was all an accident, that Ian hadn't meant for things to get out of hand. Or maybe I'll tell her the truth. That sometimes, infidelity is murder. Other times, it may as well be suicide. In the case of her father, it was both.

But for now, I say, "Someday, I hope we *all* understand why, Quinn. It's going to take us a long time to heal, but it'll happen."

"You know, I think it's a good thing. For you. You get to start over."

"I do."

"And speaking of starting over . . . see that cute guy there? On the bench?" She flips her camera around to afford me a view of a kid in a leather bomber jacket. "We're going out tonight."

"Very cute, Miss Holloway."

"Speaking of . . . Patrick and I were talking, and we want to change our last name."

Of all the things I expected my children to do in the aftermath of this mess, this one practically floors me. "Really? Do you think that's fair to your father? To your *grandparents*?"

"Do you think he cared about whether he was being fair to us? I don't want Holloway on my diploma. I just don't. And lots of people are abandoning their last names when they get married now, anyway. Women *and* men. They create a new last name for themselves. Like a combination of their names, or a brand-new name altogether."

"Really? People do that?"

"Yeah. It's more feminist that way. Equal. I mean, why should we have to abandon our identities simply because we're women? Think about it. It very naturally puts us in a position of inferiority. We succumb to that which the almighty male demands, even down to our names."

"Okay. It's up to you and your brother. You're of legal age. You don't need my permission, or your father's, but you have my blessing."

"Thank you."

"So what's your new name going to be? Quinn Thunderstorm? Quinn Awesomeness?"

"Actually, we're thinking . . . Barrett."

My maiden name. "Oh. I'd love that."

"Patrick already has the paperwork prepped, but we thought we should talk to you about it first."

"You have my blessing."

"Duh." She rolls her eyes. "We're wondering if you want to do it, too."

"I already have." It feels strange to be Kirstie Barrett again. But good. "I did it just after the divorce. I didn't want to influence you kids, so—"

"Mom, all you've ever done is influence us."

"Well, I did my best with what I had to work with. For good or bad, you got it all."

"He lied to you throughout your entire marriage."

"I know."

"Dad was pointing his finger even at *Patrick* to establish doubt. How could Dad agree to that?"

"I don't know."

"Mom? I love you."

"Aww, Quinn. I love you, too."

"Kiss, kiss," she says. "Love, love."

I walk Brady farther down the path. When we round a bend, I freeze.

Brady inexplicably doesn't make a sound. I crouch to keep him quiet and close.

Not twenty feet in front of us, an enormous doe is standing like a statue on the path.

I look to her right hind leg and see a scarred patch of hair.

We stare at each other, eye to eye.

"She's okay," I say to my dog. "She survived the winter."

The deer blinks.

"You know what? I did, too."

Brady slurps his pink tongue against my cheek.

"I love you," I say to my dog.

He howls in return, and I swear it sounds like he's telling me he loves me, too.

The deer darts off and disappears into the woods.

Chapter 53

JESSICA

I approach a table for two in the rear corner of a restaurant Kirsten suggested. It's in a neighborhood pushing the city limits, and I had to take two trains to get here, but because she's always come to me before, I can brave the burbs just this once, even in the midst of a messy February thaw.

There's a wintry mix of rain and sleet today, but Kirsten, who stands and waves the second I enter the place, looks no worse for the wear. Her hair is drawn into a high, sleek ponytail, and her knee-high, heeled leather boots don't show a single sign of wear and tear. In jeans and a fitted sweater, she looks as comfortable as I've ever seen her, despite the fact that over the past few months, her life has been torn to pieces and picked through like a yard sale. And after more than twenty years, her marriage has come to an end.

I don't know what gives, why she'd want to see me now, when we haven't spoken since the verdict.

But her smile is warm and as inviting as her open arms. "Jess, you look great. How are you?" She offers me a friendly hug.

"I'm back to rushing the elderly to hospitals, getting cats out of trees," I tell her. "You know. Usual calls."

"And the cop?"

I feel my cheeks redden with the mention of Detective Third Grade Lieutenant KJ Decker, who helped me nab the perpetrator who stole my innocence at the age of thirteen. "We'll wait and see. I'm actually applying to the force, so there's a chance we could work together."

"He's good to you?"

"He challenges me."

She sits, so I sit.

"I like a nice balance of power," she tells me. "What you do, Jessica, it's important. Prestigious."

"Thank you."

"I never had a career."

"I know."

"I have my kids, though."

"That's important, too, what you've done. It means something to raise good people."

"I wish everyone thought so." She tilts her head to one side and smiles, her gaze drifting off into the distance. "As crazy as it sounds, I'm not sorry my marriage ended this way."

"How are Quinn and Patrick holding up?"

"It's strange to say, but I think we're all okay. We're all pursuing phase two." Her smile is brighter, and more relaxed, than I've ever seen it. "That's what Quinn calls it."

"Good." I don't know what else to say. I wonder why I'm here. As pleasant as I find Kirsten Holloway, we have very little in common. And given my issues with commitment, not to mention the common thread between us being a man we once shared, a bubble of panic bursts in my nerves. It's awkward. Does she expect to do this often? Meet for lunch and exchange small talk?

I'm so not that girl.

She opens a menu. "Let's have martinis. Are you on call tonight? Can you celebrate a little?"

"I can have a drink. What are we celebrating?"

"Freedom? The end of an era?" She shrugs. "Phase two."

"So. What are you doing with phase two of your life?" I ask. "Dating anyone?"

"God, no." She closes her menu. "Honey, I've been someone's wife or girlfriend—Ian's, as a matter of fact—since Pearl Jam was all the rage." She turns to the approaching waiter. "Cosmo, please."

"Two," I confirm.

"I have absolutely no desire to jump back into all that mess again. It's time to concentrate on me," she says. "I'm helping Donna start a party-planning business, and I'm thinking of going to design school. I'm having so much fun renovating my home, and I was always artsy in high school."

"Well, if I ever own a home, I'll give you a call to help me decorate it."

"That'll be fun. Speaking of fun, I got a dog," she says. "At Have a Heart Rescue downtown. A Siberian husky. He talks, can you believe it? He howls and it sounds like words. Says *I love you.*"

I raise a brow in amusement.

"I call him Brady. I take a lot of pictures of him." She opens her shoulder bag.

I brace myself for the dozens of pictures of the pup I expect her to pull out of her purse. I'm going to have smile, nod, and say things like *aww* and *so cute!*

Instead, she produces a flash drive. "I want you to have this."

Something like discomfort kicks up in my gut.

She drops the flash drive into my palm.

In a rush, pieces fall into place, and suddenly, the Tetris game we've been sifting through with Ian Holloway has far fewer gaps.

I study her.

"You knew," I say.

"What's that?"

"You knew I was having an affair with Ian."

She returns my stare, a small not-really smile playing on her lips.

"That day at the station," I continue, "you weren't there coinciden-tally. You were looking for me."

"I wasn't looking for you," she says.

"But you knew who I was."

"I'd seen you once before, yes."

I look at the drive in my hand. "Is this what I think it is?"

"It came in the mail right after she died. Patrick found it on the doorstep, and as a matter of fact, Ian never even knew about it. There was a note enclosed, requesting more cash. The pictures aren't bad. Just you and my husband getting to know each other, but out of respect, I think you should have it. I didn't give it to Decker for obvious reasons."

The drinks couldn't have arrived at a better time. I take a healthy sip while my companion thanks the waiter and assures him he's doing a great job.

"There was only one night Jack—Ian—was at my place, and he never stayed the night."

"Is that right?"

"Were you there that night? Did you take these pictures?"

The shake of her head is nearly imperceptible. "I never said I took the pictures. I said they came in the mail. That's a very important dis-tinction. And believe me, the first time I saw the pictures of Margaux and Ian, I almost died inside. It was definitely a shock."

"Okay. So you didn't take *those* pictures. Did you take *these*?"

She reaches for my hand across the table.

Reluctantly, I take hers.

"I knew all along what my husband was. But no, I didn't follow you or photograph you. I wouldn't invade your privacy like that. If you want to know who Mr. Akers hired, you might want to ask him."

"You know, if you'd told me that day that my boyfriend was actually your husband, I wouldn't have continued to see him. You should've told me."

"I should have."

"He could have *killed* me."

"Oh, I doubt that. He's awful, for sure. But what happened with Margaux wasn't calculated. If it happened the way the DA says it did, it happened without ill intent, without forethought. It was an accident resulting from Ian's recklessness."

I consider this, and it's logical, but one thing haunts me: "He had his hands around my neck that night. It could have *accidentally* happened to me." The night he came over unannounced, he was on me in an instant, and the next I knew, I was decking him.

"Why did you stay with him?" I ask.

"When you spend your life with someone, it's hard not to rationalize. It's hard to admit when something is over. But however it happens, whenever it happens, doesn't matter. It only matters that it happens."

She clinks her glass into mine.

"To bygones."

THEN

The Third Party

Margaux approaches her building in knee-high, square-heeled brown boots and a vintage-looking minidress in a geometric pattern of oranges and blues. Her glasses are dark—no rose-colored lenses today—completely shielding her eyes from the sun, and I can guess why.

She was scheduled to terminate her pregnancy today.

When she sees me, waiting in the center of her steps, she nearly stops in her tracks. "What are you doing here?"

"I came to see how you were doing."

"How do you think I'm doing?" She holds up her left hand to prove she no longer wears the ring.

That's good. "Do you need anything?"

She looks at me for a second, perhaps wondering if she should trust me. Nothing has gone as she's planned since the day our paths first crossed.

"I want to hate you," Margaux said. "I keep thinking about how much easier it would be if I could just *hate* you."

"That's your decision. I just wanted to know if you needed anything."

"But *why?*" she asks. "Why would you assume, if I need anything, I'd turn to you? It's all happened just as you wanted it to, so why would you want to help me?"

"Because it's the right thing to do."

Finally, she sighs and says, "Come in."

I follow her into the building, then up the stairs to her loft. Once beyond her door, she gives in to the tears I'd guess she's been keeping at bay since she left the clinic. They come in like a tidal wave and nearly knock her off balance.

I catch her under the elbow and walk her to the closest chair.

"I couldn't do it," she says.

I nod. Understandable.

"He told me to charge it," she says. "He wanted to see the name of the clinic on his statement so that he'd know I did it."

"That sounds like something he'd do."

"But I couldn't go through with the abortion."

"I'm not surprised."

"You're not upset with me?"

"There's no putting this behind us now—babies are permanent like that—but we'll find a way. We, as a species, always do."

"Easy for you to say. You have an answer for everything." She rips a tissue from a nearby box. "How did you guess exactly what would happen?"

I take a seat on the cocktail table in front of her. "I'm not some kind of prophet. I didn't guess at what would come to pass. This isn't complicated; this isn't unique; this isn't special. It just happens, Margaux."

She swallows over a sob.

I pat her shoulder. "I know what's ahead of you because I was in your shoes half a lifetime ago. My whole life spread out like a blank canvas, and suddenly, it wasn't mine to paint anymore. But listen to me."

Margaux buries her face in her hands.

"Listen. I need you to do what he won't. Make a priority out of you, however impossible a feat it may seem. It's important. You're worth it. Remember you're worth it even when your days are the darkest."

She peeks at me through her fingers. "I don't know how to do that."

"There was one day I thought I'd never see the sun again," I say. "He left a bruise on my neck. You know how it happens when he's particularly revved up, and he was wild, and I felt—I can't believe I'm going to say this, but I felt like he might actually snap my windpipe, and I was excited with the prospect of being his first. The first body he'd taken, the first life he'd snuff out. I felt *needed* in that moment. Wanted, special, powerful. But the moment it was over, and he was back out the door, I was empty again. I felt used, and I hated him for it. May God forgive me, but I considered tying a knot around my neck and hanging. I wondered if the police would see the marks he'd left on my neck and suspect him of murder . . . a murder staged to look like suicide. Can you imagine anything so satisfying as watching him go down for something as irrevocable as murder? And knowing he'd finally pay the ultimate price? Taking his freedom away the way he stole yours the moment you created life together . . . a blissful thought, isn't it?"

She's not crying anymore, but she's staring in wide-eyed horror at me.

"I don't know why the thought entered my head back then," I say. "And I don't know why I didn't do it. I didn't have anyone to turn to. No one to help me. But somehow, I carried on. And the truth of the matter is, Margaux, that even if you feel all alone, even when you're thinking your family is gone, and the Akerses have wronged you and can't be trusted . . . At those times, I want you to remember that you *do* have someone. You have *me*. And if ever you're feeling the way I felt that night, I want you to call me. I'll come. No matter what time, no matter the place. I'll be there for you. He's already on to the next girl. Let it be done."

Margaux, more tears welling in her eyes, nods. "Why'd you consider taking your own life? Why not take his?"

"There were times I did consider it."

"There had to be a way . . . somehow you'd get away with it."

"No. They always suspect the significant other, you know," I whisper.

"Yes, Kirstie," she says. "They do."

"He'll come with wine and roses," I say. "He thinks he can make this right and have you whenever he wants you. You can't let him have his way."

"Of all the ways he imagined it," she says, "it won't be the way he wants."

Lightning flashes in the sky.

Margaux leans to me and kisses my cheek. "Try to get some sleep tonight."

"You'll be all right?"

"He'll never get his way again," Margaux whispers. "I promise you."

Epilogue

Kirsten

I order another round of cosmos. "So you knew about the blackmail?" Jessica asks.

"I did," I admit. "I found a demand before we left Evanston. He'd been seeing Margaux a month or two by then, and I'd already suspected a few other affairs. I had a breakdown, and Ian suggested we move. A fresh start. And it was, in a sense. I started paying attention after that. I took it upon myself to meet Margaux. We started comparing notes."

"And you knew your husband was sleeping with her all along?"

"I did. But the funny thing about Margaux: she was flawed, beautiful, and complex, but wonderful. It wasn't supposed to go this way. She'd decided to keep her baby, and I assured her we'd find a way to make it work. She wasn't supposed to give up. She wasn't supposed to end it like that. We were going to find a way . . ."

"It was your idea," Jessica says. "The money in the account for Margaux, the way the alderman was repaying what he lost."

"We had to find a way," I explain and catch a tear on my fingertip. "She was *brilliant*. So smart. So deserving, especially after all she'd been through. She deserved to go to law school, to realize her dreams. I'd be damned if Ian stole her future the way he stole mine. She wasn't supposed to give up."

"You were friends."

"I don't really know how to classify it," I say, just as I said the first time Jessica and I talked about it.

"She'll always be part of my life," Jessica says. "A milestone. Even though she never knew who I was."

"She would've liked you, I think."

We finish our cosmos.

I pay the bill.

"Let's do this again," she suggests as we exit.

"I'd like that."

She hugs me and takes a step toward the east, braving the wind whipping in off the lake.

She knows what I did.

She knows I couldn't have done it without her.

She knows Ian Holloway deserved everything he got.

We share a secret.

We share a smile.

I walk on.

ACKNOWLEDGMENTS

From the moment of inception, this novel has been something special. Never before has a novel so consumed me to the point of obsession. To my agent, Andrea Somberg of Harvey Klinger, and my husband: thanks for having the conversation, and brava to you for making this happen. To Jodi Warshaw, Caitlin Alexander, and the rest of the team at Lake Union: thank you for believing in my vision, skewed as it was in that first, hurried draft. Your patience and guidance are, as always, immensely appreciated. *Third Party* has truly been a collaborative effort, and this book wouldn't have grown without you.

One of the messages I hoped to convey with this book is that women are powerful. I've grown tired of our portrayal as catty beings always at one another's throats. I figured it was high time we depict women as strong, caring individuals with concrete principles. In short, I wanted to do something we rarely are availed the opportunity to do in fiction: I wanted to tell the truth.

Secondly, from my humble beginnings as a stay-at-home mother to two incredibly strong, talented, and vehemently feminist girls, I understand the sacrifice of one's own ambitions for the sake of the greater good. It's disheartening that even in today's climate, we're put on the defensive upon the failing of a marriage. Too many women stay in bad situations out of fear of poverty and loneliness, or due to lack of self-worth. I want to assure women that what we do, who we are, and the people we're raising are eminently important. Things need to change. Feminism is social, economic, and political equality for all. Pretty basic and easy to grasp, yes? So why are women left to choose between financial comfort and happiness? We're doing more than changing diapers and wiping noses. We are raising good people. Keep on, sisters.

To my dear friends, the Coverts: as always, thanks for the example of healthy. Your children (Margaret, Jonathan, and Caroline) are proof of all I've said above. Thanks again to Marsh and Dad-man for being there for me always.

To my mama, who is truly self-made: your perseverance taught me self-reliance. Love, love, love to you.

To Jessica Helen and Kynslee Jane, I welcome you to our family, and I thank you for lending your names to this tale. And to my brother Ken, who brought Jess and my new niece into my inner circle: while I couldn't fulfill your dreams to appear as a dirty cop on the pages herein, I thank you for lending your initials to one of my favorite fictional detectives to date. Dear readers, KJ is named for my little brother. And he really is badass.

To my sisters and cousins, there is a little bit of all of you in every heroine I write. Have fun figuring out which of you would just as soon deck a guy as kiss him. (Um, yes, Kristin. It's you.)

My girls, Samantha Mary Kristin and Madelaine Josephine Michelle: you have taught me more than I will ever teach you. For the sake of your fortitude, I pulled you with me toward a better life when I followed that doe down Harvey Avenue. Together, we've stood tall and strong. Maybe we ate too much peanut butter and "girl" cheese (why isn't there boy cheese?) in those lean years, but I wouldn't change a thing—the world is spinning in the palm of my hand because of you.

And finally, to my hunky husband, who is, as always, solid proof that love at first sight exists. He stared at the Siberian husky across a crowded room, and the pup stared back. A lock of gazes, a smile, and Joshua instantly fell in love. The last thing we needed was another dog, but we named him Brady, and he's been ruling our household for a little more than six years. He really does say *I love you.*